GORGEOUS *Gyno*

KAREN DEEN

GORGEOUS GYNO

Copyright © 2019 by Karen Deen

Published by Karen Deen
Formatted by Madhat Studios
Edited by Contagious Edits
Cover Design by Opium House Creatives
Cover Model Michael Scanlon
Cover Image FuriousFotog

About the Author

Karen Deen has been a lover of romance novels and happily-ever-after stories for as long as she can remember. Reaching a point in her life ready to explore her own dreams, Karen decided now was the time to finally write some of her own stories. For years, all of her characters have been forming story-lines in her head, just waiting for the right time to bust free.

Sitting up in the early hours of the morning with her cups of tea, chocolate, and music, she gets lost in a world of sexy, alpha men who are challenged by some funny, sassy, and strong-willed women. Bringing you unexpected laughs, suspense, and a little bit of naughty.

Karen is married to her loving husband and high school sweetheart. Together, they live the crazy life of parents to three children. She is balancing her life between a career as an accountant by day and writer of romance novels by night.

Living in a beautiful coastal town two hours south of Sydney, Australia, Karen enjoys time with her family and friends in her beautiful surroundings. Of course, when she is not shut in her writing cave bringing you more words to devour.

Contact

For all the news on upcoming books, visit Karen at:

www.karendeen.com.au

Karen@karendeen.com.au

Facebook: Karen Deen Author

Instagram: karendeen_author

Dedication

_____

This book is dedicated to all who believe in me.
That give me the support and encouragement
to find where I fit in this book world.
Eternally grateful xoxo

Chapter One

MATILDA

Today has disaster written all over it.

Five fifty-seven am and already I have three emails that have the potential to derail tonight's function. Why do people insist on being so disorganized? Truly, it's not that hard.

Have a diary, use your phone, write it down, order the stock – whatever it takes. Either way, don't fuck my order up! I shouldn't have to use my grown-up words before six am on a weekday. Seriously!

I'm standing in the shower with hot water streaming down my body. I feel like I'm about to draw blood with how hard I'm scrubbing my scalp, while I'm thinking about solutions for my problems. It's what I'm good at. Not the hair-pulling but the problem-solving in a crisis. A professional event planner has many sneaky tricks up her sleeve. I just happen to have them up my sleeve, in my pockets, and hiding in my shoes. As a last resort, I pull them out of my ass.

I need to get into the office to find a new supplier that can have nine hundred mint-green cloth serviettes delivered to the hotel by lunchtime today. You would think this is trivial in the world. However, if tonight's event is not perfect, it could be the difference between my dream penthouse apartment or the shoebox I'm living in now. I'll be damned if mint napkins are the deciding factor. Why can't Lucia just settle for white? Oh, that's right, because she is about as easy to please as a child waiting for food. No matter what you say, they complain until they get what they want. Lucia is a nice lady, I'm sure, when she's not being my client from hell.

Standing in the bathroom, foot on the side of the bath, stretching my stockings on, I sneak a glance in the mirror. I hate looking at myself. Who wants to look at their fat rolls and butt dimples. Not me! I should get rid of the mirror and then I wouldn't have to cringe every time I see it. Maybe in that penthouse I'm seeing in my future, there will be a personal trainer and chef included.

Yes! Let's put that in the picture. Need to add that to my vision board. I already have the personal driver posted up on my board—of course, he's sizzling hot. The trains and taxis got old about seven years ago. Well, maybe six years and eleven months. The first month I moved to Chicago I loved it. The hustle and bustle, such a change from the country town I grew up in. Trains running on raised platforms instead of the ground, the amount of taxis that seemed to be in the thousands compared to three that were run by the McKinnon family. Now all the extra time you lose in traffic every day is so frustrating, it's hard to make up in a busy schedule.

I slip my pencil skirt up over my hips, zip up and turn side to side. Happy with my outfit, I slide my suit jacket on, and then I do the last thing, putting on lipstick. Time to take on the world for another day. As stressful as it is and how often I will complain about things going wrong, I love my life. With a passion. Working with my best friend in our own business is the best leap of faith we took together. Leaving our childhood hometown of Williamsport, we were seeking adventure. The new beginning we both needed. It didn't quite start how I thought. Those first few months were tough. I really struggled, but I just didn't feel like I could go home anymore because the feeling of being happy there had changed thanks to my ex-boyfriend. Lucky I had Fleur to get me through that time.

Fleur and I met in preschool. She was busy setting up her toy kitchen in the classroom when I walked in. I say hers, because one of the boys tried to tell her how to arrange it and her look stopped him in his tracks. I remember thinking, he has no idea. I would set it up just how she did. It made perfect sense. I knew we were right. Well, that was what we agreed on and bonded over our PB&J sandwich. That and our OCD behavior, of being painfully pedantic. Sometimes it meant we butted heads being so similar, but not often. We have been inseparable ever since that first day.

We used to lay in the hammock in my parents' backyard while growing up. Dreaming of the adventures we were going to have together. We may as well have been sisters. Our moms always said we were joined at the hip. Which was fine until boys came into the picture. They didn't understand us wanting to spend so much time together. Of course, that changed when our hormones kicked in. Boys became important in our lives, but we never lost our closeness. We have each other's backs no matter what. Still today, she is that one person I will trust with my life is my partner in crime, my bestie.

Leaning my head on the back wall of the elevator as it descends, my mind is already running through my checklist of things I need to tackle the moment I walk into the office. That pre-event anxiety is starting to surface. It's not bad anxiety. It's the kick of adrenaline I use to get me moving. It focuses me and blocks out the rest of the world. The only thing that exists is the job I'm working on. From the moment we started up our business of planning high-end events, we have been working so hard, day and night. It feels like we haven't had time to breathe yet. The point we have been aiming for is so close we can feel it. Being shortlisted for a major contract is such a huge achievement and acknowledgement of our business. Tapping my head, I say to myself, "touch wood". So far, we've never had any disaster functions that we haven't been able to turn around to a success on the day. I put it down to the way Fleur and I work together. We have this mental connection. Not even having to talk, we know what the other is thinking and do it before the other person asks. It's just a perfect combination.

Let's hope that connection is working today.

Walking through the foyer, phone in hand, it chimes. I was in the middle of checking how close my Uber is, but the words in front of my eyes stop me dead in my tracks.

Fleur: Tonight's guest speaker woke up vomiting – CANCELLED!!!

"Fuck!" There is no other word needed.

I hear from behind me, "Pardon me, young lady." Shit, it's Mrs. Johnson. My old-fashioned conscience. I have no idea how she seems to pop up at the most random times. I don't even need to turn around and look at her. What confuses me is why she is in the foyer at six forty-five in the morning. When I'm eighty-two years of age, there is no way I'll be up this early.

"Sorry, Mrs. Johnson. I will drop in my dollar for the swear jar tomorrow," I mumble as I'm madly typing back to Fleur.

"See that you do, missy. Otherwise I will chase you down, and you know I'm not joking." I hear her laughing as she shuffles on her way towards the front doors. I'm sure everyone in this building is paying for her nursing home when they finally get her to move there. I don't swear that often—well, I tell myself that in my head, anyway. It just seems Mrs. Johnson manages to be around, every time I curse.

"Got to run, Mrs. Johnson. I will pop in tomorrow," I call out, heading out the front doors. Part of me feels for her. I think the swear jar is more about getting people to call in to visit her apartment. Her husband passed away six months after I moved in. He was a beautiful old man. She misses him terribly and gets quite lonely. She's been adopted by everyone in the building as our stand-in Nana whether we like it or not. Although she is still stuck in the previous century, she has a big heart and just wants to feel like she has a reason to get up every day and live her life.

My ride into work allows me to get a few emails sorted, at the same time I'm thinking on how I'm going to solve the guest speaker problem. Fleur is on the food organization for this one, and I am on everything else. It's the way we work it. Whoever is on food is rostered on for the actual event. If I can get through today, then tonight I get to relax. As much as you can relax when you are a control freak and you aren't there. We need to split the work this way, otherwise we'd never get a day or night off.

The event is for the 'End of the Cycle' program. It's a great organization that helps stop the cycle of poverty and poor education in families. Trying to help the parents learn to budget and get the kids in school and learning. A joint effort to give the next generation a fighting chance of living the life they dream about.

Maybe if I call the CEO, they'll have someone who has been through the program or somehow associated with the mentoring that can give a firsthand account of what it means to the families. Next email on my list. Another skill I have learned: Delegation makes things happen. I can't do it all, and even with Fleur, we need to coordinate with others to make things proceed quickly.

As usual, Thursday morning traffic is slow even at this time of the day. We are crawling at a snail's pace. I could get out and walk faster than this. I contemplate it, but with the summer heat, I know even at this time of the morning, I'd end up a sweaty mess. That is not the look I need when I'm trying to present like the woman in charge. Even if you have no idea what you're doing, you need people to believe you do. Smoke and mirrors, the illusion is part of the performance.

My phone is pinging constantly as I approach the front of the office building. We chose the location in the beginning because it was central to all the big function spaces in the city. Being new to the city, we didn't factor in how busy it is here. Yet the convenience of being so close far outweighs the traffic hassles.

Hustling down the hall, I push open the door of our office.

'FLEURTILLY'.

It still gives me goosebumps seeing our dream name on the door. The one we thought of all those years ago in that hammock. Even more exciting is that it's all ours. No answering to anyone else. We have worked hard, and this is our reward.

The noise in the office tells me Fleur already has everything turned on and is yelling down the phone at someone. Surely, we can't have another disaster even before my first morning coffee.

"What the hell, Scott. I warned you not to go out and party too hard yesterday. Have you even been to bed yet? What the hell are you thinking, or have the drugs just stopped that peanut brain from even working?! You were already on your last warning. Find someone who will put up with your crap. Your job here is terminated, effective immediately." Fleur's office phone bangs down on her desk loud enough I can hear her from across the hall.

"Well, you told him, didn't you? Now who the hell is going to run the waiters tonight?" I ask, walking in to find her sitting at her desk, leaning back in her chair, eyes closed and hands behind her head.

"I know, I know. I should have made him get his sorry ass in and work tonight and then fired him. My bad. I'll fix it, don't worry. Maybe it's time to promote TJ. He's been doing a great job, and I'm sure he's been pretty much doing Scott's job for him anyway."

To be honest, I think she's right. We've suspected for a while that Scott, one of our managers, has been partying harder than just a few drinks with friends. He's become unreliable which is unlike him. Even when he's at work, he's not himself. I tried to talk to him about it and was shut down. Unfortunately, our reputation is too important to risk him screwing up a job because he's high. He's had enough warnings. His loss.

"You fix that, and I'll find a new speaker. Oh, and 900 stupid mint-green napkins. Seriously. Let's hope the morning improves." I turn to walk out of her office and call over my shoulder, "By the way, good morning. Let today be awesome." I smile, waiting for her response.

"As awesome as we are. I see your Good Morning and I raise you a peaceful day and a drama-free evening. Your turn for coffee, woman." And so, our average workday swings into action.

By eleven-thirty, our day is still sliding towards the shit end of the scale. We have had two staff call in sick with the stupid vomiting bug. Lucia has called me a total of thirty-seven times with stupid questions. While I talk through my teeth trying to be polite, I wonder why she's hired event planners when she wants to micro-manage everything.

My phone pressed to my ear, Fleur comes in and puts her hand up to high-five me. Thank god, that means she has solved her issues and we are staffed ready to go tonight. It's just my speaker problem, and then we will have jumped the shit pile and be back on our way to the flowers and sunshine.

"Fleurtilly, you are speaking with Matilda." I pause momentarily. "Hello, Mr. Drummond, how are you this morning?" I have my sweet business voice on, looking at Fleur holding her breath for my answer.

"That's great, yes, I'm having a good day too." I roll my eyes at my partner standing in front of me making stupid faces. "Thank you for calling me back. I was just wondering how you went with finding another speaker for this evening's event." I pause while he responds. I try not to show any reaction to keep Fleur guessing what he's saying. "Okay, thank you for looking into it for me. I hope you enjoy tonight. Goodbye." Slowly I put the phone down.

"Tilly, for god's sake, tell me!" She is yelling at me as I slowly stand up and then start the happy dance and high-five her back.

"We have ourselves a pilot who mentors the boys and girls in the program. He was happy to step in last-minute. Mr. Drummond is going to confirm with him now that he has let us know." We both reach out for a hug, still carrying on when Deven interrupts with his normal gusto.

"Is he single, how old, height, and which team is he batting for?" He stands leaning against the doorway, waiting for us to settle down and pay him any attention.

"I already called dibs, Dev. If he is hot, single, and in his thirties then back off, pretty boy. Even if he bats for your team, I bet I can persuade him to change sides." Fleur walks towards him and wraps him in a hug. "Morning, sunshine. How was last night?"

"Let's just say there won't be a second date. He turned up late, kept looking at his phone the whole time, and doesn't drink. Like, not at all. No alcohol. Who even does that? That's a no from me!" We're all laughing now while I start shutting down my computer and pack my briefcase, ready to head over to the function at McCormick Place.

"While I'd love to stay and chat with you girls," I say, making Deven roll his eyes at me, "I have to get moving. Things to do, a function to get finished, so I can go home and put my feet up." I pick up my phone and bag, giving them both a peck on the cheek. "See you both over there later. On my phone if needed." I start hurrying down the corridor to the elevator. I debated calling a car but figured a taxi will be quicker at this time of the day. Just before the lunchtime rush, the doorman should be able to flag one down for me.

Rushing out of the elevator, I see a taxi pulled up to the curb letting someone off. I want to grab it before it takes off again. Cecil the doorman sees me in full high-heeled jog and opens the door knowing what I'm trying to do. He's calling out to the taxi to wait as I come past him, focused on the open door the previous passenger is closing.

"Wait, please..." I call as I run straight into a solid wall of chest. Arms grab me as I'm stumbling sideways. Shit. Please don't let this hurt.

Just as my world is tilting sideways, I'm coming back upright to a white tank top, tight and wet with sweat. So close to my face I can smell the male pheromones and feel the heat on my cheeks radiating from his body.

"Christ, I'm so sorry. Are you okay, gorgeous?" That voice, low, breathy, and a little startled. I'm not game to look up and see the face of this wall of solid abs. "You just came out that door like there's someone chasing you. I couldn't stop in time." His hands start to push me backwards a little so he can see more of me.

"Talk to me, please. Are you okay? I'm so sorry I frightened you. Luckily I stopped you from hitting the deck."

Taking a big breath to pull myself back in control, I slowly follow up his sweaty chest to look at the man the voice is coming from. The sun is behind him so I can't make his face out from the glare. I want to step back to take a better look when I hear the taxi driver yelling at me.

"Are you getting in, lady, or not?" he barks out of the driver's seat.

Damn, I need to get moving.

"Thank you. I'm sorry I ran in front of you. Sorry, I have to go." I start to turn to move to the taxi, yet he hasn't let me go.

"I'm the one who's sorry. Just glad you're okay. Have a good day, gorgeous." He guides me to the back seat of the taxi and closes the door for me after I slide in, then taps the roof to let the driver know he's good to go. As we pull away from the curb, I see his smile of beautiful white teeth as he turns and keeps jogging down the sidewalk. My heart is still pounding, my head is still trying to process what the hell just happened. Can today get any crazier?

GRAYSON

'I'm just a hunk, a hunk of burning love
Just a hunk, a hunk of burning love'

Crap!

What the hell!

I reach out to grab her before I bowl her over and smash her to the ground. Stopping my feet dead in the middle of running takes all the strength I have in my legs. We sway slightly, but I manage to pull her back towards me to stand her back up. Where did this woman come from? Looking down at the top of her head, I can't tell if she's okay or not.

She's not moving or saying anything. It's like she's frozen still. I think I've scared her so much she's in shock.

She's not answering me, so I try to pull her out a little more so I can see her face.

Well, hello my little gorgeous one.

The sun is shining brightly on her face that lights her up with a glow. She's squinting, having trouble seeing me. She opens her mouth to finally talk. I'm ready for her to rip into me for running into her. Yet all I get is sorry and she's trying to escape my grasp. The taxi driver gives her the hurry along. I'd love to make sure she's really okay, but I seem to be holding her up. I help her to the taxi and within seconds she's pulling away from me, turning and watching me from the back window of the cab.

Well, that gave today a new interesting twist.

One gorgeous woman almost falling at my feet. Before I could even settle my breathing from running, I blink, and she's gone. Almost like a little figment of my imagination.

One part I certainly didn't imagine is how freaking beautiful she looked.

I take off running towards Dunbar Park and the basketball court where the guys are waiting for me. Elvis is pumping out more rock in my earbuds and my feet pound the pavement in time with his hip thrusts. I'm a huge Elvis fan, my music tastes stuck in the sixties. There is nothing like the smooth melodic tones of the King. My mom listened to him on her old vinyl records, and we would dance around the kitchen while Dad was at work. I think she was brainwashing me. It totally worked. Although I love all sorts of music, Elvis will always be at the top of my playlist.

"Oh, here's Doctor Dreamy. What, some damsel in distress you couldn't walk away from?" The basketball lands with a thud in the center of my chest from Tate.

"Like you can talk, oh godly one. The surgeon that every nurse in the hospital is either dreaming about fucking, or how she can stab needles in you after she's been fucked over by you." Smacking him on the back as I join the boys on the court, Lex and Mason burst out laughing.

"Welcome to the game, doctors. Sucks you're on the same team today, doesn't it? Less bitching and more bouncing. Let's get this game started. I'm due in court at three and the judge already hates me, so being late won't go well," Lex yelled as he started backing down the court ready to mark and stop us scoring a basket.

"Let me guess, she hates you because you slept with her," I yell back.

"Nope, but I may have spent a night with her daughter, who I had no idea lives with her mother the judge."

"Holy shit, that's the funniest thing I've heard today." Mason throws his head back, laughing out loud. "That story is status-worthy."

"You put one word of that on social media and I won't be the one in court trying to get you out on bail, I'll be there defending why I beat you to a pulp, gossip boy. Now get over here and help me whip the asses off these glamour boys." Lex glares at Mason.

"Like they even have a chance. Bring it, boys." He waves at me to come at him.

Game on, gentlemen.

My watch starts buzzing to tell us time's up in the game. We're all on such tight work schedules that we squeeze in this basketball game together once a week. These guys are my family, well, the kind of family you love one minute and want to kill the next. We've been friends since meeting at Brother Rice High School for Boys, where we all ended up in the same class on the first day. Not sure what the teachers were thinking after the first week when we had bonded and were already making pains of ourselves. Not sure how many times our parents were requested for a 'talk' with the headmaster, but it was more often than is normal, I'm sure. It didn't matter we all went to separate universities or worked in different professions. We had already formed that lifelong friendship that won't ever break.

Sweat dripping off all of us, I'm gulping down water from the water fountain. Not too much, otherwise I'll end up with a muscle cramp by the time I run back to the hospital.

"Right, who's free tonight?" Mason is reading his phone with a blank look on his face.

"I'm up for a drink, I'm off-shift tonight," Tate pipes up as I grin and second him that I'm off too. It doesn't happen often that we all have a night off together. The joys of being a doctor in a hospital.

"I can't, I'm attending a charity dinner. It's for that charity you mentor for, Mason," Lex replies.

"Well, that's perfect. Gray, you are my plus one, and Tate, your date is Lex. I'm now the guest speaker for the night. So, you can all come and listen to the best talk you have witnessed all year. Prepare to be amazed." He brushes each of his shoulders with his hands, trying to show us how impressive he is.

We all moan simultaneously at him.

"Thanks for the support, cock suckers. My memory is long." He huffs a little as he types away a reply on his phone.

Mason is a pilot who spent four years in the military, before he was discharged, struggling with the things he saw. He started to work in the commercial sector but then was picked up by a private charter company. He's perfect for that sort of role. He has the smoothness, wit, and intelligence to mingle with anyone, no matter who they are. He's had great stories of different passengers over the years and places he's flown.

"Why in god's name would anyone think you were interesting enough to talk for more than five minutes. You can't even make that time limit for sex," I say, waiting for the reaction.

"Oh, you are all so fucking funny, aren't you. I'm talking about my role in mentoring kids to reach for their dream jobs no matter how big that dream is." The look on his face tells me he takes this seriously.

"Jokes aside, man, that's a great thing you do. If you can dream it, you can reach it. If you make a difference in one kid's life, then it's worth it." We all stop with the ribbing and start to work out tonight's details. We agree to meet at a bar first for a drink and head to the dinner together. My second alarm on my watch starts up. We all know what that means.

Parting ways, Mason yells over his shoulder to us all, "By the way, it's black tie."

I inwardly groan as I pick up my pace into a steady jog again. I hate wearing a tie. It reminds me of high school wearing one every day. If I can avoid it now, I do. Unfortunately, most of these charity dinners you need to dress to impress. You also need to have your wallet full to hand over a donation. I'm lucky, I've never lived without the luxury of money, so I'm happy to help others where I can.

Running down Michigan Avenue, I can see Mercy Hospital in the distance standing tall and proud. It's my home away from home. This is the place I spend the majority of my waking hours, working, along with some of my sleeping hours too. My heart beats happily in this place. Looking after people and saving lives is the highest rush you can experience in life. With that comes rough days, but you just hope the good outweighs the bad most of the time.

That's why I run and try not to miss the workouts with the boys. You need to clear the head to stay focused. The patients need the best of us every single time. Tate works with me at Mercy which makes for fun days and nights when we're on shift together. He didn't run with me today as he's in his consult rooms and not on shift at the hospital.

I love summer in Chicago, except, just not this heat in the middle of the day when I'm running and sweating my ass off. It also means the hospital struggles with all the extra caseload we get. Heat stroke in the elderly is an issue, especially if they can't afford the cool air at home. The hospital is the best thing they have for relief. My smart watch tells me it's eighty-six degrees Fahrenheit, but it feels hotter with the humidity.

I don't get the extra caseload, since I don't work in emergency. That's Tate's problem. He's a neurosurgeon who takes on the emergency cases as they arrive in the ER. Super intense, high-pressure work. Not my idea of fun. I had my years of that role, and I'm happy where I am now.

Coming through the front doors of the hospital, I feel the cool air hit me, while the eyes of the nursing staff at the check-in desk follow me to the elevator. The single ones are ready to pounce as soon as you give them any indication you might be interested. Tate takes full advantage of that. Me, not so much. When you're an intern, it seems like a candy shop of all these women who want to claim the fresh meat. The men are just as bad with the new female nurses.

We work in a high-pressure environment, working long hours and not seeing much daylight at times. You need to find a release. That's how I justified it, when I was the intern. I remember walking into a storeroom in my first year as an intern, finding my boss at the time, Leanne, and she was naked from the waist down being fucked against the wall by one of the male nurses. Now I am a qualified doctor who should hold an upstanding position in society, so I rarely get involved in the hospital dating scene anymore.

Fuck, who am I kidding? That's not the reason. It's the fact I got burnt a few years ago by a clinger who tried to get me fired when I tried to move on. Not going down that path again. Don't mix work and play, they say—well, I say. Tate hasn't quite learned that lesson yet. Especially the new batch of interns he gets on rotation every six months. He is a regular man-whore.

Am I a little jealous? Maybe just a tad. Both me and my little friend, who's firming up just thinking about getting ready for some action. It's been a bit of a dry spell. I think it's time to fix that.

Pity my date for tonight, Mason, is not even close to what I'm thinking about.

My cock totally loses interest now in the conversation again.

Can't say I blame him.

Just then the enchanting woman from today comes to mind and my cock is back in the game. I wish I knew who she was.

Now this afternoon's rounds could be interesting if my scrubs are tenting with a hard-on.

The joys of being a large man, if you get my drift.

There's no place to hide him.

Chapter Two

MATILDA

"Tilly, stop worrying. We've got this." TJ looks at me with his compassionate eyes.

He's a such a hard-working guy who's become a valuable team member. I take my hat off to him. He's supporting his family while both he and his fiancée try to get through studying at college part-time. They have a son, Lewis, who is the most adorable little boy with his dark skin, beautiful eyes, and tight curly brown hair. It wasn't their plan for TJ's fiancée to get pregnant at seventeen, but they've stuck together, and both worked hard to keep on their roads to their individual dream careers. Working, studying, and sharing the parenting. Amazing role models for Lewis as he grows up.

Not everyone takes that sort of life-changing news and steps up to take responsibility. No matter their age, TJ and Talesha are wise beyond their years.

"TJ, you are too good to me. You deserve this promotion. I know you won't let us down." His smile tells me my answer.

"Damn straight." He puts his hand on my shoulder to reassure me. "Now go home. It's your night off. Fleur has everything under control in the kitchen, and we have a few hours before the doors open, and I'm organized." He chuckles to himself knowing no matter what he says that I struggle to let go of control.

"Okay, okay, I'm out of here. You know you can call me. Even for the smallest question." I look at him, as he shoos me away with his hands.

Heading into the kitchen, I hear Fleur yelling at some of the kitchen staff to get moving, she hasn't got all day to wait for them to get out of her way. She is so much like me it's not funny.

"What are you still doing here?" she calls out to me as she puts down the packages that she's been carrying.

"Just checking on the last-minute things," I tell her.

"I call bullshit on that. With all the staffing changes tonight, you're nervous. Tell the truth." Fleur laughs at me as she calls me out on my anxiety for tonight's function.

"Maybe I should just work tonight. Just in case. You know how important tonight is. It's got to be perfect. Some of the board might be here, checking on us for the tender application."

She just rolls her eyes at me, turning me, then pushing me towards the exit. "Go. Home. Now. Trust me, woman!" Fleur quite clearly tells me as she walks around to stand in front of me in the doorway.

"I know. It's not that I don't trust you. It's just we've worked too hard for this to fall apart at the eleventh hour." My heart is beating a little faster than it should be.

"We've got this. I'll call if I'm worried or if we need you. So, I don't want to hear from you unless it's to tell me you're out on a date and about to go to some guy's place for a random hook-up and you're giving me his details. Understand?"

Now it's my turn to roll my eyes. "Yes, Mom. Not likely, but thanks for caring." We hug quickly, and I walk away, not convinced I shouldn't be here tonight.

"Daisy, honey. Stop knocking, if she hasn't answered it means Tilly's not home yet," I hear Hannah say as I exit the elevator.

"Tilly!" Daisy screams as she sees me start down the corridor.

"Hi, munchkin," I get out before she launches at me for a cuddle. Luckily, I manage to put my bags down, so I don't drop her.

"Daisy," her mother scolds. "At least give her time to get to the front door."

It's too late. I'm wrapped up in a little girl hug with lots of kisses on my cheeks.

"Tilly likes my hugs and kisses, she said so." I laugh as Hannah approaches us to pick up my bags for me. I'm laughing at the sweet little one who is smiling at me like I'm her Santa Claus.

"You are so right, my Daisy waisy. But I do need to get my bags off your mom and open my door before we can play. Is that okay?" I slowly lower her down.

"I suppose. But don't take too long, I'm not finished with my cuddles yet." This precious little girl makes me smile no matter what mood I'm in. She is so full of sunshine that she never lets the world dampen her spirit. I hope she can always keep that in her life. Her energy is a lot of hard work for her mom to manage on her own, though. Hannah is a Navy wife, and her husband Trent is currently on deployment. It's always a tough time for her, so I try to help where I can with Daisy. Just to give her a break. I'm not around a lot, but when I am, Daisy has dinner with me, or we go to the movies and the park, of course getting ice cream on the way home.

Besides Fleur, Hannah is my other closest friend. Oh, and Deven, of course. You never get a choice with him. Once he claims you, then you can't get rid of him. He attaches so easily. Not in a bad way, he's the most thoughtful guy I know. Maybe it has to do with being gay that he's not afraid to wear his heart on his sleeve.

We place my bags on the kitchen counter, and I turn around to pick Daisy up and kiss her in her neck and all over her face. She can't stop giggling and squirming. Hannah is laughing at us being silly.

"She is going to get too heavy soon for you to be able to lift her up like that." Hannah starts to open the fridge to grab the wine we started last night. I stop with Daisy to let her know I'm not sure I should drink tonight.

"What do you mean, no wine? Work is over for the day, what better way to relax before dinner?" Daisy is already over sitting at the little table I have set up in the corner for her. It has coloring books with pencils, books to read, and a few dolls. It was easier than her dragging everything over here when she spends time with me.

"Today has been a shit show and I'm not convinced I shouldn't go back and help with the function tonight. Might need to have a clear head, with only a moment's notice." I can see her looking at me with doubt.

"Are you being a control freak, or did Fleur actually tell you she might need you? We both know you have trouble accepting that things can operate without you." Hannah knows me too well.

"We just fired our head manager, some of the staff are off sick, the speaker for the function cancelled and I had to replace him, and that's not even the half of it. Tonight's so important, we can't afford for anything to go wrong," I mumble as I fiddle with the mail that's sitting on the counter.

"What, and you don't think Fleur can handle it? Did you sort all the problems out during the day?" she asks.

"Of course Fleur can handle it on her own. That's what we do, we run a tight ship. We both put out all the fires during the day. But ..."

"But what?" She glares at me, not prepared to let me off.

"I just have this strange feeling I should be there tonight. Just in case. You know, so Fleur doesn't have to carry all the stress. It's a masquerade ball, and you know how things can get when people drink and they're hiding behind a mask." My mind wanders off to all the things I can picture going wrong. I'm already overthinking.

"Oh, masks can be a lot of fun." Hannah looks like she's off thinking about another place.

"Do I really want to know what you're fantasizing about? Remember, there is a child in the room. Your child, actually." Her blush and giggle tell me the answer.

"Perhaps not." She pulls herself out of her haze. "You know what your problem is? You don't go out and let off steam and relax. You work too much."

"I have time off, and I go out and do things," I protest.

"Yes, with my five-year-old daughter as your date. I wouldn't call that blowing off steam in the sense I'm talking about. Take it from a Navy wife. I know how wound up you can feel when it's been too long. Nothing you do yourself can beat the real thing."

"Hannah," I hiss quietly. "Daisy will hear you."

"She has no idea what I'm talking about, silly." Hannah looks towards Daisy with her mother's love shining through.

"Daisy is one smart little girl. It won't be long before she knows exactly what we're saying and will be calling us out on it. I'm so not ready for that." We both laugh together at the thought of sharing sex talk with our little munchkin.

"Imagine Trent coping with his daughter's impending love life. We might have to make sure he's deployed for her whole teenage dating years." I can see the longing in her eyes. Although she's making a joke, she misses her husband terribly.

"Yeah, ahh, good luck with that."

I fire up the Keurig just to change the conversation.

"Look, all jokes aside. When was the last time you went on a proper date, that finished in, umm, dessert, shall we say?" Hannah is trying not to laugh at her own joke.

I'm thinking back, and I know exactly when it was. I remember it because it was a disaster.

"You know, you don't need me to answer that. It wasn't exactly something I'm proud of."

I put my hand over my eyes. It was a date that you never want to repeat. Nice guy, great company, good-looking, and a gentleman. The night was going well and then we went back to his place for a night cap. Things kept progressing nicely, and just as we were about to move to the bedroom, food poisoning hit us both. I spent the night sharing the toilet bowl with him, vomiting up our dinner. He tried to look after me, but he was just as sick. There was just no chance of a second date after spending the night watching each other spew in the toilet. Let's just say we were both happy to pretend that night never happened, and neither of us bothered to get in contact.

"That was a year ago, and you didn't even get to dessert so that doesn't count. When did you last have S – E – X, you know, like go all the way?" She's laughing while thrusting her hips back and forwards. "You know, the rumba in the slumber."

"Mommy, what's a rumba?" Daisy calls out.

We both look at each other and start laughing. So much the tears are running down our cheeks.

"I told you." I point at Daisy. "Good luck with that."

After we pull ourselves together, Daisy is sitting there waiting for her answer. "It's a dance, honey. One day when you are a big grown-up girl you will get to try it. When you are older than Mommy and Tilly, that is."

"But that's like a hundred years away," Daisy mumbles and both our egos deflate.

Starting to prepare the coffees, Hannah shrieks.

"Oh my god, I have a great idea." I turn to her jumping up and down clapping.

"Uh, are you okay, crazy lady? You've been spending too much time on your own with Daisy." My forehead wrinkles looking at my friend carrying on like a child and wondering what the hell she's talking about.

"Why don't you get dressed up as a guest and go to the function. You can wear a mask so none of your staff know it's you. You can keep an eye on everything and then pick yourself out a hot-looking guy in a suit for a one-night stand. Perfect!" She grabs my hand and starts dragging me towards my bedroom before I even have a chance to answer her crazy outburst.

"What the hell are you doing?" I ask as we stumble into my room.

"We need to find a dress. Let's see what you have." Hannah starts flicking through my clothes.

"Wait, what? I haven't even said I'm going yet. You're a lunatic, you know that. How will I even get in there without someone not knowing it's me. I don't have a ticket, and I can't tell my staff to let me in, or what would be the point of the mask?" My head is trying to catch up with Hannah who seems to be running with her idea before I can even process what she said.

"That's easy. Didn't you do the tickets? Surely you can print one out for yourself. Catch up, silly. Right, now what dresses do you have that might be appropriate. You know, hot, sexy, and showing off that body of yours." I think Hannah is mistaken about who she's talking to. Not sure I'm model material like she's hinting at.

"I don't have one," is all I can manage.

"What! You attend all these functions and don't have a gala event outfit?" She looks at me shocked.

"Correction, I *work* at all these gala events. I'm not there as a guest. I'm dressed for work in a suit. When have you ever seen me dressed up like Cinderella?" I can tell what she's thinking. "Yes, exactly. Never. Let's just forget that plan, order pizza, and pass on the coffee. Crack open the wine and drown my sorrows over my poor dating life."

"Like hell we are. Let's go." She has hold of my hand again and is pulling me towards the front door.

"Daisy, let's go. We're going over to our apartment to dress Tilly up like Cinderella." Daisy screams out and jumps to her feet.

"Yay, can I do her makeup? I will make her so pretty. I'm really good. It's okay, Tilly, Mommy lets me practice on her." The little blonde bombshell goes running past us as we make it to the door.

"Okay, let's just stop right here." I stand my ground at the door. "I don't know if I can just waltz into an event that I'm not invited to, pretending to be someone I'm not, and spy on people who might recognize me. All with the purpose of getting dessert for one night!" Hannah just stares at me for a moment. Daisy is bouncing around us. Then we both burst out laughing.

"Come on, Tilly. Live a little. All work and no play makes a very dull Tilly. Just pretend for one night that you don't have to worry about anything. What've you got to lose?"

Everything she's saying is racing around my mind. This is the same thing Fleur told me to do today. Get out on a date. They must both think I'm so boring. When did I turn into this old lady who has no social life? My mind stops and slows. Seeing a vision of me on a porch in my rocking chair. Daisy talking to me and calling me Aunt Tilly to her children. All alone with my cat on my lap. Oh crap! I don't want to be that person.

"Okay, how do you propose we make me Cinderella in three hours, with no dress or matching shoes, hair and makeup need to be done, plus, where the hell am I going to find a mask? This is one ridiculous idea."

"Fairy godmother at your service. I have a few dresses that might work. I have attended a few Navy balls, and you and I are the same size roughly. I'm sure you have some shoes that will work. Hair and makeup, ummm derrrr. I'm a frigging hairdresser. What more do we need?" The next thing I know I'm in her room and we're trying on dress after dress. Daisy is clapping and cheering, having me spin around each time. I'm probably making a big mistake and one of my staff will recognize me in the first five minutes. Sometimes, though, you've just got to take a chance.

"Oh WOW!" Hannah just stands with her mouth hanging open as I walk out ready to leave for the function.

"You look like a princess, Tilly. So pretty," Daisy whispers. I'm not sure I have ever heard her speak so quietly so it makes me a little nervous.

"Are you sure I look okay? I'm not certain if this dress shows too much of my boobs." I look down at my girls that are up and out there more than I would normally have them.

"Ummm, isn't that the idea? You look absolutely stunning. Every single guy in that room will be lining up to buy you a drink. Now, here is the mask you need. It will match perfectly and hide you from the staff." She holds up a beautiful silver mask that has feathers in both silver and burgundy color, on one side, matching the burgundy dress that I am squeezed into. I normally don't go for such a fitted dress, but I'll admit I do feel special in it. The strapless neckline is a worry—my girls are not little—and then it's fitted nicely down my waist and over the hips. From my thighs it has a split that starts a little higher than I would like but it does give me the room to walk normally and show my legs, which are probably my best asset in my opinion.

I wanted to wear the safe granny undies that would help hold all the rolls in, but Hannah insisted I needed to wear some sexy lingerie. After all, I am supposed to be going out looking to pick up. Not sure how that will go, but my Nan always said you should never leave home without being prepared for the day. So, I guess I'm leaving home prepared.

"Have you got your ticket, your phone, and that little square foil package, or a few, that will hopefully be needed later for dessert?" Hannah elbows me in the side.

"As if I own any of those packages." Been a long time since they were needed.

"What sort of dessert are you getting, Tilly? Are you having our favorite ice cream with chocolate topping, in a cone so you can have big sloppy licks?" Daisy jumps up and down in front of me clapping her hands.

"Oh, she will be hoping for some big sloppy licks for dessert," Hannah mumbles under her breath as she touches up my hair hanging down in loose curls.

"Hannah!" I gasp, thanking the lord that Daisy has no idea what she's talking about, not yet anyway.

"What? Just telling the truth. Now let's give you a last spray of hairspray and get you in an Uber and over to McCormick Place."

I close my eyes as the ozone layer loses another inch from the amount of spray she's coating me in.

"Now go and find a Prince Charming for the night. Then make sure you are home before the clock strikes six am for your morning wake-up alarm." Laughing at her own joke, Hannah motions for me to smile for a photo, and then Daisy jumps in to have her photo taken, because god forbid, we get out the camera and not take one of her. Kids are the best entertainment. Especially when they aren't yours.

Taking a deep breath, I make my way downstairs for my chariot that awaits me.

Who knows what tonight will bring?

GRAYSON

This is not how I was picturing spending tonight.

My first night off for a week and I'm stuck in a suit and starting a night of drinking and laughing with these three jokers.

I know it doesn't sound like a chore, but there are times where it's just nice to spend the night at home away from the noise and chaos.

Gym shorts or track pants, no shirt, watching some old movie that I've seen a thousand times. Curled up on the couch with my little fur friend who thinks he is a human. Falling asleep halfway through and then crawling into bed for a full night's sleep.

For most guys, that's an average night.

The life of a doctor… a full night's sleep is luxury.

Although you have other nights that you're off work, if you're on call there's never a full night's sleep. You can guarantee there will be an emergency. It's part of what I love about my job. The adrenaline rush of helping someone in their time of need.

Since I moved to gynecology and obstetrics from being a doctor in the ER, it isn't quite as bad, however no one can ever tell the babies when it's a good time to arrive. In a way, my life is ruled by little people who haven't even seen the light of day yet.

When I decided to specialize and become an ob-gyn, the guys laughed at my choice.

Mason thought he had it all worked out. Telling me he was all for a job where you get to look at women's pussies all day long. That was until I explained that I also deliver babies. That had him changing his mind damn fast. Definitely not in the plans for Mason. He doesn't plan on marriage or kids. For him, life will always be travelling the globe and hooking up with hot women. Doesn't sound too hard.

"Are you even listening to me, Gray?" Alex smacks me on the shoulder. "Since when don't you have an opinion on basketball?" Shit, what did I miss?

"You know my opinion is the only one that counts anyway," Tate says as he returns to the table with the next tray of beers. "Gray is just full of shit anyway. Tell me what you need an answer on?" He chuckles as he places the drinks down.

"Well, it's not how big is Tate's ego, that's for sure," Alex comments. "His ego's compensating for something else. Am I right, gentlemen? After all, we have all shared many changeroom showers over the years." The table erupts in laughter, well, all except Tate who fails to see the funny side of the comment.

The conversation continues to revolve around sports, and of course, ribbing Mason about what he's going to say tonight. My mind keeps drifting off to my sister Arabella. I haven't spoken to her this week and I need to check in with her. She's a lot younger than me at twenty-five. Clearly an adult, but I will never stop looking out for her. I made Mom a promise and I'll never go back on that. I make a mental note to call her tomorrow and organize a breakfast date for the weekend.

"For fuck's sake, Gray, where are you tonight? Because you sure as shit aren't here with us." Mason eyeballs me across the table.

"Sorry, man. Been a long few weeks at work and I'm needing a good long night in bed," I mumble as I pick up my beer to chug down the last mouthful, knowing it must be close to the time to leave for the function.

When I bang down the glass on the table, the guys are all looking at me.

"What?" I ask a little confused.

"It's normally me that's looking for the hook-up when we go out, not you. Fuck, you must be feeling hard up." Tate grins, standing, ready to leave.

"Seriously, you guys are idiots. I meant a good night's sleep." Although in my head the thought of a long night of hot sex is sounding mighty good. Maybe I should take on Tate at his own game tonight.

They all laugh as we make our way out of the bar. At the curb is a town car waiting for us.

"Which one of you lazy bastards ordered the car?" Lex shouts out above the noise of the traffic and nightlife around us.

"The event planners for tonight offered me a car to get to the function so I decided to take them up on it. I mean, we can't have the guest of honor turning up all sweaty from this night-time heat. I need to look my best for the ladies who will be fawning all over me and wanting my autograph." Mason laughs at himself and takes the front seat as we all slide into the back of the car. I know they say the back seat of a sedan is made for three people, but it's crap. There is no way it's made for three men with broad shoulders to sit comfortably side by side.

"Next time, can you ask for the upsize to the limo? We should never be this close to each other physically," I comment as we're shuffling trying to find the place where we fit , and we can all relax.

"Tate, if you don't move your hand off my thigh then the next issue you'll have is the gravel rash on your ass as you hit the road after I open the door and push you," Lex mumbles to him.

"Sucks to be you stuck in the middle. Thought you might just need a helping hand on working out how to get him moving, ready for a bit of action." Tate chuckles.

"Man, if you think your hand is going to give me any type of action, other than making it shrivel up, then I have misjudged you all these years." Shoving Tate's hand off his leg, both Mason and I can't help but laugh at Lex. He is the most uptight of the four of us. Hence the lawyer in the group. Always a stick stuck at least half up his ass most of the time.

"Oh, Alexander, why didn't you tell me you thought of me that way? We could have sorted this out years ago." Tate's laughing at his own jokes which is nothing unusual.

"You're a dickhead," Lex grinds out under his breath as the car slows to a stop at the entrance.

"Oh yeah, the charity sent these over for us too," Mason quickly rambles as he reaches into the bag at his feet and drops black masks of various shapes into our laps.

"What the hell are these?" Tate asks. "Did I misunderstand the kind of function this is? Not that I'm complaining. This is right up my alley." He places his on before he even exits the car.

"Tate, of course you'd be into that sort of night." I slap him on the back as I finally get feeling in my legs, standing up out of the car. "It's obviously a masquerade ball."

"Even better. Let's see what pretty little ladies we can find tonight, give them a night of mystery and pleasure. Who doesn't love a man in a black mask? Look at us sexy beasts! They won't be able to resist." He sounds like an excited kid.

There's that ego again. I often wonder how he's such an amazing neurosurgeon and top of his field. Anyone seeing him now would never let him near a hospital, let alone a scalpel and their brain.

"Tate, do you think you can try to act like an educated professional tonight and not embarrass us all? Well, me at least. I'm actually looking forward to this and the fundraiser is important to me." Mason stares him down as we ascend the steps to the door.

"Wow, give the man five minutes of fame and look what happens. Okay, precious, I will be on my best behavior just for you. Cross my heart and promise to god." Tate's sarcasm just revs Mason up even more.

"You're not even religious, you dick." I smack his arm as I walk in. I don't know if I've had enough sleep the last few days to cope with tonight. I have a funny feeling it's going to get messy. Or a little crazy. Or maybe both.

"Where's the bar? I'm going to need it to get through tonight with you three," Lex mumbles as he makes a direct line across the room, and we all follow. We look like the mafia, four tall, broad men cutting through the crowd all in black, heading straight for the alcohol.

It's time for something stronger than the beer from earlier tonight.

Leaning with my back against the bar, I survey the room.

Same bunch of stuck-up oldies with their old money, mixed with the young overly flirtatious women and men trying to find that person who can either satisfy their need tonight. Or, have enough money to satisfy all their needs long-term. It's been a long time since I've met a genuine single woman at one of these events. Mask or not, I can't imagine tonight is going to be much different. Mind you, I'm sure Tate will still leave with one on his arm and be pushing her out of his bed in the morning.

I sigh. Thinking again of my couch and cuddling up with my little dog-mate, until suddenly... I'm not sure what to think of at all.

Well, except what those legs would feel like wrapped around me later tonight.

Holy shit. The nervousness radiating off her as she enters the room has my full attention.

Tonight's just taken an interesting turn, and suddenly I'm not feeling tired anymore.

"Hey, Tate, Mason's wanting you over at the stage to help him with something." He looks confused at me but turns to walk towards the guest of honor anyway.

Now let's see who this vision is. She obviously needs help settling in.

I'm just the man for the job.

Chapter Three

MATILDA

W hy did I let Hannah talk me into this?

What if someone recognizes me? My staff will think I'm spying and don't trust them. Although it's true to an extent, the trust is not my problem. The fact that I'm a control freak is more on me than them. Fleur will kill me if she finds out. Oh god, I should just get back in the taxi and go straight home.

Standing at the bottom of the steps heading into the building I feel all crazy. I have about two seconds to make a decision, otherwise the humidity is going to have my makeup running off my face and my hair will be a disaster.

In or out? What is it, Tilly? I ask myself, waiting for some crazy voice to give me the answer.

If anyone could hear my inner thoughts, they'd think I'm a lunatic. Pull it together, Tilly. You didn't go through three hours of preening to walk away now. Imagine Hannah and Daisy's disappointment if I turn up back at the apartment less than an hour after leaving.

This is more Hannah's style. Although she is a great mom to Daisy and runs a tight ship at home, she has a crazy side. Before Daisy came along, she was wild, and says that's what attracted Trent. He loved the spunk in her, the little bit of adventure. Well, she can shove her adventure right up her ass right this minute. How the hell did her crazy turn into my adventure?

I can do this. I need to remember I am not here as Tilly tonight. I'm here as

Cinderella looking for her prince for a night, according to Hannah. Oh, and dessert, who can forget dessert!

Geez, who am I kidding? I'm here to spy on my staff and make sure the function is a success. At least I should be honest to myself. I can't fool my own head even if I've managed to fool my friend.

Handing my invitation to one of my staff, Sarah, who's working the door, I'm trying not to even speak, worried she'll hear my voice and blow my cover straight up. She looks at me strangely as I just enter without a word. I'll be one of those people that the staff gossip about in the kitchen. The weird lady who has no voice. There are always a few interesting characters we find at every event.

My heart rate is a little elevated stepping into the room, finally clear of the doorway.

Shit!

Now what do I do? It just occurred to me; I won't be seated at any table for the dinner, and standing near the wall while everyone is seated will look bizarre. I can't just sit anywhere. These things are planned long before the event. Stepping back towards the shadows on the wall, I stand just watching the whole room, quietly taking in everything from a distance.

My heart feels proud watching TJ controlling the room and staff. He looks calm and has everything happening as it should be. My breath hitches a little as Fleur floats out from the hallway that leads to the kitchen. She approaches the stage and is talking to two men at the side of the lectern. I can only see them from behind, which I must admit is not a bad view. They completely dwarf her size-wise. Fleur is what we call a pocket rocket. Five-foot-three and full of a personality that you don't want to cross. I'm not an Amazon-sized woman by any stretch of the imagination, with a height of five-foot-seven, but I still look like a giant standing over her at times.

I just watch as I see her smiling and pointing to different things on the stage. I can tell by the look on her face she is talking to them but also listening to someone talking through her earpiece. She never misses a beat and the hot suits wouldn't have even realized she was multi-tasking. One of them must be Mason White, the pilot who is the guest speaker we pulled in at the last minute. I put one foot forward and start to head over there and thank him for coming to our rescue, when I remember I'm not here working. Left in limbo and out of the shadows, I stand fidgeting with my bag. This is so crazy. What the hell was I thinking?

As I stand frozen trying to plan my next move, I hear the PA crackle and the shrill voice of Lucia on the stage announcing that dinner is about to be served so would we please take our seats. She then continues to ramble on about the way the night will run. No one is listening.

My brain is racing as she talks.

Fuck, now what do I do?

Good one, Tilly. Not so clever now, are you?

Everyone starts to turn and move towards their tables. Except one man, who seems to be heading in my direction. Shit, is he someone who recognizes me?

Turning to my right I hasten towards the toilets and decide it might be the place to hide until dinner is seated and I can work out what the hell to do. Passing two younger women exiting the bathroom, I'm relieved to find it empty. Walking into one of the stalls and closing the door behind me, I lean against the wall. No one would believe this story of my stupidity. I'm supposed to be some super-duper event planner, yet here I am hiding in the toilet trying to get myself out of some stupid idea that sounded good when Hannah rattled it off three hours ago.

Note to self: Don't listen to Hannah ever again!

Snap out of it, Matilda. You know the timeline of tonight so well, you can probably recite it backwards in your sleep. Looking at my phone, I know if I wait for five minutes everyone should be seated. There were also a few tables at the back that weren't full on the seating plan. I can sneak onto one of those. We always place extra seats just in case we need to shift someone or there is a mix-up and there are extra people.

Like me!

I find the seat closest to the back and a wall I can blend into. I feel the hairs on the back of my neck tingle from the frustration I still get looking at these annoying things. I place my damn green napkin on my lap quickly, ready for the dinner service and to avoid one of my waiters having to tend to me. Trying to avoid eye contact with anyone at the table doesn't work. There are two older couples, who from memory are some of the original list of volunteers with the organization when it started. They stopped working for the charity years ago but still attend the dinner. They like to be at the back where the speakers aren't so loud. I'm not sure why, because the way the woman is screaming across the table at me, I'm pretty sure she is completely deaf. Or forgot to turn on her hearing aid.

"Don't you look lovely, dear. I'm Esme and this is John, Gerald, and Doreen. What's your name?" I'm sure every person for five tables around us knows her name now too.

"Ma...." I stop in a panic. I can't use my name. Oh, this is getting more ridiculous by the minute. "Sorry, a frog in my throat. My name is Hannah." Sorry, Han, but it's your fault I'm in this predicament.

"What a pretty name for a pretty girl. Is your husband busy tonight?" Oh lordy, this is going to be painful.

"Yes." Short and simple. Shut her down. Come on, TJ, get those appetizers on the table so I can get her focused on eating.

"Oh. Such a pity. All dressed up and no man to spend the night with."

If only she knew she was spot-on with the truth. How am I going to find a man if I don't have the nerves to move around the function freely?

Good old Doreen then decides to join in. "In our day, you wouldn't go out without your husband to escort you. You modern girls are so different. It was frowned upon back then." I sigh, waiting for the lecture as she takes a breath. "Good on you, girlie." Now that wasn't what I was expecting at all.

"Thank you." I look over to the next table to see them being served. Finally, a reprieve from the Spanish Inquisition that I can feel coming.

Esme and Doreen start to discuss loudly the meal placed in front of them. The color, the shape, what the ingredients might be, and of course the taste. I don't feel like eating but decide to take a few small mouthfuls to test the food. You know, quality control and all.

We aren't just event planners. A few years into the opening of Fleurtilly, we decided to set up our own catering division in the business as well. That way we have complete control over the event if that's what the client wishes. We have chefs we can call in, that we completely trust and share the same visions. Likewise, for all the event staff who know exactly how we expect things to run. We found hiring agency staff just wasn't working. We would get a different group of people every time. We never managed to get exactly the result we wanted. It was a huge risk, but we took the leap and did it ourselves. With Laticia, our head chef working tonight, I know I don't have to worry about the quality, but it can't hurt to check. Of course, it's not that her mouth-watering sherried mushrooms and parmesan tart has just been laid in front of me.

I don't know why I even thought I'd be able to come tonight in the hope of relaxing and perhaps stepping out of my comfort zone. My mind is running through the timeline, ticking things off as they happen. I don't know how to take work out of my everyday thoughts. It consumes me. With minimal conversation with the other guests either side of me, I know I can't sit here for much longer. Sitting idly is not my thing. I can feel my hands itching because I should be up helping Fleur where I can.

I need to curb these nerves. I thought they would start to settle after dinner was served. So far no one has recognized me or has any idea there's an extra guest. I mean, I'm sure Fleur would have noticed an extra person on this table. She would have the layout mapped in her brain. But at this stage of the evening, things are going well so what's one extra meal.

Feeling like the air is getting thick in here, I stand and excuse myself from the table. Esme tried to start up another conversation, but I pretended I didn't hear what she was saying. People are starting to move around after the main meal and the level of noise is starting to rise. I walk briskly towards the side foyer doors that lead to what is usually the quiet area. Thank goodness Lucia insisted we make sure this was made a quiet social area due to her migraines. Not that I imagine seeing her out here anytime soon, but like everything else she was so insistent on, we agreed just to shut her up.

It's a long foyer that stretches the full length of the room. There are two separate doorways that the people are entering and exiting from. Standing out here is just about killing me, trying to keep from going inside to take control of the show. I have to keep reminding myself I'm not here for work tonight. I just need a few moments of fresh air to get myself together. Then maybe I'll have the guts to go back inside and try to talk to some men. Normally I don't have an issue. I just feel so strange dressed up and hiding behind the mask. You would think it would be easier, but for me, apparently not. I'm obviously a weirdo.

I stand with my hands on the railing, looking out at the night sky through the glass wall of the foyer, searching for the stars. I remember what it's like back home. So different. Here with the city lights always on, you can't pick out every light that is sparkling in the sky. When we were kids lying in the hammock, the sky was so bright. Fleur and I would make up pictures with the patterns in the stars. Oh, to be back in the life of my twelve-year-old self.

Life was simple. You had dreams.

You planned them, and you assumed they would just happen.

Grow up.

Start our business.

Find a sexy man.

Get married.

Buy a home.

Have three children. I sigh, my stomach twisting just at the thought of it.

All before I am thirty years old because life after thirty is all downhill.

Or so you think at twelve.

Time for self-evaluation, twenty years later at the age of thirty-two.

I have grown up and started a business. Big tick.

Then the list stops.

Frozen in time.

Who thought at thirty-two years old I would still be looking for a man? My poor ovaries are on the countdown and running out of time. I'm secretly worried that having a baby could be an issue for me. If the magical man of my dreams doesn't drop into my life shortly, then I'm going to have to resort to Plan B.

I wish Plan B was that friend from high school who promised if we weren't married by thirty, we would be each other's back-up. No such luck for me. Pretty sure that Fleur would have a real problem if she was asked to be my Plan B. She was the only one I had that connection with back then, and just thinking about it is super awkward.

No, my Plan B is freezing my eggs or going down the IVF path with a sperm donor. Not the dream I had all those years ago as I pictured a unicorn up in the stars. Should have known, unicorns don't exist and so far, neither does the perfect man. At this stage I would probably settle for at least half-decent. My nana would shoot me for settling for less than perfect. She's still living in the time when a man is a gentleman, the head of the house. He provides, he takes care of you, he reproduces with you, just not sure in what part of that description does he love you. It sounds more like he performs his duty for you.

Yeah, no thanks!

Plan B may be the way to go.

The only flaw, once again, is I need a man, even if not in spirit, at least in bodily fluids.

I smack my forehead with my hand. Snap out of it! Don't waste tonight.

I'm dressed up, looking the best I have in years. My best panties on and a mask so no one knows who I am. Start living it up a little.

I turn to walk back through the doors as the noise of Lucia's shrill voice introduces Mason White.

Not wanting to appear rude, I take a spot leaning against the bar as he starts his story.

The first words out of his mouth earn a cheer from three men all in black at his table.

Four men.

Same sort of suit.

Same masks.

One set of eyes and they are staring right at me.

For the first time tonight, my breath hitches but not for nerves or fear.

GRAYSON

Watching her move around the room, something intrigues me.

She's here by herself, that much I've worked out.

Yet she's nervous, flighty. Looking to run at the slightest thing.

I know I should be listening to Mason, and he'll be quizzing us later on what he said, but I'll be damned if I can take my eyes off her. Normally I hate a masked event, yet tonight it has my interest piqued.

The way that dress curves over those sensual hips. It hugs her body perfectly. Pity we haven't made it to the dancing part of the evening yet, though. Not sure her tits are going to stay tucked safely in that dress. Just the way I like it. The hint of what she's hiding, like the hidden temptation.

Don't even get me started on the split that runs up her dress. Leaning back gently on the bar with one foot slightly forward, the dress falls perfectly on either side of her bare leg. What I wouldn't give to be running my hand up that leg, sliding a little higher than that split, before the night's over with.

Her eyes catch me looking that direction and her chin drops a little, letting me know I'm affecting her. I'm not looking away. A gentleman would, but I'm not feeling like one right now. The filthy thoughts running through my head don't qualify as G-rated.

"Shit!" I let out a little louder than I intended to. "What'd you do that for?" I hiss at Tate who is sitting next to me.

"Because Mason is giving you the stink eye because you aren't bowing down and giving him your undivided attention. You know there'll be a test at the end of this," he whispers quietly enough that no one can hear him, but I can see Mason is watching us.

I want to stick my finger up and give him the bird, but I'm not immature like Tate. Well, most of the time anyway.

You can dress up the boy in the suit but that doesn't always make him a man. His actions will determine how he is perceived. Be the man, Grayson.

My dad reminds me of this often. I remember him saying it the first time I wore a suit. It's a day I will never forget. My dad standing in front of me telling me how proud Mom would be. Forever etched in my memory.

The cheers and clapping bring me back from my momentary mind slip. Mason walks off the stage straight towards us.

"Some fucking date you are. You weren't even watching or listening. Who's got your dick in knots, lover boy?" He slaps me on the shoulder. I could lie to him, but what's the point? I've been caught out fair and square.

"Someone better-looking than my current date, that's for sure. Great speech, by the way." I laugh as I turn to look to the bar where my mystery girl was standing, but she has disappeared again.

"Like you'd know. You didn't listen to one word I said. Just like now, for fuck's sake. Can you go dip the wick and get it over and done with?" The boys all roar laughing and start trying to find who I'm checking out. They're carrying on like a group of high school boys. If the truth be known, most of the time it feels like that's what we still are. Maybe one day we will all grow up. Well, not Tate, but the rest of us have half a chance.

Now they've all had their laugh, I need to find where she has vanished to. Every time I've tried to approach her tonight, she's been like a ghost. One moment she's there and the next she's gone. As I start to walk towards the bar, Lex yells his drink order at me.

"Make mine a scotch on the rocks, the good stuff because Mason said you're paying. Something about your punishment for not supporting your man." Again, their joke is targeting me.

"I'll piss in a glass and that's the only drink you're getting off me tonight." I keep walking, their voices fading behind me. Knowing she's not in the room and didn't pass me on the way to outside, I narrow my search to the corridor heading to the restrooms and kitchen. If I just wait here at the end of the hall, then she has to walk past me on her way back out of the bathroom. Presuming that's where she is.

I stand leaning against the wall for a while, just checking out my emails with my patients' updates. I don't want to look like I'm literally standing here like a stalker, so I'm trying to look busy. Not sure I'm too successful. Every person that walks past looks strangely at me. Including the security guard that has now positioned himself a little down the corridor from where I'm located. Okay, I must be looking pretty creepy, when you think about it. A man in a black suit with a black mask, standing outside the door to the ladies' room with his phone and not moving. Besides, if she is in the bathroom, she's taking an awful long time. This is the second time she's run there tonight and been gone a while. My doctor brain starts to kick in with the reasons she may need to visit the bathroom frequently.

For fuck's sake, you weirdo. Can't you leave work at the hospital for one night? It's bad enough you're waiting to try to talk to a stunning woman and passing the time by checking on patients. Time to take a break. They're in good hands, maybe not my hands, but they are being looked after. Go and grab a drink from the bar, and if you run into her again then it's meant to be. If not, maybe there's a reason. Who knows, she might be married or in a relationship.

The boys make sure my arrival back at the bar is noticed with their loud jeering.

"See? I told you he's a one-minute wonder. His hair isn't even messed up. Feel better now, pretty boy?" Mason goes to ruffle my hair, and the boys all push me on the arms. They catch me off guard, and with all three of them pushing from the one direction, I stumble backwards a little, falling down the couple of steps that lead up to the bar area. I'm sure I look like a fucking windmill. Arms flapping trying to grab something or someone. The guys all laugh, not doing a thing to help me.

Then it happens. Before the floor is close enough to be colliding with, I feel something, or someone, slip their arms under my armpit to slow me down. I was still going to be hitting the floor, but at least it may not hurt as much.

Like slow motion, I look up to that face, those eyes behind the mask looking down concerned at me. She is bent fully over the top of me by this stage, and all I can see is her magnificent cleavage and that leg peeking out of the prick-teasing split.

This can't be happening. All night I've been trying to get near her, and now I'm lying at her feet and look like the clumsiest man alive.

Her face has my attention. The look of concern is a pleasant surprise considering it's me that ran into her.

I hear Tate's booming voice next to me as he leans down to pull me back up to my feet, brushing me off as I find my feet. "We are so sorry, miss. He's such a clumsy man. They don't usually let him out without a leash, but he just wanted to fit in and look normal."

"Get your hands off me, moron," I growl under my breath at him.

A quiet little laugh breaks my frustration of looking like an idiot. The boys join my mystery girl in laughing at my expense. I can't help but take a deep breath and laugh with them. I can't deny I would have looked hilarious in full flight.

I take a step forward as the noise settles a little. I take her hand and bring it to my lips for a soft kiss. Slowly, holding it there, I bow and keep eye contact the whole time. The moment my lips touch the skin on her hand, my brain starts firing. Her skin is so soft, and the scent of her perfume is so delicate and inviting.

"Thank you for saving me from these childish boys. I'm in your debt now. Perhaps I can buy you a drink as repayment?" Her cheeks pink up a little and her head drops slightly for the second time tonight. It fascinates me that even with the mask on, she's still shy.

"That's not necessary." She straightens up, and I can tell she is preparing to walk away.

"No please, I insist. It's the least I can do." I turn to the bar and motion the bartender closer to us.

"What would you prefer, a wine or something stronger? You can pick anything you like because these gentlemen will be paying our bill a little later." Still holding her hand, I gently pull her with me to the bar and pull a stool over for her to sit on.

"So that means you aren't really buying this lovely lady a drink, so I get to hold her hand instead," Tate announces from behind me. Like fuck he's getting anywhere near her.

"Not a chance in hell." I still haven't taken my eyes off hers. "These buttheads behind me are my friends, apparently. Tate, the loud one, Lex, the serious one, and Mason, the ego, over there." I hear all the protests behind me.

"My name's Grayson, but you can call me Gray. And you are?" She looks torn as to what to reply. It's a little strange, but I suppose she's being cautious, I get that.

"Hannah, but you can call me Hannah." For the first time I see her cheeky smile creep up her face.

"We've got ourselves a live one," Mason announces as he drags up a few stools for us to all get comfortable.

Tate leans on the bar and places the guys' orders and repeats Hannah's order of an espresso martini.

While we're waiting for the drinks, I want to get to know her. But getting Tate to shut up is going to be an issue. It's always an issue!

"What brings you here tonight, Hannah, are you involved in the charity or just here as a benefactor like the rest of us?" I ask as Mason straight away pipes up.

"Speak for yourself. I'm the guest of honor. You are just my entourage."

"Dream on, Mason," I say, leaning out to ruffle his hair. "The only time I stood behind you was when we were lining up to see the school nurse to check us for head lice. She was so busy with the colony in your hair I could slide past without her knowing."

"Fuck off. Sorry, Hannah. Pardon my language, but really Gray! You couldn't come up with anything better than that?"

"I thought it was good," Lex speaks up from behind the others. "We're so funny we could start our own stand-up comedian act."

Hannah seems to be watching intently at the bartender that is thrown constantly between us. Just a normal day in paradise.

Her shoulders are dropping, and you can tell she's relaxing a little.

"You could call it 'four masked suits' or 'the men behind the masks.' There are so many options." Her focus is moving from one to the other around the group.

Screw this, I want time without the guys around taking away her attention.

Our drinks are placed on the bar in front of us.

"I think we should take a walk out on to the balcony and leave these annoying children behind. That way we can have an adult conversation."

I pick up my drink in one hand and link my other arm through hers. I assist her down from the stool, not really giving her a choice. However, she isn't complaining or refusing, so that's a good sign.

"Guess I will talk to you gentlemen another time." She looks at each of them, then turns and starts to walk with me.

Not if I can help it, beautiful lady.

Tonight, I want you to myself, and I intend to do whatever I need to make it happen.

Including ditching my friends.

It's not like they wouldn't do the same if they were in my shoes.

Let's see what the rest of this mysterious night brings.

Chapter Four

MATILDA

Once again, I find myself in the foyer looking out through the big glass windows. Drink in hand, this time a tall, dark, and handsome man beside me. My senses are on alert, yet I don't feel nervous, which is strange. Something about Grayson puts me at ease. Although his height and stature are a little intimidating, there is something about his eyes that show kindness. I think the inability to see someone fully makes you concentrate on the parts you can appreciate. Every time I've seen him across the room tonight, his eyes are what fascinate me.

"You didn't answer my question before, inside. What brings you here tonight, Hannah?" I almost look behind me expecting to see my friend and then realize he is talking to me. I need to concentrate, otherwise I'll slip up and this night will end way before I'm hoping.

"I was a last-minute invite through a friend that knows the event planners. She had a spare ticket she wasn't using." Technically I'm not lying, which is my pet peeve. Here I'm just manipulating the truth.

"I'm glad you accepted the invitation. You have captivated my attention since you entered the room." Gray takes my free hand again and starts slowly running his thumb over the back of it. The tingles are running up my arm, yet he has a softness about him. Looking down at his large hand wrapped around mine, I notice the strength of him. There is something about a man's hands. His hands and his arms. I'm such an arm-porn slut. Muscles, visible veins, and smooth skin.

How do I answer that comment? I'm not used to getting compliments, let alone about my looks. It might be because of the dating drought I've been on for so long, or just the men I've gone out with. Either way, it makes me self-conscious.

"Thank you. Well, you did *fall* for me pretty quickly." I need to deflect to safer ground.

"Touché, pretty lady. Touché." He smiles as he takes another drink from his scotch.

"My dickwad friends had a lot to do with it, but I'm kind of glad they did. I've been trying to approach you all night. You are like a beautiful, mysterious vision who keeps disappearing on me." Oh, this man has all the words and knows just how to use them. The tone and delivery have me quivering all over.

"Maybe I'm not real?" I try to gain the courage to get my flirt on.

Leaning forward, he whispers in my ear. "I know a real woman when I see one. Now let me show you what it's like to be treated like a treasured woman." That's it. I want to skip the flirting and just say I want that too! Show me now!

After pulling back and leaving me in a bundle of goosebumps, he smiles this positive-looking grin like he knows he has me. I want to say not so quick, buddy. You need to work harder than that. Yet my body is saying, get a room now, woman!

"What makes you think I don't already know what that's like?" I try to appear super confident. I stand tall, slowly taking another sip of my martini like he doesn't have every nerve in my body zinging around like they've drunk five energy drinks in under a minute.

"You might think you've been shown. I can guarantee it was a schoolboy attempt in comparison to what I have to offer." He leans against the glass wall with one leg crossed over the other, giving the cocky look of confidence in his bedroom skills.

"You seem to be a little certain in your skills, Grayson. Who's to say I'm interested in being shown?" Shit, now I've done it.

The challenge has been thrown out there. What was I thinking?

To be honest, I wasn't thinking, more hoping that he'll take the obvious suggestive invitation.

I have just figuratively thrown my hands in the air.

I'm all dressed up, hiding behind a mask, with a guy who doesn't even know my name. Why the hell don't I just enjoy a night of pleasure? It's not like I'll ever see him again.

"I can assure you, beautiful lady, there is no need for confidence. My skills are next-level due to my secret knowledge." He stands up straight, stepping closer, placing his hand on my bare shoulder and sliding it up my neck to cup my jaw. His thumb strokes my skin. "We both know that trail of goosebumps following my hand and the pink of your cheeks tell me you're more than interested." As he leans closer, I shiver waiting for his lips to make contact. But instead he just whispers, "Let me get a room so we can explore this more. Let me make good on my promises." He gives me the softest, lightest kiss on the lips. So slight I'm not even sure it happened.

The heat in my body is rising, and Grayson has its complete attention. I can't talk, and I'm not sure I even need to at this stage. I just eventually nod my head and his smile of victory tells me he got the message.

"No sleepover," I quickly say as he pulls slowly back to look me in the eyes.

"You're in control here. You make the rules, I bring the pleasure."

Oh fuck! My breath hitches a little. Every thought I had in my head about being nervous just disappeared. The mask on my face is giving me a false sense of bravery.

If I get to make the rules, then let it be a night of fantasy.

"No sleepovers and masks stay on. Think you can accept that?" I whisper, nervous about negotiating a night of sex with a complete stranger who I only know by his first name. Yet the excitement is electrifying and of course a little naughty. I've never been one to let my guard down and be spontaneous. My whole life is planned down to the minute detail. That's why we're successful in business, because we're good at it. I just forget not to carry it through to my personal life at times too.

"A little bit of playful hiding under that mask, is there? Now, *that* I can't wait to explore." He takes the drink from my hand and places both our glasses on a table close by. "Ready to leave?" For the last time, I debate the thought and the ayes have it on the vote.

"Yes, I'm ready to see what all this talk is about. Nothing like talking yourself up." With that, Grayson places his arm around my waist and laughs out loud as he turns me to walk towards the exit.

We only make it halfway across the foyer and Tate steps out the door with one of the young girls I saw coming out of the toilet earlier, hanging off his arm. She looks a fair bit younger than him, but who am I to judge people I don't even really know.

Both Grayson and Tate give that chin-lift thing that men do that shows they acknowledge each other and are so tough they don't need to speak words. Not sure why this continues with men after teenage years, but they all do it. I guess it's the secret nod of "I found a girl and I'm leaving to go fuck her, how about you?" To which his mate lifts his chin to say, "Good one, man, me too."

So caveman!

So fucking hot!

Grayson guides me towards the elevator. There's a comfortable silence as we wait for it to arrive on our level. I feel more comfortable that we're going to a room in a hotel. I'm not sure I'm brave enough to go back to his place. It's not a sense of danger, because strangely I feel calm and safe with him. It's more that it would be more intimate, and I might be tempted to stay the night. I want this to be that naughty fantasy that I didn't know I had. The one where you meet a sexy, sinfully handsome man, who gives you a night full of amazing sex and orgasms and is gone by the morning. Only leaving beautiful memories in his wake and no awkwardness. He will be a little naughty and a whole lot alpha.

Mmmm...even though I've just made up the fantasy, I want it, and I'm determined not to let myself get in the way of my own good time. No one is going to know what I'm doing so I don't have to explain to anyone. It'll be my own little dream.

There is something racy about being in an elevator with a sexy man. It's like the electricity rises exponentially. Grayson's hand is still around my waist and has me tucked in close to his side. His fingers slowly brush my side up and down. If this is the start of foreplay, then I'm already on board. Exiting the building, the Marriott Marquis Hotel is easy walking distance on the pedestrian bridge and makes this so much more real.

I'm actually heading to a hotel for a one-night stand with a twist.

No names and mask on. The intrigue is part of the naughty I'm feeling.

Grayson leaves me sitting on a seat while he gets a room. I hope he didn't bother paying for a view because it would be a waste of money. The only thing I'm looking forward to seeing is what's under that suit.

Two of my favorite looks on a man. A man in a well-fitted suit makes me all kinds of hot and bothered. It portrays sophistication, confidence, and someone who knows what he wants.

A nice pair of jeans that hug a tight ass, that casual look of a shirt that shows me the muscles on his arms. Both of these are my ideal outfit. Of course, a third favorite look is always going to be him naked. You'd be lying if you didn't admit that a naked man doesn't get the hormones jumping.

This whole thing is a little surreal. Five hours ago, I was sitting with Hannah listening to her come up with some crazy idea and encouraging me to go out and find dessert. Here I am sitting in the foyer of a classy hotel waiting for a sexy man to get a room for the sole purpose of us going to hook up. My life is one crazy train wreck sometimes. Imagine what Fleur would say, if she could see me now. Besides the screaming and yelling I would get when she found out I snuck into the function and she didn't know. Hence why I can't tell her about Grayson even though she is my best friend. Because then I'd have to explain where I was when I met him.

Yeah, no chance, not worth it.

It occurs to me that we must look interesting to other people in the lobby of the hotel. Still in our ball attire and the masks, no luggage. Most people would have at least taken the masks off by now. Grayson at the desk getting a room and me sitting here on my own. For anyone who cares to take an educated guess, they would know we're here for a hook-up. I start to feel a little embarrassed and self-conscious about what they're thinking. I feel people's eyes on us, which is probably stupid and not even the case. Thank goodness before I have too much time to get stuck on the thought and decide to run, Grayson returns to extend his hand and lift me to my feet.

"You look a little preoccupied, are you okay?" He gently places his hand on my arm in a purely caring way and not with any sexual energy. That makes me melt more than all the touches so far tonight. He doesn't know me, yet he still cares to check I'm alright.

"Yes, thank you for checking. Just a new experience for me. I started to get a little spooked." It just came out, but I can't help but be honest with him.

"Hannah. We can stop this at any time. We can head up to the room and just sit and have a drink together, or we can turn around and walk back to the ball. I told you before, you are totally in control of tonight. I would never want you to do something you might regret." The fire in his eyes that was there before is gone and that kindness I first saw has returned.

The use of Hannah's name reminds me of what I'm doing and the challenge I have set myself to step out of my comfort zone. Plus, a hint of guilt is sitting on me for not telling Grayson my real name.

Pulling the courage back out that I found earlier somewhere deeply hidden, I lean forward on my tippy toes to get closer to his ear.

"Or we could go upstairs, and you can show me how you can better any man I've ever been with. Well, so you say, maybe you're all talk." This time, it's him I feel a little shudder from, and the grip on my arm becomes firmer. His other arm comes around the back of me and pulls me tight against his body.

"Oh, there is no doubt I will rock your world, little one. Time for talk is done. Now it's time for action. Just so you know, I couldn't give a fuck what anyone in this hotel thinks about us. I only care what you will be thinking after I fuck you to the point you can no longer find any words to talk. Tonight is just you and me, my mystery lady."

He kisses me hard and firm on the lips, but only for a second.

It's like the promise of what's yet to come.

There's no turning back now as he walks me quickly towards the elevator. What is it with men and forgetting their legs are always longer than mine? I need two steps for every one of his, and in these heels, I have no frigging hope.

Again, with the crackling of sexual tension on the ride to the twenty-first floor. I wonder how much it cost just for the night. I can't imagine a hotel like this one offering rooms by the hour. Well, let's hope it's for at least a few hours, all this talk for only an hour would be a disappointment.

He gestures for me to lead the way from the elevator, while still having his hand on the small of my back steering me. Thank goodness because I have no idea where we're headed. With gentle guidance, we turn left and walk down past three doors to where he stops me.

Swiping the key card, I look at the green light on the lock.

I internally laugh that this is my sign to go.

Oh god, I hope this is the fantasy I'm longing for!

GRAYSON

Tonight's been far from what I was expecting when I left home.

Part of me was wanting to ditch the boys and stay in for the night.

Thank god I didn't.

The woman walking through the door into this room fascinates me. I can't quite get a read on her. There is no disputing how stunning she is and how sexually attracted to her I am. Her eyes seem to hypnotize me. Every time I look at her, they draw me in. But what confuses me is one moment she appears confident yet at times she drops her head and looks so shy and unsure.

There is no question the request for the mask to stay is to help her get through her lack of confidence at what she is doing. I have no problem with a little playing, but I don't want to push her more than she is really ready for.

Reaching the center of the room, she stops in front of me. The room is a simple one, but with a king-sized bed which I plan on making good use of. I can feel the nervous energy coming from her as she stands, unsure how to proceed. I need to make good on the promises I made her.

Stepping close so my body is touching her back, I slip my hand around her stomach. Leaning down and scooping her hair to one side, I slowly start to place soft kisses and nibble on her skin along her shoulder and up her neck. I can hear her breathing change and her body is vibrating.

"You okay, little one?" I continue to kiss her as she lets out a moan with the word yes mixed with it.

"I need you to help me know what you like. I want you to tell me what you want." My hand starts to move up her stomach and take her breast in my hand. My thumb rubs her hard nipple that is pushing through her dress.

"Everything, I want everything." Her voice is soft and needy. Like she is already well on her way to building the first of many orgasms I plan on giving her tonight.

"That's very broad. You must trust me, yet you don't know me." I can't help but push her to see how into the moment she really is.

By now I'm nibbling on her ear, and my other hand is rubbing her dress right above her pussy.

"Are you going to hurt me? Please don't hurt me." I want to stop and take her in my arms and ask her who else has hurt her, but there is no way we're stopping this.

"Never, only ever pleasure, beautiful. I want you. I intend to make you come, to fuck you hard, to have you scream my name and then to do it all again. Do you trust me to give you that?" Fuck, I'm already aching and want to strip her bare and sink so far into her. I don't know why but she has me by the balls and has had all night.

"Yes, I shouldn't but yes, I do. Don't make me regret it. Please god, Grayson. More, I need more."

That's it. No more holding back. I stand upright to find the zip on the side of her dress, starting to slip it down when she stops me.

"No, you first." She might trust me, but her insecurity wants me in the vulnerable position before her.

"Happy to oblige. Shall I? Or would you like to do the honors." I smile as I slide my jacket off and throw it on the chair to the side of us. She turns to face me, her eyes already scanning my chest even without my shirt open. They tell me she wants to yet is shy. I take her hands and raise them, placing them on my first button, holding them there as she starts to undo it. I slip my hands down her arms slightly to free her hands up to work her way down. As she gets to the top of my pants, she gasps a little as she dips her fingers into my pants to pull the shirt out and finish the buttons. I want her to take this as slow as she needs to. She's watching her own hands as they finally make contact with my skin. It starts with just the tips of her fingers, but once she starts, her hands are flat against my abs and she is getting acquainted with my chest.

Fuck, it feels good. Her touch is different. I can't explain how, but it's different. Finally, she pushes the shirt off my shoulders, and undoing my cuffs, I let it fall to the ground. I start by undoing my belt, so she knows it's okay to keep going.

"Like what you see so far?" I ask as she starts on my pants.

"Very much. Now let me see if all this talk is true on what you're hiding." She shows the first little smile since we got into the room.

"Oh, baby, I promise you won't be dissatisfied." I groan as her hand slips into my boxers and wraps around my cock that is aching. Shit, finally she is letting down her walls.

It's enough to set me off and there is no way I can wait any longer. I want her naked and spread out on this bed.

"My turn." I start again on the zipper.

"I'm not finished," she complains.

"Don't care. I want you naked. I need to see your stunning body. I want to touch you. Don't you want that too?" Her eyes tell me yes before she even opens her mouth to speak.

The dress starts to fall to the ground along with the last of her shyness.

Oh, for the love of god!

Now that is a fantasy no man will ever be able to deny himself.

My mystery woman stands before me in black lingerie, including suspenders and stockings. Top it off with her long brown hair spilling over her shoulders and falling softly over her breasts. The mask just makes her look so decadent, the forbidden fruit. I'm in turmoil in my mind if I want her naked or like this, which is driving my cock crazy.

"Fuck, you are so fucking hot, little one. Where have you been hiding?" I drop my pants, boxers and all. I'm becoming impatient. Her hands again go to my cock and balls. Wrapping around me and slowly stroking while caressing the underside of my balls. I feel like I'm going to lose it before I even get her on the bed.

"That feels so good, but I need to pleasure you first. That's the promise I made." Taking her hands, I turn her back to the bed and walk her backwards. As much as I love looking at her dressed up like a sexy goddess, I want more. Slowly I slip my hands behind her to undo the bra and let the straps start to fall from her shoulders. My hands then help to drag it off before she has a chance to feel self-conscious.

I can't wait. I bend and take her tits in my hands. I place one in my mouth, lathing her nipple with my tongue while I massage her other one. The moaning is already starting from her. Music to my ears. As I break free and look up at her face. Her head is back, and her eyes are closed as she lets herself be in the moment, feeling it all.

If she is reveling in my mouth on her tits, I can't wait for when my tongue first swipes up her pussy. Gently I lower her down to the bed and slip off her shoes. I undo the snaps of her suspenders and slowly roll the stockings down each leg, following with kisses and mapping every part of her legs for memory. Her hands are already gripping the bed tightly the more I touch her.

All she has left is her panties and her mask. As much as I would love to see her face, it's hot as hell. Something I've never done before. Sure, I've blindfolded women before who've been into that, but this is different. It is more sensual just concentrating on her eyes and her lips.

I lean over the top of her and start to kiss her. Her hands lift up, and she shoves them into my hair, gripping hard as the kiss between us deepens. Her mouth opens, wanting all of me. It's like she wants me to give her everything, just like she asked.

"You taste so beautiful and sweet, but now I want to know if your other lips taste naughty and sexy." Her body twitches as she enjoys the dirty talk.

Her legs fall to the bed as I get lower down her body. I run my nose up her pussy over the top of her lace panties which has her rising off the bed. I want to rip them off but know I need to hold back.

Hooking my fingers in the sides of her panties, I slide them off her while her body is writhing in the air.

"Grayson, please." There it is. The best sound in the world.

"Yeah, little one, hold on tight. I want you screaming my name next time." My hands run up the insides of her thighs as they try to close from the overload of sensation.

"No you don't. Relax and feel it all." Gently pushing her legs flat on the bed, I take my first taste of her wet pussy. My tongue swipes up and then presses down on her hard nub. Her body is aching for release as it continues to build towards that first orgasm that is going to shatter through her. The more I taste, the more she wants. Her groans and whimpers lead me on. Her hands in my hair pushing my face deeper tell me she is close to exploding. I know I can give her the relief she needs in one simple move. I want her to experience it and feel the sensation.

As I suck hard on her clit, taking it between my teeth, I push two fingers inside her and stroke straight on her G-spot.

"Grayson," she screams as she orgasms hard with her coming all over my tongue and fingers. I don't give her any reprieve, continuing to stroke her inside and now grabbing one of her breasts, pinching and pulling on her stone-hard nipple. She is thrashing and screaming under me until her body floods my mouth again. I gently release everything and stroke her while she comes down from the high she's hit. The smile on her face is one of utter bliss.

"Believe the talk now, beautiful?" I whisper in her ear as her eyes open to see me hovering above her. I kiss her and our tongues dance together while she tastes herself on me.

"Gray," is all she can say.

"I know, now let me fuck you, baby. Let me show you how much more there is for your pleasure." She lays there like a limp rag doll with all the energy depleted from her body.

"I don't know if I can," she mumbles.

"Oh, I know you can. Let me show you." I run my finger up her slit again and watch her body come to life. "See? You think you can't, but your body wants more. Tell me you want more too."

"I want more. I need your cock inside me. No regrets."

That's right, baby, no regrets. But I doubt you will be able to walk away like you think you can.

I lean over the side of the bed to grab my wallet to pull out a condom.

"Fuck!" I'm rummaging through every section and there are none to be found. It's been that long. "Shit." By now she's leaning up on her elbows looking at me confused.

"I don't have a condom. I'm so sorry, I can't believe I've done that. Don't suppose you have one." She just giggles at me. That is not helping my throbbing dick who is on a massive promise.

"No, my friend told me to pack some. I should have listened to her. Sometimes the hotel has them in the bathroom products." She lays back down as I spring off the bed towards the bathroom.

"Thank fuck, you are a genius," I yell as I'm suiting up, walking back towards the vision spread before me. It's tight and obviously not the extra-large size, but it will do tonight. I don't care if I'm squeezing in.

By now we are both getting desperate, and the moment I'm above her, Hannah's legs come up and hook around me as I sink into her.

Oh good lord!

Never have I felt anything like it.

Her head tilts back as she breathes through the initial pain of taking me. After that first few moments that we both need to savor the pleasurable pain, her pelvis starts to rock slightly. Yeah baby, I want that too.

"Now try to tell me this is not the best fuck you've had." With that, the sex explodes between us and we both go hard at it. Clawing, kissing, biting and fucking. It's intense and heavenly. I don't care what she says, it's the best sex I've ever had. There is something different this time.

"Gray, yes Gray, more, I'm so close." She's screaming, and I can't hold on anymore.

"Now, come with me now." As we both explode together. I feel like the amount of come pulsing from my body seems to go forever. That's what happens when you haven't had sex for a while, then you decide to break the drought with the hottest woman you have ever fucked.

I pull out to tidy her up and hopefully lay together for a little while so I can get to know her better before we head for round two, if I'm lucky.

Kneeling on the bed, still between her legs, I look down as I go to take the condom off. Only to see the tip flat.

This is not good. Even without my knowledge I would know this is not ideal.

"Argh, Hannah. Please tell me you're on birth control," I tentatively say.

Her head whips up off the pillow quickly to look at me.

"The condom appears to have split. Might have been a little small for me." What a way to kill a moment.

"Yes, I get the shot. But please tell me you're clean." Her eyes are full of fear.

"I swear on my mother, I am clean as a whistle. I'm tested regularly. There's no fear of that, so it seems we can both relax." The tension shifts from her body and I lean over her.

"I'm sorry that happened." I don't want to lose the moment. I stroke the bottom of her cheek. "Can I take the mask off now? See all of your beautiful face not just your mesmerizing eyes." I wish I'd kept my mouth shut and just kissed her.

Pushing me backwards, she's up off the bed and dressing.

"Woah, wait. It's okay, we can leave them on. I just was hoping to see all of you. Please, Hannah. Stop." She's still grabbing things and shoving her stockings in her bag.

"I shouldn't have done it. I need to go. Thank you. Yes, eleven out of ten." With that, she is dressed, shoes in hand, and heading for the door.

"Hannah. Please wait, I'll walk you down for a cab." After discarding the condom, I'm trying to pull my clothes on as I hear the door bang.

For fuck's sake, how did this happen?

My damn mystery woman disappears from me again!

Chapter Five

MATILDA

Why do they have to make the alarms on phones such annoying noises? Okay, yes, I know it's obvious, I just answered my own question.

Seriously, though, this morning I want to pick it up and throw it across the room. My limited amount of sleep is not making me very pleasant. Well, even less than usual. Because I haven't turned off the alarm, my phone starts vibrating and making noise as it warns me this is the second time it's had to say, "get up, lazy bones." I'm one of these people who sets several alarms, each five minutes apart. I hate being late, so it's my safety net against sleeping in or hitting the snooze button. After the second alarm has already gone off, I can now picture the little person in my phone standing there, hands on hips saying, "now get up, woman, don't make me have to come back here a third time to wake you or there'll be trouble." What the fuck is wrong with me?! Now I'm imagining little people in my phone. Because that's normal...NOT!

I stretch my body out as I lie on the bed, before I attempt to get up. There are muscles hurting that haven't been sore in a very long time. Except for the last ten minutes of my stupidity, I couldn't stop playing the night over and over in my head when I got home.

OMG Grayson was not lying when he said nothing before would compare. I was so worried about getting out of there I even admitted it to him, which I'm sure fueled his ego.

55

But holy shit balls, that sex was off-the-charts hot!

I know I didn't want to tell anyone, but I'm not sure I can keep all that to myself. I also know Hannah will be here at some stage to get all the gossip, and I know there is no way I can lie to her. She will read my face straight away.

BEEP BEEP BEEP

Shit, now I'm pissing off the little person in my phone. Okay, little alarm person, I'm getting up. I definitely need a shower, to wake me and soothe some of these muscles that are letting me know they're still there after all this time.

Feeling half-human and like I can face the day after a shower, a coffee, and piece of toast. I'm now just finishing off my hair and getting ready to leave for the office when my phone chimes again to alert me to an upcoming appointment. Not that for the life of me I can remember what it is. My brain is foggy this morning. Gray fog, and not as in the color grey.

Appointment: Friday 8.45am Dr. Fontain

Oh crap. I totally forgot that was this morning. Normally I would take extra care preparing my body, shall we say, for my gynecologist appointment. I look at the time and realize I don't have time to do anything about it now. It's already almost eight o'clock. It will take me at least thirty minutes to get across town to her office. I hate being late for appointments, so I need to leave. Maybe if I get there early enough, I can go into the ladies' room and freshen up. I grab a razor and cloth from the bathroom and then head to the door.

Taking the first step into the hallway, I hear Hannah and Daisy opening their front door. The smile on her face lights up as she sees me.

"So how was dessert last night?" she says and I'm blushing.

"Did you have the chocolate on top with the cherry?" Daisy asks, getting excited again thinking of ice cream.

"I had the whole works." Hannah gasps while I laugh. Daisy claps thinking I'm lucky. Oh, honey, I certainly got lucky.

"I can't stay and chat, I'm running late for an appointment."

"Bullshit you are, get back here right now, young lady," Hannah yells after me as I speed walk towards the lift.

"Mommy, that's a bad word. You said we aren't allowed to say that," Daisy says as Hannah is trying to close her door.

"Yes, but Tilly is being naughty, so she deserves it." I chuckle as I jump into the elevator and close the doors as she is yelling at me that I better wait for her. I'm wicked, but I can't do it this morning. Tonight, over wine, now that will be a different story.

By then I will be busting to tell someone.

"Hi, Lisa. How are you?" I approach the receptionist in Dr. Fontain's office. She looks up from the desk with puffy eyes and not her usual smiling happy self.

"Oh, hun, are you okay? Looks like you're having a tough morning." I stand waiting to run around the counter and hug her if she starts crying again.

"Hi, Matilda. Sorry, it's been a tough one alright. Dr. Fontain has been called away in the early hours of this morning as her mother's had a massive stroke. They aren't sure what's going on at the moment. The family's all at the bedside with her. She is such a lovely old lady. Always making us morning tea or just popping in to say hello." Lisa has water in her eyes again. "I can't imagine what they're all going through." She mumbles a little behind the tissue that she's using to wipe her face.

"That is so sad. My heart goes out Dr. Fontain and her mom. What awful news. Is there anything I can do for you? Would you like me to go and get you a coffee while you start cancelling your clients?" I feel a little helpless and don't know what else to offer.

"Thanks, but that's fine. We have a friend of Dr. Fontain's due to arrive any minute to take over her appointments today. We don't want to reschedule because we just don't know how long she could be gone for. It just creates too big a backlog. So, Cindy is going to take you through and get you set up, if that's okay. That way we won't be running behind. I hope you don't mind another doctor. Yours is just a routine checkup anyway, right?" Lisa looks at me with despair. I can't say no. I've been coming to Allison since I arrived in Chicago, and we've become good friends. I mean, we don't socialize outside of here, but I tell her my deepest darkest secrets at times. We laugh over stupid things and she just gets me. She is more like my GP than my gyno. To be honest, I very rarely see a GP these days.

I don't want to let Allison down, either, by making a fuss.

"Sure, whatever you need me to do. That's okay. I'll be in and out before you know it and keep you running on time." In my head I'm also cursing because now I won't even have time to freshen myself up either. This morning is turning into one disaster after another. That will teach me for going out last night and getting home late. Lack of sleep is not good for my little brain.

Cindy takes me into the examination room, handing over my gown and running through the normal procedure. Go into the toilet and pee in the cup. Get into the gown and come back out. Hand her the sample then get myself up on the table ready. This has to be the most uncomfortable medical appointment there is on the planet. Guys can argue a prostate exam is bad, having a finger stuck up their butt for thirty seconds. Please, give me a break. We are splayed out like a turkey with our legs up in stirrups while they spread everything wide open for the world to see. Take a look inside, take a swab, stick some weird ass instruments inside us, and then to top it off, take one of those swabs and scrape our insides until they get enough flesh to put under a microscope.

Oh yeah, men have it so hard! Poor bastards.

That's not even taking into account the whole birthing a baby the size of two footballs through a hole that won't even fit a tennis ball. Plus, the joy of a monthly visit from the period and hormone fairy. Who, let me assure you, some months is more like she's a devil carrying a pitchfork and is out to lynch any man she can find or any woman who looks sideways at her.

Safe to say the deal men got is the golden ticket in the lottery of reproduction.

Lying back on the bed looking up at the ceiling, I start to try to imagine myself in the warm water on the island in the picture. Allison has covered the ceiling in pictures to take you away from thinking about what you're doing here. I love it. Her sense of humor is great. She has also photoshopped herself in the background of the pictures so you can play Where's Waldo while you lie there. The pictures get changed regularly.

Cindy comes back into the room to collect my sample.

"Dr. Gray has arrived and will be in shortly, I'll just go and test this for you. Just lie back and relax." She leaves the room again.

Who is she kidding, just lie back and relax?

Firstly, this is a gynecologist appointment which is bad enough, and secondly, it's with a doctor I don't know. I now have to expose my most private part of my body to her and let her touch it. Yeah, just relax she says!

I can feel my heartbeat getting a little quicker as I start to feel anxious. God, can they hurry up so we can just get this over with and I can get on with my day?

Go back to swooning over those strong hands from last night and what Grayson did with them.

Those eyes, oh god, those dreamy eyes.

A knock on the door wakes me from my daydream.

Oh, fuck me dead and twice on Sundays. It's those eyes!

Staring at me from the doorway and walking straight towards me.

The sound of the door shutting behind him can't even make me move.

Oh god, I need to get out of here.

Shit!

Shit shit shit!

I'm frozen and can't take my eyes off him.

Maybe I'm mistaken. He could be a brother, a cousin, or just a lookalike.

Until I see the little scar on his chin. Dread slams into me.

It's Grayson, I'm sure of it.

For fuck's sake, my life is a train wreck.

Only I could have a mystery guy I plan on never seeing again, then he turns up in my life again less than eight hours later.

What is he doing here?

In the doctor's room, in a doctor's coat, with a stethoscope in his pocket. Coat open and his shirt fitting nicely across that chest. The one last night I explored every inch of.

Oh crap, the name registers – Dr. Gray!

His eyes haven't left mine either. He hasn't said a word.

No, surely, he can't recognize me. He only saw my eyes. I don't have anything on my face that will give me away.

Bingo!

He thinks my name is Hannah. Even if he is suspicious, my name will be different, so he'll just think he's seeing things. That's perfect. I need to snap out of it and pretend I don't know him. That I don't know what those plump perfect lips taste like, and how his tongue circled my mouth as he took control.

Snap out of it, you idiot. Just do the appointment and get out of here ASAP. Make up some crap about how you're just here for a possible urinary tract infection. There is no need for an examination. Just test my pee and get out of here. I don't even know if that's a thing, but that's all my crazy head can come up with. Slowly sitting up on the table, I come face to face with Grayson.

Who apparently also goes by Dr. Gray.

Or in my world.

Grayson the Gorgeous Gyno.

A quick shake of his head, and he looks down at his chart again.

"Matilda, hello, I'm Dr. Gray. I apologize for the change of plans this morning. Unfortunately, Dr. Fontain has family issues to deal with. She has asked me to look after her caseload today until she knows more. Lisa tells me you're okay with this, and that's very kind of you." He reaches out his hand to shake mine. As soon as I touch it, I can't help but shiver. His expression tells me he felt something too.

Now I'm back to the same problem as last night. If I speak too much, I'm going to give away who I am. Hannah, you owe me big time. Once again, remember the rule.

Never listen to Hannah!

So instead of answering him, I just nod my head.

"Right. Let's get on with the examination so you can get your clothes back on. You're shivering a little so you must be feeling a little cold." He smirks as he turns to pull the trolley with the tray of instruments on it towards him.

"If you can just lie back down and we'll get you set up in the stirrups and we can start. Then we can chat about any issues when we finish. How does that sound?" What is it about that voice that has me all sorts of giddy? Damn, I can't even tell him I don't need an examination because that means talking.

Fuck, I give up. What does it matter, he's seen it all anyway. Touched it, licked it and fucked it. I need to stop thinking about this otherwise he's going to be looking at one wet turned-on pussy.

Is there a shovel big enough to dig a hole for me right now, so I can crawl down into it and just die from embarrassment?

How is it possible that last night's fantasy has become today's nightmare?

Seriously, what even is my life!

GRAYSON

"Hey, Lisa. Have you heard any more from Allison on her mom yet?" I rush into the front of my friend's office. It was not the phone call I was expecting at four am. Especially after only just getting to sleep.

Allison and I went through med school together and both ended up specializing in the same area. Over the years, we've helped each other out on different occasions and also quite often discuss cases we need a second opinion on. At times it helps to have a woman's opinion on certain things. I know all the technicality of the female body, but nothing is as valuable as firsthand knowledge.

There was a time at college where we were flirting around each other, but then realized before it was too late, we were just really good friends and should keep it that way. I'm so glad we did.

It was awful to hear her in tears as she tried to tell me this morning what was going on while she was on the way to the hospital. The best thing I can do for her is look after her patients and keep her business going as much as I can. It will mean pulling some big days between her load and mine, but I'll pull in extra help if I have to.

"Hi, Gray, not much. I got a text about an hour ago to say no change. She's still in the ICU in a coma." Poor Lisa has tears spilling down her cheeks. By the look of her, I'd say they aren't the first tears for the day. I think we're all in shock. Even when you're a doctor, it still doesn't make you immune to these sudden medical episodes.

Walking around the desk, I put my arm around her and give her a hug, showing we're all here to support each other. Rubbing her arm a little, I know I need to get started so the day doesn't get any worse. Luckily Allison only had morning appointments and afternoon rounds in the hospital. I'm rostered on afternoon shift today so I can cover her rounds with mine, and then manage some sleep sometime early tomorrow morning. Nothing I haven't done many times over the years.

"Okay, let's pull it together and get things underway. Who's my first patient, and please tell me they didn't already bolt because I'm a guy?" Lisa lets out a little giggle and hands me the file.

"Matilda Henderson. Routine checkup and smear. Cindy already has her in the exam room and got you set up." Just as she's finishing, the phone on her desk starts ringing which cuts our conversation off.

Dumping my bag in Allison's office and dragging on my coat, I start scanning the file as I head down the corridor to the exam room. I see Cindy head into the back with a specimen jar, so I know my patient will already be ready to go.

Entering the room after knocking so as not to startle her, my feet freeze as I lock onto those eyes.

Holy shit, it can't be her.

But those eyes!!

The same ones that had me hypnotized all night.

Hannah.

Fuck, it has to be her.

No, but that's not this patient's name. I fumble with the file to look down again.

Matilda Henderson, that's not even close to Hannah.

Looking up again, she is staring right at me. Looking like she is freaking out. Why is she freaking out too? Is it her? Shit, I don't even know what the hell is going on. One thing I do know, though, is I need to find out more about this woman. Otherwise I'm going bat shit crazy and I have no idea why.

You need to pull this together. You are a professional and also helping out a colleague. Do not fuck this up, you idiot. At the same time, she seems to snap out of her freak out and sits up on the table.

We are eye-level, and I'd know those beautiful eyes anywhere. They're her eyes. No matter what her name is.

I need to get to the bottom of this.

I start to introduce myself and put my hand out to shake hers. I deliver my best bedside manner speech which almost derails when I touch her. There is that feeling again. The one from last night. The one that's different and I can't work out why. I feel her shiver at our touch too.

Try as I might, I can't get her to speak. So, I just need to be the doctor here and put all this weirdness aside. I would never forgive myself if I missed something because I was too busy worrying about a woman who may or may not be my mysterious date from last night.

"Right. Let's get on with the examination so you can get your clothes back on. You're shivering a little so you must be feeling a little cold," I say to her, waiting for her reaction. I'm trying to call her bluff, but still she stays silent. She's going to have to talk sooner or later when we get to the question part of the examination. If she's trying to hide from me, let's see how she goes trying to get through this taunting.

"If you can just lie back down and we'll get you set up in the stirrups and we can start. Then we can chat about any issues when we finish. How does that sound?" I wait as she reluctantly lies back down on the bed.

If I was a responsible doctor, I would tell her that I know who she is and ask if she wants me to get another doctor for her. It's what I should do, but I can't help the pressing need to know who she is. This is the only way I'm going to find out. I'm still hesitating, feeling guilty for not saying anything, but surely, she would be saying something if she is uncomfortable. Maybe it's not her.

"Okay, just relax for me, and I'm going to lift your legs now." Placing my hands on her ankle and lifting, I see her close her eyes and bite her lip. "Are you okay, am I hurting you?" I worry that I've done something wrong and we haven't even started. She shakes her head and I continue on. After getting her set up with her legs up, and I explain what I'm about to do, still she keeps her eyes closed. I wish she would open them. That's how I can read her. That's all I had last night, and they were like an open book telling me her story.

I start my preliminary look over her vagina and skin around it. My toes are curling in my shoes. Trying not to show any reaction to what I'm seeing.

It's her.

Fuck, there is no doubt.

The small birthmark on the inside of her right leg just to the side of her vagina confirms it. This beautiful lady innocently lying here is my mystery woman, and she has no idea who I am.

Why did she tell me her name is Hannah? Oh shit, I hope she's not married or something bad like that. I wheel my chair across to the file on the counter and breathe a sigh of relief.

SINGLE is written in the marital status.

Just get on with it and then talk to her and explain who you are. Christ, I can't tell her right now while she's lying there, legs in the air.

This is so fucked up.

Sliding the speculum in, she tenses, which is normal, but still eyes tightly closed. It's as if she doesn't want to look at me. It makes me wonder if she recognizes me on some level. Which would be awkward considering she ran out on me and was Hannah last night.

"I know this part is a little uncomfortable so please tell me if I hurt you at all. There shouldn't be any pain, just discomfort." Winding it out, I encounter something that in all the years I've been practicing I've never seen.

I can't help but start laughing, although totally unprofessional. But who wouldn't laugh at seeing their own cum inside a woman they're examining? Her eyes open wide and look shocked at me laughing.

"I'm sorry, I'm not laughing at you. Just wondering. Can you tell me, did you have intercourse in the last twelve hours?" I could've said twenty-four, but I'm an ass and want to prove this without a doubt. That they are my little swimmers having a great time inside her body. All staying nice and warm while they race for the end of the marathon that luckily none of them will win.

"Yes," she quietly whispers as her cheeks blush. Argh, she has a voice. Let's try a bit more.

"Well, he must have been a very well-endowed man, because you have been stretched considerably. It looks like you also had unprotected sex, which is very irresponsible in this day and age." I can see the fire spark up in her eyes. Here we go, I've got her now.

"Not that I would consider it any of your business, but no, he had one of the smallest penises that I've ever had. Plus, we did use protection, but he was so useless he didn't put it on right, and it leaked. Condom must have been too big for his pin dick." Oh, little one. Two can play at this game.

"I would say, the medical evidence here says otherwise." I want to really get her fired up, but I know I still need to get the smear we need and retain some doctor-patient relationship. I decide to stop talking until she is dressed and sitting on the bed. Then it's game on, beautiful.

"Almost done," I say as I slip the speculum out and clean her up. I see her shudder every time I touch her. It's hard to look at her like this in a clinical setting, when only hours ago I was devouring her and claiming this very part of her magnificent body. I learned a long time ago how to keep my doctor's coat on at work, however, I can still enjoy a woman's body outside of here.

"You can hop up and dress now. I'll give you a minute and will be back shortly to finish the appointment." I can see she's still nervous and flighty. Just like last night. Ready to run at the first opportunity. Part of her, though, I can see is ready to give me a mouthful for my cocky comments before, pardon the pun.

I walk outside the room and just lean my back against the wall. My head's spinning and I don't know how to tackle this. I want to tell her who I am and that I recognize her. But I'm just not sure how she'll take it.

A few minutes have passed, and I know the fun is about to start as I turn to walk back in.

Sitting on the bed with her back straight and her game face on, I take a seat and grab the file as I wheel it towards her.

"We are nearly done and then you can get on with your day." I raise the pen ready to fill in the answers.

"Now just for the records, checking your name, if you can tell me." I look her straight in the eye to see her reaction.

"Matilda Henderson," she says without batting an eyelid.

"You know, you don't look like a Matilda. I imagined your name as something different." Moving on quickly so she doesn't have time to reply, I ask more questions just on her general medical history.

"You are currently on the birth control shot which is due again in four weeks' time. I advise you to make sure you're on time so you don't leave yourself unprotected, what with your prior history of disregarding protection. Can't be too careless now, can we. You might want to mention to your boyfriend to buy better condoms next time." I look at her with a smirk on my face. She is trying so hard not to react.

"He is not my boyfriend, just some dickhead I thought might give me a good night. Turns out I was wrong." Matilda, Matilda, Matilda. If you really thought that, then you wouldn't be sitting there ready to draw blood from me.

"As discussed before, the medical evidence doesn't lie, and I'm sure he would have been a proper gentleman to you. I can't imagine a pretty lady like yourself would attract anything but a man who knows how to treasure you." I emphasize the word treasure just to put the nail in the coffin.

"Are we done here?" She jumps off the bed and grabs her bag, stalking towards the door.

"Yes, your results will be back in a week, so be sure to check in with Lisa if there are any issues." There she goes, running again. I follow her out to the reception where she is bypassing Lisa and has her hand on the door handle.

"Thank you for seeing me today, Hannah. I really enjoyed seeing you again." She stops and slowly turns to stare me down.

"Dr. Gray, did you say your name was? I'm so bad with names. Just so you know, that man we discussed? He may have been a gentleman last night, but he is certainly an asshole today. Thank you for pointing that out. Now I won't make the same mistake again."

Just like last night, the sound of the door closing signals my mystery woman disappearing from my life.

Again!

Chapter Six

MATILDA

"**W**hat a jerk!"

"I can't even work out what I saw in him last night." I rant to anyone who will listen as I stomp with vengeance down the sidewalk. I should've got a cab but I'm too furious to sit still.

"How dare he make comments about having sex and being irresponsible. It was his fault. What a douche. He knew. He knew all along who I was." People are staring at me talking to myself. I don't care. I need to vent, and I'll be damned if they're going to stop me.

Standing at the traffic lights mumbling to myself, a lady lightly put her hand on my arm to ask if I'm okay. She startled me at first.

"Thank you, yes, I'm fine. Just letting off steam. Men are just assholes." I start to laugh a little at my ranting.

"Honey, I feel your pain. Whatever he did, don't you let him get away with it." She smiles at me as she starts to cross the road on the walk symbol.

"I won't, thanks," I call to her as she disappears in the crowd. "It's not like I'll be seeing him again anyway."

Now I'm hot, sweaty, and still pissed off when I finally make it into the office. Marching straight past Fleur's office, she just stares at me with her mouth open while she's stuck talking to someone on the phone.

My bag makes a loud bang as I dump it on my desk, and then I storm into the bathroom.

Standing in front of the mirror taking a deep breath, I close my eyes. Slowly releasing it. I can feel my heart still beating hard against my ribs. Another big breath and it's starting to slow finally.

I don't think I've ever been so angry with a man in my life. Actually, that's a lie. There was that one guy all those years ago who shall remain nameless. Besides him, this will have to rate a close second. Slowly pulling myself together, freshening up, I head back to my office. Walking through my door, I find Deven sitting in my seat with his feet up on my desk and Fleur on the couch. Both sets of eyes zero in on me like laser beams. They're not saying a word, just waiting.

"You can wait all you like. I don't want to talk about it," I mutter, swiping his boots off my desk.

"Bad luck. There is no way you are storming in here that upset, then not sharing. It's either something really terrible, or it's super juicy. Whichever it is, you obviously need to spill it. Come on, we're waiting," Deven, our resident gossip queen, taunts me.

"Seriously, don't you have something better to do with your morning? Pretty sure we aren't paying you to sit in the boss's office and be annoying." I lean over him to turn on my computer and try to continue as if they aren't here.

"Now that's where you're wrong," Fleur says. "*This* boss is happy to allocate her half of paying his wage to give him time to help me get you talking." They both start laughing at me. My body language must be giving away my frustration.

"Unlike you two, I actually have work to do. Hurry along, children, and go look for your gossip elsewhere." I wave my hands trying to shoo them out.

"Tilly, I haven't seen you this worked up about anything since the great Ice Sculpture Fiasco of the Debatore wedding. You remember the one where the sculpture turned up as two naked people with the guy and his erect penis. They got the deliveries mixed up." Fleur is laughing as I smack my hand on my forehead.

"There is no need to remind me of the details. I'm pretty sure that day is imprinted in my memory bank loud and clear." I can't help laughing as we all remember the look on the mother of the bride's face when the wrapping was dropped to reveal the *large* statue, shall we say.

"I've never managed to learn two new skills so quickly, as I did that day. Got my ice sculpting certificate and a diploma in rearranging floral arrangements to hide a nude statue, all in twenty minutes." It felt good to laugh for the first time since getting out of bed. This morning was such a shit show that I need to start again and just move on. Shelve Mr. Tall Dark and Handsome for another time, when I can unpack and dissect what the hell happened.

After the laughing settles down a little, I'm just about to try to get rid of them again, when we all hear the front door of the office open. Deven stands and leaves my desk to greet the client so we can at least look a little professional.

"This isn't over, you know," Fleur mouths at me.

Turns out just to be the delivery guy with a bunch of flowers from Lucia to thank us for last night. The client from hell is at least happy, which is a bonus.

"I haven't even got to tell you about last night yet." Fleur looks at me weirdly. "Come to think of it, strange you weren't on the phone first thing."

"I had a gyno appointment this morning so was a little distracted." I take the flowers and put them on my desk. I need the cheering up today.

"On that note, I'm out." Deven throws his hands in the air. Mental note made that next time we need to get rid of him just start talking about our lady bits and he will squirm and run.

I laugh a little. "Now what do I need to say to get you to run away too?" I stand with my hands on my hips.

"Let's see, I think I'm here for the long haul. I think it will take a while to unravel those knickers out of your ass to start with. My guess, it has a lot to do with the tall, dark. and handsome man who was one of the Fuckalicious Four at the ball last night. The one you left early with after you skulked around the event thinking I wouldn't notice you there." My mouth drops and I'm trying to get words out to deny it, although it's going to be useless. I'm hopeless at lying, and if she already caught me out, what the hell is the point? The one person who knows my every nuance is eyeballing me with the biggest smirk on her face.

"How the hell did you know?" I fall back into my chair. Slowly she gets up, closes the door, and then takes the chair at my desk so we are nice and close.

"Tilly, you have been my best friend since we were four years old. I know everything about the way you walk, smile, laugh, flick your hair, hold your head, and every other little thing about you. Besides, you think I wouldn't notice the weirdo that was just wandering around on her own, trying not to be noticed yet stood out like a flashing beacon to me. You know me better than that." Leaning back and making herself comfortable, she continues with her rant. "So, we will unpack the need to spy on me at a later date. Right now, though, you need to spill the tea on what happened with mister dark and delicious."

I groan and put my face in my hands. "You won't believe me even if you hear the whole story," I mumble.

"Give me the whole thing, from start to finish, and I'll be the judge of that. Do I need coffee?" She laughs to herself watching me like I'm dying trying to get the courage to start my story.

"This is more of a wine and chocolate type of story, or even tequila shots, but I think it's against the rules of drinking to start at ten-thirty am. Just for the record, though, I was not spying on you." Fleur rolls her eyes at me to let me know she doesn't believe me but is prepared to leave it for the moment.

"Come on. Time's a wasting, woman," she tries hurrying me along.

"If I can offer you one piece of advice before I begin. Never listen to Hannah. Her ideas suck!"

"Please, do tell, I'm sure this story just got ten times better." Fleur starts to giggle. "I suppose both of you are going to blame poor Daisy next. I mean that five-year-old is pretty smart."

Thirty minutes later and I've laughed, yelled, and cried through the whole drama-length edition of my masked night and morning with the Gorgeous Gyno.

"He may be twenty out of ten for the sex and perfect night. That does not excuse him for being a dick this morning. How did he even know it was me? Why didn't he say something?" I was still wound tight like a spring getting it off my chest.

"Let's be a little fair here. You didn't say anything either." Great, now my friend is on his side.

"You're supposed to suggest we tie him to a tree and shoot flaming arrows at him, trying to hit him in his dick. Isn't that what best friends do?" I stand up to pace the room.

"In your warped head, maybe, in the real world we just walk up to him and knee him in the balls then tell him that's for being a total douche. Or we send Deven down to sort him out. That man can bitch slap like no one's business.

What will it be, the knee or the bitch slap?" Trying to keep a straight face, we both lose it and the laughter overtakes us.

"I still think the arrows are the best idea." The tears are running down my face from laughing. Fleur walks to me and hugs me tight.

"I'm sorry that after the perfect night with the sex god he ended up being a jerk. At least you got your fantasy and finally got laid. You need to forget what happened past the minute you ran out and took your Cinderella moment. Just look at it this way, he turned into the pumpkin, not you."

"All jokes aside, are you okay?" Fleur looks straight at me to check I wouldn't lie to her.

"Yeah, I'm okay. It just really sucked how it ended today. Last night, there was something in that room. A feeling, an electricity that was bigger than just great sex. I think that's why I freaked and ran. I didn't know how to cope with that. It was just supposed to be a one-night stand, a bit of fun. Now the joke's on me. Even today when he was doing his best to be the biggest jerk, he was still setting my body on fire, my heart beating and hoping the appointment might turn into something else. How stupid is that?" I feel like an idiot. I'm a grown woman, yet a guy whose last name I still don't know, has me all tied in knots.

"It's not stupid at all, a little funny when you look from the outside in, but definitely not stupid." We both hug again and then get on with talking about the actual function and how the staff went. She told me about TJ and all the awesome things he did and improvements he's bringing to the team. I knew we did the right thing with giving him more responsibility. Time passes and our stomachs are letting us know that lunch should be next on the agenda. Deven for once has stayed out of the office and let us get through my girly crisis.

"I can't believe we've been talking so long, and still you haven't said sorry for spying on me. Seriously, what possessed you to sneak into the ball?" Fleur says joking but part of her is still worried I didn't trust her.

"In all honesty, I just felt bad for leaving you with a function that was holding together with strings at one stage yesterday. You convinced me you didn't need me, so I went home. Then Hannah was talking about me being so high-strung and blamed it all on no sex for over a year. Or if you want it in child code language, I was sent out to find some dessert for the night to mellow me out."

Fleur just stared at me and then spat her water out across the room. "So, your deliciously hot gyno was dessert. Oh, that's gold. Fucking Hannah is so hilarious. Seriously, if that was just dessert, imagine what it would have been like if you were served the whole three-course meal before you took flight. There would have been no walking today and instead of asking if you had sex last night, he would have asked if you had been to a mass orgy."

"Fleur, that's disgusting," I scream, slapping her arm. "Why do you even think these things. Like you even know what that's like." She drops her head slightly and her cheeks pink up .

"Oh. My. God. Fleur! Tell me you haven't been to one." I know she's more confident than me but seriously, this is next level.

"That's a story for another lifetime. Now how about we get some lunch?" she mumbles.

"Fleur, what lifetime? Your lifetime and my lifetime are the same lifetime. What the hell have I missed? I need the gossip immediately!" I give her the stink eye that secretly says I can't believe you haven't told me this.

There isn't any talking happening. A lot of playing with the hem on her skirt, crossing and uncrossing her legs. I'm waiting and not letting her out of this. The door bursts open with Hannah and Deven barging in. I'm not sure who Hannah is talking to. Just one of us or all of us. Perhaps it's just anyone who will listen. What I do know is the chance to get the story out of Fleur is gone. That will have to wait, but not for long, that's for damn sure.

"You!" Hannah finally stops and points straight at me. "You are so damn cruel. Running off on me while I juggle three bags, locking a door, and coping with a five-year-old who is jumping around excited because you mentioned dessert. She wanted ice cream for breakfast before school. Because if Tilly got the chocolate topping with the cherry on top then she wanted it too. For Christ's sake, woman. You better start talking and tell me every sweet thing that happened and with whom." Standing in the middle of the room with her hands on her hips, I understand why Daisy thinks she's crazy. I'm starting to think she might be right.

"That's my signal to get us some food. Han, are you staying for lunch?" Fleur asks as Hannah doesn't take her eyes off me.

"Depends if it means I get the dessert story served with my salad?" Fleur signals Deven to get his phone out to start the order.

"Not a chance, cupcake. You're on lunch duty, Fleur. I'm not missing out on the gossip a second time today." Deven tries so hard to assert some authority.

"Deven, out!" all three of us yell at the same time.

"You are all moody cows, you know that, right? How is a man supposed to keep up when you shut me out?" He turns, huffing as he walks to the door. "You can all order your own lunches, bitches." Mumbling, he keeps walking.

"I pay your wages, remember that conversation," I yell at him.

"Whatever." He gives me the finger over his shoulder and keeps walking.

"Tell me again why we keep him around?" We all laugh at Fleur as she starts the lunch order on her phone instead. "I'll sort it out and catch up when I get back. I'm sure the second time round is going to be even funnier."

So glad everyone is getting so much amusement out of my nightmare. Who needs enemies with friends like mine?

GRAYSON

How I've managed to get through today is a miracle.

A total of three hours' sleep, in the last thirty-six hours.

Twenty-three consultations of Allison's patients in the office then fourteen in the hospital.

Sixteen of my own patients and then an emergency C-section to deliver twins at eleven pm just to make the day finish on an adrenaline rush.

Not even taking into account my mystery woman.

My head is still a mess thinking of the woman I knew as Hannah is really Matilda. The appointment this morning has thrown me.

I woke up this morning after dreaming of a woman who ran out on me and left me wanting more. I had no idea what I did to make her take off like that. The night was perfect, and for me it was the best sex I'd ever had. Watching her lose herself beneath me was beautiful. But I still can't rationalize the memory of screaming the name Hannah as I reached the peak of my orgasm inside her, only to find out that's not even her name.

Her eyes just looked deep into my soul as I took her breath away.

Then she was gone. I finally drifted off to sleep in my apartment after leaving the hotel thinking of how I could find her again.

Never in my wildest dreams did I picture walking in to her propped up on my examination table, half-naked.

I'm good at my job because of my calmness and professionalism. I threw every single part of that out the window this morning. I was stunned and hypnotized by her eyes once again, only to have my curiosity turning me into a crazy idiot. The things I said to her were so not called for. Yet the guy inside me hurt at the deceit and her running off just took over. Then to have her say I had a small dick and the sex was shit, that was like a red flag to the bull. Seriously. I should have walked out and let the girls reschedule her. I should've known though that she had worked out who I was.

The most annoying thing while I was examining her was, that even in the peak of my anger, how much I wanted to take her and kiss the hell out of her. Those plump lips that last night tasted so frigging good. My dick wanted to do a whole lot more, and in all the time I've been a doctor, never have I been attracted to a patient. I've now broken that rule.

Staring at the ceiling from the bed in the doctor's night quarters, I still can't get Matilda out of my head. Last night she was this beautiful enchantress and today she was a strong, feisty woman who captivated my every thought. The hard part is now I know her name and all her details, I need to decide what to do with that. Professionally, I can't use it. Personally, man, I want to.

I need to stop thinking and start sleeping before another emergency happens and I can't function.

Rest assured, Matilda, I'm not done with you yet. Not even close.

You can run, but know that I will chase you.

Somehow, someday, we will meet again.

"Seriously, Ally, I am going to hang up on you shortly. It's only been a week since the stroke, and I stood in for you at the office. It was not trouble at all. I'm just so glad your mom is slowly recovering to her old self." Sitting in the chair in my office looking out the window, I'm just relieved that everything is now heading in the right direction.

"How are you holding up?" I ask when she stops long enough for me to get a word in.

"I slept a full night last night for the first time since it happened, knowing she is finally out of the woods. Plus, Dad stayed at the hospital last night with her, so I know she wasn't lonely." Allison sighed.

"Ally, have you met your mother? As long as she is talking there's no way she will be lonely. She probably has every nurse in that hospital in stitches laughing at her. I'm surprised she doesn't have a list of every eligible doctor in the place for you already." I start to laugh down the phone.

She groans at my comments.

"Do not even mention that. You'll jinx me or send her ideas through the universe. That woman drives me insane. When will she realize I don't need a man? Well, that's not entirely true, they are a little useful at times, but that one use does not outweigh all the other annoying habits." I can hear her keyboard tapping as she's talking to me on the phone.

"Really, that's your opinion on the whole male species? I personally do not have any annoying habits to speak of. I can assure you." I pull the phone from my ear as she screams down the receiver at me.

"What the hell! This is me you're talking to, Gray. You know, the girl who spent all those years of college with you, who worked all those night shifts with you, and now I'm still cleaning up dramas after you. Want to tell me about what the hell happened with one of my favorite patients, Matilda Henderson? Why she walked out of my office calling you an asshole?" There's silence on the phone from Allison waiting for me to reply.

Fuck, I was hoping that would slip by Lisa's memory or she would keep it to herself.

"What are you talking about, Ally? Oh shit, look at the time. I have to run, literally. It's Thursday and it's game day with the guys." I try to dodge her which is pretty pathetic.

"Don't you dare think you're getting out of this. Did you examine my patient when you already knew her?" She was trying to be forceful but it's not even close.

"Well, technically no."

"What the hell, Gray, what does that even mean?"

"I didn't know I knew her, until I saw some evidence to the contrary," I mumbled a little, knowing I'm about to get strips torn off me by the one person who can do it and get away with it. Well, besides my sister, who tries although I pretend to let her get away with it.

"Oh, this is going to be good, I can tell. Spill it now, and don't you dare try to bullshit me. What details did you see that gave you this big revelation, hmmm?" I can't tell if she's pissed or just pushing me.

"Let's just say one you will be okay with, and one you may or may not want to yell at me for. Are you listening?"

"I'm hanging on every word and can't wait for this," she says sarcastically.

"Now, now, no need for the sarcasm. Here goes." I pause, knowing this will go down a treat. "I was doing the preliminary external examination and a birthmark on her thigh just near the crease caught my eye. It may have looked very familiar to a woman I had met the previous night, who in my defense told me her name was Hannah and we were wearing masks." I try not to stop even though there are noises coming from Ally. "Then, the next thing that confirmed that she was that woman may have been the remains of a good time that was had by all." I pull the phone as far as possible away from my ear. I knew she would scream but it was louder than even I imagined.

"What the actual fuck, Grayson. You better start explaining, how could you have not known who she was?"

"It was a masquerade ball. We both had masks on, all night, until she ran out of the room at the end." Shit, I probably shouldn't have added that part. "Plus, she said her name was Hannah. Now stop freaking out. It's fine. We worked it out by the end of the visit."

"By working it out do you mean her walking out of my office calling you an asshole? I swear to god, Gray, you are on your own if this comes back to bite us on the ass. I hope your insurance is up to date. Luckily, I love you like a brother and you're always there for me, otherwise right now I would be striking you off the Christmas card list. Seriously. I can't believe you fucked her then examined her. Wait, hang on, what the hell did you say about seeing the remnants of a good time? Please tell me you did not sleep with my patient bareback? You are not that stupid, surely!" Now the penny is dropping for Ally. I was wondering how long it would take.

"No, I would never do that, you know me better than that. I spend my days dealing with the shitstorm that creates. The fucking condom broke. Weirdest fucking thing ever to see that in there. Never will that vision leave me. So freaky."

"I forgot how disgusting men are and you have just taken the cake. Thank god Matilda is far more responsible than you and takes her own precautions. Lord knows this world does not need any little Graysons running around. Especially if I have to deliver them. I'm not sure my love extends to bring into the world the devil's spawn." Now she's starting to giggle.

"Wow, I'm so offended right now. Imagine how cute he would be. Plus, the world always needs more geniuses. If it's me that needs to step up to provide them, then it's a sacrifice I'm willing to make. Now you can calm down because I am sure Matilda is fine and you have nothing to worry about." Looking at my watch, which is now vibrating against my arm, I see it's time to move.

"As much as I'm enjoying this little chat, I really need to go. You know how Lex gets if I'm late to anywhere." Standing while I'm still talking, I walk into my office bathroom to change. Putting her on speaker, I listen to the lecture of don't go anywhere near Matilda or use her information for my own purpose.

"Yes, Mom, now go sort out your life and call me with any questions later that you have on my notes. Love to your mom, and tell her I'll be in over the weekend when I'm off shift."

"I'm serious, Grayson," Ally yells down the phone.

"Oops, bad reception, can't...you...go...love..." I hang up to her laughing and giving me shit.

Ally is like my sister that is old enough to almost be the mother that I need sometimes. I love her dearly, just not the kind of love that keeps you warm at night.

With my crazy life as a doctor, I'm not sure I'll ever be lucky enough to find that.

Currently I don't know if I could even manage a relationship.

However.

That's not to say I don't want it.

Who doesn't need to feel loved?

It's been a long time.

Chapter Seven

GRAYSON

"You work the closest and you're always the last one here. Seriously, dude." Just as I knew he would, Lex is into me for being thirty-five seconds late.

"Whatever. Ally was on the phone and giving me a grilling. Have you ever tried to stop her in the middle of a rant? I doubt it. Try it someday and then come talk to me. Now let's play ball," I tell him.

"I bet I could stop her from talking," Tate yells from across the court, thrusting his hips at me. I just glare at him as he chuckles to himself and starts off down the court with the ball. They all know how protective I am of her, along with my sister. He does it all the time, just to get me going.

"Yeah, start running, it's safer." I sprint off to chase him down. I need this. Burn off the irritation that's mounting. Partly from the woman who just screamed at me several times and the other part from the woman who visits my dreams at night and I know I fucked up with. Both are as frustrating as the other.

"What is with you today, man? How are we supposed to win if you aren't concentrating?" Mason squirts water at me from the fountain.

"Sorry, Mas, you should have traded me for another pick early on in the game." I laugh knowing there is no reserves bench.

"Trust me, I would if I could. Want to share your shit mood?" The boys all stop as Mason walks back to the park bench we're all sitting on.

"It's a long story. Not sure we have time right now. We all need to tap out in the next five minutes." I can imagine as soon as I tell them, that the jokes will last for hours. Maybe I should blurt it out now and get it over and done with.

"I'm in surgery this afternoon so I'm out now. Who's around tomorrow night, dinner and beers?" Tate looks around.

"Good for me. I'm on mornings so I'm free. How about you two?" I ask.

Both Mason and Lex are nodding.

"Great, let's meet at Timothy O'Toole's Pub at seven. That work for everyone?" Tate starts backing away as we all agree and starts his run back towards the hospital. I'm off for the rest of the afternoon now, so I think I might go for a run to make up for all the time in the gym I've missed, working solidly for the last week. At least tonight I know I'm going to get a full night's sleep without being called into the hospital. I'm off the on-call roster for the next week, which is heaven.

Thinking now an hour later and at the end of my run, it was probably a pretty stupid time of the day to head out. The heat and humidity have me nearly dying as I walk back into my office. I look like I've been swimming instead of running, with how wet I am. Sweat is running down my face and my tank top is saturated. Maybe tomorrow the gym might be a far better option. When I pass by my secretary, the little giggle and stupid grin let me know something isn't quite right. Between my game with the guys and my run, I've been gone nearly three hours, I'm starting to wonder what I've missed.

"What's going on, Catherine, should I be worried?" I keep walking only hearing her trying to hold in her laugh.

Grabbing a cold water bottle out of the bar fridge in the hallway, I turn the corner into my office, and it all makes much more sense.

"Damn, Allison. Bet you think you are so fucking funny. Well, my girl, you will pay for this one," I say out loud to no one as I walk over to my desk to the bouquet of condom balloons, all different colors and sizes. There is a card which I'm sure will be just as hilarious.

Dear Grayson
Just in case you slept through this college class,
this is what a condom looks like.
Save the universe from little Grays

and make sure you use them.
From the doctor who cares
but also wants to hurt you A LOT
Ally xoxo

All I can hear is Catherine losing it outside my office. I turn to see her videoing my reaction.

"Remember who pays your wages, Catherine." I laugh as I give the phone the bird. "That's for you, Ally. Just remember karma's a bitch, my friend. One day it will come back and bite you on the ass, and I hope I'm there to laugh the loudest." Catherine disappears, and I'm sure that video is already shooting across the internet to Ally's phone as we speak.

"That better not end up on any social media, missy, or there will be trouble," I yell out to her desk.

"Not me you have to worry about," Catherine yells back as I hear her typing away on her computer a message which I'm sure is to Ally.

I must admit, it's pretty clever. I can't even imagine where she got this from and I'm not sure I want to know. Or how she got it here so quickly. Now the next challenge. How to get it out of here and home? I'm not sure it's the right look for a professional gynecologist's office.

"Catherine," I call, "I think I'm going to need your help with these condoms." Oh shit, that didn't come out right. "I mean packing them, not using them. Sorry." Again, there's a fit of laughter coming from her desk. Oh man, how the hell am I going to live this one down? Wait till the boys hear about this. No point hoping they won't. I bet Ally will send them the video just for the fun of it. Come to think of it, she probably already has.

It's going to be a long afternoon. Thank god Tate is in surgery for a few hours. So at least that will keep my phone from blowing up with stupid memes. One day I'm sure he will grow up, I just can't see it being anytime soon. Wait until tomorrow night when they hear the story that prompted the present from Ally. Maybe I need to fake sickness and hibernate. It sounds like a good option.

It's amazing how more in control of your life you feel after a good night's sleep. I consider getting more than six hours is the guideline for normality in a doctor's life. Last night I got eleven which is totally unheard of for me. I feel like I am so full of excess energy, even after my gym session and working the morning shift at the hospital.

"Come on, Memphis, let's go out for a walk and see Aunty Bella. She's been a bit quiet, so we need to go visit. I think she's hiding from us. What you think, boy?" My little buddy looks up at me, tail wagging. Not really understanding or caring what I said, except for the words walk and Bella.

I can't even describe what type of dog he is except for an awesome one. He was a rescue puppy I got from a shelter when I finally got my own place about eight years ago. Buying my condo meant no longer begging a landlord for permission to have a pet. When I walked into the adoption area, he bounded straight over to me and plonked his butt down on my feet. It was like he was calling dibs on me, making sure I couldn't actually move to look at any of the other puppies. When I picked him up and looked at his cute little face that was black with white patches, he licked me up the cheek and I was sold. It was more like he claimed me rather than me choosing him.

That first night we were home, I had Elvis playing in the background and he stood in front of the speaker and whined like he was singing along, then after a while he curled himself up right there and slept through the rest of the album. I knew he was meant to be my family. Of course, the only obvious name was Memphis, the place where magic and love was made.

"Go and get your lead." I look down at him and he is off down the hallway to the front door where it's kept. By the time I get there, he's sitting on his back-side, up straight, lead in his mouth, waiting patiently. "Good boy." I attach it and we are off to play big brother. I know she's at home because I can see her active on my snap map. That's the good and bad thing about technology. You're never invisible. Even if you think you are.

The afternoon weather today is superb. Not as hot as the last few days and a slight breeze which makes it perfect. Memphis trots along like he owns Chicago. This boy has attitude which I'm sure has nothing to do with how spoiled he is. Thinks he's human, I'm sure. Heading up the lift in Bella's apartment, I wonder what she's up to. I know she thinks I'm annoying, but I made a promise to Mom years ago that I would always look out for her. So far, I'm doing just that.

Memphis is sitting patiently at her door, tail wagging like a floor sweeper. I can hear her coming and so can he. His tail speeds up and starts thumping the floor.

"You know you give away who it is, Memphis, with your tail banging. You take away our element of surprise." I lean down to rub the top of his head with my knuckles as she opens the door.

Bella drops down to get attacked with affection. "How's my favorite boy?" By this stage his paws are up on her shoulders and he is all over her.

"I'm doing great, thanks, how about you?" I answer as she totally ignores me. "Good to know who is loved more," I say as I walk past her and into her apartment.

"Memphis, of course. Why do you even question that?" She follows with him at her heels and closes the door.

"To what do I owe this pleasure, big brother?" Bella asks sarcastically.

"Do I need an excuse to visit my sister?" I open the fridge to grab a bottle of water for me and pull Memphis's water bowl out from under her sink that she keeps for his visits. She fills his as I swallow down mine.

"No, you don't. So, what's new?" The perfect opening for me.

"What's new is that I haven't heard from you for over a week. Except for a few one-word answers on reply texts. You know that makes me stress." I lean against her kitchen cupboard while she just rolls her eyes at me.

"Seriously, Gray, I'm not a child anymore. You know I'm responsible for people's lives just like you. Time to let go." She laughs as she comes in for a hug.

"Like that's ever going to happen. You might be responsible for people's lives. Well, guess what, you are one of the lives I'm responsible for. So, suck it up."

She pulls away and heads over to fall into her chair in front of the television where I join her. "Gray, when you promised Mom you would take care of me, I was five years old and you were fifteen. That was twenty years ago. You have done your job. I'm sure Dad also has the job under control. He's just as bad as you. I might have missed out growing up with a mom in my life, but I ended up with two parents. I'm sorry Mom put that on your shoulders, but it's time to stop worrying about me. I promise you'll always be the first person I come to if I need help. It's time you just spent your energy finding yourself someone else to worry about. A girlfriend, perhaps, that maybe you could eventually call a wife. Then even a daughter who you could smother rather than me."

I place my arm around her and draw her into my side for a hug. I know she's right, it's just been my pledge for so long I don't know how to let it go. Dad has sat me down so many times and told me that Mom never meant it to be forever, but I can't get the memory of that day out of my head.

Mom felt just generally unwell for a few months, nothing specific, just not herself. Dad was busy with work, so she didn't tell him. She just kept going, doing her day-to-day things, being the amazing mom she was for all of us. Arabella hadn't started school yet, so she spent time with her during the day then was always there with food for me when I walked in the door from school. Then she was the chauffeur for me and usually at least a few of the guys for any practices or after-school activities we had. She never said a word to any of us.

Until it was too late.

After collapsing at home in immense pain, she was rushed to the hospital. Dad flew in from New York where he was on a business trip to be by her bedside as they did tests. The results devastated us all. She had Stage 4 cervical cancer, and it had spread to her liver. There wasn't anything they could do except give her chemo which was only to prolong her time. It wasn't going to cure her. She and Dad decided against it and let her live her life out as best she could without becoming unwell with treatments.

At first, I was angry.

Angry at cancer, angry at her for ignoring the symptoms, angry at Dad for not noticing and taking better care of her. Just angry at the world, as a fifteen-year-old boy is when he's told his mom is dying.

One night, Mom asked me to come and sit with her in her room. I sat on the bed with her while we talked. Reminisced. Laughed and cried together for hours. She explained how she hadn't really had any symptoms and that is why it is known as the silent killer. Then we talked about her wishes for my life. She begged me not to let this overtake me and make me bitter and mad at life. Take my time, grieve, and then make the best of my life that I can, for myself and for her.

That was the night she asked me to promise I would look after Arabella. Mom knew how devastated Dad was going to be when she was gone. She was the love of his life and I would need to hold the family together, until he was strong enough again, to take over. I promised I would never let anything happen to my baby sister and that the three of us will always stay together and as close as we were then. I would make her proud of me. I laid down and curled up in my dying mother's arms and sobbed myself to sleep like a little boy.

She was gone three days later. I didn't know until years later my dad had sat outside the door of their bedroom on the floor listening to the whole thing, silently crying for the love of the strong woman he married and the sadness we were all about to endure. She knew her time was coming and had taken time with all of us to say her piece before she left us.

It was then I decided I would become a gynecologist. Hoping I could make a little difference in the world and save other families going through what we had.

"Do you still remember her?" Bella quietly whispered into my chest.

"Yeah, Bella, like she was here yesterday." I spoke into the top of her head as I kissed it softly.

"Tell me a memory," is her reply. This is what we do. From the time Mom left us, I tried to make sure Bella always knew Mom. Only being five when our mom died, her memories of her are limited, but she has as many as I have in my heart. I have shared every single one of them multiple times. One day I will be doing the same to Bella's kids, telling them about the grandmother who would have loved them so dearly.

After we sat and talked for a while, I look at the time and realize I need to get moving so I'm not late for dinner with the guys. Memphis is sleeping soundly in his bed that Bella keeps for him when he stays over if I'm out of town.

We both laugh at the little snore coming from him.

"Leave him with me tonight if you're going out. I could use the company. I'm off work tonight and tomorrow so I'll bring him back in the morning." She looks a little sad, which is not what I came over to do, but I know leaving Memphis here with her will be a good idea.

"Okay, and don't think I didn't notice how you managed to get out of telling me what has been going on in your world lately. That conversation will happen tomorrow. Got it?" I tap my finger on her nose as she smiles up at me. "Just tell me, are you okay?" I look her straight in the eyes so she can't dodge me.

"Yes, Dad, I'm fine." She stands up on her toes and kisses me on the cheek, then opens the door for me.

As I'm about to leave, she puts her hand on my arm gently.

"I love you and will always be grateful for you in my life." I hug her as tight as I can and we both separate. Trying to break the mood, she then pushes me into the hallway outside the door.

"Now screw off and find some woman to take home tonight while I babysit your child. Tell the guys I said hi." I just laugh and nod. I walk away knowing there is something not right with my sister, I'll try again tomorrow.

It's okay, Mom. I've got her. I always will. Just like I promised.

Sitting at the bar, I made sure I was first here. I'm not giving them any more opportunity to get on my case. There'll be enough ammunition with what Ally will have sent them and then my Matilda story will give them plenty to last weeks.

If I'm lucky, maybe they will have forgotten.

Right, and the sky is green.

Lex never forgets a thing. His legal brain listens, catalogues, then files it in the correct folder, only to be drawn out at a later date, quoting word for word. No wonder he was on the Dean's Honor List at college graduation.

Just as Mason taps me on the shoulder and nods to the bartender for one of the same, we hear Tate entering the pub. That man is always the life of the party. No matter where he is, he's the loudest. The only time I've ever seen him quiet is when he's operating on a brain. It's like you are looking at a totally different person. The intense concentration and focus he shows are what make him a top neurosurgeon. That type of surgery is powerful and needs stamina for the long hours each operation can take. I think that's part of the reason he's such a wild one out of the hospital. He works hard and then plays harder.

"Where's our anal friend?" Tate says as he pulls up his bar stool.

"Not up mine, that's for sure," Mason says as he takes his first sip of his beer. I just laugh at them both.

"I don't know, I haven't heard from him, but you can be assured I'll be pointing out the time when he gets here. He never manages to miss it when one of us is late." I signal for another beer and one for Tate.

We fill in time chatting about our day and the sport we're looking at on the television screens. Finally, Lex arrives to cheers from us all. He looks pissed and just orders a beer and a shot. Downing the shot, he then turns to us with his beer in his hand.

"Thank fuck it's Friday!" To which we all clink glasses together and cheers to that. One of the things about being friends for over twenty years is we know the times when you need to just shut up and let someone be. Right now is one of those times for Lex. Work must have kicked him in the ass today, so we just go on discussing the boxing match that's about to start on cable.

I thought I would have to do something drastic to save me from the interrogation, but Lex arriving late and pissed at the world has taken the attention. Well, that is until the steaks are placed down in front of us at the table. Tate then pulls out his wallet and flicks a condom packet onto the table.

Shit.

Then Mason and Lex follow.

"Apparently, you're in need of some of these, Ally tells us. Care to explain, lover boy? My guess is it has something to do with a cute little lady you escorted out of the ball last week." As Tate finishes his speech, they're all laughing and waiting for me to talk.

"Is this what had you playing pathetic basketball yesterday?" Mason adds his little bit in too.

"You're all about as funny as Ally. That woman needs to be taught a good lesson. She thinks she can play with the big boys. I'll get her, don't you worry." I start to tell them everything that happened. Well, not everything, just the boys' bullet-point version that's needed. As usual, Tate cannot keep his mouth closed.

"If you just shut up and let me finish, you'll know the answer. So, it turns out my first appointment of the day was her, Hannah—or actually, Matilda, to be precise." I try to continue only to have Tate reply.

"You know this is just like one of those soaps that the nurses watch. Wait, let's get popcorn." He sniggers.

"Shut up, asshole." I throw a chip at him from my plate.

I continue, until I get to the part of Matilda running away again after finally confirming she knew it was me.

"Of course, then Lisa, Ally's secretary, turns me in, and she's all up in my grill yesterday about it. Then thinking she's fucking hilarious with the condom delivery." I finish the last mouthful of my beer and sit back in my seat while they're all enjoying teasing the hell out of me and my life.

"You have to admit, though, that it was a pretty awesome idea. Who doesn't need a bunch of condom flowers? I wish she would send me something special too." Tate is trying to poke me to bite again.

Lex can't resist throwing back at him, "The only thing she will send you is a bunch of barf bags for all the crap that comes out of your mouth. You know how much she loves to listen to that."

This continues for a while until they get all their jokes out of the way. Then finally Mason asks the first serious question since I started.

"All jokes aside, man, you liked her, didn't you?" They all go quiet for the first time of the night.

I don't have to think it over, my answer is straight off my tongue.

"There is something about her. I don't know what it is, she just fascinates me. The fire in her is a massive turn-on. Too bad I can't track her down. All that privacy crap."

Lex just shakes his head at me. "Gray, you'll be lucky if you don't end up being slapped with a medical lawsuit for examining her before you admitted you knew her, not to mention you were a dick to her. Therefore, if you want me to stand up in court and convince a judge you're a good guy just extremely stupid, do not—I repeat, *do not*—use her personal information to chase her down. Are we on the same page here, my friend?" The doctor part of my brain is nodding, yet there is a small part of my brain wanting to ignore him and turn up on her doorstep.

"Besides," Tate adds, "she'll probably add a clause in that lawsuit that she wants compensation for the false advertising you used the night before, telling her you were going to be the best sex she had. We all know that's not possible."

"You are such a dick, Tate, you know that? I'm still confused why we're friends with you," I mumble.

Tate grins and keeps going with his ego. "Because you all need me, to keep my awesome talents rubbing off on you."

Lex rubs his chin. "You are my biggest worry, Tate, we all know that. There will come a time when I am seriously bailing your ass out of jail for finally fucking the wrong woman. I mean, I'm sure you've already been with half of Chicago, so at least some of them must have been married. Or the other even scarier thing is, the chance of having a child support claim for multiple children you have running around this city." He actually looks serious about how much he worries about us.

Mason laughs. "Lex, you need to chill out. We're big boys, and if we get ourselves into trouble then you can kick our ass then. We don't expect you to save us. Well, in saying that, if I ever need anyone, it better be you standing up there." He slaps Lex on the shoulder.

Lex just shakes his head. "See? You do expect me to save all you stupid idiots. I should have walked away from you three troublemakers that first day at school. I'm sure they sat you with me to see if I would make you all behave." He sighs and runs his hand through his hair.

"Like you are such an angel, Alexander Jefferson the third." Tate puts on his poshest voice. "We all have stories that are to the contrary. So, stop with the holier-than-thou crap."

We all start to laugh, even Lex. No matter what happens in my life, I know these guys have my back.

Talking about what everyone else is up to in their lives, the conversation turns to Mason and his new job as a charter pilot on a private jet for a client. She's a high-profile business magnate.

"Basically, I'm just on standby for whenever she needs the jet or is letting someone else use it for business or pleasure. Don't get me wrong, I'm at the airport every day doing checks and maintenance and I have trips booked in. But my job also means if she needs to fly at any time, I need to make it happen. She rewards me very well for this privilege." He smirks a little which tells me there is more to this story than he's telling us.

"How the hell do you get a job where you get paid to just wait around until someone needs you?" Tate asks.

"You become a doctor." I laugh. "It's just we seem to be needed more frequently than a trip every week or so in a fucking private jet. Good for you, Mas. After your years of flying in the military, you deserve a cushy job." He just nods and takes a drink. I know things still haunt him, but he assures us he has it under control.

We spend the next few hours playing pool and debating the problems of the world, how we know all the answers and can fix them if people would just listen to our wisdom. I drink more beers tonight than I have in a long time. It feels good to let go and just relax. No work to worry about, and it makes everything else seem less of a drama.

While the boys are finishing up a game of darts, I sit just letting my mind drift a little. Those eyes keep calling me. I just wish I could work out a way to find them. She may have left last week thinking she hates me because I made her feel that way. I knew she had the power to weaken me. Stupidly, I thought if I was a jerk, then even if she knew it was me then she wouldn't want anything to do with me. It worked exactly to plan. But the moment she left, I regretted every word I said. I was such an idiot. It's funny how six beers will let you admit how stupid you can be. Opportunity totally lost with her, because I'm too scared to feel anything.

We're at the point it's time to call it a night and get an Uber to get us all home, when Tate pipes up with his exciting news. He looks like the cat that ate the canary and that concerns me before he even opens his mouth.

"Hey, Gray, I forgot to tell you. I got the list of my next rotation of interns. Guess which sexy little doctor is going to be spending every day and night with me for six months." The slap on my chest from him makes me shudder.

"Fuck no. Get her moved. You are not having Arabella working under you. I know what happens with your interns. Working under you, literally, they all seem to get extra-credit marks from the teacher. No fucking way. I'm talking to the boss tomorrow." The beer has lost the warm glow I was feeling. That sober, clear head is back and there's no way Tate is going anywhere near Bella.

"Calm down, Dad," Lex says, putting his drunk arm around my shoulder. "She'll learn a lot from Tate, you know he's the best neurosurgeon we know."

"He's the only neurosurgeon you know, idiot," I spit my words frustratingly at him.

Mason is the only sober one out of the four of us, due to being on call to fly his jet at any time.

"Gray, settle. He wouldn't be stupid enough to touch her; she's your sister and also like a little sister to him. You know he'll look after her. She's probably safer with him than that other guy he works with. His reputation is worse than Tate's and that's saying something." My mind is scrambling to rationalize.

"Yeah, what he said. Bella is my little sister too, man. There is no way in the world we are letting Zoran near her. Trust me, bro, if they don't suck his dick, they fail." He is way drunker than I am. "Plus, she will kill you if you get involved, you know that. To be honest, I'm almost as scared of her as I am of Ally when she gets going. Just let her stand on her own. She's a grown woman, who knows what she wants and where she's heading."

That's what worries me. What if she doesn't need me anymore?

Then I'm on my own.

Something I never really thought about.

Until now.

Chapter Eight

MATILDA

This week feels like it has been the longest one ever.

At least it wasn't the disaster of last week, though. As much as I want to forget the events that happened, a certain doctor just won't leave my mind. It always starts with thinking of the jerk he was the last time I saw him and ending with the stomach flutters remembering the man in the mask, the way he made me feel. Sleep is not happening like it should, and lord knows I need good sleep. I want to totally forget him; it just seems I'll require different thoughts to replace Grayson in my head.

Marching into the office on Friday morning, I'm ready to put my plan into action. All is silent and the offices are empty. It's not unusual. I tend to arrive early and get my head in the right mindset for the day. I need to work hard on that this morning and then start the day fresh. Today is going to be called 'get rid of Grayson' day. Let's see how that all works out.

"Morning, sunshine," Deven calls out as he comes swanning in the front door. I can smell him before I see him. Well, technically not him. The smell is wafting from something far better than Deven.

Coffee!

"I knew there was a reason I love you. You're worth more money."

He laughs passing mine to me. "Always happy to accept any pay raise you want to give. I'll be your coffee bitch any day for more money. Who wouldn't?"

I just roll my eyes at him. "You know you're already paid way more than you deserve, just because it stops you from complaining. You do need to do some work to justify the money that just mysteriously lands in your bank account each week." I lean against his desk as he's unloading his man bag of all his electronic devices.

"Really, why? I like how it just arrives each week and then I can go spend it. Working is overrated. I know that's like swearing to you, but it's true. You should try it sometime. Oh, that's right, you don't have a life outside this office." He smirks, standing far enough away so I can't reach to slap him.

"My life is perfectly fine, thank you," I snap back.

"So I hear. One-night stand with a hot doctor and you're running the opposite direction. What is wrong with you, girlie? If I found a hottie who knew what do with his hands, I'd be tying him up, so he couldn't run away. Just think of the possibilities. If you don't want him then share with your pal." He plonks down in his chair pretending he's dreaming of my hot man.

"You've never even met him or know what he looks like. Plus, he's not gay, that, I can assure you. He is more than happy playing with my team. He's also a dickhead. Good looks don't make the man." My thoughts drift off to the night we were together and how gentle he was with me, a considerate lover. Yet nothing is perfect.

"I'm not after the gentleman, the day after the event. I'm just looking for the asshole, he sounds much hotter in my books."

"Deven, seriously, you are such a man whore. One sniff and you're out there chasing down the poor guy, gay or not." I laugh as I pick my coffee up ready to head to my office.

"I've never met a man yet who can resist this charm and good looks." He runs his hands up and down his torso. "Oh and of course my big ..."

I hold my hand up to stop him before he even gets part of the word out. "Let's go with personality, shall we?" By now both of us are laughing which is a good way to start the day and try to get rid of my thoughts.

Chatting together about the mundane things we have on the agenda for today, it's the first Friday in a month we have no function booked in. After the week it's been and my lack of sleep, having tonight off couldn't come at a better time.

We can hear Fleur before she even gets through the front door of the office.

I'm sure she thinks we know what she's saying because her eyes hit mine as she opens the door like she's expecting a response.

"Well, aren't you excited?" She stands with her hand on her hip waiting for the answer.

"I probably will be once you tell me what the hell you were saying out there." I stare at her to let her know I'm not joking.

"Seriously, so deaf!" I don't even argue with her. "I had an email this morning. We have a meeting at two pm at the hospital to discuss our successful tender proposal. We did it!" Fleur screams at me as she reaches out and grabs me tightly. I barely have time to put my coffee down.

"Are you kidding me?" I quietly whisper. I feel like I'm in shock. Then it sinks in and the whisper is taken over by my much louder voice. "Are you freaking kidding me! Finally, we have landed a big fish. Fleur, we did it!" I can't contain the excitement now.

We both start jumping up and down, shouting over top of each other. Deven just keeps laughing at us acting like a couple of twelve-year-old girls who have just been given tickets to a Shawn Mendes concert.

"If only the stuffy high-society people on the hospital board could see you now, they might regret the decision." Deven drips with sarcasm.

"Fuck off!" We both yell at him at the same time then break out into a giggle. We slowly calm down to take a few breaths.

We have worked so hard on this contract tender proposal. Hours and hours of reworking numbers and coming up with the right ideas for function proposals. It's the next rung up the ladder for our business. This will mean expansion and running two arms of the business. One that will concentrate on the big functions for the hospital and the other to still run as we do now, on private functions. It will mean splitting the two of us at different times across the functions, but it will be worth it in the long run. In the initial phases, though, we will need to work hard and be hands-on as we are now. It also means no social life for the next twelve months while we get this off the ground.

"Right, now that you two have finished with the crazy, can we get sorted with time, place, and what's needed for this meeting? You know, the actual important things that I'm sure were in that email. Or did you stop at the first line that said successful?" I look at Fleur and then we both turn to face Deven, knowing that what we are about to do is going to send him into a meltdown.

"Deven, you know those times when we say never pick on the bosses? Well, now is one of those times." We both start giggling as we start messing up his desk. Tipping out the paperclips, pencils, knocking the Post-it notes on to the floor, running my fingerprints all over his computer screen. While Fleur finishes destroying his desk, I start drawing on his white board. He is squealing and carrying on behind me.

"Who's the twelve-year-old now?" I say. "Your squeal is like a kid throwing a tantrum. Happy cleaning." We both head to Fleur's office laughing and leaving our assistant absolutely losing his shit about messing up his desk and touching his things.

He is one of those fastidious people who has everything in its place and knows if anything has been touched. We love to play games on him when he's not in the office. We just move one thing on his desk and wait to see how long until he notices. It's become our chocolate cookie betting pool. I'm really good at it, not that my thighs need the extra cookies. Plus, he is so crazy that it doesn't take long for him to get it and yell at us for picking on him and being bullies. Yeah right! We are the two women who keep this guy employed while he is making sure his hair is perfect and that he has lunch organized for himself and us.

"I can't believe we got this contract, Tilly." Fleur looks up at me from the chair at her desk. "We need to get started on what we need to take to this meeting. Deven might think he has it all worked out, but I read every last word of that email in case I was misunderstanding it. We're meeting the board at two pm, and then after the meeting, we spend time with Kitty Ellis who is in charge of all the function coordinating at the hospital." We both just sit back and stare at each other while we're taking it all in.

"You read out the list and I'll take notes. No time to waste. Let's get on this now." I grab the tablet on her desk, and we get started.

Exiting the taxi, briefcases in hand, we both walk towards the front door of Mercy Hospital. I'm not one to get all sweaty, but with the nerves that are building, I can feel the beads of moisture running down my back. Thank goodness I have a dark navy dress on, so it shouldn't be noticeable. My black pumps allow me to walk with confidence like I own the place, even though I'm dying on the inside. We take the elevator to the administration level with the boardroom.

There is something about a hospital that makes you feel strange. It's the smell and overall vibe, I think. It can be a place of immense sadness or extreme happiness, and a whole lot in between. Several doctors and nurses walk past us as we stand in the waiting area for the chairman of the board of directors. I know they don't meet every new contractor that is appointed at the hospital. I'm guessing we get the privilege because they want to make sure that they're happy with who is running their many functions. I'm guessing each one of the board members has at least a part of the hospital that they're attached to for different reasons.

"Ladies." An elderly man comes towards us with his hand outstretched to greet us. "I'm Thomas Collum, the chairman of Mercy Hospital. Thank you for meeting with us today. Come on through and meet the board." The butterflies I was feeling while waiting have just taken flight in my stomach, and I quietly take a big breath. I can see that Fleur is twitching slightly too. I don't blame her. This is a big deal for both of us. We need to nail this meeting, and the pressure to get the first function perfect will be crazy.

After sitting with the board for an hour, I think we have been told in five different ways what is expected from us. How unhappy they were with the last event planners and what they did wrong. I have a feeling this is not going be an easy job until we get their trust. It won't be a problem for us, but there will be lots of hard work involved.

"Thank you for your time, everyone. We look forward to working with you all," Fleur says in her sweet professional voice. Not the one that was screaming in the highest pitch at the office earlier today, right in my ear.

"Thank you, ladies. Kitty will meet you outside in a moment and brief you on the next few functions." Thomas opens the door for us and basically sends us on our way. I'm sure their time is valuable.

Once the door closes, we both look at each other and roll our eyes. There are some serious old farts in that boardroom. I'm not sure they're ready to move with the ideas we will be bringing to the table. Oh well, at least we don't have to get approval from them. I wonder what this Kitty will be like. She could make or break how successful this job is going to be.

"I think the average age in that room was eighty-five for the men and seventy-five for the women," I whisper to Fleur as we stand waiting, trying not to look like idiots standing here doing nothing.

"Surely there has to be a mix of younger people that can take up some positions. All they'll be judging about our functions are how good the cups of tea and supper are." We both have a little giggle together. "Plus, they'll all need to be lunch functions because they need to be in bed by seven pm." We both try to keep our laughing to whisper level.

I can hear the fast clicking of heels approaching down the corridor. There is someone on a mission heading our way. Around the corner she appears. Tall and all legs. Hair pulled back into a tight bun. Black skirt, fitted and straight, showing her perfect figure. White blouse with a neckline that falls down to a perfect V between her breasts. This woman is model material. A perfect ten.

That red lipstick, stern lips, and the way she is looking at us tells me she is a powerful woman who won't take any crap. I have no doubt this is Kitty Ellis, and this may not be as easy as we think.

"You must be the ladies from Fleurtilly, I'm the head of operations at Mercy Hospital, Kitty Ellis. Pleased to meet you." Her hand extends to us, and I know before I even shake it that it will be like shaking the hand of a man. It will be firm and a power exchange. I admire women in roles that make the world stand up and take notice. Just in the first ten seconds, I can tell Kitty is one of these women.

"Hi, Kitty, I'm Fleur Florentine and this is Matilda Henderson. We're pleased to meet you and excited to be working together." My assumptions on the handshake were spot-on. "What did you have in mind this afternoon?" Fleur takes the lead on this meeting as she has done most of the liaising with the hospital tender as the contact person.

"We will head to one of the meeting rooms and look at the upcoming schedule and work out our plan of attack and how we will work collectively. I oversee all the operations in the hospital, but I don't have time to be concerned with minor details," she says as she starts to head down the corridor, assuming we will just follow her. Fleur turns to me, rolling her eyes, as we both step off to follow her like little puppies. That's what we need to do until we settle in, and then we will start to show we are professional businesswomen too, that don't need to be treated like children. But to begin with, softly, softly, as they say.

Entering the room, there are already another woman and man both seated at the desk. Introduced as her PA and the head of the legal department who has all the contracts that are needed before we can continue any further. Included in these are privacy and non-disclosure agreements. Our tender contract runs for two years, which will give us enough time to wow the board and use the contract as leverage to land other large corporate tenders. Signing a contract with the hospital to be the exclusive event planner for all their charity and corporate events is huge. The main people who attend these events are business-people or the wealthy who are on boards for other charities. The new contacts will be endless.

"Now, we have several functions on the calendar over the next three months, so you will be thrown in the deep end, I'm sorry. With the last company leaving us rather unexpectedly, we are a little behind the eight ball. I hope you are as efficient as they tell me you are." Kitty lays out a calendar on the table. My heart starts to do that anxious racing that I do on the day of a big event.

Holy shit! That calendar is crazy. What have we taken on?

I can see Fleur's body language giving off the same vibes. Neither of us bats an eyelid at the super dominating Kitty. We can't let her know that we're crapping ourselves on the inside.

"We will have you organized in no time," I say, dragging every bit of confidence I have out to make it sound convincing. The reality is we're good at what we do and are both as determined as the other to nail this job.

"Absolutely. Let's start with next week and work through the first month's functions to get started, shall we." Fleur opens up her laptop and starts tapping away at the calendar program we use while I pull up the form we use for the briefs on each function.

We have been at it for around an hour when we finally get to the last one that is listed for a Friday night four weeks from now. The venue, the Blackstone Hotel, has already been booked with some vague arrangements in place, but it's up to us to pull this together and implement any changes we need.

"This is an important event that I want you to give your full attention to. It's a new charity that is being started by one of our doctors at the hospital and his family. This man is very important, and I want you to make sure everything is perfect. Dr. Garrett is honoring his mother, so we want this to be everything the family is hoping for. I will have my PA send you the brief and organize for a meeting with Dr. Garrett's father Milton early next week so you can talk to him about your visions. Dr. Garrett is a very close friend of mine, if you know what I mean, so make sure there are no screw-ups. Otherwise I will take it personally." Kitty almost purrs when she says his name. What she should have said is I'm screwing Dr. Garrett so don't fuck this up or else.

Don't worry, Kitty Cat, we get the message loud and clear. Bend over backwards for Dr. Garrett and stay away from him because he's yours. I can picture the claws coming out if we even look like going near him. Can't wait to meet this Dr. Garrett. The way she's speaking about him, he must be someone pretty impressive. Little does she know it's the last thing on my mind. With this new job, I won't even have time for a date with my vibrator let alone a real man. Your man is safe, Kitty.

We spend another hour running through security issues with all events, but especially the ones here in the hospital. We will be working closely with Banister Security who handles all the needs of the hospital and its staff. It's unfortunate in the modern world it has to be a major risk factor that is managed carefully.

My mom's biggest concern when I was moving to the big city was that I'm more at risk for the craziness in the world. I tried to tell her I have just as much chance of being hit by a bus, but it doesn't stop her worrying. It's just what moms do, I suppose.

Kitty shakes our hands again and then stalks off down the corridor on her next mission. Her heels clicking as she looks for her next victim. After she rounds the corner, we both look at each other and burst out laughing, covering our mouths trying not to be loud. Slowly, we make our way over to the elevator, not a word spoken. Both of us just try to hold it together until we are in the safety of the four metal walls so we can really let it out.

Thank god the elevator is empty as the doors slide closed.

"Oh, my fucking god, what a witch," I let out after holding it in for two hours.

"A bitch with balls, as Deven would say," Fleur blurts out in between giggles.

"I bet the amazing Dr. Garrett is some weedy little guy that she gets to push around and ties up in the bedroom. She's probably one of those dominants that's into leather and whips." We both look at each other.

"Not that there's anything wrong with that," we both say to each other at the same time. We continue to laugh all the way to the ground floor. We try to pull ourselves together to look professional as we walk out the main entrance of the hospital. I've got a feeling this is going to be one big adventure. Let's hope that the reason the last company walked away from this job is not because it's too hard to deal with Kitty. Only time will tell.

"That's enough for one day." I sit back in my chair in our conference room in the office.

"Don't you mean one week? This one has been huge," Deven says from where he has two laptops and piles of folders all spread around him.

We've been brainstorming all afternoon after we got back from the hospital and putting action plans in place. Luckily, we don't have a job tonight, so it allowed us to get straight into it while it's all fresh in our mind.

"That's a great start for next week, and we have a plan to work off starting Monday morning." Fleur starts shutting things down and tidying up.

"Why don't we just leave everything here and convene Monday morning seven am to get a jump on the week. Are you guys okay with that?" Both nodding at me, I can feel my shoulders starting to drop a little knowing that we're feeling confident on our direction.

Deven stands in between us with his arms around our shoulders. "I don't know about you two, but I need a drink. Who's up for a nice glass of bubbles to celebrate the two badass bitches in town who are going to totally rock this contract."

"Best thing I've heard all day!" I reply while I rest my head on his shoulder. Probably not the smartest idea to head out drinking when I'm so tired, but who cares. We all deserve to celebrate this achievement.

"Let's get out of this place and get a drink into us, do some serious partying," Fleur announces as we break apart. "It's not very often we get to hit the town on a Friday night or get Tilly out partying. Look out, Chicago!"

Lordy, what have I agreed to? This must be the universe's way of helping me forget Grayson. Being busy at work is a simple remedy, but drinking and partying with these two could get really messy. I have a feeling I'll regret this tomorrow.

Four hours later and I've had way too much bubbles and not enough food. Dev is dancing with a hot-looking guy, which looks more like dirty dancing from here. There is plenty of grinding happening. I doubt he'll be coming home with us. Lucky guy.

"I'm done," I lean forward to tell Fleur as we stand on the platform up near the bar looking down at the mosh pit of hot sweaty bodies rubbing up against each other. I can see she's torn about staying or leaving with me. "I have to go home. My head is spinning and I'm bordering on vomit territory. No thanks."

She smiles at me. "You are such a lightweight. No wonder you don't go out partying all the time. Let's get you home. But I warn you, if you puke on me, we are no longer friends." I laugh because she says that all the time, and I think over the years I've done it about six times. She's still my best friend and would never leave me in my time of need. Fleur on the other hand can hold her liquor like a sailor. "You just hold the table up here while I go and interrupt Dev and tell him we're leaving. Don't fall over or do anything stupid, okay?" She grins as she stalks towards the dance floor.

How rude. I'm not that bad. Well, maybe. I know walking out on to the dance floor would be a challenge right at this moment, yet if you give me some water, I'm sure it wouldn't be a problem.

"Let's walk a little to get you some air and sober you up a bit. Then when you've had enough, we'll flag a taxi. Okay?"

"Yes, Mom," I mumble to Fleur as I link my arm in hers to stabilize myself. I pretend it's because I love her and want to give her a hug, but we all know I'm having trouble walking on my own.

"You drank me under the table tonight, my Tilly girl. What was that all about?" Fleur asks as we slowly wander down the sidewalk.

I think about it and I'm not sure I want to share my real motivation, but as usual, my filter mixed with alcohol results in the flood gates opening on my inner thoughts. My best friend knows that. She's using it against me right now.

"Celebrating being happy."

Her face says it all. "Yeah, nah. Not even close. Spill it, missy." Why does she have to be bossy when I can't defend myself?

"You play dirty. You know when I drink, I talk. No fair. You're supposed to be my bestie."

She starts laughing loudly. "Why do you think we're walking and talking? I'm not stupid. Now, what is sitting on those shoulders that you need to offload?" I know she loves me, but she really sucks as a friend.

Pausing for a moment, the little drunk girl in my brain opens the door and out it all comes.

"Why was he the perfect gentleman that fucked me so good and then turned out to be an asshole? Why couldn't he just stay in my dreams as that Prince Charming?" I'm standing still now, trying to explain my thoughts. "I mean, I don't want a boyfriend, but lordy that man is so delicious and knows exactly how to please a lady. He breaks my drought and then leaves me high and dry. That really sucks, you know!" By now I'm getting worked up and stamp my foot like a little girl having a tantrum.

Grabbing my arm and getting me walking again, I can see her grinning at me.

"It's not funny!" I raise my voice to get her to stop smirking at me. We have turned the corner on the street and a small crowd of people are heading towards us. I try to walk as straight and tall as I can, so I don't give away how drunk I am.

"You know how to get over Mr. Hottie is to do it again. Hook up with another man, and if that doesn't work then try another. By the time you get to number four, he will be a distant memory."

I'm horrified at what she's saying. I wouldn't even know where to start. "Fleur, I'm not a slut, you know," I scream on the top of my voice. Again, no filter or volume control apparently. "Just because I don't know how to get over the best sex that was out of this world with a gorgeous gyno, doesn't mean I go and fuck some random stranger." By this stage, we're close to the group of guys walking towards us.

Too close.

"I'll be your random stranger," one of the guys calls out as they get closer.

Goddammit, I need to learn to keep my mouth shut when I drink.

"Don't even fucking think about it, Tate. There is no way you can compete with this gorgeous gyno!"

Oh fuck!

That voice. I'd know it anywhere.

Why does this keep happening to me?

I stop dead and pull Fleur close to me. She is looking at me then the men who stopped in front of me.

Grayson, so close I can feel the energy coming from his body.

I can smell his aftershave. That scent that haunts me at night when I lay in bed touching myself.

"Best sex in the whole world, Matilda. I'll take that as a compliment," he says then leans forward and whispers in my ear, "I told you no one would compare. Would you like me to remind you?" My damn body is betraying me again. Every time he's near me, it's like he casts a spell over my senses.

"Holy shit, you're the mystery woman from the ball? The one we chatted with and called Hannah." One of the guys, Tate I think, says as he goes to step closer to me. Grayson shoots his arm out and glares at him to step back. What the fuck was that about?

"This, my friends, is Matilda, who likes to go by Hannah when it suits. Now, who might your friend be?" Grayson's deep voice breaks my trance.

I'm struggling to talk from a combination of embarrassment and being so close to Grayson again. Thank god for my bestie.

"Fleur, I was actually running the ball that night." One of the others steps forward. "Mason, isn't it? You were our speaker." She laughs a little as they all start to talk to her and leave me standing staring at Gray like I'm hypnotized.

For a man I was never going to see again, why does he keep turning up at the weirdest times?

"Not the first time I've had you speechless, little one," he says in a low voice. One that takes me right back to that room and the pleasure of that night. "Come home with me, ride my cock, and I can have you screaming in no time." His words snap me out of my dream.

"What the hell. As if I'll go anywhere with you. I'm not a booty call. Remember last time I saw you? Does the word asshole ring a bell? Now you are a douchebag asshole. Let's go, Fleur." I grab her by the arm and start dragging her down the street. Funny how I can walk faster and soberly now.

"Your loss, little one. Until we meet again," Grayson yells out to me as I walk away from him.

Again!

This is becoming an annoying pattern.

Chapter Nine

MATILDA

"Aren't you supposed to be my best friend?" I scold Fleur as we stomp down the sidewalk as quickly as my heels will carry me.

"What do you mean? Slow down, woman, you'll break an ankle," she growls back at me.

"You know, the best friend who was going to knee him in the balls for being such a dick to me? What happened to that best friend, huh?" I stop to glare at her. Like it's her fault I just made an idiot of myself. "For fuck's sake, why does he bring out the bitch in me every time? Why didn't you stop me from opening my stupid mouth?"

"Umm drinking champagne, remember, results in no filter! Plus, how could I attack those balls on such a fine specimen of a man. Actually, times that by four. I was right from that night at the ball. Now the masks are off they are the Fucka-licious Four. Now, if you don't take advantage of that, just stand back, woman, and let me choose. Or better still, maybe I will take them all for a ride."

I slap my forehead at Fleur's spiel. "Don't you dare touch Grayson, or I will take those flaming arrows I talked about and use them on you!" I start off down the road again to the sound of loud laughing from her.

"You don't want the asshole, but you don't want to share him either. Hmmm, let's see how that works out for you, Tilly."

I keep stomping forward and know I need to go home and go to bed. My plan when I woke up this morning was to forget Grayson.

What a massive fail that was. Fleur thinks I'm stomping down the road because I'm pissed at her. But really, it's because I'm pissed at how turned on I am again.

His touch.

That voice.

The breath on my neck.

Every damn time brings me to my knees.

If we were anywhere else, being on my knees in front of him sounds perfect.

"Tilly, slow down and stop being such a drama queen. Let's get a taxi and go home. You need to sleep off the hangover that's coming." Her words rattle in my head. Oh, Fleur, that's not the only thing that will be coming tonight. That man might infuriate me, but he makes me so hot under the collar that I know what's going to happen once I sneak under the covers tonight.

Water runs down my back as I stand in the shower hoping the heat and steam will clear my head. One day I will remember the headache that follows the morning after too many bubbles. I love champagne, I'm just not sure it loves me. Well, maybe it has something to do with the quantity I consumed and the lack of food lining my stomach last night. You would think at my age I would know better.

Come on, Tilly, time to suck it up and get on with the day. I promised Daisy a trip to Lincoln Park Zoo today. There is no way of getting out of it. That little girl will murder me if I try to suggest we postpone. Maybe her infectious energy will wear off on me. That or three coffees before I leave the apartment might help.

I can't believe it was Fleur dragging my drunken bum home last night. It's normally the other way around. I wasn't slurring my words, but I certainly was under the influence of the alcohol that alters my sensible brain filter. Not that it happens that often but still, between her and Deven, if we're out partying, I'm usually the most sober. Wait until Hannah hears about this. She will be pissed she missed it.

By the time I'm on my second coffee, the bangs low down on my door tell me that my little partner is ready. Opening the door, she comes bounding in like a kangaroo.

"Look, Tilly, I'm a bouncing tiger." Her smile reaches all the way up her cheeks. Please can I tap some of that energy. "You know, like from Pooh Bear, a bouncing tiger. Boing, boing, boing." She cracks me up, even with a pounding head.

"Daisy," I hear Hannah calling across the hall. Her guilty face gives her away.

"Have you brushed your teeth?" I ask, trying to put on my serious face and not laugh.

She looks down at the floor, all the bouncing stopped, and shakes her head back and forth.

"Off you go then. No teeth then no zoo. Skedaddle, missy." She takes off back home with the speed of lightning, thinking she might miss out on today's adventure. What is it with kids and clean teeth? I can't think of anything worse.

Within two minutes, the voices were coming back in the front door. One bouncing tiger and one growly grizzly momma bear.

"I swear to god, that child is going to have no teeth left by the time she's ten. They will rot and fall out. Are you sure you don't want to adopt her? I promise she's cute most of the time. Well, some of the time, actually for about five minutes a day if you're lucky." Hannah drops her bags in the kitchen and grabs a coffee mug. "There is no way we're leaving before I get one more load of caffeine into me."

"Me too," I mumble to myself only to have Hannah turn and look at me a little more carefully.

"Well, well, well. Is someone a little under the weather this morning? Those look like champagne eyes to me."

There's no point denying it. I need someone to give me some sympathy. "Too much celebrating last night after our hospital meeting," I grumble, filling my cup with that third coffee I knew I would need. "Blame Deven. He suggested it. Fleur kept filling my glass."

"And you kept drinking them." She laughs out loud at me. "Pretty sure it's your fault. How messy did the other two get?"

"Who knows about Dev, we left him grinding some guy on the dance floor at the bar. Let's just say Fleur was the responsible one getting me home last night."

Hannah spits coffee across the kitchen counter. "Are you kidding me? Fleur is never the responsible person between you two when drinking is involved. Where was my invite? Hmm?"

"You were holding down the home front with the bouncing tiger over there. It's like the universe was playing some cruel trick, I'm sure. Besides losing my rambling filter with each glass of champagne I drank, on our way home we ran into Grayson the jerky doctor."

Again, the coffee ends up on the counter.

"Seriously, can you warn me when you're about to say something that is going to make me laugh? I'm not sure much of this coffee has been actually drunk yet. I'm getting good at decorating your counter, though." Madly wiping down the mess, she's glaring at me to keep talking.

"Don't you dare leave me hanging. What happened?"

I don't even know how to answer her. "We spoke briefly, he offered me sex, I turned him down, and then I stormed off down the street like a two-year-old while he was laughing at me. Yep, that about sums it up." Just as she's about to ask for more details, we're interrupted by Daisy who is getting impatient waiting to leave for our adventure.

"There is so much more to this story, I'm sure. Don't worry, I have all day to torture you and drag it out of you. Hope you've taken painkillers, because a day with Daisy and a hangover can be enough to make your head explode, spoken from experience." We both laugh, clean up our coffee mess, and head out the door to spend the day together.

A few hours at the zoo and I remember how hot, smelly, dusty, and noisy it is. Between the animals and the children who are like animals, you can hardly hear yourself think. Finally, Daisy is slowing down and the words are only coming out at half the speed. I'm still laughing on the inside watching Hannah trying to explain what the monkeys are doing. The horny male jumping on the female who's just sitting there minding her own business. He then starts wildly humping her and making monkey noises at the same time. Of course, all the adults start laughing, which means Daisy is asking questions as to why we're laughing and what they're doing. Hannah makes up some wild story about him getting a piggyback ride and the noises are like when we laugh from fun. I have to walk away, otherwise I'm going to lose it and that would wreck it. I think it will be my best memory from today.

Finally, we're sitting on the grass having our picnic lunch while Daisy is playing with the kids in the play area. I slowly lie back on the blanket and close my eyes, letting the sun warm my skin and sweat the alcohol out of my system. I could easily drift off to sleep, catching up on last night and the week of no sleep that I've had.

The world is at peace until Hannah pokes me in the ribs.

"Ow, what was that for?" I open my eyes to see her staring at me.

"You know exactly what it was. Don't you dare go to sleep. Now we're alone, you have stories to tell me, woman. That bullet-point explanation this morning won't cut it, you know." Ugh, I don't know if I want to go over this again. It was humiliating enough the first time.

"You got the gist of it this morning. There's not much more to tell," I try brushing her off.

"Not a chance, Tilly. What is it about this guy that has you all tied up in knots? For someone you've only spent a few hours with and had two brief meet-ings since, he has you going crazy. This isn't like you." Hannah is so right.

"Well, to start with, it's not like they were two normal meetings since then. Remember one was me flat on my back, legs in the air and open for the world to see. Not my ideal date, I'm sorry to say." I sit up and lean back with my hands behind me.

"I don't know, on your back, legs open, sounds like a great date to me. I can't remember the last time Trent had me in that position, so stop complaining." Hannah half laughs but I can tell she's also sad about missing him.

"Oh Han, I'm sorry, you don't want to hear about my drama."

"Bullshit. If I'm not getting any, I need to live through you. Now get back on topic. What is it about Grayson that has you all flustered?"

I sit there staring out into the park. I don't know if I can put my finger on the exact thing and why I can't seem to wipe him off my mind.

"That first night, he was so wonderful. Not just the sex, which was unbeliev-able. The way he spoke to me. The intense electricity that was between us when we were near each other. The attraction to him was instant when I spotted him across the room looking at me. He treated me like a lady. Never once did I feel scared or in any danger. I had this undeniable trust in him. We shared something amazing in that room that was so much more than sex. It was such a connection that I panicked and ran. I told myself it was just one night, but what he made me feel, I knew if I stayed I would find it hard to walk away in the morning." Finally, I'm getting out everything that has been in the back of my mind all week.

"Why is it a problem if you both wanted to take it further than one night?" Hannah asks, pushing me to keep going.

"I don't have the time to commit to a relationship. Especially not now with the hospital contract. Fleur and I have worked too hard to get here. I can't let her down and slack off now." Daisy calls out to her mom to watch her climbing the play fort. It gives me a moment to breathe.

"I'm just having trouble trying to match the Grayson I met that night with the arrogant Dr. Gray that turned up the next morning. He let me be embarrassed, knowing who I was and not saying a word, instead being a jerk in the appointment. Then last night on the street, he wasn't the same man I first met. It was like he was this super confident guy who just wanted a good fuck. I thought I was more than that the first night. Stupid me."

Hannah leans over and hugs me. It feels good to let it out. "Maybe he was just meant to be that one-night stand and nothing more. I don't know, but what I do know is the universe is trying to tell you something. Otherwise why does he keep showing up in your life? Maybe he was as embarrassed as you were that morning after, so he was trying to hide that. Last night, maybe he had been drinking like you had, or it was a really bad day at work." She shrugs at me.

Part of me wants to listen, but the stubborn part says no, he's just a dick. The smooth gentleman was an act to get me into his bed. "I don't know what to think, Han. All I can say is that if I don't see him again for another ten years, it will probably be too soon."

Hannah shakes her head at me.

"I think the universe's vision might be a little different to yours. Mark my words, I think this is far from over. Hold on for the ride, baby."

I hope she's wrong.

But do I really?

GRAYSON

The rhythm of feet pounding on the ground is what I need this morning. I woke up with a slight headache, not from the beers last night but from her. Instead of my mystery woman, I should call her the sleep thief. Every time I see her it just makes sleeping worse.

Why she affects me so easily I don't understand. One minute she's the most beautiful woman I have ever met, that night was sensational. Since then, she is so snarky and just wants to rip my head off. Strangely I find that just as sexy as the quiet shy beauty of the ball. Maybe it's because I'm not used to women treating me like that. There are so many that just see me as a doctor, which to them means status or money. Then there are the society bunnies who know I come from money. They just want a place in the inner circle, not having to do a day's work for the rest of their life. None of it is about me. Or there are the honest women I come across that are just looking for a casual good time.

Matilda is none of those. She might have thought she was just after a good time, but that night was more than that. I felt it and I know she did too. Then when she found out who I was, instead of her latching on, she ran the opposite direction. Twice. I mean, what the hell is that? Mind you, I was being a jerk both times.

Last night she caught me off guard. I had a few too many beers. Tate had just pissed me off telling me Bella's interning with him, and then I hear her talk about me being the best sex she ever had. Then Tate offered himself to her, my brain went into overload, and I snapped. She is mine, I want her, and all I could think in that moment was how I would like to take her to my bed. Tate the shit-head, being intoxicated, gave me shit the whole ride home in the Uber. I love him like a brother, but last night I wanted to kill him. I had fucked up trying to talk to her again, and he was just making it worse.

Getting closer to the end of the run, with Elvis singing *A Little Less Conversation* in my ear, I couldn't agree more. I need to find a way to see Matilda and have a normal conversation. No distractions, no hostility, and apologize for what I said and did. I need to show her that's not me. Wanting to do this and working out how to achieve it are two different things. Pulling my earbuds out of my ears, I slow, ready for a drink of water. Mason and I slow up as we get closer to the fountain. He messaged me this morning telling me, not asking, that we were running, and I better be there. The other two are probably too hungover.

"You were a bit slower than normal this morning, Gray, still sweating the beer out?" Mason is leaning forward to take the first drink.

"Probably. That and lack of sleep this week," I mumble.

"I don't believe either. You've been worse off before and still kept up. As for lack of sleep, man, you are a doctor. You don't ever sleep properly. My bet is Matilda is rattling that cage of yours and you don't know how to handle it." Smartass. He is spot-on, but I don't know if I want to admit that to him.

"That look on your face tells me I'm right on the money. Don't try denying anything. Why aren't you doing anything about it?" He starts stretching his legs on the park bench.

"Fuck, if I could get five normal minutes with her then I would. I can't contact her without the risk of a lawsuit. Every time I've run into her randomly like last night, things have been a disaster. What am I supposed to do?" That there is the crux of the problem. I want to find her, but I can't. For years I have had women that I'm not interested in throwing themselves at me. I finally find one who has me standing up and taking notice, and I can't do a damn thing about it.

"Firstly, you stop sulking. Man up and work out a way around it. Talk to Ally. Matilda is her patient. Surely, she can contact her on your behalf. You know her last name. Stalk her on social media, for god's sake. That's what the rest of the world does these days. Surely you've had those crazy girls send you nudes before, even when you don't even know them. Totally nuts if you ask me, but they do it anyway." He wipes his face with the front of his tank top to mop up the sweat.

"I don't know, Mas, I feel weird invading a woman's privacy like that. I'm thirty-five years old, not eighteen. Surely, I can find another way. I'll think about it and come up with something, somehow. She seems to keep popping up, so who knows. Enough about me. What's going on in your world? This new job working out okay?" I need to think about something else for a while.

"This job would have to be a pilot's dream job. A Dassault Falcon X8 jet plane that's all mine to captain. A boss who is hot and feisty. I get paid to be at her beck and call. What more could a guy need?" He laughs to himself.

"Isn't it frustrating, sitting around waiting?" I've finished stretching so we start walking again to head home.

"Sometimes. It doesn't happen all the time. This week I have five days of flying her from New York, Seattle, Washington DC, Portland and then down to Florida with a round-trip home. Weeks like that are more common than the waiting around. Paige has the jet for convenience because she flies so much. She's not one of these rich ones who has it as a status symbol. That's why I took the job. I love to fly, not sit in a hangar and wash the jet every day."

"You know that sounds ridiculous, don't you? What did you do today, dear? Oh just wash the jet, not much." Mason smacks me on the shoulder, laughing at me. "I mean, you probably wash the jet more than you wash your car. You know, the one you hardly ever take out of the garage." When you think of Mason's life, it's not anywhere near a normal one.

Changing the topic of conversation, we switch to our plans for the weekend and plan for catching up to watch the ball game tomorrow. We split off as we get closer to our apartments. Both living in The Loop, it makes it easy to run together in Grant Park. It's good for the body to get out in the fresh air and clear the mind. Now to plan the rest of my weekend before I head back into another busy week at work being on call.

"What do you say, Memphis, we take a drive out to see your granddad for the rest of the weekend? I could use a change of scenery. While he's home, we should squeeze in a visit. Let's see if Bella is up for a little road trip."

Dad travels a lot for work as an HR arbitrator. He gets contracted to come in and sort out disputes in companies between management and the employees. It's usually at a boiling point with the risk of strike action or they've already walked off the job. He never knows where he'll be or when he will have to go. He doesn't always get a lot of notice. After Mom died and we'd grown up, it suited him. He can come and go as he pleases, at any time, and not have to worry about anyone else. Probably why he has never met anyone else. In some ways he's like a doctor the way he is on call.

Grabbing a few things and receiving a yes message back from Arabella that she will be ready in twenty minutes to be picked up, I take Memphis down to the car with me. He is so placid he travels really well. Dad still lives in our childhood home in Norwood Park. It's too big for him but is close to the airport, so he won't sell it or move from it. He bought the house for him and Mom when they got married. He says there are so many memories in the house he can never get rid of it. As much as life would be so much easier for him in the city, I'm glad he kept the house all this time. It's where I feel closest to Mom. There are times I need that.

When Bella jumps in the car, I can't wait very long before I blurt it out. She's stuck with me and can't get away, so it's the perfect time.

"Why didn't you tell me you've been put on Tate's intern rotation list? You know you need to get it changed, right?" I know it came out too harsh, but I can't help it. The protective big brother is in the house.

"Seriously, Gray, is that why you invited me to come home with you? So you can lecture me all the way there, and then get Dad on your side too? Turn the car around and take me home. I'm not in the mood for this shit." She turns and stares out the window.

Now that's not quite the reaction I expected. I don't know whether to push it or leave it alone. I can't help myself and need to have my say now that I've opened my mouth. If she is going to be annoyed, I may as well get it over with now than try again later.

"No, Bella, I didn't invite you just to talk to you about this. What would have been nice, though, is if I had heard it from you instead of Tate. I just think it's a really bad idea." I can't say everything I'm thinking because that's just not the conversation you want to have with your sister, or even be thinking about.

"This." She waves her hands between us. "This is why I didn't say anything. I knew you would go all psycho and stick your nose in where it isn't wanted. He is the best neurosurgeon on staff at Mercy. He's like a brother to you, the only person you would trust to operate on that pea-sized brain of yours, yet you don't trust him with you sister. That's just fucked up, Gray!" I hate to admit she has a point. "If you're worried about him hitting on me like he does all his other interns, you're crazy. Best friend's little sister." She points to herself. "Never going to be interested or game to go near me. Won't happen. So, tell me what the problem is?" This is the most fired up I've seen my sister in a long time. I knew last week something wasn't right with her. I hate that I've stressed her out by her worrying about my reaction.

Looks like I'm not winning any brownie points with any women around me at the moment. The only award I'm in contention for is the giant douchebag award. I need to get my life together.

"Listen carefully, because you will probably never hear this again. You're right. I should trust both you and Tate. I didn't look at it the right way. I'm sorry for being so overprotective. I can't turn it off. You do know it comes from a place of love, though, don't you?"

She slowly turns to look at me from her window. The silence in the car tells me it's taking a while to sink in. Eventually she starts to softly smile. "Do you think you could repeat that so I can record it? You said it yourself, I'll never hear it again." She starts to get her phone up, pointing in my direction. "Ready and action."

"My sister, Bella, is the most annoying sister ever." She groans and smacks me on the arm. "I'm glad that is now on record. Just be careful, Bel, I don't want you hurt. Just pretend Tate is any other doctor and keep working hard like you have been, okay? Don't give anyone a reason to say you got an advantage because you know him."

"You do know I'm a big girl now. I've got this. Trust me." She puts her head on my shoulder and kisses the top of it. We then continue to drive home while Memphis sleeps soundly in the back seat, snoring like a champion.

Bella leans over and turns up the music. We both start singing to Elvis songs, totally off-key but neither of us care.

Turning into the driveway at home, a sense of calm comes over me. Home is always good for the soul. In a way, cleansing.

Maybe tonight I'll get some sleep.

Although if Memphis keeps letting out dog farts like he has in the car, he'll be out on the back porch. That's enough to stop even the heaviest sleeper being able to breathe.

Opening the car door, he runs towards Dad standing on the front porch.

I have a feeling this could be the only grandchild he gets, at least for a while.

Not that Memphis is complaining at the extra love he gets being the only fur baby.

"Hey, Dad." I embrace him.

"Hi, son, you look tired. Is everything okay?" He pulls back looking at me carefully.

"Yeah, Dad, it will be. Good to be home." I give him another hug and head inside.

Within an hour, I'm fast asleep on the couch in front of the television with Memphis curled up on the floor in front of me.

Yeah, sometimes you just need to go home to find your center.

Chapter Ten

MATILDA

A rriving at work early on a Monday is worth it. We have just hit eleven o'clock and the whole week is scheduled. We've started the process of hiring some more staff to cover the new functions. Deven is off getting the coffee, I'm publishing all the new rosters to the staff, and Fleur is replying to all the weekend emails and sending out all the orders we need quotes on for the new functions.

"We've got this, babe," she says as she looks up from her computer at the other end of the table in the meeting room. Just a reminder to us both to breathe and trust ourselves.

"Sure do. Challenge accepted, and we are already winning." We both return to what we're concentrating on.

"Oh shit, wasn't planning on that today, but check your calendar. We now have a meeting with Milton Garrett this afternoon at five o'clock at The Blackstone Hotel. Kitty Cat told us not to be late. The fucking hide of her. I already hate this bossy bitch. At least give us some professional credit." Fleur curses and then goes back to replying to her new favorite person.

Normally I would just let Fleur go so we can use both our time efficiently, but we don't want to piss off the queen of the hospital and her doctor boyfriend. I look at my calendar for this afternoon and start sending off a message to a client asking if I can shuffle the time forward a little.

"Okay, I'm set. I've moved my four o'clock to three o'clock so that should give me plenty of time to make it there. How are you situated?"

Fleur is busy replying to a text message. Her face looks intense. "I might be a little late, you'll have to start. Thank god Kitty won't be there so she won't know that you started on your own. How hard can it be? It's not like we haven't done a thousand of these types of functions before. I'll send you the email she sent with the meeting details. Do you want to take Deven?" she asks with a smirk on her face.

"God no. I can cope on my own, thanks. He drives me insane on the initial meetings. I know he thinks he's an event planner, I just don't think he gets that his job is the assistant who is to be seen and not heard in these meetings. One day maybe he'll get there, just not with me." We both laugh to ourselves.

After spending the next few hours in the office, I make sure I arrive a little early for my first appointment, so I don't get held up. Thank goodness, they're a repeat customer so super easy to deal with and already trust our work. Signing off on their function quote, I'm now standing outside The Blackstone Hotel thirty minutes early. I decide to read through the brief again before I head inside. It is a standing function of drinks and canapes, three hundred and forty guests approximately. In the Crystal Ballroom which is the most spectacular room. If I ever get married, I would want it in this room. So Old World, and high-class elegance. Chandeliers and beautifully sculptured ceilings. A spectacular view and the room edged with an old-fashioned balcony where guests can mingle. I've seen it set up for a wedding full of flowers and soft furnishings. Fit for a princess. I push that thought to the back of my mind so I can concentrate on this meeting. The charity is called Maxine's Angel Foundation. Okay, let's go and show them what we can do to help them.

Standing in the Crystal Ballroom admiring everything, I hear voices behind me as the woman from the front desk shows Milton Garrett in to meet with me. Walking towards me is a tall distinguished-looking gentleman. Grey hair and clean-shaven. Dressed in a navy suit that looks like it fits him perfectly, shoulders back, he strides towards me with purpose but has a gentleness about him in his eyes. As he gets closer, his smile is warm and immediately puts me at ease.

"Good afternoon, I'm Milton Garrett." He extends his hand that takes mine in a gentle yet firm handshake. One that tells me he sees me as an equal. I already like this man.

"Mr. Garrett, I'm Matilda Henderson. Lovely to meet you. My business partner Fleur Florentine will be joining us in a little while, she's just finishing off another appointment. Thank you for agreeing to take us on such short notice for your function. We are trying to pick up all the hospital's work and get every-thing settled quickly."

"Firstly, please call me Milton. My children already make me feel old enough. I actually think it is I who should be thanking you. I know it's a big ask to come into a function with such a short lead-up time. I hope it won't be too stressful for you." What a lovely man. His voice makes me think of my dad. Gentle and kind, yet I think if needed they can pull out the sternness.

"Oh, you needn't worry Mr.— I mean, Milton. This is what we do every day. By the time we walk out of here this afternoon, everything will be organized, and you will just need to show up on the night. Now, let's take a seat shall we and get started. I'm sure you're a busy man and your time is valuable." Before I even get a chance, he pulls a seat out for me to sit on, and we settle at a table to get started. He makes me feel like a lady.

"You have no idea how much better I feel already, Matilda. You seem so much more on the ball than the last planner we spoke to. Oh, I'm sorry I forgot to say, my son will be joining us shortly too. This is really his baby, and I'm quite often called out of town quickly for work so he will be your contact person for everything from today onwards. My daughter is also part of the board, however she is still studying, so I would prefer you only go to her as a last resort. She has enough stress on her plate at the moment. Including a big brother who seems to think he knows what is best for her, much to her disgust." We both have a little laugh. "My son should be able to handle everything you need. If he can't, he will get in touch with me or make sure he finds someone to help you with whatever you need."

"That sounds perfect. Your son is Dr. Garrett, I believe? I'm assuming he works at Mercy Hospital and that's why they're involved in this function. From what we were told, he is very highly thought of there."

"Thank you, yes, I'm very proud of both my children. It was difficult for them, especially my son, to see their mother sick and pass away, and they both have dedicated their lives to medicine because of it. Maxine was the best mother and a beautiful soul. She lived for the kids. My son wants to start this charity to fund the treatment of cervical cancer for those on low income who can't afford treatment. Maxine had the best treatment that money could buy at the time, but we couldn't stop the cancer as it was so advanced when she was diagnosed. However, there are women out there whose cancer is detected far earlier than Maxine, but they can't afford the best treatment that they all deserve. So, we are trying to have a place for these women to get help and get that treatment straight away to try to stop the disease before it takes hold. It started out as my son's idea, but my daughter and I have the same vision. I'm sure you will get on well with my son. He has a big heart and is very passionate about the cause." I can see the love in Milton's face for his son.

I hear a noise from behind me as the voice of the woman from the front desk shows someone into the room. Probably Fleur arriving from her appointment.

"I hope I can live up to that speech, Dad."

I freeze.

That voice. I would know it anywhere.

For fuck's sake, not again. Damn Hannah and her universe!

"Here he is. Matilda, this is my son Dr. Grayson Garrett. You can call him Gray if you wish. His name is such a mouthful the hospital just calls him Dr. Gray for short." I can't take my eyes off Milton as I feel Gray standing by my side. "Matilda, are you okay?" Milton inquires. I must look like a frozen statue.

"Oh, um, yes, sorry." I turn to see the face that can't seem to leave my life, with a cheeky smile on his face. I put my hand out reluctantly but acutely aware I am here on a professional basis. "Hello, Dr. Garrett. A man of many names it sounds like." I straighten a little trying to fend off the spark I'm feeling as he hangs on to my hand for longer than is necessary in a handshake.

"We meet again, Matilda. It seems we are destined to keep running into each other. How are you today?" So very smooth is our doctor.

"Do you two know each other? How wonderful. This will make the process so easy. In fact, I'm sure I won't be needed at all. I can leave you two friends to sort it all out." I nearly choke on the word friends.

"Thanks, Dad, yes we know each other quite well. It will be lovely to spend some time together again, talking. Won't it, Matilda?" I just want to knee him in the balls. He knows I can't do a damn thing here except play along with his little game in front of Daddy Dearest.

"Of course. Although I'm sure we could use your input too, Milton, there's no need for you to think you can't be involved as well. It sounds like a family affair." I smile at Gray like we're playing a chess game.

"No, dear, it's okay. Like I said, it's Grayson's baby, so I'll leave you both to it. I have to fly out later tonight for work, so it'll be fantastic if I have a bit of extra time now to get a bite to eat before heading to the airport." He stands and places his hand on Gray's shoulder. "I'm off to Boston for a few days, I've let Bella know. Keep an eye on her for me. I'll be in touch."

Turning back to face me, he takes my hand in both of his. "It was so lovely to meet you, Matilda, I'm sure you will make this an amazing night. I hope to see you again soon. Have Grayson bring you home for dinner one night. Any friend of his is always welcome in our home." He pats Gray on the back again and leaves the room.

I'm sitting here stunned and trying not to choke on all the words that have just been spoken. If only Milton knew how we are *friends*, for want of a better word. I'm sure I wouldn't be so welcome in his home if he knew I was just a floozy who slept with his son after knowing him for less than an hour.

How the hell have I gotten myself into this mess?

Fleur, hurry up, I need you to rescue me.

"Matilda, please relax. You look like you're about to take flight. I'm not that scary."

I just glare at him. Scared isn't the word I would use. I just know that being around him for longer than five minutes could definitely be a problem for me. Already my insides are fluttering just looking at him.

It's like a change comes over his face. It softens and those eyes that had me hypnotized before, have returned.

"I'm actually glad we've run into each other again. I need to apologize and say sorry for being such a jerk the last few times I've seen you. I don't know what came over me. Please believe me when I say that is not me. I should have told you who I was when I recognized you at the appointment."

"Yes, you should have. That was so unprofessional. You took advantage of me," I snap at him.

"Well, it would have helped if I knew your real name. I think we can both take some blame here, don't you?" He raises his voice slightly, and I can tell he's trying really hard not to. In all honesty, he has a fair point.

121

"That is true, I apologize for that. But I need to know, how did you know it was me? I thought the wrong name had me safe from being found out."

He dropped his face a little, and for the first time I can see a little pink on his cheeks, blushing. Not what I was expecting from our cocky Dr. Gray.

"Please don't take this the wrong way or in a creepy way." He pauses for a moment and raises his head again to look my in the eyes. "First, your eyes had me confused, they were the ones I had been picturing since you ran out and left me. That wasn't what confirmed it, though. You have the most beautiful birthmark on your inside thigh, just near the place I very much enjoyed exploring that first night. As soon as I saw it, I knew for sure it was you."

Now I can feel my cheeks burning like crazy. I know I'm bright red and there is nothing that can stop it. Trying to slow down my breathing, I go to stand up and put some distance between us when Gray leans forward and puts his hands on my cheeks.

"Please don't be embarrassed. I will never forget that night. It was pretty spectacular. You weren't the only one who thought it was the best sex they've ever had."

He's too intimate. I can't do this here. I'm supposed to be working. I accused him of being unprofessional, and here I am letting him touch me.

I jump out of my seat like it's on fire.

"Gray, we can't do this now. I'm working for you. We need to do that. I mean work, you know, the function. Sort out things, make some plans. Oh god, you have me rambling like a schoolgirl. Lord help me."

He stands and takes my hands in his and starts to laugh. Not just a little laugh but a deep belly laugh. I can't help it. It's infectious. Before long, we're both laughing loudly and from deep inside. It feels so good.

Pulling himself together to stop laughing, he guides me back down into my seat.

"Relax. Let's just breathe and start again. We have a job to do, so let's get through that then we can chat, okay? I'm sure we can act like grownups for at least thirty minutes." His smile will get me to agree to anything.

"Sure. But purely work. No more mention of that other meeting. Let's totally wipe that." I let out a nervous giggle as he extends out his hand to take mine and shake it.

"Hi, I'm Grayson Garrett, board member for Maxine's Angel Foundation and a gyno...actually, let's just say a doctor at Mercy Hospital." Right in this moment he is the masked man from the ball. His eyes are twinkling and captivating and his smile so warm.

"Hello, I'm Matilda Henderson, but my friends call me Tilly. I'm an event planner which I hear you need some help from. Perhaps we should start with a bit of planning." We are both acting very professional to the point I think I can handle this. Until Gray breaks protocol again.

"What a good idea, on one condition. Have dinner with me tonight when we're finished. Let me make it up to you for being a quote – asshole – unquote." He motions his fingers in the air to accentuate his joke.

"I don't know if that's such a good idea, Grayson." I hesitate. I want to, but I know I shouldn't.

"How about we get started here and you can decide when we finish. How does that sound? Come on, Tilly, give me a chance to prove myself."

"Okay then, but just to seeing how I feel when we finish this. I'm not agreeing to dinner just yet. Don't get too excited." I smile at him and relax a little for the first moment since he walked into the room.

"Deal." He shakes my hand and then sits back on his chair, crossing one of his legs over the other, and stretches his arms up behind his head. "Now, what have you got to show me that will impress me?"

Oh yeah, this is going to be kept really professional.

GRAYSON

What is it about this woman that she keeps falling in my lap? Every time I turn around, she's here.

Thank god.

Finally, I can start on the right foot with her. Well, hopefully.

At least I've been able to apologize, and we're talking civilly to each other. Now I just need to get her to agree to dinner.

Time to pull out the Garrett charm.

"The two main objectives you have are to get the charity visibility and people learning about its purpose. Plus, of course, to raise funds to get the charity off and running. Is that correct?" Tilly looks up from her tablet where she is recording everything she needs. I'm finding it awfully hard to concentrate on what we're talking about.

"Essentially yes, that's right. We need to get our vision out there. With so many good causes in Chicago, it's important that we snag people's interest and leave them wanting to know more. Any suggestions you have to help with that would be wonderful." She taps away again, making more notes.

We go through my thoughts for the function and how it will run, the food, the entertainment, and speeches. Watching her work is such a turn-on. The confidence and professional way she's running the meeting makes me realize that there are two sides to my Tilly. That first night she was so unsure and just wanted to give up control to find her pleasure. This Tilly here in front of me now. There is no shyness, just complete domination of what's happening around her. That is just as hot as the sensual woman I first met.

Before I realize it, we've been talking for an hour and getting close to wrapping up the meeting when her friend comes rushing into the room. Everything is now clicking in my head. Her friend was managing the masked ball and Matilda was a guest. I'm sure there's a story as to why, but that can be a question for another day.

"I'm sorry I'm so late. My last meeting was running late and then traffic was a killer." She's looking down at everything in her arms until she gets to the table and attempts to slow down and get herself together.

"It's fine, we're almost done," Tilly reassures her. Finally unloading her arms, she looks up. "Fleur Florentine, this is Dr. Grayson Garrett, the infamous Dr. Gray." Tilly is already laughing at the stunned look on Fleur's face. I reach out and take her hand to shake it. Her mouth drops open and then finally the words come streaming out.

"Holy shit, it's you. The asshole. One of the Fuckalicious Four. Crap." Matilda's hand slams over Fleur's mouth to stop anything else embarrassing come out.

Matilda is bright red and scowling at her.

Fleur is still staring at me and processing it all.

I'm laughing so hard there are tears building in my eyes.

"Fleur, for god's sake be professional. What has gotten into you!" Matilda is scolding her in a stern whisper.

"That would have to be the best reaction I've ever had from a woman. I'm not sure I can say it's a good reaction. But a reaction, nonetheless. One that will need a little explaining, I think." I smile as Matilda is trying to drag Fleur into a seat so she can get her under control.

"Grayson, I'm so sorry. *We* are so sorry. I'm not sure what's wrong with her, but it won't happen again. If you could perhaps forget everything that just fell out of her mouth, I would greatly appreciate it." Matilda's face is still red, which I think is partly embarrassment and part anger at her friend.

With that, Fleur snaps out of wherever her head has taken her to.

"Dr. Garrett, I am so sorry. That was so rude and unprofessional of me. Now, does someone want to explain to me what's going on here?" I can see her starting to eye me up and down. She's like the mother lioness when someone is threatening one of her cubs.

"Fleur, stop. It's fine. We have been chatting and cleared the air. I have also done all your work while you weren't here. So, you can calm down now." Matilda has her hand on Fleur's arm, which in a way looks like she's trying to hold her back a little.

"Okay, so we aren't kneeing him in the balls or shooting flaming arrows at his dick?" Matilda's face just drops into her hands with a groan, hearing what Fleur has just said.

"I sure hope not. I must say though, Fleur, I think you and I are going to be great friends. That, and I might just buy a jockstrap while you're around. You know, just in case I piss you off or something." We all look at each other and the awkwardness is broken. I have laughed more in the last hour than I have in the last month. These girls are real, no pretentious bullshit. Just themselves, which is so refreshing.

"All I will say before I shut up for a while to save my image. Yes, Grayson, you better be careful. Always be on alert. You hurt her again, I will come at you. Now we have that cleared up. Can we catch me up on the function I've probably just ruined any chance of us running? But please enlighten me anyway." I look across at Matilda who still looks mortified. Trying to put her at ease, I reach out and place my hand on top of hers on the table.

"It's fine, Tilly, I'm not worried. Relax."

There it is again. That crazy sensation I get every time I touch her.

As quick as I feel it, she pulls her hand back and it's gone. Fleur looking backward and forwards between the two of us now with a stupid smirk on her face.

Matilda starts shuffling papers on the table and is all of a sudden totally engrossed in her tablet looking for something.

"Well, Fleur, I think Matilda has everything already under control so I'm sure she can fill you in later. We were just getting ready to wrap up the meeting. The only thing left to be decided was if Tilly agrees to come to dinner with me. Maybe you can help her with the decision." I keep looking at her, only seeing the top of her head as she isn't game to look up. "Perhaps that could be the way to make up to me the totally unprofessional greeting I received when you arrived. I'm sure with a lovely dinner in my stomach and a glass of wine, I would forget it was even said."

Fleur starts laughing as Tilly's head whips up to glare at me. "That's blackmail! I was going to say yes anyway." She then realizes what she has blurted out.

"Perfect, then no need for the blackmail. Mind you, I would really love to know more about the Fuckalicious Four? Maybe you can explain that over dinner?" Both her cheeks pink up a little.

"You're crazy, you know that, and I am not saying anything about that. Not even one word. Understand?" Tilly is finally relaxing as she giggles at me. Now that is what I love to see.

"What, no invite for me?" Fleur stands with her hands on her hips and a sly smile.

"No," both Tilly and I say at the same time.

"Wow, I see how it is. Be five minutes late to a meeting and you're already out of the popular group. Well, you two have fun and don't have too much to drink. We know how that ended for both of you the other night." Fleur shakes her school-teacher lecture finger at both of us.

"Yes, ma'am. I promise to have her home by curfew." I stand up with my hands behind my back like a good schoolboy.

"Oh god, what the hell for? That just sounds boring. Just make sure she makes it to work in the morning...or not."

"Fleur, seriously, where the hell is your filter tonight? I have no idea what's going on with you two, and I'm not sure I want to know. Just dinner. I agreed to just dinner, two associates or at a stretch friends, having a meal to talk. Do you both understand now? Lordy, I have a feeling you two are going to be trouble together. And it will be aimed all at me." With that, she stands and picks up her bag ready to leave. I signal for them both to start their way to the exit while I try not to make it too obvious how I'm watching Tilly's ass from behind. The view is definitely one I could get used to.

"Be good or be good at it," Fleur calls over her shoulder as she's about to get into her taxi. I laugh while Tilly is blushing for the about the tenth time today.

"I'm so sorry about her. I'm not sure what has gotten into her. She would never normally act like that with a client."

"That's the thing, I'm not exactly a normal client, am I? Don't let it worry you. I think she's great. She was just protecting you at first, probably with good reason, and then after that she was just having fun at our expense. I have a feeling there will be more of that as we go along, and I for one look forward to it. Now where would you like to go for dinner, my treat?"

Watching Tilly, her shoulders are starting to relax again now that it's just the two of us. I can see she loves her friend, but she was making her uncomfortable and that's the last thing I want. Tonight is about her getting to know the real me, not the asshole she thinks I am.

"I'm in your hands tonight, so you choose."

"Argh, my hands are my strongest asset, so you are definitely safe in my hands. Let's see what mischief we can get up to then." I take her hand and hook it into the crook of my arm as I turn to walk down the sidewalk.

"Friends, remember." Tilly looks up at me as we walk along.

"Mhmm," I say, which is followed by a chuckle. Tilly just rolls her eyes and starts laughing.

A strange feeling washes over me as we walk that there's more at play here. This beautiful woman on my arm has tried three times to run from me, and every time the universe places her right back by my side.

One thing I do know is that whatever it is, I'm sure as hell grateful and promise not to screw it up this time.

Well, I'll try.

With my track record, promise might be too strong a word.

Chapter Eleven

GRAYSON

"It's warm out tonight and neither of us is dressed to be walking great distances. Let me get the car and take you to one of my favorite restaurants, Ocean Prime, down on the river. The food is amazing, and we can relax and get to know each other." We stop on the pavement and it's like Tilly is thinking about it in her head. "Look, you trusted me so many times already, I think a simple car ride is not even close to what we've done." I turn her to face me. "We can walk if you like. Your choice."

"No, it's okay, the car ride is no issue, unless you're a bad driver?" She smiles a cheeky smile.

"I think we've had this discussion before at how I excel at lots of things. Driving is also on that list. Just so you know. Now let's get the car and get in some air conditioning. There is only one time I like to sweat, and it's not standing on a sidewalk on a warm night." Taking her hand this time, I lead her to the carpark, listening to her tell me how hopeless I am at making suggestive comments all the time. She is so right. I'm not doing it by accident. It keeps her blushing and I love it.

"Let me guess, it's not when you're exercising either?" Her eyes sparkle when she's up to mischief.

"You could say I'm working out and getting exercise, just maybe not how you're picturing. Or are you picturing it right now, you dirty little thing. You told me to behave and here you are saying things like that."

"I can never beat you, can I?" Tilly's laughing at me as we approach the car. "You always have a comeback better than mine."

"Not a chance. What do you not get about me being pretty awesome at just about everything in my life?" I open the door for her to hop in.

"Except being humble," I hear as I'm closing the door on her. She is cheeky. The more I get to know her, the more I like it. I need someone to challenge me and who will also fit in with my friends. Lord knows there are some very big personalities in the guys.

Driving out of the carpark, she's looking around the interior of the car.

"You don't like?" I ask her, hoping she doesn't dislike my car. I'm rather fond of it.

"The opposite. I love it. When I'm back home with my dad, he loves all things cars. We would spend hours at car shows just looking at all the fancy ones, the new ones, and the totally over-the-top muscle cars. Not having a brother, I was the only one who let him drag me along. I secretly loved the time with him on our own." She's running her hand along the interior dash leather.

"I'm so glad my Audi is passing the test. I might have a soft spot for a nice car. I figure if I work long hours then I deserve a treat. Not that I get to drive it much. In the city it's such painful driving. Taking it out for a good run in the country, now that's a good day. You'll have to come the next time I go. If you're a good girl, I might even let you drive." I turn to her, smiling at her smirk.

"I suppose you'll tell me you're the better driver too."

"Of course, that's a given." I look back at the traffic in front of us heading up South Michigan Ave, making sure I don't run up anyone's ass and cause a crash. The last thing I want to do is ruin that driving reputation in the first thirty seconds.

"We'll see about that. I'll have you know I've done four fast laps in a Nascar at Daytona. My lap time was pretty impressive." The look of accomplishment on her face makes me laugh.

"Wow, I have a lot to live up to then. I'm guessing me delivering the baby of one of the top Nascar drivers, who I can't name for privacy reasons, doesn't count? It was an emergency delivery while they were in town for a race and then he let me drive his Nascar to say thanks. That doesn't count?" I try to keep the straight face

"Are you for real? Humility really isn't in your vocabulary, is it? Every single time, you one-up me." She's slapping her forehead, and I can't hold it in anymore. My laughter bubbles out and she looks at me suspiciously.

"Nah, just joking. But you totally fell for it. You know you're cute with that little competitive streak. I'll have to remember that for future reference." Now that comment earns me a slap on the arm.

By the time we get out of the car at the restaurant, it feels like we've known each other for years. The conversation is flowing so easy and she seems to be relaxed around me. I probably shouldn't have, but I place my hand on the curve in her back as I guide her to the doors. It might be an intimate move, but she doesn't seem to react or mind. It just feels natural.

Being seated near the window, it means we get to enjoy looking out at the nighttime activity, and it's a little more cozy than being amongst all the people. The restaurant is abuzz, and we're lucky to get a table. I think it helps that I'm a regular. It has such a warm atmosphere with all the brown leather seating and the gold lights and furnishings. The guys and I have eaten here many a time and frequented the bar that serves some of the best cocktails in town. Not that I'm a cocktail lover, but I have been known to taste one or two.

We continue to talk about just general life, our jobs, friends, the foundation. We can't seem to venture into personal questions. Every time I try to go there, she steers it back to safe territory. It's like she doesn't want me to get too close. Little does she realize that's exactly what I want to do. For obvious reasons, but also to really get to know Tilly, not just the Matilda I'm chatting to now.

I feel like there are two women in her world. Matilda the professional businesswoman, who is efficient and slightly guarded at all times. Then there is Tilly who I've seen glimpses of. Even if one of them was under the Hannah disguise at the time. Tilly is the one who was naked in bed. Shy and a little unsure but with a playful side that's dying to be unleashed, I can tell. I need to stop this thought, otherwise I'm going to embarrass myself when we stand to leave. I won't be the only one standing up.

"Your dad said you have a sister, that she's studying to be a doctor too. Where is she based?" Tilly asks in another change of subject.

"Currently she's at Mercy too. Believe it or not, she is about to start a rotation of neurosurgery and has Tate as her head doctor. I just lost my shit over it when you ran into me the other night when we both had a little too much amber fluid under the belt. He is my best friend and one of the biggest man whores in the hospital. I was a little peeved. Bella made me see that I trust him with my life, so I should trust him with my little sister. She had a fair point. I'll be warning him, though, don't you worry." When I get off my soap box, Tilly is laughing at me, her hand over her mouth trying to hide it. "What's so funny?"

"How old is your sister?" she asks.

"Twenty- five. Why?" I reply.

"Your dad did mention you were an overprotective older brother. I can definitely see that already. She must love you." Tilly is still trying to hold it together.

"Most of the time, yes. When I'm being the big brother, not a whole lot. You nailed it in one. Now let's not talk about my sister. I'd rather talk about you." Again, I try to swing the conversation around to her.

"I'm pretty boring, not much to tell. Grew up in a small town. Have an older sister who is off travelling the world, currently working her way across Europe. Mom and Dad happily married and still living in the home they moved into after their wedding. We are the typical American family. Even have the family dog and cat. Mind you, they hate each other, but they make it work." She laughs at the memory of her family pets.

"I have a rescue dog who is my best friend. I can't even tell you the breed, or mixture of breeds, but I wouldn't know what to do without him. After a bad day at work, he's nice to come home to for that wagging tail and the cuddles that he loves."

"I can't picture you with a dog." Tilly looks at me genuinely.

"Why is that?" I'm a little confused.

"Well, it must be hard to compete with your ego at home. Usually the pet rules the home, yet I'm not sure there's room for two alpha males in one place." She starts to laugh after struggling to keep a straight face.

"I don't know if I should take that as a compliment or not. Maybe you'll have to come and meet Memphis to see who the boss of the house really is."

She looks at me with a grin. "Your dog's name is Memphis? Did you choose that?"

"I did, but that was after he chose me at the rescue center. It was love at first sight for both of us. Be careful if you meet him, he might claim you too." The words that have just left my mouth actually give me a warm feeling. I would love to see her in my home with my boy. He's a smart dog. I know he'll trap her heart too. The perfect wingman.

The waiter had been to the table with the bill, which Matilda tried to pay half. No way, no how, is any woman ever paying for a dinner when we're out together. My parents raised me better that that. My father would whoop my ass.

"Can I drive you home please, Tilly?" I ask hopefully as we exit the restaurant. What I wanted to say was I'm driving you home now. I'm trying to keep my 'alpha,' as she called it, in check and not appear like the jerk she thinks I am.

"That would be great, thank you. It's probably a little out of your way, but I would appreciate it. I don't drive around the city during the day. I find it easier to use taxis or Uber. I'm not sure where you live, but I live north in Uptown, so if it's too much of a pain, I can order a car." I can see she is hoping to get a ride, but as I would expect, doesn't want to put me out.

"It's perfectly fine, happy to do it. Doesn't matter where you live. You know how much I love to drive my baby." She rolls her eyes at me as we head back to the car. Pulling out of the carpark, she casually asks where I live. Luckily, we're already in the car and moving.

"In The Loop, it keeps me close to the hospital when I'm on call." It doesn't take long for the reaction I'm expecting.

"Gray!" she yells. "I am so far out of your way. You should have let me call a service. I feel so bad now. Why didn't you tell me?" Her eyes are fixed on me with fire in them.

"Because it wouldn't have mattered if I lived in the back of butt fuck nowhere, I still want to drive you home. You've met my dad, right? He wouldn't be impressed to know I let you take a car service home after dinner." The fire in her eyes is gone and she's relaxing into the seat again.

"So, you aren't really a gentleman. It's just you're scared of your father." Her smirk tells me she's baiting me.

"Very funny, missy."

"And butt fuck nowhere, really? Want to explain where that is, because I can't wait to hear this one or see your house there." We continue to chat for a short while until we get closer to her suburb.

"I suppose this baby has a pretty impressive sound system too." She has no idea. Pressing a few buttons on my steering wheel, the music comes to life. I see her grin even though the music is loud. I start to turn it down, but her hand reaches over and stops me.

"No wait, I love this *Shallow* song. Who knew Bradley could sing like that?" She starts to sing along. Her voice is so sweet. Nothing like when Bella and I did carpool karaoke. I could sit here all night and listen to her angelic voice. Just as it finishes, she realizes where she is, and her cheeks color at exposing something about herself.

The song changes, and Elvis starts blasting through the speakers. Burning Love, to be exact. As the song starts to really get going, I feel like I've been hit by a brick.

"Holy shit, it was you," I burst out. As I pull into the spot outside her building, Tilly's head whips around to look at me.

"What are you talking about?" Looking confused, she has her hands clasped on her lap.

"That day outside the building, the woman I nearly ran over the top of, literally." Her hand goes to her mouth as the gasp escapes. "I was running listening to this song and then you appeared from nowhere and disappeared just as quickly. I can't believe I didn't remember that." I look at her and the vision of her face in the back of the taxi comes racing back to me.

"Oh my god. What the…" She looks at me dumbfounded. "Hot, white tank top, it was you." She just sits there for a moment and then blurts out, "Damn Hannah and her universe crap." Collecting her bag at her feet, she looks ready to run again.

Oh no you don't, little one.

This running stops right now.

This is all too much. For the last few weeks, this woman has been turning up in my life. What is going on? I just don't understand one little bit. Maybe that's the point. We aren't supposed to understand.

I place my hand on her arm before she bolts from my car.

"I think I'm beginning to like this universe. Tilly, you can't deny there has to be a reason we keep running into each other. Otherwise it's just super random and weird."

"Hannah told me as much as I fight it, the universe has other ideas."

"Is that a bad thing?" Please say no, Tilly.

She just looks at me for a moment and then drops her face with her insecurity. My heart skips a beat until she shakes her head side to side a little to tell me no.

Thank god.

"I know you want to run, but at least let me walk you to your door, please." I lift her chin making her look me in the eyes. "We take this as friends and see what happens from there, no pressure."

"Okay," she quietly whispers and then starts to open her door. As I make it around to her side of the car, she's already pacing towards the door of the apartment building. She might have agreed for the escort to the door, but she is still running.

We don't talk as we enter the building or the elevator. When we reach her floor, she just exits, and I follow like an obedient puppy. It's late so all is quiet or just a low hum of the television as we pass doors. Finally, she stops in front of what I'm guessing is hers.

She turns to look at me after retrieving her keys from her bag.

"This is me. You aren't going to stalk me, are you?" I can see her attempt at humor is trying to take away her nerves and break the tension.

"Only if you want me to, Tilly. It won't be stalking, though. It will be so much more than that. Open the door and I'll leave you to head inside like I promised." As hard as that will be. The key turns in the lock and she steps in one foot and hesitates. I can see she's thinking. Slowly she turns to say goodbye.

"Goodnight, Tilly." I lean forward slowly to kiss her cheek.

As I get closer, though, she turns and kisses me squarely on the lips.

The shock of her taking the leap has it being a quick peck.

She steps back and I follow her into her apartment.

No way can I leave it at that.

I pull her head back and give her a kiss that will leave her wet long after I've left. She moans into my mouth.

Fuck, she is killing me.

I'm torn, I promised I would not take the night too far, yet she's giving me all the signals she wants me to stay. As we break apart, I lean my forehead down on hers and she wraps her arms around me. We stand there for a moment until her hand moves and I hear the door quietly closing behind me.

I'm still unsure how far I should be going so I continue to test the waters.

"I can't do this, Gray. You're a client" she whispers as I trail kisses down her throat. I place both my hands on her face and have her complete attention.

"Yes, and I'm a doctor and a man and I was fucking you before I was a client, so tell me why I need to stop, because I'm at my breaking point. I want you bad. You have turned my world upside down, and I need more. I need to feel you again. All over. Every part of you. I want to kiss you, taste you, and I want to cuddle with you until the sun rises. No need to run this time. Don't you want that too?"

"God yes, Gray. All of it. I just..." I don't give her the chance to say another word. My mouth lands hard on hers and devours the lips that have been taunting me all night. It doesn't take long and her body is pressing hard against mine and she's kissing me, as urgently as I'm wanting her.

She pulls away, murmuring to me.

"Just once more." Like she thinks she's not already mine.

"In your dreams if you think that. Once will never be enough. Tomorrow you'll be lucky to walk." She giggles a little and kicks off her shoes. Then standing on her tippy-toes, she starts to push off my jacket. For someone who is hesitant, she's leading this show. I'm happy to let her take this first part, but when it comes to the real action, that's when I want the control of her pleasure. A gentleman never comes first, and if he does, he better be making it up to his lady tenfold.

MATILDA

I should be stopping, I try, albeit not very hard.

There is just this magnetic pull, and every time he's near I can't think clearly.

It's just a raw need to get naked. Enjoy every part of him and let him take me to another place full of pleasure.

That one night was enough to know I want more. As much as I try, I have absolutely no restraint.

"I knew you'd come around to my way of thinking," he whispers as he nibbles on my ear while I'm undoing his buttons. He makes it hard to concentrate on the job at hand. My knees go weak and my body is screaming for his touch in all sorts of places.

My legs barely working, I'm stepping back so I can see his abs, and he grins down at me as I run my hands over him. The hussy in me wants to lick every part of him. Oh god, what is he doing to me? I'm never like this with men. Yet Gray, holy shit, he makes me want to be all sorts of naughty and have him spank me for it.

His finger runs down my jaw as he tilts my head up.

"What are you thinking? Your face is telling a story, and I think it's one I might be interested in." His hand slowly slips down my arm and up again.

"Thoughts that I have never entertained, before you," I whisper, not wanting to tell him yet needing him to hear me loud and clear. His groan tells me which it is. Before I can even take a breath, he is on me.

Drawing my body to him.

Tilting my head to the perfect angle for him to kiss me with so much passion, I think I may have set off the beast.

So much for me taking my time and savoring his body. He's already unzipping my dress, and I feel it falling off my shoulders while he's still continuing to kiss me. I fumble with his belt wanting him naked as quickly as he's stripping me.

What is it about this man? For the love of god, I just want to be fucked within an inch of my life, and it can't happen quick enough.

Leaning down I grab his wallet that has fallen on the floor. "This better have the right sized condom in it this time." I giggle while he just takes it from my hands and pulls out what we need. I drag him to my bedroom leaving our clothes strewn all over the living room floor. We make it to the bed, and I push him backwards. He falls heavily. Well, he is a large muscly man, after all.

I didn't get to explore much last time, so I want to feel and taste it all. Gray looks up at me with a wicked smile.

"Like what you're seeing, little one?" His voice is lower now and I can tell he's holding back from taking me. He is indulging my fantasy.

"Very much so." I start crawling up his body to take his boxer briefs. Dragging them down over his cock, it slowly comes into view. I hope the moan I just made was inside my head, but by the look from Gray I know it wasn't.

My hands slide back up the insides of his legs as I'm sitting on my knees between them. He lies back taking in the view, with his hands up under his head. The ultimate position. I wish I could capture it in a photo. His abs tense and that set of V muscles that lead down to his cock stand strong. They are like arrows to the promised land. My hands run over every inch of his chest. The little bit of hair, that makes him feel rugged, tingles the tips of my fingers. Looking up, I see his jaw clenching. He's hanging on by a thread. Time to give him a little show too.

I very slowly place my hand around his throbbing cock and slide it up and down a few times. Bringing out the little soft groans from him. On the next up slide, I keep my hands going up to around my back and release my bra. It is not as sexy as the first night, but his eyes tell me it has the desired effect. Pushing the straps down my arms, the satin bra falls forward and on to his hardened cock. His eyes are starting to roll a little, and I'm not sure how much more he can take. I place my hand over the satin and drag it up his shaft. His hands are moving to grasp my hips.

Hard.

"Tilly," he moans almost like a guttural growl. I want to push him over the edge, and I know just how.

"Mmm," I let out as I lean forward and take him in my mouth as deep as I can.

"Fuck! Tilly, you need to stop." I shake my head, but on the third time I'm sliding him out, his hands grab my head and drag me up towards his face.

The way he starts to kiss me, it's like he's never going to see me again. His hands roam all over my back and ass as I lie completely flat on top of him. He grabs my ass cheeks and squeezes them to push me hard down on him. The heat in the kiss has me now grinding against him.

It happens so quickly. Gray flips us so he's on top of me and I'm pinned to the bed. My heart races and my body is throbbing. I want him to touch me. I also want him to take me and give it to me with all he has built up. We are both wired and ready to let go. He pulls back onto his knees and rips my panties off me. He freezes for a moment, just taking in everything he's seeing. I can't breathe just watching him. He leans over to grab the condom and slowly rolls it on like even his touch on his cock is nearly pushing him over the edge.

Both his hands move forward to show my breasts attention as his mouth lowers down and he takes the first swipe through my folds with his tongue. It's slow and deep, ending up with him sucking my nub until I explode and cry out. I can't hold it any longer. Riding the high, I feel him enter me with one deep thrust.

Wrapping my legs around him, Gray lets go of all the pent-up sexual tension I had built every time I looked at him and touched him. I feel like he's giving me more than his body. This feels like so much more. I can't think or talk. My breathing is heavy, the moans are broken, with the occasional *oh god* that I can manage to scream in between gasping for the air my body is craving.

"Can't hold on much more. Come with me, little one," Gray gets out through his gritted teeth as he continues to hold on and not come before I do. That thought is enough that it pushes me over the edge once again. I can feel him let go too. Those last pulses inside me make me shudder as he pushes as deep as he can go, creating pleasure for us both.

His weight on his elbows so he's not crushing me, his head drops to my chest. I can hear him catching his breath as I take my hands and run them through his hair. Still connected, I feel the closeness like I never have before. Gently he slides out and rolls to the side, leaning down and kissing me softly and tenderly. Not like before, where it was frantic, hot and demanding. This is trying to tell me how that felt. The emotion and connection we both felt.

It's crazy when we've only known each other a few weeks. Yet it's like our bodies know each other from another lifetime.

"Let me clean you up, beautiful." He softly speaks to me as he rises from the bed, walking towards my en suite. Not closing the door, I watch him in all his glory dispose of the condom and grab a cloth, running it under the warm water for me. Why does he have to be so perfect?

I lie back like a princess while he wipes me over. No guy has ever taken such care of me. When he returns, he climbs straight onto the bed, grabbing the blanket at the end of the bed and pulling it up. He then places his arm around me and draws me so close I end up lying half on his body while he cuddles me. Not that I'm complaining one bit.

I have no idea what tomorrow will bring, but the way I feel right now is something I'm not used to.

It's confusing yet calming.

It came from nowhere, and I don't know what to do with it.

This is why I have avoided anything serious. I don't have time for these thoughts of confusion in my crazy world. Yet I know I'm not going to able to keep running, nor will Gray let me.

"What's wrong, baby? I can hear your breathing getting faster," Gray mumbles as if he's already half asleep. His hand is rubbing me so softly on my back which is like a lullaby to a baby in trying to calm me down.

"Gray, I don't know what's happening. What is this between us?" I lean up on his chest to look at him.

"Beautiful, don't overthink this. It's whatever we want it to be. Friends, lovers, partners, husband and wife, there are options." He starts laughing at the panic he must be able to see on my face.

"I'm joking. Just relax. Why don't we just keep being friends and date a little bit to see if you can cope with me. I know I'm a lot to take on, my personality, my life, my career. Oh, and god forbid my family and friends. Once you assess all that, you'll likely kick me to the curb anyway." His other hand is now holding my face and stroking my cheek.

"I wasn't looking for anything like this. I just feel like I'm at the top of a roller coaster after going through a few of the ups and downs and getting close to the top of the big dipper that launches into the corkscrews. I know I'm crazy, but I'm used to complete order in my life. You..." I pause, waving my hands up and down over his body, then lean and kiss his lips lightly.

"You are the total unknown that happens in an event. It has me scrambling trying to work out how to manage it. Keeping the world calm around it."

"Yes, but you always work it out, don't you? It never derails the event, does it? Everything still turns out perfectly."

Looking him in the eyes, I realize he has a point.

Why am I trying so hard to fight this? Instead of just letting it take its course, whatever that may be.

I know exactly why.

Heartbreak.

No one wants their heart broken. I had it once and never want to feel that again. It hurts too much.

Pulling my head to him, Grayson kisses me again, trying to make me understand what he's feeling, making me realize how serious he is about this.

"Just try, Tilly. Can we just try to date? You must admit it's been pretty great so far. Well, apart from a few verbal spars, but hey, this make-up sex was so worth it." That cheeky grin sucks me in again. Every damn time.

"I can't believe I'm even saying this." It's like he's holding his breath. "Let's take it slow. Especially until after the foundation launch event. We need to separate business and pleasure."

Within seconds, Grayson is cheering like a schoolboy.

"Shh, you'll wake the neighbors." I smack him on the chest.

"Now that is where you are wrong, little one. Me making pleasure my business is what is going to wake your neighbors, and they better get used to it." As he grabs me, I know that speech about going slow has gone out the window as soon as I said it.

Holding me tightly, Grayson lets me know exactly what is happening between us. To be honest, on the inside I'm screaming like a schoolgirl too, as he says the words out loud.

"You. Are. Mine."

The rest of the night is hot, heavy, and a whole lot of burning love.

Chapter Twelve

MATILDA

Mmmm. Stretching my arms above my head, legs out straight, I can feel every muscle in my body. In a good way. So good that I feel like a bad little girl. Thirty-two years old and I feel like a nineteen-year-old after a wild night out. I start to giggle a little because the honest thing is, I wouldn't know what that was like. I've always been on the conservative side.

Until now.

Since a certain hunky doctor showed up.

I roll over, realizing I'm alone in bed.

Where is he? A moment of panic that he's left runs through me until I see his clothes folded on my chair beside my bed and my dress from yesterday lying over the ottoman.

My anxious feeling starts to settle down when I hear faint noises coming from the kitchen and the smell of coffee is starting to call my brain awake.

Sliding out from under the warm blankets, I start to pull my robe off the hook and head to the bathroom to make myself presentable.

Just sitting down on the toilet, I hear the banging on the front door. I'd know that rhythm anywhere.

Fuck! Daisy's here.

Jumping up and trying to pull myself together, I run only to make it to the living room as my little buddy is already standing inside the door. Hands on hips staring up at a giant towering over her, shirtless and with a towel wrapped around his waist. He looks slightly confused as he gets a lecture from her about answering the door without all his clothes on. I want to laugh, but I know this is going to be a challenge to sort out first.

"Daisy, what are you doing here so early on a school day?" I walk into the room and catch Gray's eyes that are reading, *please help me.*

"Tilly." She runs towards me and takes a leap into my arms. "Who's he?" She points with aggression to Grayson who is still looking a little confused.

"He's..." I hesitate, trying to think how to explain this. Before I can continue, the hot guy in the towel with the big ego beats me to it.

"I'm her boyfriend, Gray, pleased to meet you." I glare at him as he walks towards us with his hand outstretched to Daisy. All her confidence is gone, and she's burrowing her head into my neck as he gets closer. Not sure he's picking up the daggers I'm throwing his direction yet.

"Sweetheart, this is my friend."

"Boyfriend," his determined voice jumps in again, this time glaring at me. I get a flashback to last night, the words *'you are mine'* feeling so good as he claimed me.

"This is my boyfriend Grayson, but you can call him Gray. Now he is going to go and put some clothes on before he catches a cold, isn't that right, Dr. Gray?" He's smiling now, having won the silent argument between us.

Then in a delayed reaction, I hear Daisy whisper, "Doctor." Then she's squirming to get down.

"I want to be a nurse when I get big like Tilly and my mom. One that looks after people, you know, the ones that are sick. Do you make people better?" Before Gray can answer, I hear the next problem for my morning coming across the hall through my open door.

"Daisy, stop chatting and hurry up with the milk, you'll be late for... holy fucking shit balls." Hannah's eyes nearly pop out of her head.

Her face turns bright red.

Her hands land on her cheeks, not knowing what to say or do.

I can't help but laugh.

"Hannah, Grayson. Grayson, my friend Hannah, and before you say a word, you, bedroom and clothes." I point to Gray. "Daisy, turn on the television and I will pick up your mother's jaw." I smack Gray on the chest as he walks past me.

"I love it when she gets all bossy," he says over his shoulder as he disappears, laughing at the bombshell he's left in my living room.

"Mommy, you said bad words. Lots of them. Dr. Gray opened the door without all his clothes on which is also naughty, and Tilly is telling me to turn on the television even though she knows I'm not allowed in the mornings." The hands go back to the hips again. "You are weirdos today, I'm glad I can go to school soon." She just turns matter-of-factly and walks to the remote and hits the button, searching for the cartoons.

I walk past Hannah who is still frozen to the spot with her mouth open. I lift her chin and keep walking to close the door.

"Oh no you don't, you little hussy," she whispers and grabs my arm, dragging me to the kitchen. "Spill now! Why is there a hot—actually, that's not enough. An *extremely* hot, drool-worthy man in only a towel, in your apartment at seven am on a weekday?"

"You act so surprised. Yet you sent me on a mission to get a life and find dessert. Well, you know I'm such an overachiever, so I brought home the whole meal." Opening the fridge, I pull out the milk I'm guessing Daisy had to come to get and got sidetracked.

"Is that the asshole doctor? The one I told you the universe keeps handing to you on a platter?"

"The one and only. I turned up for a new job yesterday, and the good doctor is my new client." I finish making the coffees Gray started.

"Matilda, holy shit, you slept with a client. Whatever will we do with you?" Her shock has worn off and now the laughing is starting.

"Shh, remember Daisy's here, and I already feel unsure about the whole client thing. He just puts up very convincing arguments."

"Too right I do, I don't care one bit and neither should you." He comes up from behind me, kissing my temple, sliding his arms around my waist, and reaching out to Hannah. "Nice to meet you, Hannah. I believe I have a lot to thank you for, including the borrowing of your name by a certain lady trying to hide from me."

Hannah just stands a little stunned.

"Oh for god's sake, Han, he's just Grayson, snap out of it," I let out, a little frustrated at how much Gray is affecting her.

The next thing I know I'm getting smacked on the ass from him.

"Enough of that. I'm pretty special. Just ask me, I'll be happy to rattle off all my best features," he says from behind me.

Throwing my hands in the air, I signal I'm giving up.

"Seriously, how do you live together, you and your ego? It would be such hard work. Now Hannah, you need to get Daisy to school. Remember, milk, late for school, all of that." I wave the milk in front of her face to get her snapped out of her trance.

"Umm oh yeah, yep, yes that, right umm, school." She is still a mess.

"Hannah, get a grip, woman, seriously." I grab her arm and drag her to the door. "Daisy honey, take Mom home, have breakfast, and see if she can manage to get you to school on time." Daisy is up, television turned off, and she's skipping over to the door as quick as she can.

"You have so much to tell me, this is not done," Hannah whispers at me as I push her through the door.

"Yes, when you can string a sentence together, that is. Have a good day." I laugh as I close the door and wander back to the kitchen.

I just stand at the door for a moment admiring the view. Grayson leaning with his back against the kitchen counter. Barefoot in his black pants, white shirt with sleeves rolled up so I can see the arm porn that I love. Top buttons undone to give me a peek of the chest, and then I find the cheeky smile. In no hurry, he slowly picks up his coffee and sips it, placing it back on the counter. He then holds mine out for me. I move towards him, and just as I get close enough, he puts the cup back on the counter and grabs me around the waist, pulling me tight against his body, wrapping me up.

As he leans down and slowly takes me in a tender kiss, slipping his hand into my hair, I can feel so much electricity running between our bodies. He pulls back, looking down at me.

"Morning, little one."

"Morning," I say, my head still dizzy from the kiss.

"Well, that wasn't quite how I thought the morning would go." He lifts me up and walks backwards, placing me on the other kitchen counter. My legs now curl around the back of his thighs and arms around his neck. Looking into those melting eyes.

"No, far from it." I giggle a little. "Sorry about that. Daisy is a whirlwind and normally Hannah is not that ditzy. I love them both dearly, though."

"I can tell that. Obviously important in your life. Now maybe I can get back to breakfast."

"Oh yeah, what's for breakfast?" I ask, wondering what he found in the kitchen.

"You," he states, full of confidence as he slips the tie on my robe undone. Letting the silk slide open.

"Grayson," I gasp as his hands run over my body, sending goosebumps everywhere.

"Yeah, baby." He smirks looking at me.

"We have to get to work," I mumble, trying to concentrate.

"All in good time. I planned to bring your breakfast to you in bed, but I can't resist this beautiful sight." He places his hand on my chest and slowly pushes me backwards to be lying flat on the counter.

"I don't think you understand how stunning you look. I need to show you what you do to me." I hear his zipper sliding down and his pants dropping to the floor. I lean up on my elbows to see the view. He's already sliding the condom down his cock that is more than ready to go.

"Where did that come from?"

He just smiles at me. "I make sure I'm always prepared for you. I never want to be caught out again." He looks so satisfied with himself as he runs his finger along my folds to find me more than ready.

The first thrust, we both groan, and he just stays still letting my body accept him. Then slowly he starts to move and we both continue to pant and enjoy every moment.

"Need to remind my girlfriend, this is happening." His thrusting gets harder and quicker like he's marking me as his. Just in case I didn't get the message last night.

"Be mine, Tilly, I'm already yours." He's almost pleading with me as we both race to that climax. Here on my kitchen counter.

In all my naked glory, I scream the only thing I can.

"Yes!"

Rushing through the office glass doors, I find Fleur and Deven standing there with their arms crossed and stupid looks on their faces.

Deven looks down and taps his watch.

"Not a word from you two. Not a fucking word!" I say as I hurry past them into my office to get my computer on and set up for the day.

Damn Grayson, he was in no hurry to leave this morning as he had a late start. I, on the other hand, had great difficulty leaving his warm arms and magic hands.

"Sleep in, did we, princess?" Deven asks as they both follow me into my office. "Or was it the Prince Charming in your bed that kept you awake all night." Both he and Fleur start laughing.

"Get all your smart comments out now, let's go. I know Hannah will have messaged you both all the gossip. Now let me give it to you in bullet-point form, so we can get on with work."

They're both laughing harder now, seeing the discomfort on my face at being the center of their jokes.

"Yes, I slept with Grayson. Yes, he stayed the night. Yes, he was fucking amazing and yes, we are now seeing each other. Got it? Good. Now, can we get to work? I'm running behind." With that I sit into my chair and open my emails for the day.

"Look, Deven, our little girl's all grown up. Her first real boyfriend. How cute is that. Do you think we need to have the birds and the bees chat?" Fleur puts her finger on her chin dramatically.

"I think the dreamy doctor may have that talk all under control. It's safe to say he should know how babies are made."

"That's it, you've had your fun, now out. Get to work. I only want to hear from you if there is an emergency or it is work-related. Understood?"

They both link arms and turn to leave, laughing at their own jokes as they close the door behind them.

I drop my head onto the desk. Oh lordy, this is going to be a nightmare with those two, I can tell. It's like this even before Deven has met him and started commenting on his body.

I sit back in my chair just trying to take in the last twenty-four hours and how my life has been turned upside down, shaken sideways and then stood upright again. This time yesterday I was just organizing to meet a new client.

Today, I have a new client, been fucked within an inch of my life, and have a boyfriend. Who, after only knowing him for such a short time, I know will crush me, if he ever walks away.

My phone chimes with a text message.

I look down to see the name on the screen.

GG

He saved his number for me in my phone last night.

His put in his initials GG for Grayson Garrett.

For me, all I can think of is:

GG – Gorgeous Gyno

A smile comes to my face as I open the message. It's short and simple but means more than a thousand words.

GG: I will thank the universe every day for bringing you to me. GG x

My heart is melting and finally I know I can't walk away. This man is everything I wanted and certainly what I need. Now I pray the universe just teaches me how to get this right.

GRAYSON

I'm standing at the nurse's station, filling in patient records, having just done patient rounds on some new moms. I've always looked at the babies as something I might want one day. So now, how can one night with one special lady have me looking at them so differently this morning? I picked up little Coby and he was wrapped up so tightly. So peaceful, all pink and new. While I held him and chatted to his Mom and Dad, I could see the unconditional love in their eyes after only a short time. This is the part of parenthood I never really noticed before. It's like a switch was triggered last night, and that scares the hell out of me. I need to dampen down this new sensation. I already make Tilly nervous about being so serious. If I tell her about me thinking about kids, that'll be enough for her to pick up and take off again. I finally just got her to agree to stop running. I don't want to give her another reason to change her mind.

"That humming tells me this little boy got laid last night. Finally decided to get rid of the frustration, my friend?" Tate walks up behind me, slapping me on the shoulder.

"You are such a dick sometimes, you know. Actually, most of the time. Just because I'm humming means nothing. But if I did, I'm a gentleman and never kiss and tell." Two of the nurses at the desk look at us and just laugh. Both mumbling about what a load of shit, us doctors love to brag. They could be right, but not this doctor and not this time.

"Let's walk and you can fill me in. I'm on my way to X-ray, and I want to run something by you. You done here?" I nod and we start down the corridor.

"Pretty sure I just said I don't kiss and tell." I walk, smiling to myself, wanting to drag this out a little just to annoy him.

"Yeah, right. Who is she and where did you pick her up?" I don't have much time for this chat, and if I'm being honest, I want to share my news with a friend. The sooner they know and get all the ribbing out of their system, the better, then I can organize to have Tilly meet them properly.

"Really, I don't have time for this stuff. We aren't teenagers anymore. I ran into Matilda last night. She's the event planner for the foundation as it turns out. Which led to dinner and me leaving her apartment this morning as her boyfriend." He stops walking, and I stop and turn back to look at him. He's looking at me strangely.

"You really like her, don't you?" It's the most serious I've ever seen Tate except for in the operating room.

"Yeah, I do. I never believed in that sappy stuff, but I think she's the one," I say quietly.

"No shit, it's written all over your face. Wow, man. That's great, I hope it works out for you." I'm standing here feeling like I'm in a parallel universe. Seeing Tate so serious about Tilly and me is something that just doesn't seem normal.

He puts his hand on my shoulder and gives it a squeeze, then starts walking again.

I follow on behind him, wondering what to say next. Things have gotten a little awkward. Not in a bad way, just a different way.

"What did you need to discuss with me?" I ask, looking at Tate and trying to get his full attention again.

He looks at me and shakes his head.

"Right that, umm. Oh yeah, you know, that patient we looked at last week with the brain tumors that had the spots on the cervix? Just wanted to let you know I'm monitoring your test results and when we get the rest back, we'll chat, okay?"

I've known Tate for a long time and that's the biggest load of bullshit. He didn't want to talk about that. There's something else going on, but he's stalling.

"Everything alright, buddy? You seem distracted," I ask as we stop at the end of the corridor that leads to X-ray.

"Yeah, yeah, all good." He runs his hand through his hair and drops his gaze to look at the floor.

"Look, if it's about what I said the other night about you and Bella." His face shoots straight up, and his eyes could peel paint off the wall behind me.

"What about me and Bella? She's your sister," he says rather snappy.

"I know, and I shouldn't have given you a hard time about conquering her on your rotation like all your other interns. That was wrong of me and disrespectful to both you and Bella. I know you would never do anything to hurt her. She's like a little sister to you too. Sorry, man, I really am." I put my hand on his shoulder and he flinches slightly.

"Yeah, she's your little sister so totally off limits. We all know that, we hear it loud and clear. Gee, look at the time, I better run. Catch you later." With that he's off and through the doors, not looking back at all.

What the hell just happened?

Like I said, an alternate universe in here today.

I'll talk to the guys and see if they know anything about Tate. I've been so caught up with Tilly that maybe I've missed something.

I've finished with rounds, so it's time to head back to my office and prepare for the clinic visits this afternoon. Wandering back the way we just came, my mind drifts off again to this morning. What a beautiful way to wake up. Tilly was lying on her stomach next to me. Her brown hair sprawled all down her back in soft waves. Her back was in full view as the sheet had slipped down. Her peachy complexion and smooth skin, a vision with just the top of her back-side peeking out of the sheet. She was facing me, and I could feel the soft breaths. It was like every time she exhaled, I breathed it in, and she fed life into me.

I laid there for about an hour just watching her. I know it sounds creepy, it's just she mesmerizes me. I actually can't believe I found her again. Got a second shot for her to get to know the real me.

For the first time in a long time, I think it's going to be hard to concentrate on work today. All I want to do is find a way to see her.

What has she done to me?

Since when have I ever acted like this over a woman.

I'm at my desk and fully immersed in the scans for a twenty-five-year-old woman who I have to deliver the dreaded news to in a few hours that she has cancer and it's terminal. It has spread, and at the moment the best we can do for her is to give her treatment for palliative care. This is the worst part of my job. How can you tell someone news like that and not be affected yourself?

Cancer sucks and I wish I could do more.

Whatever we're doing, it still isn't enough.

The ringing on my phone brings me out of my thoughts. A welcome break from the intensity.

"Dad, how's your trip going?"

"Hi, son. All good. Everything is resolving as I was hoping. We still have a little way to go, but we have them on the right track now. I just wanted to check in on how the meeting went with Matilda. Are we underway with all the organizing?" There's something about the voice of my dad that always makes me feel good. He has a really calming tone, and I can understand why he's so good at his job.

"Everything is arranged, the meeting went fantastic, so did dinner, and breakfast was good too."

Dad's chuckle lets me know he knew all along she was more than a friend.

"Why do you think I'm calling? I saw the way you were looking at her from the moment you saw her. Plus, Matilda couldn't look any more stunned at seeing you than if the President walked into the room. There were some pretty big sparks firing in that room, son."

I laugh at his descriptions. My dad is excellent at reading body language.

"Let's just say, my great persuasion skills convinced Tilly to become my girl-friend and get to know me better than the first few times she met me."

"I'm sure there's a story there for another time. You're really taken by her, aren't you?" Dad's voice gets a little more serious.

"More than I know what to do with yet. I have this overwhelming feeling she might be the one for me. I know it sounds crazy, but it's just this strong feeling in my gut." I sit back in my chair looking out the window.

"Then I don't doubt she is, Grayson. When I met your mother, not another woman ever looked the same compared to her. She had laid her claim on my heart. From that moment on, my heart didn't want anyone else, ever." He went a little quiet as he talked about Mom, and my heart hurt for him.

"We all know how much you loved her, Dad. She did too. But she wouldn't want you to be alone forever. You do know we would be happy for you if you found another woman to have in your life, don't you?" As hard as that is to say, it is what Bella and I wish for him, happiness.

"I know, Gray, it's just no one has ever been worthy of taking her place. I still look in the hope one day someone might. But so far, I still live with Maxine's love holding my heart. When she's ready, she'll let go and give it to whoever she picks for me."

It's so hard to hear my dad talk like that, but it also brings warmth knowing how much my parents loved each other.

We talked for a few more minutes until he was called away and it was almost time for me to head down to the clinic.

At least I don't have any worries about my dad accepting Tilly or being concerned that she's dating her client. Now I just need her to meet Arabella, which could be a little more interesting. She complains that I'm overprotective, however in Bella's eyes, no one is ever going to be good enough for her big brother. We have a very special bond that whoever we both meet will need to understand. You can't go through what we did and not be as close as we are. I know Tilly is perfect, so Bella will see that too, I'm sure.

While my mind is floating on the happiness of the new woman in my life, I take that strength as I walk down to try to deliver the worst words someone wants to hear.

You have incurable cancer.

Fuck you, cancer!

Chapter Thirteen

GRAYSON

Today has been a tough one. They happen and you really need to take care of your mental health in a job like this so you can continue to be the best you can. Normally, I would run it off and then the body uses the endorphins to calm me again.

Tonight, it's the last thing I'm thinking of. I want to see Tilly and wrap her in my arms. Let her be the energy to calm the soul. I didn't even ask her plans for tonight this morning when we left her apartment. I was too busy getting that last kiss and last touch before I let her walk away from me. The rate I'm going, I'll lose my tough guy image when people see me around her. She makes me so soft.

Walking out of the hospital, I push her name on my phone. I hope I'm not interrupting anything important or she's still at work. Being after six, it's still light and the air is warm. I can feel the sweat already starting under my shirt.

"Hello." There it is. That voice I've been waiting for.

"Hi, beautiful. What no, 'Hi handsome' or 'Hello there, big boy'?" I can't help myself, I need to break my mood.

I hear her giggling on the other end of the phone. Music to my ears.

"Considering I'm at the park with Daisy, that may be a little awkward, but sure, you just pretend I said all of the above. What are you up to, are you still at work?" My heart is already beating faster and my plans are already formed.

"Just in the car now. Tell me what park you're at and I'll grab Memphis and meet you both there for a play date." I hesitate a little. "That is, of course, if that's okay? Sorry, I shouldn't have just assumed." I need to keep myself in check. As much as I want to storm into her life and plant myself right beside her, I'll scare her off. Slowly, Grayson, that's what I need to keep telling myself.

"You're an idiot, of course I want to see you, but let me ask my date. Daisy, Gray wants to know, can he bring his dog to the park to play with us?" I hear a scream in the background getting closer to Tilly. I hear Daisy's voice loud and clear down the phone.

"Yes, yes bring the puppy. But put your clothes on first." Her little voice is so loud I'm guessing she is screaming into the phone. I chuckle to myself as Tilly obviously takes control of her phone again.

"Sorry, she just stole it from me. How's your eardrum?"

"Lucky it was already connected in the car, but all of Chicago now knows that I need to wear clothes more often apparently, so there's that. I'm guessing that was a yes to meeting up with you." I'm already trying to get home as quick as possible.

"Looks like you passed the test. Maybe not you, but I think Memphis may have been your wingman with Daisy. She loves dogs but can't have one. So be prepared to be smothered. Well, Memphis anyway. I hope he likes kids." She sounds so happy and carefree. I forget what it's like to feel that sometimes. Just to enjoy the simple things.

"Perfect. Daisy can cuddle Memphis, and I can cuddle you. Double date. Now where am I heading to? And you better be ready to be kissed within an inch of your life when I get there."

"Grayson. Remember five-year-old girl, keep it G-rated." I can't help but laugh at that.

"Hey, that kid has seen me nearly naked in just a towel, kissing you is mild. Now, woman, give me your location before I lose my patience and hunt you down."

"Calm down, big boy."

"Ah, now that's more like it. Continue."

"Oh for god's sake, will I ever get to have a normal serious conversation with you? Actually, forget that, I already know the answer. We're down at Clarendon

Park. There's a dog-friendly beach here, Montrose Beach, we can take Memphis to if you want."

Just hearing her already thinking about my dog makes me feel good.

"That sounds perfect. I know the one, I've taken him there before. I'll be as quick as I can. The traffic isn't too bad. I assume Daisy will have to be home soon, so I'll hurry."

"Gray, don't rush. I want you here in one piece, please. It's okay, we'll wait. Message when you get here."

"Will do. Looking forward to seeing you. I missed you today."

"Me too," I hear her quietly say, not much more than a whisper. Looks like we need to work on that confidence. I want her screaming to the rest of the world, I'm hers.

"See you soon."

"Bye." Her voice is gone and the music cuts back into the speakers, and my foot presses a little harder on the accelerator.

———

I look back at Memphis sitting up like royalty on the back seat. His dog seatbelt on and knowing he's off to somewhere special because we've been in the car that little bit longer than normal.

"Are you ready to meet my girl? I think you'll love her. She has a little playmate for you. Be nice to Daisy otherwise it could be a problem, okay? Best behavior."

Plenty of people will look at me like I'm crazy talking to a dog. He knows what I'm saying. The love of a pet is without judgement. If you love them, they'll show you their love back just as much. Usually in slobber with face licks, whether you want them or not.

We pull into the carpark, and I get him out on the leash. He knows to wait, but I can tell it's almost killing him to sit patiently.

I can hear Daisy coming before I even see her. Yelling at Tilly to hurry up so she can pat the dog.

As they come into view, my body starts to let the tension of the day go. Part of me feels guilty because that patient from today doesn't ever get to let go of that tension. I have to keep telling myself that to help them I need to keep looking after myself.

"Dr. Gray, Dr. Gray, we're over here!" Daisy is calling out as she runs to me. She's so cute she thinks I can't see her. When she gets older, she'll understand the magnetic pull your heart has when its other half is close by. You feel them just as much as see them, and your eyes will find them even in a sea of people.

I give her a wave, so she knows I see her. Tilly is smiling the biggest grin walking behind her. I'm not sure of the connection between them all yet, but whatever it is, they're like family even if they aren't the same blood.

Memphis is pulling tighter on the lead to get to this little girl who is obviously making a beeline to him. I try to pull him in, but his legs are pushing hard to get to her. I don't want him to overrun her or frighten her by jumping up.

"Memphis." I use a stern voice which stops him in his tracks and allows Daisy to approach him first.

"Hi, Dr. Gray, can I pat him, what's his name, does he like to play ball?" She's almost jumping out of her skin.

"Hi, Daisy, just call me Gray. You sure can pat him. Just like this." I kneel down so I have full control of him, not that I really need to worry, he's being really gentle with her. "That's it, he is loving that pat." His tail wagging, Memphis is in heaven.

I stand up again, leaving Daisy to give him the attention while I take Tilly in my arms and kiss her. Not the way I want to, but I did promise to keep it G-rated.

"Hi, little one," I whisper in her ear as I snuggle into the crook of her neck, just taking in her smell and the feeling of being home. She shivers a little and then pulls back.

"Are you okay?" she asks softly, looking concerned at me.

"I am now." I take another kiss and then reluctantly release her from my grasp. "Long day at work." The look on her face tells me she knows what I mean. It's like it kicks her into action.

"Daisy, do you want to take Memphis over to the beach so we can throw the ball for him?" Tilly asks her.

Her little eyes light up and look up to me with a question she clearly wants to ask and isn't quite sure of.

"Would you like to take his lead, and I will just hang on to the end bit?" I offer, knowing it's what she wanted.

"Yes please, Gray, can I do it? Will he run?" she asks, a little worried.

"Not if he wants his dinner tonight. He will be good for you, I promise. Plus, I'll help you too." We start out towards the beach, Daisy and Memphis on one side of me and Tilly on my other side. I reach out, taking her hand in mine.

This feels so good and totally natural.

I should be freaking out about now, but strangely I'm not. I could get used to these kind of afternoon walks. Beats running kilometers to burn off my stress, any day, hands down.

After showing Daisy how to throw the ball for Memphis, she started doing it herself, and the two of them are having the best time. Lots of laughing, squealing in fun, tail wags and barking.

I pull Tilly down to sit on the sand with me, between my legs. Pulling her back against my chest and wrapping my arms around her. We just sit in silence watching, and it is so peaceful. I love that we don't need to fill the air with words. Just being together is all we need.

"She's pretty cute, isn't she?" Tilly is watching Daisy like a hawk as she still runs around with Memphis.

"Yeah, she is. Full of life I'm sure, does she ever slow down?" I ask.

"Yes, when she falls asleep." Tilly giggles to herself. "That's why I try to help Hannah out with her. Trent is deployed, and she's on her own without family around. It's hard work. I'm like an adopted aunty in a way. I get just as much out of it as they do." I knew there was a special bond between them.

"That sounds like you really love her like your own," I comment, still watching Memphis to make sure he's behaving.

"The way I'm going, she may be the only child I ever get in my life." That makes me stiffen a little.

"Do you not want them or is there a reason you can't have them?" My doctor brain is going flat-out trying to think back to when I examined her. Did I miss something?

"Yeah, silly, you need a man to make a baby. Geez, I thought even you would know that." She turns her head to look up at me, a big smile on her face.

I can't help but laugh.

"That's easily solved. You can tick that one off the list. But do you want them, kids, I mean?" Her face starts to look a bit more serious now.

"I've always wanted children one day. I was just starting to think my time is running out. I was starting to think I might need to have a Plan B. I know that sounds silly, but I just don't want to miss the boat. Who knows, maybe I can't even have kids." She turns back and looks out to the water. I let her have a minute and then I can't wait any longer.

"What is your Plan B, Tilly." I quietly speak while resting my chin on the top of her head, letting her know she doesn't need to look at me.

"I haven't done anything yet, but maybe to freeze my eggs just in case. Then that would also give me the option of IVF later if I still couldn't find a man who wanted me." Every calm muscle in my body is as hard as a rock. I stand up, dragging her up with me. Before she even has time to breathe, I'm on her. Kissing her like she needs this kiss to keep living. I'm probably too over the top, but I need her to know.

"Does that feel like a man who doesn't want you? Fuck, Tilly, if I could I would give you practice at making babies right here, right now. Understand?" By this stage, I have her face in my hands and just want her to really see I mean everything I'm saying.

"When the time is right, I will happily give you ten kids if that's what you want." Before we get to finish the conversation, I feel a nudge in the back of the leg from Memphis. I look down to see him there, but no Daisy. I quickly look up to see her sitting on the sand quietly on her own. I move before I even think. Running down to where she sits, I crouch down in front of her.

I can hear Tilly following, but I didn't wait.

"Daisy, are you hurt? Did Memphis hurt you, sweetie?" She has little tears running down her cheek.

Tilly came up next to her by now.

"Daisy," she whispers, rubbing her back slowly.

"I miss my daddy. He kisses my mommy like that. My mommy misses my daddy too. I hear her crying sometimes at night when she talks to him." I know she hardly knows me, but I can't see a little child crying. My instinct just kicks in. I pick her up and stand up with her, giving her a tight cuddle while she cries into my shoulder. Just quietly I whisper in her ear that she's okay. Tilly is looking at me and I can't make out her thoughts.

"It's time we get Daisy home, her mom will want her in the bath and then tucked up in bed ready for school tomorrow." Tilly holds her hands out to take her, but Daisy won't let go.

"I'll carry her if you can put Memphis on his lead and walk back with him." She smiles at me as we turn for the car.

By the time I drive us all back to the apartment, Daisy's over her tears and too busy introducing Hannah to Memphis, her new friend. We let her have a little play and then tell her it's time for her to go home. She isn't happy with this but goes anyway. Hannah seems a little more relaxed around me this time.

"I'm just going to walk them over and have a little chat with Hannah for a minute." Tilly gives me the little wink that confirms what I think. She wants to tell her about Daisy's sad tears at the beach. I really feel for her.

"Just make yourself at home, and I'll be back in a minute and we can talk." She closes the door and I'm left with Memphis sitting at my feet wondering where he is.

"What do you think we're going to talk about, boy? The crazy I pulled tonight talking about fathering her kids, or the fact I gave her an M-rated kiss on the beach instead of G-rated and it made Daisy cry? Either way, I think I'm in trouble. What do you think?" He just walks over and plonks down next to a little table and chair in the corner that's obviously there for Daisy. I hate to tell these girls, but Memphis has obviously claimed them all, just like he claimed me all those years ago. Now he's Team Daisy, and it looks like tonight I'm on my own to fight this battle.

"Thanks, traitor. You're supposed to be on my team. Where's the bro code? Mates before dates, huh?" He just looks up at me then puts his head back on the ground and that's it. I start to laugh at him when I hear the door open behind me.

"Back again." Tilly walks in and straight across and into my arms. Okay, maybe I'm not in too much trouble.

"Is she okay?"

"Yeah. Hannah said there have been a few tears lately. Since she started school, she finds it hard seeing the other kids with their dads. Just a learning curve. If they lived on base there would be other kids like her, but in her class, she's the only one. Poor little munchkin. I guess tonight it was just another time it made her think of her dad. He's due home in six weeks, so let's hope that helps."

I take a deep breath and just hold her a little tighter. I know I need to finish the conversation we were having at the beach, but I'm not sure if I should just let it go until she brings it up. There is no way she didn't understand what I was saying. Maybe I should just leave it for now.

"Can I order us some dinner before I head home?"

Her head whips up. "You're going home?" She looks disappointed.

Day made!

"I need to take Memphis home. I don't have his food or bed." I brush a little piece of hair off her face and tuck it behind her ear.

"Okay, I understand." My super-confident Matilda looks like a sad little Tilly now.

"Let's see if we can turn that frown upside down. Come home with me. Pack a bag and stay with me tonight. We can go now and pick up dinner on the way. What do you say, beautiful?" I slowly tilt her chin up so I can softly kiss her on the lips, trying to persuade her.

"Do you mind?" Oh my precious Tilly. Do I mind taking you home to my bed? What do you think?

"Of course I don't. Let me see, hmmm, cold bed on my own. Lying there dreaming of you all night." I hold my hands like scales. "Or sleeping with my beautiful girl with me all night and living my dream. Gee, I wonder which I should choose. It's a tough one."

"Don't be cheeky." I get the ever-increasing light smack on the chest for teasing her. They're becoming more common. I must be doing something right.

"I'll message Hannah to let her know in case she needs me. Then I'll throw some things in a bag."

I kiss her on the top of the head when I let her go. "Give her my number too, in case she can't get hold of you for some reason. Tell her she can call anytime." She just mumbles something as she heads into her room. I take a seat on the couch, picking up my phone, and decide to message the guys to see if they know anything about Tate. Then I shoot a message off to Bella asking if I can meet up over the weekend for breakfast, hoping to introduce her to Tilly. Maybe Dad can meet us too.

Hearing Tilly talking, I'm guessing it's to Hannah. Her voice is getting closer as she comes from her room with her overnight bag. Memphis is just sulking next to Daisy's toys, because we took his friend away from him.

He's the most human dog I know.

"Yes, sweetie, you have a good sleep too. Yes, he is." She looks at me and hands the phone to me, mouthing to me it's Daisy on the other end.

"Hello, sweetheart." I keep my voice low.

"Hi, Gray, thank you for letting me play with Memphis. Can he come again another day and I promise not to cry?" Daisy's voice is so soft and sleepy on the other end.

"Of course we can. He would love that, and so would I. And you can cry on my shoulder anytime you want, okay, sweetheart? Now you go and have a nice big sleep ready for school tomorrow. Sweet dreams." I pass Tilly the phone back, but Daisy has already hung up.

"Here I was laughing that Memphis may have claimed all you girls today as part of his humans. Now I have a feeling I've been claimed by Daisy as one of her humans too."

Tilly stands on her tippy-toes and kisses me on my nose. "As long as she knows you were mine first, she only gets to borrow you. Now take me home, good doctor. Show me this bachelor pad you two boys live in."

"As you command, princess. Memphis, home." With that, he's up and sitting waiting at the door. Looking very proud of himself, his lead in his mouth. Looking up at Tilly with those pleading puppy eyes that he's so good at.

"Hey, buddy, news flash. She was mine first. So, you can back off too. Got it?" He drops to the ground and sits his head on his crossed-over paws sulking.

She bends down and gives him a pat and cuddle. His tail wags and he gives me the sucked-in loser look.

"It's okay, Memphis, I can share," she says, loving him up.

"Good for you, woman, because I can't. Let's get moving, so I can show this dog who's the boss around here, and who gets all the loving from the pretty lady."

She takes his lead and opens the door.

"Geez, jealous much?" She walks down the corridor with a cheeky little bum wiggle while walking my dog who is strutting his stuff right beside her.

Great, now I'm competing with a dog.

Seriously, what is even happening in my life.

It's turned crazy… and I couldn't be happier.

MATILDA

Spending the night at Grayson's apartment was a little more impressive than mine. His is about twice the size of mine, and the building's much nicer. One that has the security guy at the door and views good enough that you can admire both day and night.

Last night was just as amazing as the night before. Although, the only little interruption this morning was the dog needing to go out to pee. Being the gentleman he is, Grayson got up. He took him down and then came straight back, stripped off, and jumped into bed with me and tickled me with his cold hands. Still such a little boy at heart.

We've been lying here a little while, and it's still early. Although I usually like to get to the office early, I'm content here. Plus, I need to clear this up. It's been playing on my mind since yesterday.

"Gray, can I talk to you about yesterday?" I feel his body tense up a little bit underneath me.

"Sure, little one. What do you want talk about?" I think he has a fair idea.

"Remember when we went to dinner two nights ago and agreed to date and take it slow, then by yesterday we're very deep into a serious conversation about you impregnating me ten times? I just felt a little freaked out. Everything is moving so fast. I feel overwhelmed. Don't get me wrong, I am so happy right now. You coming into my life is nothing I was expecting or wanting. Yet I can't let you go." He gets a big smile, proud of himself.

"I'm just worried that we've skipped the whole dating bit in the middle. We've gone from meeting a few times to talking about children. What part of that is the slow bit we agreed?" I try to show I'm not upset, it's just a little over-whelming.

"I'm sorry. I was worried yesterday after I said it that you would panic and run. I was so relieved when you just let it go and moved on. I know I'm a little much, the weird thing is not usually with women, though. You are totally different. You consume my world, in a wonderful way. I'm trying to tell myself in my head to back off, but I can't seem to put my words into actions."

I fall back onto the bed laughing at Grayson saying he's trying to go slow. "I don't think either of your heads have any intention of backing off." I'm giggling now and he's making it worse by tickling me.

"Such a funny lady, aren't you. Thought you wanted a serious conversation, yet, look at you." Struggling to stop, he's smiling down at me knowing he doesn't care that I'm making fun of him.

After we roll around on the bed a little, both laughing, tickling and kissing in all sorts of places. We finally settle enough to hold a conversation again.

"I've got an idea," Grayson announces like he has invented the wheel.

"This sounds very serious. Should I be scared?"

"You're quite the funny little one this morning, aren't you. No, this is a serious one. Why don't we plan a few dates. I will organize a date, totally a surprise. You just turn up and have to go along with my plan. Then you get to do the same thing on a different night, or day for that matter. As much as it pains me—yes, severely pains me—to say it. I will even refrain from the naughty part of the date if that is what you want." He looks like he's having a heart attack the way he's faking the pain in his chest.

"What, no dessert on the date? Are you for real?" I appear shocked.

"Wow, I'm dessert, am I? That sounds like some kind of fantasy I could really get on board with." His playful nature's gone, and the sexual tension is rapidly building as he now pins me with his body and drags my hands above my head.

"Does this dessert involve whipped cream and chocolate?" His voice has now lowered, and I can tell he's picturing what he would do with that.

"If you're a good boy then maybe one day if you're lucky." I lift my hips to put pressure against his groin to give him the hint of where I want this to go.

"Now, baby, do we agree on the dates?" he asks as he starts to lightly kiss across my shoulder.

"Mmm," I moan a little. "I love the idea." My body is really starting to react to him as he leaves my hands and I know not to move them. Then slowly he slides his hand down my arm and makes its way down the side of my body as he continues to taste every part of my shoulder and up my neck.

"Then I need to get my fill now because, apparently, then I'm on a diet for a while with no dessert. So, I better make this extra special. I think I'll attempt every dessert on the buffet before I leave, shall I?"

Before I even get to answer, he's touching my breast and moving his mouth to it. Taking my nipple in, his teeth make me moan loudly with both pleasure and pain. I think I'm going to be late for work again. I couldn't care one bit.

After I have been completely loved with no doubt of what we're feeling is real, Grayson expects me to be able to get out of bed. He's already in the shower and yelling for me to be joining him. I know if I do that there is no way I'm getting out of here to work anytime soon. I lie here a little longer just rethinking this morning's discussion. It's really quite sweet. We are grown adults, yet he wants to take me on a few dates, so I feel like things are going at the right pace. Am I really that crazy that I can't just accept that there is something special here?

Emerging from his bedroom, I can smell the coffee which is the injection my veins need. I only get a step into the living room and Memphis is at my feet wanting some attention.

"What's wrong, my big boy, did you feel left out?" He gets as close as he can to my body to let me know he's special too and needs my attention.

"I told you, Memphis, she's mine first and you get her when I'm finished wearing her out. I think I'm getting good at it."

"Your human is such a dreamer." He lifts his head to look up at Grayson as I scratch under his chin.

"And he is such a traitor." To which Memphis gives a little bark to defend himself.

I walk to Gray in the kitchen that I could probably fit my bedroom in, watching him buzz around preparing a meal for us along with coffee. There is a platter of fresh fruit, yogurt, and croissants.

"This is impressive, do you cook much in this kitchen or is it just for show?" Waiting for him to respond I take a seat at the counter.

"I'll have you know, I'm a great cook. Remember the talk we've had several times? You keep forgetting." He places a plate and my coffee in front of me

"Yes, I get it. You're awesome at everything. I know, I've heard it before." He chuckles, very pleased with himself. Kissing the top of my head, he takes a seat next to me.

We both start to devour the breakfast. I think we've worked up quite the appetite.

I sit back, sipping my coffee after I've had my fill of the food.

"So what have you got planned for our first big date, Mr. Garrett?" I hope that he just slips and lets it out as he's distracted.

"Nice try, little one. It's a surprise, otherwise where's the excitement?"

"Maybe spending time with you is surprise enough?" I pause and look at him. "Actually, I think this is a ploy. You have no idea what you're doing and you need to stall for time. I'm on to you, Dr. Gray. I better not find out that you have some super secretary that you're going to get help from."

"Well, that is my secret, isn't it? You'll just have to wait and see. Now we just need to work out a night that will suit. I know you have functions that you need to work on, and I have night shift for the rest of the week at the hospital."

Grabbing my phone, I check my diary.

"I have Friday night after six pm free, or Sunday all day and night. Do either of those work for you?"

"Both. Friday is my date night, and you get to pick Sunday, day or night." He looks at me waiting. I try to think on the spot quickly.

"Sunday during the day. I just thought what I'm doing. Plus, I can't wait until the nighttime to see you. What a waste of the day, when I could be getting this." I reach over and wrap my arms around him.

Just when I'm snuggling in, Grayson's phone goes off. It's a different tone to what I've heard from his phone before.

"Shit, sorry, baby, I need to take this." He stands and starts walking towards his bag on the table and pulls out his tablet.

"Dr. Gray." He stands, listening intently and looking at something on his tablet. "Okay, yes, I'm on my way in. Get Dr. Fontain to attend to her, and let her know I am ETA of fifteen minutes. I want that fetal monitor left on and surgery on standby. I'm not liking the sound of that." A brief pause and he's saying goodbye and hanging up. I have already worked out we need to move fast. I'm rushing into the bedroom to grab my bag that I had packed, and I'm back at the front door where he has his briefcase on his shoulder and talking into his phone, to Alison I'm guessing. There is a whole lot of words that make no sense to me, so I just follow and wait until he's finished.

He ends the call as we enter the elevator.

"I'm so sorry, baby. Welcome to the life of dating a doctor. There are going to be times this will happen. Sometimes it'll be at the worst time, but I can't help it." He looks torn. Medicine is his life, but he doesn't want it to be a problem in our life.

"It's okay, I understand, and I knew that when I agreed to be your girlfriend. That's what you do. You bring babies into the world and you try to look after people. At times it's going to take priority."

He turns to me and takes my face in his hands.

"How the hell did I get so lucky to find you? My perfect little one." He then kisses me with all the gratitude he feels.

Five minutes later, he's on the way to the hospital and I'm on the way to work, late again, and preparing myself for the same carry on as yesterday.

Nothing they can say will bring me down from the cloud I'm floating on.

My GG.

Can life get much better than this?

It's almost too good.

Should I be worried or just try to go with the flow?

Only time will tell.

Chapter Fourteen

MATILDA

The start of my week was a whirlwind but one that has my heart fluttering.

I haven't seen Gray since leaving him on Wednesday morning when he was rushing to deliver a little baby girl into the world. I had to work Wednesday night, and he was on night shift. I came home to a single red rose on my doorstep. As I bent down to pick it up, there was a little noise behind me, and an envelope came shooting out from under Hannah's door.

I smile thinking he already has the girls on Team GG.

Putting my bag down and boiling the kettle for a nice green tea before bed, I smell the rose as I place it into a glass. I've never had anyone give me a single rose before, so I don't have a vase for it. Must rectify that, in the hope I get more.

I take my tea and sit on the couch with my envelope, wondering what's inside.

To my beautiful Matilda
Thank you for understanding this morning
Now you know what my life is like
You will always be the most important person in my life
Just sometimes being a doctor, patients will temporarily come first

It is not easy to take on, but I hope you see enough in me
to take the risk of the good and bad.

Roses are Red
Sky is blue
Lonely was my Bed
Until I found you

I hope this shows you I am listening.
Slow and sappy at your service.

Can't wait for our date
GG x

I didn't think there was any way he could get more perfect than he already is. Yet this has just taken that to a new level. Where has he been hiding all this romance? Somewhere under the cocky, overconfident joker exterior, it seems.

I know he's working so I get ready for bed and sit with my cup of tea and think what message to send. I need to compete with his note that has me swooning hard. It's not like I can just write back the word, *Thanks*. Talk about pressure. Finally, it pops into my head.

Tilly: What a beautiful surprise to come home to.
You have started your collection of firsts.
First red rose received.
First love letter.
First happy tears from words.
Let's see what you can add to your list of my firsts, as we get to know each
other.
See you in my dreams
LO (Little One) x

I hover my finger over the button then press send. Snuggling down into my bed feeling weary, I wait to see the dots dancing on my screen. Nothing appears for ten minutes, and I resign myself to the fact he could be in surgery or just busy with a patient.

My body is tired, and sleep is trying to overcome me. I haven't had much sleep the last two nights with Grayson keeping me awake—or occupied is a little more accurate. Not that I'm complaining one little bit.

I really want to say goodnight to him and hear his voice, but my eyes have shut and the sound around me is lowering as sleep claims me. The sandman is sprinkling his dream dust and I slip off to slumber land. The last thing I remember is getting the faint smell of Grayson as I snuggle tighter to the pillow he slept on.

That damn alarm. I swear one morning I'm going to smash it. Getting up is not what the problem is. It's just the annoying noises they use. Who wants to wake up to dings, bells, constant ringing, or a peaceful set of wind chimes. I mean, seriously, who wakes up to wind chimes and is happy about it? Not me, that's for sure. I stretch out and hear my phone drop to the floor off my bed. Oh shit, that's right, I fell asleep waiting for Grayson to reply.

I lean down grabbing it and sitting up quickly. I try to focus the bleary eyes.

GG: I'm happy I made you smile.
Challenge accepted, beautiful.
Open your front door.
Can't wait to wine you, dine you and ...
x

I throw the blankets off and run to the door, pulling it open so fast I almost rip it off its hinges.

Sitting on the ground is a basket with four muffins, all different flavors. I can smell them. They're freshly baked and still warm. Tucked in the side of the basket is a card.

For my Little One (LO)
For your list
First basket of fresh baked breakfast muffins.
Enjoy.
GGx

I stand there frozen at the door. What have I started? This man is pulling out all the stops to show me that he's the expert at dating too. Does he have to be the best at everything he attempts? I mean, seriously. My Sunday date needs to be spectacular to beat all of this. Plus, we haven't even made it to Friday yet. I desperately want to call him and hear his voice. I know he will be asleep after just coming off night shift, so I've got to refrain, which is so hard. I snap a photo of my cute little basket of muffins and send my own version of a morning message.

Tilly: My muffins are warm and smell so sweet.
What a shame you aren't here
You could have eaten breakfast
or maybe dessert too.
x

I'm sure he will wake up and groan at my message. Nothing like a little flirt first thing in the morning. It's payback for making me miss him like crazy, when I should be happy that we're slowing down.

Maybe that's his motive. He's showing me slow is not really what I want. I'm beginning to think slow is a little overrated myself. Not that I'm telling him that. His ego doesn't need feeding at all.

I take a quick shower and head off to work early. I'm awake and a little hyped up on butterflies so I may as well be at work using the energy. I have evaluation sheets to fill in from last night and prep to do for today's small luncheon we have at the hospital for the board members. We just need to provide food and a staff member to serve. However, we decided that one of us should be there to supervise this early in the contract. Fleur was going to go, but she has an urgent meeting for one of our functions next week. There's been a problem with the committee, and she's basically going to sort out a cat fight between two women. Seriously, we're event planners not classroom teachers sorting out playground spats.

I wrap up my muffins to keep them warm and take them to the office with me. Mind you, one will be breakfast for me on the way. I don't always eat much in the morning. The coffee is the important brain starter, but these are just too tempting.

"Thank Gray for me," Deven mumbles through a mouthful of blueberry muffin. I have no idea how this guy can be so fastidious with everything in his life yet talk with a mouthful of food, every damn time.

"I'm sure he'll love to know his present to me is being spat all over the office as you speak. For god's sake, Dev, finish your mouthful." I roll my eyes at him, and he pays absolutely no attention to me and keeps talking as he walks towards Fleur's office.

I've been in the office for a few hours now and got everything I need done, finished with ease. I have an hour to kill before I need to be at the hospital to take delivery of the catering platters. I'm busy looking up things to plan my Sunday date for Grayson. I know what I want to do, I just need to sort out the logistics and schedule. I mean, I can't have a whole day date and not have a plan. It will do my head in otherwise.

I just can't decide if we have a three-way date with Memphis or leave him at home. I will plan it out, then make a decision.

This is the most fun I've had in a long time. My whole life revolves around my business of planning things for other people. I love it and I'm good at it. I've never sat back and planned something fun for me. A special event that I want to be just as perfect as if I were doing it for a customer. In some ways this is more important than those events, because it's for someone I care about and the day is trying to show him just how much.

"Hey, shouldn't you be leaving to get to the hospital?" Fleur calls out from her office. I look at my phone. Shit, I totally lost track of the time. I was totally engrossed in my date planning. Seriously, most people would just take this so casually. Yet I'm not most people, am I?

"Thanks," I yell as I rush past her on the way out to jump in a taxi. I'm meeting TJ there who will serve the food. We're going all out with our top person. We need to keep the board happy and instill confidence in our work.

TJ is standing outside the hospital right where he said he would be. Looking very dapper as usual. I jump out of the taxi, apologizing for being a little late.

Getting inside out of the heat is a blessing. I'm sure TJ is appreciating it too in his black pants and long-sleeve white shirt.

"How's the family? Is Lewis still keeping you up wetting the bed?" I ask him as we ride the elevator together.

"They're great. Yeah, he's trying, bless him, it's just not happening yet. We just keep trying every night. Even though the washing of sheets kills us, but it's what you do. Poor Talesha is exhausted. I try to help where I can, but she just hasn't been feeling very well either, which doesn't help." He goes a little quiet.

"Has she seen a doctor, TJ?" Again, he looks down.

I answer for him.

"I'm guessing they're too expensive?" I ask.

"Yeah, we save our health insurance in case we need it for Lewis. She'll be okay. I think she's just tired from overdoing it. We'll be fine." I get the feeling he's trying to end the conversation so not to feel embarrassed.

"Please promise if you need help you'll come to us. Okay?" He nods as the doors open on our floor and arrive in plenty of time to be setting up the conference room before the food arrives and the board members with their special guests.

I get engrossed in setting out the room, giving everything the extra little touches, while TJ handles the food delivery and storing. We both finish and high-five while taking a breath. Knowing we have a few minutes, I decide to quickly go to the bathroom before we start. Otherwise the next thing you know you've been crossing your legs for two hours and if you don't get to pee in the next thirty seconds it'll be too late.

I'm walking quickly as I come around the corner, not paying attention to where I'm going, too busy checking emails on my phone. I run into a firm chest and startle as I feel myself being grabbed so I won't fall. Oh god. How embarrassing.

Then I hear the voice. The one that makes me tingle.

"Hands off or I'll cut them off." Half-joking, half-serious.

Looking up, I see Tate's face and the cheekiest grin as he starts to wrap his arms around me. Normally I would be freaking out, but I know he's trying to send Gray crazy. I get the giggles as I'm pulled out of his arms and wrapped in the ones that feel like home.

I snuggle into his chest a little when he tilts my chin up to kiss me.

"Hi, little one," he whispers as he gently kisses me and my stomach flutters as usual.

I happily take it then my brain kicks in, reminding me where I am. I pull back, trying to distance myself a little.

"Sorry. I'm working, I shouldn't be doing that here." I start smoothing out my shirt and skirt, making sure I look presentable.

"Baby, it's okay. Just relax." I can feel myself getting a little anxious. Then I remember I have just nearly knocked Tate over.

"Oh god, where are my manners? I'm sorry, Tate. I wasn't looking." He just laughs and puts his hand on my arm.

"It's a bad habit of hers running into men's chests," Gray mumbles.

"No problem, Matilda. Just relax. Otherwise big boy next to you is going to blow a boiler in a minute worrying about you. I mean, look at his face." With that we both look at Gray who is not happy at Tate's hand on my arm, plus that I pulled away from his embrace.

"Fuck off, Tate." He pulls me to him again and away from Tate, so he has to let go. I start laughing at him.

"Hey, I'm not a possession. Chill out, Gray." With that, Tate roars laughing at him.

"I knew you two would be trouble together," Gray mumbles.

My phone then beeps, and I look to see TJ saying it's showtime. Shit, and I didn't make it to the bathroom. Looks like I'm crossing my legs again for a few hours.

All I want to do is stand here and cuddle Gray and let him know how much I missed him last night. But I can't.

"I have to run. My meeting is about to start, and they're arriving. Call me later." I turn to leave and they both laugh behind me.

"We know. We're heading to the same meeting. Come on, I can see you're getting stressed." Gray takes my hand and starts walking. As we get to the corner, I pull my hand back. He frowns.

"Not here," I whisper. He understands. He's not happy about it but reluctantly accepts it.

I move into the room and to the corner to stand with my hands in front of me and not saying a word as TJ does the same. Our job is to be seen and not heard. Normally it's easy. But with Gray and Tate in the room, this is going to be incredibly hard. Gray is trying not to be obvious that he can't take his eyes off me. Tate, on the other hand, I can tell is making his life hell and trying to wind him up.

As more people file into the room, the seats fill up.

Then I hear it.

The sound of Kitty's heels storming down the corridor. Making sure everyone knows she is about to make her entrance.

The sound of talking gets lower as she enters through the door, everyone looking up at the whirlwind as she arrives. As I knew she would, she just walks straight past us without any acknowledgment, not even a smile or lift of the chin.

I whisper to TJ who she is, and he rolls his eyes to let me know he has her worked out in the first thirty seconds of seeing her. I watch her walk down the room, and my body is already tensing. There are several seats near the front, but she makes a beeline for the one next to Gray. As she sits, she pulls her chair very close to his and leans all over him, her hand on his arm. I feel the hairs on the back of my neck stand up.

I grab the water jug and storm down the room. If she doesn't get off him, she'll be wearing this water in her lap shortly.

As I come up behind them, I can see Tate's shoulders shaking trying to hold in his laughing. I push between her and Gray to fill their glasses.

"Water to keep you cool," which I probably say too sternly

"Can I have some too, miss?" Tate puts his glass up between him and Gray for me to pour the water into. With my back to her, I focus on Tate who is mouthing the words 'keep calm' to me. He's right. I'm working, and I need to stay professional.

I take a big breath and then turn back to the devil woman who's not happy with me.

"Oh I'm so sorry, Kitty, I didn't realize it was you. How are you?" She just glares at me and doesn't respond for a minute and eventually a one-word answer, of 'Fine'.

"Dr. Garrett, nice to see you again. Thank you for the lovely dinner the other night. How is your father?" My sweet voice may be a little too much, but it's the best I can do.

"Miss Henderson, it truly is nice to see you again. I too enjoyed dinner and the lovely dessert. I hope you liked the appreciation gift I sent for the hard work you've been putting in on my behalf." The cheeky bastard. He always manages to turn it into something sexual.

"Yes. Thank you, Dr. Garrett, I do aim to please. Now, can I get anything for you all before you start? Coffee, tea, or cold drink perhaps."

"I'd like some popcorn, if you have any?" Tate says while trying to keep a straight face.

"Popcorn, why would you want that? You are such a weird person." Kitty sits back in her chair shaking her head.

"I love popcorn when I'm watching a show, sorry, I mean presentation," Tate says, and Gray chokes a little on his water.

Kitty leans over to pat him on the back, but I'm having none of that.

"Perhaps you need to stand up, Dr. Garrett. Give yourself some breathing space." I step back as he pushes his chair out and steps away from Kitty and Tate.

"I think I'll just walk outside for a moment to the restroom before we get underway. Excuse me." As he goes to leave, he winks at me and nods toward the door.

Tate starts to talk to Kitty I think to distract her. Gray walks out of the room, and I return the water pitcher to TJ to refill and start the rounds of serving the room. I let him know I will be back in a minute. Looking at the clock on the wall, we still have fifteen minutes before anything starts.

I get halfway to the bathrooms when a door opens, and I see Gray and his hand signaling for me to come through the door. As soon as I get in past the door, he closes it and is on me.

He kisses me hard and presses my back to the wall next to the door. His hand is on my breast and the other running up the back of my thigh under my skirt.

"Oh, you certainly do please, Miss Henderson." I giggle quietly. "Do you know how hot you are when you're jealous? Fuck, I'm so turned on. I want to take you right here, but I don't have time." My mind goes to all the things we could be doing, but I need this job. I need to stop taking risks.

"Save that thought for later, big boy."

He groans in my ear as he leans his forehead on the wall next to my head. "You are killing me," he whispers.

"Nope, but I will kill her if she puts her hands on you again. Mine. Remember that." With that, I slip out from under him. Straighten myself and open the door and walk out with a smirk on my face. I know he won't be able to leave that room for a few minutes, until he calms his cock down.

I, on the other hand, am racing to the restroom to pee before I wet my pants.

I can't be concentrating on the evil Kitty Cat in there and trying to stop myself from peeing while the presentation is on.

Having sorted myself to look my best, I return from the bathroom just in time for the CEO of the hospital to be coming down the corridor. I slip into the room in front of him and take my position with TJ to the side, seeing he has the room all under control and I'm really not needed. Now knowing what Kitty is like, I'm not leaving. I'll be making sure that I'll be working all the boardroom events where Gray is concerned. That woman has claws and she's trying to latch them into him. When I tell Fleur, she'll erupt like a volcano. She already hates her for the way she treats us. This will just take the cake as far as she is concerned.

By the time the presentation was finished, I had a totally different view of Tate, when he was standing in front of the board as Dr. Tate McIntyre and presenting his proposal on the research grant he's supporting about brain cell transplants. It was all way above my head. He stood there and had the attention of the room the whole time. I also saw when Gray turned into work mode and was not paying as much attention to me. This was one of those times where he needed to put being a doctor before me, and I'm perfectly fine with that.

Packing away the trays and plates into the cupboards after we had cleaned them, I can hear Tate, Gray, and Kitty behind me. I want to turn around but know I can't make it obvious.

"Why don't we meet for drinks tonight, Gray? You know that bar we used to go to. The one you take me to on the dates we enjoy. I just need to speak to this new caterer and tell her to pull her socks up and then we can make arrangements." Her voice and words have turned me to stone.

He dates her.

How could he not tell me he isn't available, that he has a girlfriend? She thinks they're an item still. It all comes flooding back at the interview. Her saying we had to take extra care with her boyfriend Dr. Garrett. I totally forgot everything after the shock of meeting Gray again with his dad. All these names are the problem.

I don't do this. I promised I would never get caught out like this again.

TJ is right next to me. I whisper to him I need to get out of here and he can finish up. I grab my bag that's on the counter in front of me. Quickly starting for the door, both Kitty and Gray call me at the same time. I pretend I don't hear them. Which is impossible, but I'm not ready to look at either of them in the eye.

I might hate her guts, but I don't date cheating men.

"Miss Henderson, I need to speak with you about your services, and where you could improve," Kitty's shrill voice is calling after me.

"Later, Kitty," Gray growls and I can hear his footsteps behind me and closing the gap at a rapid pace. "I need to see her in my office about the foundation function. Now!" he says as he catches up to me entering the elevator. Taking my arm, we both step in and the doors close behind me. I try to pull away from him, but he isn't having it. I push the ground floor, and he pushes the level-three button.

There is silence because I know if I open my mouth I will either yell and scream or cry, and I don't think this is the place for either.

The elevator slows for level three, and I prepare for the Mexican standoff when I refuse to get out. My disadvantage is that there is no one else in here with us. I take my arm from him, cross them, and just stare at him.

"I can do this all day, babe." He pushes the button to keep the doors open.

Just as I'm about to say my piece, a couple and their newborn baby come into the elevator. He gets a little smirk because he knows I won't make a scene now. Fine, asshole, you win this round, but I will win the war.

I stomp my way out and he follows me. Then I realize, I have no idea where I'm going. I stop and wait for him to walk in front of me. Probably looking like a spoiled child throwing a tantrum in the process.

I'm already coming up with the speech I'm about to let loose on him. We stop outside a room with his name on the door. He unlocks it and then signals for me to follow him in. I stand just inside the door still with my arms folded. I hear the door close and lock. I feel him behind me. I can't breathe, I'm so upset.

He slowly comes around in front of me like he's circling a wild beast with caution.

"If I talk, are you going to listen?" He looks me in the eye.

"Mhmm" is all I reply, holding the anger in.

"What you heard, you have totally misunderstood. Yes, I did date her a few times over the last couple of years. Single dates for a bit of company. Have I slept with her? Yes, once, which I totally regret because now, I have this problem. The one where in her head she believes we're still dating. I haven't taken her out in over nine months. Yet she tells anyone who will listen that we're dating but that we're just two busy people so find it hard to spend time together." He pauses, waiting to see if I'm still with him. Or if I'm even taking it in. I'm hearing it, I'm just not sure what to make of it.

"If I'm being honest, I actually feel she may have a mental illness. I'm not about to say anything because she has the power to turn the board against me and cause me to lose my job. My work here is my life and too important for the foundation that will be based from here. I've just been humoring her up until now. It didn't matter before because there was no one in my life that mattered." He pauses, his eyes full of emotion.

"Until now. Until you."

He then moves slightly closer, testing the waters with me. My arms are still crossed so he isn't wanting to set off the firecracker.

"Tell me what's going on in that head of yours, little one?" He slides a little closer again, taking a piece of stray hair and tucking it behind my ear. "Let me know what you need to say, let it out."

Deep down, I know he just wouldn't be that kind of guy. The last few weeks he has been with me, I can feel what he's feeling. It's not fake. It's so real. I need to trust what I've been feeling and let him in. I slowly lower my arms by my sides, and he reaches out softly and pulls me into his arms. Wrapping me tightly with my head on his chest. Right where I can hear his heart beating. That feeling of home tells me that trusting him is the right thing.

"Who hurt you, little one? Who took away your trust? There's more to this than Kitty."

I know I need to tell him, but I don't know if I can tell him it all. "Henry." I pause as the hurt surfaces again. "Henry Porter," I whisper.

"Do you want to do this here? We can wait until we're at home?" I shake my head no. I need to tell him now so I can bury it again.

"He broke my heart. We had been together for a few years after high school. I wanted to move to the city with Fleur, start out business. He kept saying no. So, we kept putting it off. Until we both knew it was now or never. I told him to come with us, but he wouldn't leave Williamstown. I promised to go back on weekends, and we would do long distance. He said he wanted that. Jerk even said when I've finished playing with my friend in the city then I can come home to stay. I should have told him to fuck off then." I pause taking in a few breaths to keep me calm.

"When we got here, things were crazy trying to get the office, find work etcetera. It took a few weeks before I got back home. I felt bad so turned up for a surprise visit. Only Mom knew I was coming." I can still picture the look on his face when I walked into our apartment we'd been sharing above the garage where he worked. It was just one big room so when you opened the front door you could see everything, including him fucking Lucy Olson on our bed with her wearing a pair of my shoes I'd left behind.

The tears started to slide down my face.

"You don't need to say it, Tilly. I can guess where this is going. You found him with another woman."

The loud sob escaped my body, pulling out pain that had been buried for a very long time.

"Beautiful, I'm so sorry. I will never do that to you. I promise you. You can trust me. Please tell me you know you can trust me." Deep down I know I can, but once you've been burnt, there's always that niggle that will haunt you. I can't tell him that, so I just nod my head and try to calm myself down. I really need to be pulled together before I can tell him the rest.

"I'm so mad at Kitty for making you feel like this. I should have put a stop to it a long time ago," he mumbles into the top of my head when he kisses me.

"She's a bitch. I hate her already and I don't hate many people. But I swear if she touches you again, I don't care about the contract. She and I will be having words. I shared a guy once and didn't even know it. I definitely won't be doing it again."

"I'm not him. I will never touch another woman while I'm with you. I don't share. Ever!" I can see he's getting wound up a little.

Then his phone goes off, and I know the rest of the story will have to wait.

"Fuck." He grabs his phone on his desk.

"Yep. On my way, will be scrubbed in within five minutes." Dr. Gray is in the room.

"Fuck, Tilly I have to run. Stay, wait for me. I'm so sorry, this is an emergency. Fuck." He's running his hands through his hair as he takes off out the door, and I hear him running down the corridor. I'm really starting to understand how intense his life is.

I can see where the comedy and cockiness in him comes from now. It's the barrier that protects him from this.

From the life and death.

The memories and the pain.

The helplessness.

From the love and the loss.

Can I be the person to help him with that? I just don't know.

My life is always controlled, planned, and calm. Sure, chaos happens in my work life, but my job is to solve and fix it. Grayson's chaos can't be fixed, his life is designed around chaos. Can it even be controlled? I have no concept. Will I cope with something I have no control over? I have no idea. They say opposites attract, and in so many ways we are. I'm so scared of having my heart broken again that part of me is thinking I'm just finding reasons to end this before it really begins.

Truth is, I feel more for Grayson than I have ever felt for another man. Even the man I thought broke my heart all those years ago. Looking back, that's nothing to what I would feel if Grayson hurt me now.

Today with Kitty just has me thinking. How badly do I want this? How hard am I prepared to fight for him? I could sit here and continue crying, waiting for Grayson to comfort me like he asked. Or I can be the strong woman I have become in the last seven years, get up and get on with my day.

Nothing that bitch can say or do is going to wreck what I feel.

This time I'm not running, I'm going to stand up and hang on to what is mine.

Put this on your list Grayson – You're the first man I will fight for!

Chapter Fifteen

GRAYSON

E xactly like I told her.

There will be times being called on as a doctor will interrupt something major. Like now.

Running down the corridor to surgery to scrub in for an operation, and all I can think about is the beautiful woman I've left in my office having just fallen apart.

Standing there crying, hurt and confused as to what happened in the conference room. For the first time ever that I can remember, I wanted to ignore that pager on my phone.

Once I heard the case, I knew I couldn't wait, lives depend on me. The doctor in me just kicked into my normal routine. I need to block out thinking about Tilly, as hard as that is, as I scrub up for the emergency C-section of a mother with twins, where one twin is in fetal distress. It's go time, as I push into the operating room trying to appear calm and take command of the room.

Mom is being anesthetized as there is no time for the epidural to kick in.

"We will get this done as quick as we can, Dad. You will be holding your babies and smiling with your wife before you know it." As much as I'm trying to reassure him, he looks terrified.

Luckily the babies are thirty-seven weeks, so as long as we get them stable after being born, there is no reason why they won't be on a normal ward within twenty-four hours.

"Let's get started, everyone, so we can bring these little babies into the world."

Everyone takes their position as we make the first incision. No matter how many times I do this, I still hold my breath every single time, hoping that I get it right.

Standing in the room with Mom who's still groggy but getting her first cuddle of her twin boys is the ending to an intense hour in all our lives. The adrenaline is starting to calm, and I just want to get out of here and back to my office to Tilly. I hope she just closed the door and curled up on my couch, waiting for me to come back and make it better. Reality is I doubt she'll be there. Either way, I want to get back there to find out.

Turning the handle and finding it locked is not a good sign. I can feel it, before I even unlock the door. She's gone. I'm still on shift so I can't go after her, and I know she's working tonight. I need to hear her voice.

To know she's alright. That we are alright.

Then I will deal with Kitty once and for all. To hell with the repercussions. I won't have Tilly treated like that by anyone. I'm not hiding her. I want the world to know that Dr. Grayson Garrett is off the market, for good.

"Over there, Stuart. Hi, Gray, sorry, busy setting up a function." Her voice tells me that the confident, professional Matilda is back.

"Sorry, I know you're busy. I just need to know you're okay. To hear your voice." I stare out the window of my office at the outside world, that at times feels like it is so far away from the bubble of the hospital.

Her voice is a little quieter this time.

"Yes, I'm fine. Don't worry about me. I've pulled myself together." Sighing. "Grayson?"

"Yeah, baby?" I want to reach down the phone and touch her.

"I'm sorry I overreacted today. It took me back to a place I promised I would never go again. But I'm okay." Her voice tells me she isn't, but neither of us can do anything about that today and I know she needs to be on the ball at work.

"Tilly, you don't need to apologize for anything. Well, maybe the blue balls in the hospital room earlier today, but I'm sure you'll help fix that soon." She has a quiet giggle. "You told me to save it for later, baby, and he's still waiting."

"So bad. We always end up back here." Tilly's voice sounds just a little lighter now. "I have to go, Gray." She might be happier, but the goodbye is still hard.

"Okay, but what time will you finish tonight? Can I come to see you after my shift?" I just want to hold her.

"I'll be exhausted and so will you. Tomorrow night is our date. Let me miss you before then. I'm looking forward to it. You better make it impressive; I've been working hard on mine."

"That's not the answer I wanted, but I don't have a choice. I'll give your condolences at the funeral of my blue balls." We both have a little laugh together. "Just so you know—because you seem to be a poor listener—I excel at all things, little one. Including dates for my girlfriend. You better hang on to your lace panties – yes, that is a hint – and you will receive further instructions tomorrow. Go and be the super boss and kick some ass. I'll call later to say goodnight if I can."

"Now I can't wait. I really need to go. Talk soon." She goes to hang up and stops. "Gray, thank you for being you. You have no idea how special you are. Bye." With that, she's gone. Not even giving me the chance to talk. In a way it's probably better. I was getting close to blurting out words that she should never hear for the first time on a phone call. I have a feeling it won't be long, and she will be adding that to her list of firsts.

The rest of the night shift is quiet which is just as I was hoping. I spend a few hours in my office catching up on patient reports that needed to be done. I haven't seen Tate since this afternoon at the end of the disaster presentation meeting, so I send him a message to let him know I'm in my office if he's having a quiet night too. It's the sort of thing you do wish for as a doctor, to be bored on shift. Because it means no one is seriously sick.

Reviewing scans that have to be done today, I hear my door open and look up to Tate walking in with food.

"Oh god, you must have read my mind. I'm starving but couldn't be fucked to do the order." I get up and walk over to the couch where he has placed the bags on the coffee table.

"See, that's your problem. There are plenty of nurses who will do anything I ask if I just use the old McIntyre charm. Including place my order, take delivery, and bring it to me."

"Christ, do they want to eat it for you too?" I laugh as I drag out a satay chicken that will do me just nicely for my belated dinner.

"No, see, the clue is they want to eat *me*. They will do anything, poor little souls. They just want a go with the man that is well-known as the best in town." Tate settles back with his beef curry.

"Tilly thinks I have a big ego. She obviously hasn't met yours yet." I just laugh and shake my head.

We eat while dinner is hot, plus you learn as a doctor when you order food, eat it straight away. You never know when you'll get called away and for how long.

"Is Matilda okay now?" Tate asks as he places his empty food container on the table.

"I'll say yes, but I haven't seen her to confirm properly. We were in the middle of an intense discussion when I got paged for an emergency C-section. She understands, but the timing sucked, big time. I wanted her to wait but she had another job tonight. I've spoken to her but until I see her, I'm not entirely convinced."

"What the fuck was up with Kitty, though. That was a load of bullshit. We all know she thinks you're hers, but to be honest I thought it was a bit of a joke. After today, I'm convinced that to her, she believes every bit of it. You need to be careful, buddy." Tate is now leaning back on my couch with his head laying back like he's taking a little time out.

"I just ignored it because there was no one to care anyway. But now it needs to stop. The thing that worries me is how much power she has. She can make life hell for me and for Tilly and Fleur." The day is catching up with me too. I lay back like Tate and close my eyes for just a minute.

His speech a bit slurred like he's trying to fight sleep, Tate keeps his eyes closed as he gives me something to think about.

"You know how to stop her. Make a big grand public gesture to let the world know you're with Matilda. The foundation dinner will be perfect, because the board is there and so is Kitty. Worth a try," he mumbles, and I'm sure he's now already asleep. We both have pagers set up on our phone so we're still reachable no matter where we are. I've never slept through a page yet, not even when I'm in a deep sleep. My body knows that sound, and I can be awake in a matter of seconds and dealing with the issue. You learn to power nap at times to just top up after an intense surgery or after a busy shift. The adrenaline high needed in the peak of an emergency also has the low that follows which makes you tired. That's why the twenty minutes of power nap can be enough to recharge you.

That is, of course, until the phone goes, and the cycle starts all over again. This time it's a car accident, multiple victims, and one of them is a pregnant woman who needs assessing. Even though I'm not rostered on to emergency, Tate's phone was enough to have me awake.

I decide to join him to see if I can help at all.

As we reach the ER, there's a lot of noise, crying, screaming from the casualties, and yelling from the ER team. Tate is straight into room four where he is being directed to a patient with a head injury. I stand at the desk assessing the situation, waiting to see if I'm called.

The next ambulance comes through the door with a young lady holding her stomach and looking very frightened. She's looking behind her where I see her partner carrying a little boy, trying to keep up, and that's when he looks up and I recognize him.

"TJ, isn't it? You work for Matilda. What happened?"

"Dr. Garrett, please help Talesha. Please, her stomach hurts. The seatbelt hurt her in the accident. Plus, we're not sure, but we think she might be pregnant. She's been later with her period and we have just done the urine test but nothing else. One was positive and one was negative. So we don't know. Please, she needs to be okay." The emergency ob-gyn is already seeing to the known-pregnant woman who was in the accident. There were multiple cars involved so there are ambulances coming in behind us.

"Trauma room six," I tell the paramedic "Susy, I've got this one in six, possible abdominal injuries and potential pregnancy." I put my hand on the back of TJ and push him towards the room. "Let's go. I've got this, TJ, I'll look after her and the baby if there is one hiding in there." With that, the time to talk is finished, and I'm assessing Talesha who is in a lot of pain. I order blood work and the ultrasound machine. At least that way while I'm waiting on blood, I can see if we have a little peanut in there or any internal bleeding.

As I'm palpating her abdomen, she's trying to be brave in front of her son but there are tears. TJ is pacing behind me and his little boy is tired and sleepy but very confused about all the noise and what is going on with his mommy.

"Tell me what happened tonight," I ask to help me understand what she's been through. Talesha starts to try to answer, but each time I touch her it's difficult so TJ steps in.

"I had just finished work with Matilda, and Talesha was picking me up. Lewis was asleep in the car. We started to head home and then from nowhere the car in front of us was hit from the side by a car that ran a red light. That pushed him into us and then we were hit from behind too. Lewis and I are fine, just a little shaken, but the steering wheel pushed back and hit her in the stomach as well as the seatbelt pulling on her. We could barely get her out. Is she going to be okay? God, please, is she alright?"

From what I can feel, I think it's just bruising, but until I can see what we have inside, I don't want to get his hopes up.

"We will know soon enough. Now why don't you take a seat and take a few deep breaths. Do you want to call anyone to come and help you with the little one?"

He shakes his head at me sadly. "No, it's just us. Our little family." Talesha puts out her hand to take his. The love between these two young people is more than I see in some couples twice their age.

"Well, let's see if we're going to grow this little family or not. Sit and try to relax a little and let's hook up this ultrasound and do a scan to see what we can find." I'm not sure what they want the answer to be, but we are about to find out.

Modern technology still always amazes me, even though I use it and experience it every day. In such early days of a pregnancy, it's hard to see the fetus on an ultrasound. If this doesn't show anything, we may have to do an internal one, but let's see what we get here first. Running the scan over her organs, there are positive signs there's no internal bleeding. The pain is probably just bruising and the muscles from tensing up for impact, which will be sore for a while. She's only tiny so not too much fat stores to protect her.

As I slowly move the wand across her uterus, I find what I suspected. A little peanut who is nicely cushioned inside Mom and protected from what has just happened. Instead of saying anything, I turn on the sound and pick up the faint heartbeat. My guess is she is about eight to nine weeks, maybe even ten weeks.

They both look at the screen, their faces frozen and just totally silent. Listening to the strong little beat that is nicely ticking away.

"Congratulations, you are going to be parents again. The baby seems fine and in no distress at all. About nine weeks along, give or take a week. But everything seems fine with you both. I think you're just severely bruised and will be sore for a while, and I would like to keep you in for observation overnight just to be sure." The tears are rolling down both their faces. TJ leans down, holding his son who is finally asleep in his arms from exhaustion, and kisses Talesha. Giving her a smile to reassure it will be okay.

"It's okay, I'll be fine at home. Thank you," she says quietly. TJ gives her a glare, and she shakes her head a little. I've seen this unspoken conversation many times before.

"Okay, let's wait until all the blood tests come back and then we can talk about it. In the meantime, the nurse will take your blood pressure and a few other things we need. TJ, do you want to come and help me fill out some details I need? Why don't you put your little boy in bed with Mom while we're out there? I'm sure he'll sleep better, and Mom could use a cuddle too." I see a bit of twinkle in her eye as he places him down on the bed next to her and he snuggles into her. Even in pain, he makes her smile, and she feels at peace that he is safe. We walk out of the room and away so she can't hear us.

"Can I get you a coffee, TJ, or a water?" I offer just trying to relax him. He declines and I can tell he's nervous.

"I know you work for Matilda, and from what I saw today she must think highly of you to have you at the hospital function. I also remember you running the ball. Is that your full-time job?"

"Yes, sir. I also study online trying to get my business degree. We both are. Little Lewis decided he wanted to come into the world a lot earlier than we had planned on having children, but I wouldn't change a second of it. It looks like Talesha might have to put her studies on hold again for a little bit and give up her job. That's okay. We can manage." His face tells me he isn't so sure about that.

"Can you answer me honestly. Is Talesha saying she'll go home because you can't afford to be here?" He hesitates and then just looks at me with his shoulders back like the man he is, even with a big weight on those shoulders.

"Yes, sir, but if you say she needs to stay, I will find a way to pay. She is more important than anything in this world. Her, Lewis, and this new little baby." He rubs the back of his head with his hand trying to take in that they're having another child.

"Okay, hear me out for a moment. You've probably guessed that Tilly and I are seeing each other. So, I know what it's like to have someone you would do anything for too. You're important to Tilly, so therefore I need to look after you. Talesha is now my patient. So while she is under my care, I can waive all her costs. That way we can get her settled and make sure both she and the baby are perfectly fine. It also means you don't need to stress, and you can concentrate on looking after Lewis while she's here. How does that sound?" He looks totally dumbstruck. Like he's either dreaming or has just won the lottery. Either way, he doesn't know how to process it.

"TJ, just breathe, man. I don't want you to faint on me."

"Why...why would you do that? It's very kind, but why? There are other people who need it more." That right there is the reason I am paying his way; even in the hardest time of his young life, he's thinking of others.

"Sometimes the universe places the right people in our life for a reason. Matilda has proven that for me. Just think of it as my way of saying thank you to the universe. It's your time to get your gift from the universe. When the time is right, I know you will pay it forward to the next person who needs it."

He bursts into tears and throws his arms around me to show me how grateful he is.

"Now let's get that coffee and sort out the paperwork. I'm just about to get off shift, so I'll get Talesha settled and then I can give you a lift home. I'm guessing your car is written off. So that way you can get Lewis into bed and then get some sleep yourself. Come back in the morning and your girl will be much better. How does that sound?"

"I am so grateful to you. You will never understand. I will pay this forward, that you can guarantee, Dr. Garrett. I know why Matilda picked you. She sees the good in people."

"Please, call me Gray, and right back at you, buddy. She obviously sees the good in you too."

We get everything sorted, and I wait outside giving him a moment to say goodbye. I can't stop thinking about Tilly and how upset she'll be about TJ. I'm just glad she also wasn't caught up in the accident. I know it's selfish. I only just found her, so surely God isn't that cruel to take her away from me. Deep down, I have a fear of loving someone unconditionally only to have them taken away from you. Like my mom. I don't think I could go through that hurt again.

"You have my number, if you're worried or need anything, just call me. Otherwise I will see you at some stage at the hospital tomorrow. Get some rest," I call out to TJ as he walks slowly up the steps of their building. It is one of those old brick buildings with three stories above the street level and an apartment or two down below the street level. He told me as we were chatting on the way home that they live on the first floor in a one-bedroom apartment. They gave Lewis the bedroom, so he has some space to play and a quiet place to sleep. They have a pull-out bed. It works for them, and from all accounts they seem very happy. I wonder how they'll handle the new baby coming and a reduction in income.

Driving away, I am reminded how blessed my life has been in some ways, never having to worry about any of these things. My mind starts to gather some thoughts that I need to work on before I share them with the world. One thing is for sure, though.

There is no way I'm going home without seeing my girl tonight. Today has been totally crazy and full of so many reminders of how fragile life can be. I can't close my eyes tonight without knowing she's okay. Whether she likes it or not, in ten minutes, she will be in my arms and I'll feel like I can breathe again.

This is one time I'm actually glad she doesn't have a doorman. Otherwise I would be fighting with him at two minutes to midnight to let me in. Yet it also makes me worry about her safety, along with Hannah and Daisy.

By the time I get out of the elevator and am standing outside her door, it is one minute past twelve. Rather than knock and wake everyone up, I message her.

GG : Here is your next first.
Your first home-delivered dessert.
Awaiting you on your doorstep.
Before you argue, technically it's now Friday morning!!

I hear movement inside and the door peeks open. I see a sleepy little face through the gap. She's smiling as she opens a little more and leans on the side of the door.

"This is very sneaky, Dr. Garrett. How am I supposed to learn to miss you when you turn up here looking all kinds of sexy for a late-night booty call?"

I walk in and take the door from her hand, quietly closing it.

"Now that's where you're wrong. I'm not here for a booty call, although if it's on offer, who am I to turn it down?" I slowly run my hands over her hair and down the back of her head to her back. Pulling her closer, I just take her in. The way she feels against me, the way she smells, her breathing on my neck. The thumping of her heart I can feel through her very thin sleep shirt.

"I can't end this day without seeing you. I need to know you're okay. To feel it. Otherwise there'll be no sleep tonight." I pull away slightly to see her face. She looks so tired and drained. I touch her lips gently, trying not to get carried away. I've promised to slow down, and tonight I just need to show her I care. That's all I came to do. I sweep her off her feet into my arms and carry her to her room. Placing her in her bed, I sit beside her and kiss her again.

"Gray, what are doing?" Her sleepy smile looks up at me with a hint of confusion.

"I'm not breaking my promise. I came to see you, now I'm tucking you into bed safely and leaving you to sleep and miss me." She goes to talk, but I shut her down and kiss her again. A little deeper than a moment ago.

"Close your eyes and dream of me. Wait for your first clue tomorrow. I can't wait, little one." I kiss her on the nose and walk out of the bedroom, leaving her totally stunned but still with a little smile.

Just as I make it to the door, I hear her call to me.

"First midnight kiss." With a beautiful little giggle following it.

I flick the lock on the door, close it, double-check it's locked, then walk down the corridor with the weight finally lifting off my chest and a smile on my face.

And a pair of very blue balls that aren't appreciating me heading home.

A cold shower is in the cards before bed.

A little later after arriving home, showering, and trying to take away the ache while I keep thinking of my girl, I'm now sitting in the dark. Scotch in hand, Memphis snoozing at my feet while I look out at the city lights twinkling. The stars in the sky looking down on me. I've been thinking of my mom more than I have in a long time, wondering what she would think of Tilly. Would she be fussing over her like she used to do for me and all my friends? I can imagine them together, both teaming up against me in the best way. Would I be sitting with Mom asking her opinion on if she's the one, can she see what she means to me? A single tear slides down my cheek. One I haven't shed in a very long time.

Taking another slow sip of my scotch and feeling the burn as it slides down my throat, I know my answer. It's been there all along.

Mom would love Matilda just like I do. I know it's too soon to tell her, but I know deep down I have already fallen in love with her. All my doubt about what Mom would have thought disappears when I realize of course she does. She handpicked her and sent her to me. Even when I was too stupid to know that, she kept bringing her back until I finally got it right.

Memphis stirs and looks up at me with those eyes that tell me he's listening to my thoughts.

"Yeah, boy, we need to keep this one. She's the special one. The one we get to love for the rest of our days." He wags his tail in the air. "Now just help me to get it right and not screw it up. Okay, buddy? Be my wingman for me. I need you." I lean down and pat him on the head and get up to walk to bed. Placing my empty glass on the table, I pause at the window.

One last look up to the stars, I blow a kiss to the sky.

"Thanks, Mom, she's perfect. Just like you. Love you."

Laying my head on the pillow, I'm finally ready for sleep.

I'll need it to get through today.

Chapter Sixteen

MATILDA

I awake to another cute message on my phone from Grayson. Explaining how beautiful the funeral was that he held in his manhood's honor. He was sad I couldn't attend but knew it would be awkward when I was the cause of the blue ball's disease they died from.

His sense of humor is perfect. We both get each other on that level, and I never feel I have to hold back.

My reply saying it was good while it lasted has my phone ringing instantly.

"You knew I would call, didn't you, cheeky girl? There is no way we are anywhere near finished. You know, if you fixed the issue then there would be no need for the funeral." He laughs although it sounds a little husky like he's just woken up.

"You had your chance last night to fulfill their dying wish, you chose to leave. No guilt here." We both laugh together.

"Morning, beautiful," his rough sexy morning voice says down the phone. It has me tingling and wishing he was here with me.

"Morning. I hope my message didn't wake you at all?" I wasn't thinking when I sent it that he had been on late shift a few nights in a row.

"You can wake me anytime, in person would be better, but anytime regardless." He pauses and then I hear him sigh. "I have some news for you, but before I tell you, just know that everyone is fine, and I will make sure that continues."

I sit straight up in my bed already panicking about what he's going to say.

"Last night, TJ, Talesha, and Lewis were in a car accident and were brought into the emergency room while I was there." I gasp and grab my heart. "The boys were fine, but Talesha was in a lot of pain. There was a little complication to that, so we were a little worried. Anyway, I can't tell you everything due to client confidentiality, but just know after everything, she's perfectly fine. I kept her in overnight just to be sure, and will be off to check on her shortly."

I take a minute to process it all. "Oh, Gray, you aren't covering up anything, are you? You really promise they're okay, all of them?" I feel a little teary just thinking how scary it must have been for them.

"I would never lie to you about that. They have no car, every one of them is fine. Talesha is going to be sore and bruised for a few days, but besides that, all good. I will check on her first thing when I get to work and message you. Okay?"

I feel relief just hearing his voice over the phone letting me know that beautiful little family is okay.

My brain starts racing back to the conversation yesterday with TJ.

"Crap, Gray, can I pay their hospital bills? I know they can't afford it, and their insurance won't cover it all. I need to call TJ." I'm up and getting dressed as I put Gray onto speaker.

"Tilly, stop and breathe. I've already taken care of it. I have waived my fees and will pay any of the other costs they need. I see it all too often where they would have left last night because of cost. I know they're important to you. I told TJ I would take care of it. He's a good kid. I can see he deserves a break."

I can't talk, the tears are running fast now.

"Tilly, please don't cry. You know I hate when you do that. Especially when I'm not there to wipe them away."

Sniffling, I try to pull it together. "Where have you come from, Grayson?" I whisper. "How did I get so lucky?" I'm trying to pull it together.

He doesn't reply but I can hear him still breathing on the other end.

"You just keep doing these things that are minor to you but are huge to everyone else. If you were here right now, you would be getting breakfast, lunch, and dinner. Plus, lots of dessert." We both burst out laughing. It was either that or I would be crying again. Happy tears, of course.

"Don't move a muscle, I'm on my way. Because let me assure you, I am currently starving!" I can hear him moving out of bed.

"Stop right there, big boy. We both have work shortly, you have a special patient to check on, and a date to plan. I'm not sure you can fit in eating from your favorite restaurant." I can't help pushing him with a bit more flirting.

"Fuck, you're going to get punished when I see you. Currently, my balls that I thought had died are letting me know they're still there. Alive and well and in a world of swollen hell. You are such a tease, my little one." His groan fills the speaker.

"Oh god, I know that groan."

"That's right, baby." His voice is lower and a little breathy. "This is what you do to me. Tell me what I do to you." Our call has gone from playful to hot and heavy in seconds. "I need to picture you to get me there. I can't turn up at work like this."

I don't know what to say, this is new to me. I just start describing what I'm doing. "I'm already standing in front of the mirror in the bathroom, looking at my near-naked body." There's that deep groan again.

"Get naked, touch yourself. Tell me how it feels."

I pull off my sleep shirt and drop it to the floor along with my panties. Slowly I run my hands over my breasts and feel that my nipples are hard and super-sensitive. I can't help it, my breathing is getting louder and faster.

"That's it, baby. I'm imagining feeling you myself. Where are your hands? Tell me everything."

I want to close my eyes, picture him behind me looking into the mirror, his hands sliding over my body.

"My breasts, oh god, Gray, I wish it was you too." Now it's me moaning from my own touch and the noises he's making while he's getting himself off.

"Slide your hand down your body. Run your finger through your pussy. Tell me how it feels, baby, are you missing my touch?"

"Oh fuck, so wet and sensitive. Gray, I want to come. I feel so turned on thinking of you jerking off to my voice. Help me come." I'm whimpering as I start to really rub hard against myself. My legs are starting to feel weak and the shudders deep in my stomach are building.

"Fuck, Tilly, I want you here coming over my cock. Listening to you moan is so fucking hot. I want you to keep rubbing while you use your other hand and pull hard on your nipple, pinching and twisting it so I can hear you scream." I can hear him grunting and his words aren't flowing as freely as he talks. He's almost there too.

"Gray, oh god Gray, please, oh god."

"Now, baby, come now. I'm there sucking on your clit, licking every bit of you."

That is all I need, the vision of him on his knees in front of me, taking what is his. The memory of that feeling is enough to push me over the edge. Screaming out as I ride the wave and fall forward on to the bathroom counter to keep me standing upright. My body shudders as I listen to him making the same sort of noises and his breathing heavy.

"Holy shit, Tilly. Now that was one hell of a wakeup call." He sounds proud of himself while I let out a little embarrassed giggle.

"Mhmm. Not what I was expecting. I think I need to buy you a dictionary. Your definition of slow is a little different to mine."

"This is my slow, if I was normal speed you wouldn't be leaving your apartment—well, only to move to mine. This is as slow as it gets, baby. It's called compromise."

I look at myself in the mirror again, cheeks still flushed. I need to get to work.

"Time for me to shower and get to work."

"Ughhh, seriously, you are a cruel woman, Tilly." Gray laughs at his own words.

"You, on the other hand, have a dirty mind. Now I need to shower and be out the door on time. I don't want to be late tonight. I have a hot date with this guy. Some doctor who I literally picked up one night off the floor."

With that, Gray is laughing loudly down the phone and I know I need to finish up.

"Can't wait for my first clue. Now go shower yourself. I have visions of a dirty little boy lying on his bed covered in his own sticky mess."

"You got it, boss lady. Have a good day and enjoy your date with the hot sexy doctor. I hear he's alright."

"I'll be the judge of that. Now go. Oh, and by the way. Another for your list. First phone sex. Amazing." I don't give him time to respond otherwise I'll never make it to work. Hanging up, I start the shower, jumping in to freshen up, ignoring Gray as he's calling me back. I've got to get organized and off to work to start what will be a special day. I just have this gut feeling about it.

Arriving in the office, I fill Fleur in about TJ, and we call him together on speaker phone. He tells us about last night and the surprise news that Gray left out. I know he couldn't tell me, but I'm also glad because it was TJ's news to share. When things settle down a bit, we need to have a good talk to TJ and Talesha and see how we can help. Maybe she can do some clerical work from home for us. We're going to need more office staff as we grow, so it could help us both. In the meantime, the fact they are both safe is all that matters

"Gray is one hell of a guy, Matilda. I am still in shock. I don't deserve it, but he made me promise that one day I'll pay it forward. You know I will, as soon as I can."

"I can't think of anyone more deserving, so stop that nonsense. We all know you will when the time is right. Now just take care of your family and get Talesha better so she can start growing that little bean for us to be able to spoil." I try to let TJ know that Gray wouldn't have done it if he didn't believe he deserved it.

"Better be a girl, I want to shop for pink frilly things this time," Fleur pipes up from beside me.

"Haha, let's just wait and see. That's a while away yet, so don't get too excited with the shopping trips."

"Argh, have you met me? Shopping is my middle name. Any excuse is a good excuse." TJ and I both laugh at Fleur who is being serious.

"Yeah, we get it, Fleur. Anyway, we better get some work done, we have an event to get sorted for tonight. Plus, I have a date with Gray. Not that I know anything about it yet. I suck at surprises. You know I like to know exactly what's going on." They both start to snigger. Wait, they know something by that reaction.

"What the hell is going on? Spill the details now or you are both struck off my Christmas card list." I'm staring at Fleur with my best intimidating look, which is obviously useless as she laughs and tells TJ I'm giving her the stink eye.

Neither of them is giving much away, and it's killing me.

"I have to go and head to the hospital now, but I do have a message from Gray for you, Tilly." TJ makes me hold my breath.

"Clue number one. Dress casual but pack a bag with a change of clothes. Enjoy, bye."

"What was that? He hung up. What does that even mean! Fleur, you better tell me what's going on. No secrets, bestie, remember?"

Fleur is waving her finger in front of my face.

"Uh, uh, uh I'm not being blamed for ruining the surprise. Just suck it up and enjoy the fun. You wanted him to date you and sweep you off your feet. You need to let the poor guy do it. Now write it down on this sheet and wait for the next clue."

She slides a handwritten sheet to me.

Matilda's FIRST date with Grayson
Clues to find the treasure
1.
2.
3.
4.

Prize: The man with the biggest ego in town. Dr. Grayson (Gray) Garrett as your slave for twenty-four hours. To be used however you choose.

I can't help but laugh out loud. The man is a lunatic.

"Yes, your boyfriend is pathetically soft. Wonder if his friends know about all this," Fleur yells from her office, where she is just sitting at her desk.

"Don't you dare, Fleur. I will kill you." I sit writing my first clue on my paper.

I have no idea what the clue means but I can't wait for the next one. I need to message him.

Tilly: First clue received
Date commenced.
Game on.

GG: First guess?

Tilly: No idea. Driving me crazy.

GG: Mission accomplished. Have fun

Thank god we have an event today to occupy me. Otherwise I will go crazy trying to piece this together. I try to get through my morning paperwork that needs to be done while working on some plans for upcoming functions. I look over a few things for Grayson's foundation, but there are some questions about things I need to talk over with him. I know if I call him now, he'll think it's an excuse to get a clue out of him.

Even though I have been working, my mind is still on my first clue.

Why will I need a change of clothes? Will I get sweaty, dirty, wet? The list is endless. Or does he mean a change of a different sort of clothes, like casual to dressy? I want to message him to explain, but I know I need to be patient. Not my strong suit.

Deven and Fleur are both calling out to me to grab my things and hurry up. We need to head to today's job. We're down TJ and have called in his second-in-charge to cover him. It's a smaller function, so she should be fine with Fleur there guiding her too.

As I get to the door, here is Deven holding out a bright red juicy apple to me.

"Clue number two." He waves his hand all around the apple like a game show hostess. "This is dessert for part of your date." Then he hands it over to me with a smile.

"What does that mean?" I scream at him. "Come on, Deven, I won't tell him." I grab him lightly on the arms and pretend to shake the answer out of him.

"As if he would be stupid enough to tell me anything. Everyone knows my loose lips sink ships...or plenty of seamen. Whichever you think works."

"Ugh." Both Fleur and I groan at the same time.

I stand staring at the apple for a few minutes. I'll give him one thing. He wasn't joking when he said he was good at this. I know my date is great but just a totally different thing to this. As frustrating as it is, I love how much effort he's gone to and how hard he's thought about things. I take a deep breath and smile at my friends.

"You've got to admit, he's pretty cute. Who would have thought from those first few meetings when he was such an asshole?" They both look at me, roll their eyes, and walk out.

"What, are you two jealous?" I scurry along behind them.

"Yes," Deven cries.

"Not a chance," Fleur tries to get me to believe.

We're all still laughing about it and trying to put together the first two clues as we walk through the foyer. We wave at Cecil who is already opening the door and hailing a cab for us.

"Watch out for crazy running men, Miss Henderson. Luckily he caught you that day." He chuckles to himself as we step out onto the sidewalk.

Little does Cecil know what he witnessed that day. He certainly caught me. Hook, line, and sinker. I just hadn't worked it out at that stage.

The function is set up earlier than expected. That's always a bonus. Fleur calls me over and says there's one box left sitting on that table over there.

"Can you check what it is and deal with it? Then you should leave. Go home and get ready for this super date." I'm walking across the room when I notice it has a number three on the top of the box. I turn to look at her, and she smiles and walks away, making herself busy. It would seem Grayson has everyone in on this date. The only one that has no idea what's going on is me.

I lift the lid to reveal a small blanket in the bottom. Two roll pillows and a box of popcorn. Sitting on the top of everything is an envelope with Gray's writing again.

My Little One,
Your wish is my command
Slow is the name of the game
This box contains necessary equipment for your magic carpet ride.
See you soon
GG x
P.S. the date starts earlier than you think so get a move on.
I'm done with wasting time.

My head is spinning. Nothing seems to link together. The clues are so cryptic, he's not making it easy. All I know is I need to take my box of goodies and get to my apartment. There's no time on the note, I just know I need to be ready earlier.

"Fleur, do you know anything? I'm going crazy," I yell across the room. She isn't there and all I can hear is laughing from the kitchen.

"Get out here, woman, right now. You are Team Tilly not Team Gray." My box under my arm and my bag over my shoulder, I turn to go and find her when she comes through the swinging doors smiling.

"For god's sake, did he at least tell you what time I need to be ready?" I'm almost pleading with her.

"Nope, my job was to deliver number three. That's all I know."

"Oh, for fuck's sake. You are all scratched off the best friend list. Don't you dare expect a message after the date because I will be as radio silent as you all have been. You all suck." I stomp out the door in a panic I'm going to be late. Plus, I have no idea what to wear, or take as spare clothes.

Sitting in the back of the taxi on the way home, my palms are sweaty. I have butterflies in my stomach. I feel like a young girl on her first grown-up date. Why am I surprised? This is what I asked him for. To slow down, to feel special. Get to know each other. Make an effort for more than just sex. I was just expecting a few dinners and maybe a stroll in the park. Grayson always seems to make everything bigger and better. He has told me jokingly, many times, how he excels at everything. Now I'm beginning to think he means it. I need to share this excitement. I know I don't do it often enough because life is crazy, but there's one person I can count on who will really understand me, understand how important this is to me after everything I went through. I push the contact in my phone.

"Hello, my beautiful Matilda." My mom's voice almost brings tears. I miss seeing her.

"Mom, I'm sorry I've been busy. I know I'm a terrible daughter."

"Sweetheart, don't be silly. Your business is growing, and it takes a lot of energy."

"Thank you. How are you and Dad? Is he out in the garage working on the car?"

She laughs in the phone. "Tilly, you know your dad. Where else would he be? We're both doing just fine. What's happening in your world? How are you and Fleur? Everything okay?" Mom is just running through the normal questions.

"I met a man. Grayson. I'm going on a date tonight, but he's already technically my boyfriend and I panicked, so he's slowing things down for me, but I think it's too late, Mom. I think I've already fallen, and I don't know how to deal with that." I can't stop and everything is pouring out.

"Slow down, sweetheart. Take a big deep breath and start again. You have a boyfriend whose name is Grayson." She's waiting for me to fill in the blanks. I look at my watch knowing I'm running out of time until I will be home. After telling her the brief story of what has happened, there's a silence at the end of the phone.

"Mom, are you still there?" Then I hear a little sniffle.

"Mom, what's wrong?" I ask, wondering what I said to bring tears.

"I've waited so long for this. A phone call that has you so scattered you don't know which way is up or down. You've found your one. I don't even need to meet him, I can hear it in your voice. You thought you loved Henry, but it wasn't even close. It took the right man to show you that. I can't wait to meet him. Don't wait too long before you bring him home. Your dad will want to meet him. You know how protective he was after your heart was broken."

"He makes me smile, my heart flutter, challenges me, and opens my eyes to things I haven't seen before. We have this connection that is like no other. But how do I know for sure? I've been wrong before. I don't want my heart broken again." The taxi is getting close to home now.

"Honey, you already know. Before you even called me, you knew in your heart. There is no way you would have let him this close if you were truly worried. You just need me to remind you that you deserve this. It's time to let someone in, Tilly. Not just a little way, but the whole way. Right to the center of your heart. The place that only one soul ever fits. Grayson's soul."

This time I have tears running down my cheeks as we pull up to the curb outside my apartment block. "Thanks, Mom. You knew just what I needed. It's time, isn't it?"

"Yes, Matilda, it's your time. Now go and enjoy this amazing treasure hunt date he has planned and call me tomorrow to tell me what in god's name everything means. I'm good at crosswords, but puzzles do my head in."

I wipe the tears and pay the driver, grab the box and step out of the taxi. Putting the box down for a moment, I put the phone to my ear again.

"Love you, Mom, and thank you."

"Anytime, Tilly, just maybe a little more frequently might be nice." I giggle and agree to call tomorrow.

In a world of my own, I rush out of the elevator towards my door to find another note stuck to it, with a big number four drawn on it with colored pencils. It is decorated with flowers, hearts, and a few puppy dogs. Well, they look like dogs let's just say.

Placing the box down, I pull the envelope off the door which says:

Read before you open the door.

My darling Matilda,

Not having any control of this is hard for you, I know.
Just think back to that first night when you let go.
Tonight, I want you to let go of Matilda who needs structure.
Get dressed in the clothes we have left you and bring the bag.
I have the key to the lock so no peeking.
Remember what it felt like that night of pure mystery.
Let tonight be one of intrigue.
This time I'll show you how a true date of firsts should be.
You have fifteen minutes until your car arrives.
Don't be late.
I've waited long enough for you to come into my life.
I don't want to waste a minute more.
GG x

I can't breathe. I feel faint from the emotion that's running through me. I didn't even hear Hannah open her door or come up behind me. When she put her hand gently on my shoulder, I jump with a little squeal.

"It's just me." I turn and fall into her arms.

"Hey, why are you crying?" Hannah laughs at me.

"Because I'm so happy. I know I'm crazy. He'll kill me when he finds out he made me cry. Don't you blab!" We both hug tight and then my brain remembers the time limit.

"Oh god the car, fifteen minutes he said." Fumbling with my keys, Hannah takes them off me and opens the door. The noise of my door opening then brings Daisy out of her place with another box.

"I'm not allowed to open this. Dr. Gray said they are special for you. For your date. He said this will be dessert." I blush and Hannah can't stop laughing.

"Okay, Daisy, we've done our part, now we need to let Tilly get changed and not miss her ride for her date." She leans in and gives me another quick hug.

"The universe did good, Tilly. He's a keeper. Enjoy." She then pushes me in the door of my apartment and closes it behind me. Rushing into my room, I realize Gray must have had Hannah's help with my clothes, using her spare key.

Laid out on the bed is a pair of denim cut-off shorts with a white shirt. A navy stretch tank top for under the white shirt. My flat brown shoes and a broad-brimmed floppy straw hat. True to his word, the bag next to it is full but locked. Then next to it is another bag with a note asking me to fill it with all my clues. It's then I remember I haven't opened the last box.

This one I have a little idea what it could be, so I decide to keep it a surprise for later.

Standing in front of the mirror, dressed and ready, I take a photo and send it to Grayson.

Tilly: First time I'm lost for words.
Ready when you are.

The dots are typing straight away.

GG: So beautiful you stole my words too

There is a knock at the door as I open the message. I know it's him.

I almost run to open it.

I throw myself into his arms.

"Welcome to your first date, baby." He grabs my face and kisses me with so much pent-up emotion I know there is no way he's going anywhere when this night is finished except straight into bed with me. It's a given.

"I'm so grateful the universe brought you to me." I can't wait to tell him.

"Me too, little one. Me too."

He kisses my nose and picks up my bags.

Time to solve his treasure hunt.

Even though I already have my prize.
Standing right here with me.

Chapter Seventeen

GRAYSON

I don't know how I managed it, but the vision of beauty standing before me tells me I have succeeded in my surprise clues.

Her flushed cheeks, the sparkle in her eyes, and the smile that lights up her face. I have achieved what she wanted. To be swept off her feet and feel the exhilaration of that first date. Me being the overachiever I am, I may have super-sized this first date. At our age, it needs to be bigger than a date at the burger bar and a drive up to make-out point, for some kissing and a bit of groping if you're lucky.

"Are you ready, baby? I have a fun date in store for us." I stand there with her bags at her door.

Her giggle tells me she's excited.

"Gray, this date started at one minute after midnight this morning. You have had me smiling, laughing, crying, yelling, and maybe a little moaning during the day. I feel like we are just building to the climax."

"You have such a cheeky way with words. Let me assure you there will be a climax, that's a given. Now the car is waiting for us, so let's get moving." I stand back so she can lock the door and start walking towards the elevator. I turn to wink at Hannah and Daisy who are spying through a crack in the door. I mouth thank you to them and I hear Daisy giggle and Hannah telling her to shush while giving me a little wave. With that, their door is closed, and I am off behind Tilly again admiring that cute ass. The one I love in a business skirt, but right now, lordy. Those daisy dukes are hot and definitely doing it for me.

"Can you give me a little clue, please?" She bats her eyelids at me in the back of the hired car.

"I did, you've had four. Not my fault you haven't got it yet." She does this cute little pretend pout on her face.

"Okay, just because you look so cute. Let's just say when I think of first dates, the ones that make you all nervous, it makes me think back to my childhood. So, we are going to revisit that time for both of us. That simple first night of fun and trying to do things to make me look good and win you over." This is so much fun, having her hanging on every word yet not really giving her enough to work anything out.

She throws her head back against the seat and just sighs.

"You are killing me, Gray. I give up."

"You can't give in yet, the date and night are just beginning. Come on, I don't take you for a quitter. Start thinking outside the box." I can see her looking out of the car trying to work out where we are and what direction we're heading. I have deliberately asked the driver to go a different way than the normal direct route just to make it harder. The added bonus is I get to spend a little longer with her nice and close in the back of the car.

As we start to get closer, the skyline opens to see the giant wheel. Her eyes widen. I can see her starting to piece together stage one.

"Navy Pier, you're taking me to Pier Park to the sideshow rides. I love the Pier. How did you know?" She's bouncing up and down in her seat.

"I didn't, but it makes it even better that you do. You ordered slow, and to me that meant you wanted the fun and flirty times that go with teenage dating. So here we are, your first stage of our date."

She looks at me a bit shocked.

"This is just the beginning. I have lots in store for you." With that, I step out of the car and take her hand to help her out too. She goes to get her bags and I stop her.

"It's okay, they're being taken care of. I'll race you to the carousel; we should start off mild and work up to the Light Tower." Knowing she has a competitive streak like me, she's off running before I can even blink. I catch her quickly and pick her up one-armed around the waist. Whirling her around as we both laugh,

I lean down for a quick kiss. Hand in hand we then proceed through the gates and onto enjoying the rides.

A few hours have passed, and we're taking our last ride on the Centennial Wheel. The sun is just starting to slowly set as we cuddle enjoying the views over Lake Michigan and the buildings of Chicago.

"The view is so beautiful from up here, especially at this time of night." I know she's talking about what she's seeing outside the glass walls. For me, the most gorgeous view is right here beside me.

"Yeah, little one, the view is stunning." I kiss the top of her head while we just enjoy the silence. That is part of the thing that makes Tilly so right. We don't need to always talk. Just sitting in the quiet can be just as soothing.

Exiting the ride, she looks up at me and just smiles.

That simple gesture is perfect.

"For your list. First kiss on the Centennial Wheel and first, first date at a carnival. Nice work, Grayson. You're winning already."

We're both laughing as we head to the exit gates with our bag of cotton candy and carrying the big stuffed fluffy dog I won on the strongman in the carnival games. Of course, I will be boasting about that for years to come.

"We can skip the rest of the date then?" I ask her, stopping her from walking and turning her towards me.

"Not a chance, I need to solve this puzzle!" I take her hat off her head and kiss her on the forehead. Holding her face in my hands, I leave my lips on her for a moment, soaking in the feeling that's between us. She lets out a quiet little sigh.

Pulling back, we both show the words that aren't yet spoken, purely with the looks in our eyes.

"Turn around for part two then, and see if you can work out the clue." Her excitement has her spinning instantly to see our transport to the next destination.

"Oh my god, Grayson!" she squeals.

"Finally, someone acknowledges my status in this world," I try to say, but I'm not sure I was heard over the squealing and then her leaving me for dust and heading straight to the horse and carriage waiting for us.

Watching her closing her eyes as she cuddles into the horse tells me part two is a winner too.

"Tilly, meet Pepe and our driver Tony. Pepe is sharing our date with us for a little while. He will be working hard to take us to our next bit of fun for the night." That's when I see the lightbulb moment in her eyes.

"Aha, the apple for dessert is for Pepe. His reward. Very clever and so cryptic. I'm never going to win puzzle games against you. I bet you can solve those mystery novels by halfway through the book too. That's why I stick to my romance books. There is nothing wrong with the imagination side of my brain."

"You're getting closer to the prize now, baby. Just so we're clear, though. While I'm around, you won't need an imagination. The real thing is always ready and willing. Now let's not keep Pepe waiting for his dessert." I wink at her as I help her up and into the red open-air carriage. The seats are red leather and the carriage is beautifully restored with the old-world brass lanterns on the side, a black roof that sits behind our head ready to pull up if it rains. In all the time I've lived here, I have never taken a carriage ride. Tilly is ticking her own firsts on my list too.

I pull her in tight next to me and we just enjoy the soothing sounds of the horse hoofs as they trot along the street. Being a Friday night, the street and roads are busy, however the hum of a busy city in a way can be soothing too. After a while, we fall into a little chatter about different sites that after living here for a few years Tilly still doesn't know much about. I'm happy to be her tour guide. Having grown up here, I love Chicago. It has a special feel to it. The people, the places, and the opportunities are amazing. I know I'm biased, but traveling over the years, I always love to come home. Looking down at my girl snuggled in, I finally realize I was missing a piece to my personal puzzle. Now my picture is complete.

Pulling to a stop outside Millennium Park, Tilly sits up still looking a little confused.

"Gray, I don't have my bag to give Pepe my apple." She looks a little sad.

"Do you really think I would let a little detail like that slip? Come on, give me credit." I step down and take her around the waist, lifting her into me for a sneaky cuddle before I slowly put her down.

"Any chance you get, Dr. Gray, you are hopeless." I don't see her complaining though when I wrap her in my arms.

From behind her, she hears a voice.

"Here is your bag, Mr. Garrett. The rest is set up and waiting as requested." The look on her face is priceless.

"What now? I'm not sure I can take many more surprises."

"Sure you can. I have it on good authority that the heart is a strong muscle. It can take lots of fun for hours at a time." I wink to her and then take the bag from the gentleman, thanking him, and I earn a slap on the arm for my comment from Tilly. Doesn't hurt to keep the thought in her head. I am a mere male, after all.

I unzip the bag to reveal her apple sitting right on top. Passing it to her, she takes time to nuzzle with Pepe and give him his reward. It is obvious she's spent time around horses before now, the way she's standing and handling him. I snap a picture of her with the chestnut's head bowed and her eyes closed as she kisses him on the nose. This woman does not have a mean bone in her body, I'm sure of it. Her goodness shines through at every opportunity.

Giving her the time to enjoy her cuddle, Pepe then starts to get a little restless and we thank our driver as he guides the carriage out into the traffic again.

"Now where are you taking me to, sir?" She's almost in another world now living on her happiness.

We start walking into the park, heading for our destination.

"Do you remember your third clue?" I ask as she whips out of her back pocket her list I gave for her to fill in.

"Always come prepared is my motto. But I remember it word for word anyway. I'm trying to put it together with being in the park." She starts talking to herself out loud, working through her thoughts.

Just as I think she is almost about to guess, we walk into the clearing of everyone set up in the outdoor movie theater. To the back, there is a lady standing near our pillows that are set up on a picnic blanket. Placed on the blanket is our picnic basket, and to the side is our box of popcorn. As I guide her closer, she freezes and gasps, working out that it's ours.

"Thank you, Sally, for watching this." She nods and tells me she will be back later to collect it all.

"Gray, I just can't even...I just... Oh god, you are so incredible. I can't even describe what I'm feeling."

"Then I'm getting it right. I wanted you to feel special. To show you it might seem fast but even if it's slow, for you to still see how right it is too." The kiss she reaches up on her toes to give me is perfect. One that is full of what she is feeling. Soft and tender.

"Now let's eat, all this fun is making me hungry." We sit and the previews start up on the screen. I start serving her from the antipasto platter and pouring her a glass of champagne.

"I've got it." She almost knocks the glass out of my hand. "Wishes and magic carpet, it's the *Aladdin* movie, isn't it? You are so clever." One of the things I asked her to do was let go of Matilda for the night and relax. In her place I have Tilly who is like an excited little girl experiencing all these new things.

"You are my whole new world, Gray. I don't think I'll need any more wishes." She leans over and kisses me again.

I can handle more nights like this.

Just us and totally carefree.

"Me too, baby, me too."

Sometimes it's the simple things in life that can bring the most joy. I've never thought about a kids' movie in the park, good food, good wine, and a beautiful woman curled up in a blanket by my side before. I've been missing out. Then again, it really is the company that has made it what it is. Tonight has been so much more than perfect. I can't remember the last time I was so relaxed.

I hear Tilly singing the songs quietly as the movie plays, and I love her voice. Visions of her standing rocking our little baby to sleep singing a sweet lullaby comes into my head. I'm way ahead of myself, but the thought doesn't scare me like it would have a few months ago. Still, that is a thought to be kept to myself for the moment. Tilly is not quite ready for that.

As the credits roll up the screen, I have a feeling my very excited date has just about fallen asleep. Just like half the kids that are here with their parents. She's lying on her side with her head in my lap, all warm and snug in her blanket. I have been lightly playing with and stroking her hair. I may have found the calming trick for my little one. I mean, who doesn't like to have their head stroked while they lay and relax. I start to laugh a little to myself thinking about how I love to have my head stroked, my other head, but I'm not sharing the joke right now. Like I said, I'm just a mere man.

"Baby, it's time to go. You need to wake up." I lean down and kiss her temple.

"I'm not asleep, just totally relaxed. You have sent me into a state of serenity. I don't know if I can move."

"That's okay, I'll carry you." My comments have her sitting up slowly.

"No way. I'm too heavy for that."

I just scowl at her. She knows I'm not impressed with that comment, but we both let it go for now.

Sally has quietly stepped in and started to pack up our things. Tilly, being the person she is, wants to help, but Sally insists that she leaves with me. I pick up the bag that has followed us around for the date.

"Are you too tired for the last stop? Or can you hang in there?" I put my arm around her as I guide her down the path towards the car that is waiting for us to go to the last stop.

"I'm not missing one single minute of this night. Lead on, Prince Charming." She looks up to me and smiles.

"Wow, I made prince status before I even got to the end of the date. I'm rating pretty high here, little one."

"What's the clue for our next stop? You know we're running out of time? Your night is almost up. Not sure you can cram much more in."

"Never doubt the master. I have saved the best for last. This last one will blast you out of this world with excitement." This brings a deep laugh from Tilly. She may have been sleepy before, but this has got her back up and her eyes twinkling again.

The hired car is waiting as booked at the edge of the park. We are whisked away, heading south of the park, and again leaving my girl wondering where we're heading. It doesn't take long for her to piece my comment together, yet she doesn't know it all just yet.

"That clue was perfect, Gray. Blast me out of this world."

We stand at the front doors of the Adler planetarium, looking at all the people leaving a function that has been held here tonight. To the side I see Monica waving us over.

"Let's go, baby, we only have limited time for this one." She looks a little confused but follows anyway.

"Hi, Dr. Gray. Just inside to the left and follow the signs. Lucas is in there waiting. You have fifteen minutes before we need to shut it all down." I give her a big smile to thank her as we push through the door and head to the planetarium telescope.

"Grayson, what is going on?" Tilly giggles, tagging behind me as I rush down the corridor. I spot Lucas waiting at the door for us.

"Hey, Lucas, thank you so much for this. How's the family?" I ask as we follow him inside into a dark room.

"Anything for the man who brought my little terrors into this world safely. They're doing just great, thanks. Now here's a flashlight. Walk to that little dot you can see in the middle of the floor. Then stop and wait for me." I can feel Tilly moving closer to me in the dark.

"Gray, I'm so confused."

"I know, but just trust me. This will be the highlight."

We make our way to the spot, and I put the bag down, turning Tilly so she's facing me. Just as I do, the roof above us lights up with the stars in the night sky. All bright and twinkling like they're so close you can touch them.

"Oh Gray, it's so beautiful. Stars. Just like home, without the city lights. I have missed that so much." Her face is fixed on the roof, and I can't take my eyes off her.

"When you told me that I have given you so many firsts, I decided to take that one step further. This star that Lucas is showing you now is your star, Tilly. For now and forever, that star is for you. No matter what happens, that star will always look down on us."

Tears are streaming down her face. "What is the star called?" she whispers, looking up as the telescope zooms in and Lucas highlights it.

"I named it for you. It's called Grayson Matilda which stands for first love." I place my hands on her wet cheeks and lower her face to look at me. "I can't hold it in anymore, Tilly. I've fallen in love with you. Total crazy love." Lowering to kiss her, she pulls back slightly.

"Wait." She pauses and my heart stops. "I never believed I could feel this, but I am so in love with you that you have found your way into my heart to a place I have hidden from the world. Now kiss me." We both giggle as we kiss with all the passion that has been building all night. Our lips meet and there is hunger as I feel like I am devouring her. Our tongues are dancing around each other, and I know this could very easily become more than kissing in a split second if we don't pull back.

"Take me home, Gray, I think you've earned dessert." The way she's looking at me, we'll be lucky to make it home.

"So, you opened box number four then." I laugh as we both look back up at our star one last time.

"Nope, I've left it so we can share that one together. I figured anything that had the clue of dessert was an *us* present." Even in the dark of the room with only the stars shining on her face, I can see the blush of what she thinks is in that box.

Slowly the stars start to disappear, the room getting lighter. Our time here is over and it turned out just how I hoped.

Back in the car and being driven to my apartment, both our hands are wandering to places that aren't exactly for public display. I can't stop kissing her and whispering things I'd like to do to her in her ear. That blush that I've put there, I want to keep for the rest of the night.

We barely make it in the front door, clothes coming off, hands everywhere. I'm not having the first time I make love to her be over the back of a couch.

I pick her up and carry her to my room, legs wrapped around my waist while she kisses me, taking my breath away.

I gently lay her down and just take a minute to really appreciate the beauty in front of me.

"What about the fourth box?" she whispers.

"It can wait for the next round. Right now, I just want to make love to the woman who has taken my heart." Crawling up the bed over the top of her, our mouths lock again and the fireworks ignite.

"I just need to suit up." I lean to the side of the bed to reach my drawers, but Tilly is trying to stop me.

"You know I'm clean, I trust you. Make this the perfect end to the perfect date." I know that this woman is it for me, there will never be another. Tonight, she is giving herself to me and I already know, I'm never letting her go.

"My little one, I will never take this for granted. It will only ever be you tonight and always."

As we join for the first time with not a physical or spiritual barrier between us, our fate is sealed. I'm hers and she is mine. Just like it's written in the stars.

"We really should have showered this chocolate off," Tilly mumbles as she starts to wake up. She's lying on my chest which is still covered in smears of sticky chocolate residue from last night's shenanigans with the contents of the last box.

"Nah, that would have taken the fun out it. Plus, it gives me an excuse to clean you up this morning before I make you dirty again." I'm not sure either of us have the energy after last night, but I'm happy to try.

"You are a sex maniac, you know that?" Tilly leans up and rests her chin on my chest looking up at me.

"Morning, beautiful." I drag her up my body to kiss her. "Mmm chocolate for breakfast."

"I'm not surprised, the amount you kept rubbing on your cock for me to suck off, there's bound to be some left on my face. You are a naughty man, Dr. Gray."

"Only with you, my girl, only with you. Now let's shower and clean up. All good things unfortunately come to an end. This work thing is definitely over-rated today."

"I'm showering, you're in charge of coffee." Tilly tries to get up.

"No way. We are showering together and then if you're lucky, I'll make you coffee and breakfast. Actually, let's start with dessert first." Tilly jumps up and runs for the shower with me hot on her tail. The sound of her giggle is pure joy.

That's all I want to hear, for the rest of my life.

Tilly in my bed, in my home, happy.

If I play this right, soon it will be our bed, our home.

With the shower taking longer than normal, I decide that breakfast will be a little simpler than I was intending. Fruit, yogurt, and pastries. Of course, coffee too, otherwise I might lose Tilly if I don't provide strong caffeine first thing in the morning. I leave Tilly to shower in peace after I washed her, made her dirty again, and then when I offered the second wash I got booted out.

I hear the door open and know it will be Bella bringing Memphis home. I had her babysit him last night just in case I ended up at Tilly's place. Even though we stayed here, it was nice not to have to worry about him getting me up early. I hear his little feet come running across the apartment looking for a pat. I crouch down to say good morning.

"Dude. Clothes would be great. The visual I just copped from under that towel was not fun," Bella says as she walks into the kitchen shielding her eyes.

"Now you know what to aim for in your future man."

"Really, for god's sake, Gray. Why would you even put that thought in my head that I should compare my future man to my brother's dick? You are such a weirdo sometimes." I walk towards her and put my arm around her shoulder.

"You love this weirdo, though."

"I would love this weirdo even more if he was clothed." Bella is trying to get out of my grip when I hear Tilly coming from the bathroom.

"Hey, big boy, can I finally have the keys to the padlock? I need to get dressed." As she appears with a towel wrapped around her fresh from the shower. Thank god she wasn't game enough to come out naked.

"Oh shit. Sorry." Bella starts laughing as Tilly, pink-faced, backtracks into the bedroom screaming at me. "Gray! Get your ass in here right now!"

Hearing her voice, Memphis is off chasing after her to see his girl.

As I come into the bedroom, she's crouched down giving him some love and telling him his daddy is in big trouble.

I just laugh, unlock the bag, and walk into my wardrobe to get dressed so I can properly introduce Bella to my girlfriend.

"Stop laughing, before I put you on a strict no-dessert-ever diet." She's trying to wrestle with her bra and is failing miserably. I walk over to offer my help.

"No touching, you. Get over there. You are in the doghouse for not warning me. I can't believe the first time I meet your sister I'm naked in a towel talking about keys and locks. Can you imagine what the hell she is thinking? Gray, seriously, concentrate on me."

"Oh baby, but I am, you look so fucking sexy when you're angry and standing there in stockings, heels and lace underwear. Let me assure you, I am certainly looking at you." I duck as she throws a pillow at me.

"For fuck's sake, Gray. Out now. Go and apologize to your sister for having to see that. No one needs to see me near naked this early in the morning." I walk over and grab her, pulling her into my body.

"Matilda, stop stressing. My sister will love you just like I do. This'll be a story we will laugh about for years."

I feel her collapse into me.

"I just want her to like me, and I'm afraid that wasn't a very good first impression."

"Finish getting dressed and then come out and meet her properly. You will see how it made no difference. Bella is just like me. She'll think it's funny. Now hurry up, we both have to leave for work soon and I haven't fed you yet. Well, let me rephrase that. I haven't fed you food yet." I start laughing, walking away as she's groaning at my joke.

"Get used to them, Tilly, they will never change."

"Great!" is all she yells at me from the room as I leave.

"Be nice, she's freaking out in there," I warn Bella as I grab the coffees off the counter, ready for Tilly to walk out any minute.

Her face as she walks out tells me how anxious she feels.

Before she gets to the kitchen, I hand her the coffee. "Here, take a big drink and it'll help."

She smiles, pulls back her shoulders and walks confidently towards Bella. Matilda is in the house now. "Hi, Arabella, I'm Matilda, but my friends call me Tilly. I'm so glad to finally meet you. I'm so sorry about earlier, the whole towel thing. Your brother neglected to tell me you were coming by." She goes to put her hand out to shake Bella's hand.

I couldn't love my sister more than I do right now.

"Come here, silly." She grabs Tilly and hugs her, laughing. "I'm excited to meet the woman who has stolen my brother's heart, clothes or no clothes." They both start laughing and the moment is broken. "Plus, anyone who has Grayson threatening me to be nice to you because they have him scared is a goddess in my books. Welcome to the family." They hug again, and I know everything is going to be perfect.

Smiling, I walk to hug them both, but Tilly puts up her hand.

"Nope, you're still on the shit list." With that, both girls take a seat at the counter and start chatting, eating all my breakfast, and Bella is more than happy to share all my shit habits with Tilly.

"Hey, I didn't invite you here to make me look bad. Remember, Bella, you are Team Gray."

She waves her hand at me and smiles.

"Pfft that boat sailed the moment you flashed your dick at me this morning and told me to compare my next boyfriend to it. Team Tilly all the way, bro."

Tilly nearly choked and sprayed her coffee across the counter.

"You what? Oh Gray, seriously. No wonder your sister wants to kill you at times."

"That's it, I'm on my own now. Not only did Memphis ditch me, now Bella too. That's some serious power you have, little one. Can you at least leave me my friends for Team Gray?"

The girls both laugh together.

"Take it from me, you don't want any of those boys anyway. They're all jerks just like this one." Bella points at me and takes her last mouthful of coffee. "Try growing up in this city with four big brothers. Hell, I tell you, pure hell."

My phone goes and we all stop, knowing what it means.

Once again, the call of my doctor life cuts a moment short.

Only this time, it's a good thing. I have a feeling the girls are just getting started.

"Go, I'll get a cab," Tilly says. I lean down and kiss her, grab my keys and bag that is always ready at the door.

"Love you." I blow her a kiss and close the door hearing my sister gasp and blurt out the words "Holy shit."

I agree, holy shit is right.

Holy shit, my life is perfect.

Finally.

Chapter Eighteen

MATILDA

Gray walks out the door, rushing to his hospital call. Bella looks like she's in shock.

"Holy shit," she says as she turns to look at me.

I can feel the way she's looking at me. She wants to know more. About me, my life, who I am, and what my intentions are with her brother.

I don't blame her. I would be the same with my sister if I ever saw her. It's a bit hard to be protective from the other side of the world.

"You're really it. His special one. I never thought I'd see the day. Dad told me it would happen, but I never believed him. He said when the time is right, each of us will find that person who will make the world stop." She reaches out and takes my hands, squeezing them.

"I know it's quick, and lord knows I tried to slow him down, but I've fallen in love with him. His charm is hard to resist, and when he wants something, he doesn't give up," I start talking fast to explain. Bella gets the most beautiful smile on her face.

"Promise you won't hurt him. I've never seen him like this. He has fallen hard. If you don't feel the same, please tell him now, don't drag it out. Because looking at him, I doubt he intends to ever let you go."

I squeeze her hands back. "Him never letting go is fine by me. Bella, Gray and I are on the same page. I can guarantee I would never have let it get this far if I wasn't looking for more than a fling. He has my heart and I'm not asking for it back. I gave it willingly." Now it's my turn to make another person cry. Bella has tears running down her face.

"He told me once when we were both drunk talking about Mom. Missing her. That he was never going to commit to any woman, in fear of her leaving him like Mom did. His memory is of the only woman he had given his heart to leaving him and breaking it. He also watched my dad's heart shatter and never heal. For you to break down every barrier he thought he had, I know you are it for him. But if you walk away, it'll be the last straw. His heart would never mend again. I know it's heavy, but I need you to know. He's not as tough as he seems."

My heart has just burst, for the love this woman has for her brother. The short meeting that I had with their father, I can see where they both get their tender side from. I know I would have loved their mother too if she raised children to be this loving.

"Bella, I promise I won't hurt him. Thank you for caring so much for him. He is blessed to have a sister like you."

She bursts out laughing. "Can you tell him that when he's complaining I'm being a pain in his ass? Which will be regularly, just warning you. I'm hoping you will be a bonus for me and keep him off my back. I love him, but he needs to remember I'm not ten years old anymore. Team Tilly, remember, so help a sister out." I already love Gray's sister. We are going to get along like a house on fire.

"I have loved meeting you this morning, but I'm really sorry I need to leave for work. I wasn't expecting to be staying here last night. Even though Grayson obviously was. He had my friend Hannah pack a bag with my work clothes for today and everything I needed. He just forgot my laptop and work bag, so I need to call into home on the way."

Bella just grins at me and points to the bag near the front door.

"What the hell? How in god's name did he get that here?" I can't believe he even thought of that.

"He had me swing past your apartment last night after you left, to pick it up from Hannah. Oh my god, Daisy is the sweetest little girl. She almost wet herself when she saw I had Memphis with me. I ended up staying for a glass of wine with Hannah while she played with Memphis. Daisy is cute and your friend

Hannah is so funny. We all need to go out for a girls-only night. It would be so much fun."

"You think Hannah is wild, wait to you meet Fleur and Deven. Now that would be a crazy night out. We have to do it. Gray might kill me for corrupting you, but he will just have to suck it up. I can't wait. Let's organize it for after the foundation function. By the way, is there anything you would like to contribute to the night?" Her face drops a little and all the sparkle leaves.

"Bella, what's wrong? What is it about the night that's worrying you?" She shakes her head and then stands up, trying to show me it's all good.

"I need to go so you can get to work. Oh, look at the time, I need to get moving too. I'm so glad to finally meet you. Look after my brother. Thank you for coming into his life." She leans in and gives me a quick hug and is scurrying towards the door.

Before I even have time to stop her and say goodbye properly, Bella is gone. I have no idea what the hell is the issue with the foundation function, but I intend to find that one out. Bella doesn't seem as on board as the others.

Grabbing all my things, I make sure Memphis is fed and has water. I have cleaned up and locked the door, now finally heading to work. I can imagine the reception I will get from the two class clowns. All I know is I have not had enough sleep to be able to deal with them. However, nothing is going to bring me off my high today.

Grayson loves me and that's all that matters.

It's that simple really.

The morning goes as I expected.

I arrive at the office to Fleur, Deven, Hannah, and Daisy all sitting waiting for me. Hannah figured she may as well come in for the date debrief to save me repeating it twice. There was oohing and aahing, screaming and laughing. Of course, they didn't get every detail, but it was fun to share my excitement. I had already called my mom from the taxi like I promised I would. She's already wanting me to bring him home so they can meet him. Normally I would find an excuse to avoid that, but this time I can't wait to see her and have Grayson meet my family.

Luckily, we have a function to prepare for so I could cut them off. Otherwise the coffee would have spread into lunch and beyond while they pumped me for information. Deven just keeps telling me to stop smiling so much and then gives me a cheeky grin. Fleur on the other hand just keeps asking about his friends, hounding me for a group date ASAP. Hannah left telling me how jealous she is and to keep enjoying dessert which then triggered the asking for ice cream from Daisy. A normal morning all round, really.

Heading out of the office, my phone buzzes in my pocket of my pants. I have my hands full so decide to wait until I'm in the taxi to look at it. Fleur is right beside me and we're juggling a few boxes and bags each that need to go to the function.

"We really need to buy a van, you know. It would make life easier. It's not like the budget won't allow it," Fleur complains as we're loading into the taxi.

"Who's going to drive it? It's not like either of us want to do it. I hate city traffic and you're hopeless in anything bigger than a matchbox car," I reply while we slide the last of the bags onto the back seat.

"Well, maybe we need a driver too. Can we make him good-looking, with one of those chauffeur hats? Oh, and no shirt." She looks back at me from the front seat, while the taxi driver just rolls his eyes.

"Because that wouldn't be weird at all, would it." I remember my phone and grab it from my jacket pocket.

GG: *Should I be worried what my sister told you after I left?*

Tilly: *Depends, what things have you got lurking in the dark?*

GG: *Nothing, but I'm sure Bella will make up some.*
Was she okay though, nice to you?

Tilly: *Of course. She is lovely, we got along great.*

GG: *Thank goodness, I didn't want to have to divorce my sister.*

Tilly: *Wow, what a compliment. But don't ever feel you need to put me before her.*
I know you two are close.

GG: *Thank you but it's okay. You are both in your own special place.*

Tilly: I miss you already

GG: Me too, little one. Please tell me I can sleep over tonight.
I don't want to sleep alone
The boogie monster might get me.

Tilly: You should be more afraid of what I might do to you!

GG: Promises, promises. I can't wait for that!

GG: Damn pager is going again. Will message soon, don't panic if I don't.
Just busy

GG: Love you xx

Tilly: Totally understand. Love you xx

I didn't realize we've just about arrived at the function place. I look up from my phone, probably with a stupid lovesick grin on my face.

"No guesses who you were messaging. It's written all over you face. Is this how it's always going to be?" Fleur gets out and starts unloading the parcels.

"Absolutely, so get used to it and no bitching. You told me to go out and get laid, so I did. It's your fault. No one to blame but yourself." I'm still on the high from my message with Gray, so I'm not letting her bring me down.

"Well, can you tell me to go out and get laid, so I can go off and find my own damn Prince Charming? You know whatever we do, we do together." Walking in the doors, getting out of the heat, I laugh as I drop my boxes. Thank god they aren't breakable.

"Everything except that. I've never, nor will I ever, share a man with you, and as for a gang bang, it's off the table for me, thanks." I'm trying to pick my boxes back up while I'm still laughing and not succeeding very well.

"Don't knock it until you've tried it."

I gasp and put my hand over my mouth. "Fleur Florentine, you little hussy. I never!"

"Oh shut up, you. Get to work so I can go home and leave you to it. It's my night off and I might just go man shopping. You never know what I might find out there in the shadows." She has the stupid grin on her face that tells me she means it.

"For god's sake, woman, can you not go lurking in the shadows? At least stay in the light so you know what they look like." We both put our boxes down, laughing, but take a big hug.

"So happy for you, Tilly, you know that, don't you," Fleur whispers in my ear.

"I know. Your turn will come. I know it. He will be perfect for your crazy." I squeeze her tighter and then we both move to get on with the day.

Not long after I send Fleur home and the function is getting underway, my night dive-bombs. Standing near the door and just monitoring the room, I hear the feet and the shrill voice that make my skin crawl. Just when I was thinking tonight was going to be a piece of cake.

"Ugh, well, I can already tell this will be a crap event, if *Fleurtilly* is running it," Kitty says quite loud to her friends near her. I feel the hairs on the back of my neck stand up and my muscles clench. I can picture Tate's face at the hospital telling me to just breathe. Which is a far better option than what I really want to do to her.

I keep repeating in my head, *just ignore her, just ignore her.* She's not worth it. I hear through my earpiece that one of the bar staff is looking for the extra bottles of champagne. I walk away to deal with that while I can hear her in the background, continuing to badmouth us. This woman is trouble, and I need to be very careful with how I react to her.

During the dinner service, she sent her appetizer back because it was cold, her main meal wasn't cooked right, and the dessert tasted funny. I mean, really, Kitty, could you not have thought up something that's an interesting story? I suppose it's because you're just a boring person. I dealt with each of the problems she made up and kept a smile painted on my face. Her friends by this stage are getting a little embarrassed at all the fuss she's making. The night is a meeting for businesswomen in the medical field. It can be bad for business if she keeps badmouthing us. I don't know what to do without losing my cool. Feeling frustrated, I message Fleur for advice. Being a little removed from the emotion, I'm hoping she will calm me down.

It doesn't help much when her answer is to dump a drink in her lap, and if that doesn't work to just knock her out cold. Not sure that will be a great business move in front of all these potential customers. Great, I'm going to have to deal with her. Things are getting towards the end of the night and she's getting louder the more she drinks. Even if it isn't about me, I would still need to go over and calm her down. This bitch is just about to make me snap. I can tell by the looks on the rest of her table, they've all had enough too.

Taking a deep breath, I walk over, taking one of my staff with me.

"Hi, Kitty, just wondering if you could perhaps lower your voice. It's getting a little loud and disturbing the rest of the event." I want to say so much more, but I have put on my most polite, sweet voice.

"Fuck off, you low-life cheating whore. Is that loud enough for you?" She looks back to her friends hoping for support, but they're all cringing trying to ignore her.

"Look at her prancing around here like some sweet little thing. But really she just runs these functions so she can seek out the rich men she can trap in her lair." This is going way past drenching with a drink or knocking her out.

"That's enough, Kitty. You've had too much wine. I'm calling you a cab."

"What, are you shutting me up, so people don't know the truth that you stole my boyfriend? You tramp." Richard, who is standing with me from my staff, starts to lift her by her arms to help escort her out of the room as everyone is stopped and staring.

"Grayson Garrett is mine. I'm going to be Mrs. Dr. Grayson Garrett. He is just waiting for the right time to ask me. When we aren't so busy. He loves me." She's still yelling as she stops cold in the middle of the dance floor nearly making Richard fall over. Standing there, she spots the two people storming in the doors. I see them too and my heart skips a beat at the same time my eyes meet theirs.

Normally I would be furious, but I'm so relieved to see Fleur turn up at an event on her night off and bring Grayson with her. I don't know how she did it, but I'm so glad she did.

I want to run to him. I feel like a schoolgirl in some ways, wanting to say to him "Kitty is being mean and picking on me." Yet it is so much more than that. If there is one thing I can't stand, it's women who try to bring other women down for self-gain. That is what she's trying to do. By badmouthing my business, she's hoping to get us removed from the hospital contract and therefore away from

Gray. I hate to tell her nothing will keep me away from him now. No matter where I'm working.

"Kitty." His voice is stern. The women in the room take notice. Some of them know who he is and the others are finding out.

"That's enough. You will apologize and then leave. This has got to stop." As he steps towards her, she tries to throw herself into his arms. There is no way he is letting that happen, holding her at arm's length.

"I know you're only using her until the foundation function is done. It's okay, I'll wait for you." This woman is crazy. She can't see it.

"Kitty, stop this! We are no longer together and never will be. I am in love with Matilda." He looks past her to find me still frozen watching the show.

"Love. You can't love her, she's so beneath you. Just a party host. We can be the power couple of the hospital." The tears are now coming. I see Fleur roll her eyes. She has had enough.

"Come on, Kitty, you're embarrassing yourself. Let's get you in the cab. Tomorrow will come soon enough for you when the regret and killer headache move in." Fleur and Richard are now escorting a crying, pitiful woman outside. Part of me feels sorry for her, but it is a very small part.

Once the doors close, he's stalking towards me on a mission. I might be working but I couldn't give a damn. He pulls me into his arms, and I burst into tears. I have never been made to feel so small in all my professional career. I don't know why I give her the power, but I can't seem to stop it when she attacks my two weaknesses.

The thought of being cheated on.

And Grayson.

"I've got you, little one." His hand is rubbing my back in circles as I try to pull myself together.

"You should be at the hospital." I sniffle into his chest, not interested to look up at all the people staring.

"I was almost finished, and Alison arrived early for her shift. So she signed in to cover me when Fleur called."

"How did she find you?" Then I realized the client data base, Grayson is in there for the function. "Never mind, she could track down the President if need-ed." With that we both have a little giggle.

"Let's get you into the kitchen and cleaned up. Let these women all find something else to look at." With the adrenaline high from the fight-or-flight response starting to come down, I can't stop my giggles. It's that or tears.

"You know they aren't looking at me. They're eyeballing the hot doctor in the room. Admiring his ass."

"You are too much. Only you could say that at a time like this. Just know they can all look as much as they like, but no touching. It's only for my girl. The badass one standing right in front of me now." He turns me and we make our way to the kitchen as I hear Fleur taking command of the room again, and the noise of women starting to talk gets louder.

After a cup of tea, a big piece of chocolate cake that was left over, and several kisses and cuddles from Gray, I finally convince them all I'm okay. By this stage, everyone has left, the staff have everything packed, and we are ready to head home for the night.

"Thank you for being my cavalry," I tell Fleur. "I don't care what she calls me, but I don't want your name dragged down too. We've worked too hard for this." I hug her as we go to let her out of the cab we're all sharing home. Gray insisted we take her home first and then we'll head to my place, after we pick up Memphis.

"Too right we have, but nobody gets to attack my bestie like that. If I couldn't get Superman here, then I would have taken her down myself. With a great amount of pleasure. The woman is one crazy bitch." We hug and she gets out, but then ducks her head back in so she can leave us with one more comment. "Be good you two, and if you can't, at least be good at it." She then closes the door and I can still hear her laughing to herself as she enters the front door to her building.

"Kitty may not be the only crazy lady around here," Gray whispers to me as he pulls me to his side and holds me tight. I can feel the tiredness starting to creep in.

Stopping at Gray's place, we pick up Memphis and his supplies and climb into Gray's car. I offered to just stay there, but he insisted I needed to sleep in my own bed tonight. I'm kind of glad. There's nothing like your own bed and surroundings after a long day.

Memphis gets excited as we entered the apartment even though it's eleven thirty at night. He races over and sniffs around Daisy's table and toys. Gray decides to put his bed there because he obviously feels at home right there.

Getting organized for bed, we leave the bedroom door open though just in case he needs us.

Starting to strip off my clothes, Gray hands me my sleep shirt that is on my footstool. I feel a bit shocked. He sees my confusion.

"You just need sleep and a cuddle tonight, little one. There is plenty of time for that tomorrow, I promise." He is lying down in the bed with his boxer briefs still on, showing me that he would still be ready if I asked for more, but to be honest, he's right. He always seems to know what I need more than I do. Holding his arms open, I climb in and snuggle in my special place. Tucked under his arm, my head on his chest and my leg hooked over the top of his, I feel like this is home. My safe place.

Tonight, I need this.

Shutting my eyes, I feel like I'm safe.

Because Gray is my home now.

"Really, that is not romantic. It's disgusting." I try to open my eyes to push Gray away after feeling him lick my cheek. Being in a dead sleep, I'm struggling to function.

"What are you talking about?" I hear him mumble behind me. Then I realize he's behind me and the wet tongue is in front of me. My eyes are open and I'm sitting straight up in mere seconds. Seeing a very happy Memphis with his tail wagging, proud he has me awake and there's someone to play with now.

I let out a little squeal as I sit up, which he takes as a call to play. Jumping up onto my bed, he's trying to nuzzle between me and Gray for pats and attention. Gray's not impressed as he's also still half-asleep.

"Memphis, down now," he yells at him. Immediately he's off the bed and sitting patiently waiting for his next command. When Gray doesn't move enough, he starts to whine which tells me he needs to go out for the toilet.

"I'm already awake, I'll go." I start to move, only to be pulled back onto the bed.

"Not a chance. Relax and stay here. We have unfinished business." He stands, trying to adjust his cock that is standing up nicely with a morning woody. "That's right, even in my sleep being near has this effect."

I laugh a little and then snuggle back under the blanket. "Can you please put some clothes on this time? I don't want to scare Daisy again. Twice in one week and she may need therapy before the age of ten."

"You will pay for that when I get back. Memphis, door, now, time's a wasting." Picking up his pants and shirt from yesterday, he throws them on, going barefoot because it's quicker. I hear him talking quietly to Memphis as they leave and head for the elevator. If he's lucky, he won't have woken Daisy yet. Otherwise it'll be a challenge to even get back inside.

It's not long before I hear the front door open again. The trot of Memphis across the floor to his bed and footsteps heading this way.

"You have a funny old lady that lives in this building. She just tried to chat me up. Then when I stubbed my toe on the step, she tells me I owe her a dollar for the bad word. To get you to drop in later with the money. She knew I was staying with you. Is she the stalker of the building?" By now he's stripped to naked and climbing in with me.

"No, she's just an old lady who lost her husband and is lonely. You can't blame her for hitting on my sexy boyfriend. We'll call and see Mrs. Johnson later today. You'll love her, but you know what I'm not loving is your cold feet."

"Is that right? Well, you need to warm me up then, baby. Get naked and let's see how hot we can make it in here." I don't have much of a chance before he's helping me to strip off, and this time, he's lying back waiting for me to take control.

"Tell me what you want, baby, what do you need from me?" The fact he knows I need some control after yesterday makes me twinge all over.

"Hard." I stammer a little. "I don't want gentle. I need you to own me. I'm yours, not her." My words are soft but with purpose. He reads me like a book.

"You tell me to stop at any time."

I nod quickly. I'm not good at asking for what I want, but I'm getting better.

"I want you here on the bed, ready for me to take my pleasure." He stands and walks to the bathroom while I lie down. He returns with the tie from my robe.

"Hands out," he commands, and I can feel my pussy getting more excited by the minute. He wraps my hands together then ties me to the headboard. I've never been tied up before, but it feels exhilarating to have no control now in what Gray is going to do to me.

His hands are now roaming my body, and I can't help but moan every time he skims past my clitoris but doesn't give it the attention it's craving. The smile on his face as he kneels over me tells me my sexual frustration is pleasing him.

"I want to touch you," I blurt out, looking at his cock with the first little dribble of pre-cum leaking out.

"Maybe so, but is it what you need? I don't think so. What you need is to suck me off so I'm nice and hard, and then I'm going to pound you into next week, just like you deserve."

My heart is nearly beating out of my chest, and I know my legs are quivering and a little twitchy waiting for what he's promised.

"God yes," is all I can get out before he's above me and sliding his cock in and out of my mouth. I've never felt so desperate to please him, trying to take him deeper and deeper each time.

"Fuck, Tilly, the way you suck me, I can't hold on, it's so fucking good." I don't want him to stop. I want to make him fall apart, but he has other ideas. Before I can finish, he moves off me and then flips my body over on to my stomach.

Grayson is behind me and lifting me up by my hips, so my ass is in the air and I'm on my knees. He's rubbing his hands over my ass cheeks, and I'm already moving up and down trying to find my own rhythm to get some relief.

I feel him nudge me a little with his cock, and then he slams into me with no notice. Hard and fast. I can't breathe. He's not giving me any break, just slamming into me over and over again. It is the most amazing feeling. I can feel my body building and taking all the pleasure he is making me feel, just how I asked.

Just when I think I can't take much more, he leans forward and whispers in my ear, "You want me to own you? Then I am taking every piece of you now." I'm hardly forming normal thoughts as I'm so close to exploding in an orgasm, when I feel a wetness at my tight rosebud that has never been entered before.

"Oh, fuck, Gray." As he pushes his thumb in and out of my ass, I totally let go. Screaming and coming so hard, I lose my vision, as the stars take over and the sounds of Grayson still slamming those last few times until he fills me to the brim are a little distant.

He falls forward, and his breathing is hot and fast on my neck.

"I own you, and only you, Tilly. Never will I own another body or soul with such passion. Just like you own every part of me."

He starts to kiss me lightly and whispers over and over how much he loves me and that will never change.

In all the times I have tried to be this strong independent woman.

This is the one place I didn't realize how much I crave to be dominated for my pleasure.

Life won't quite be the same again.

Instead I think it will better and perhaps a little naughtier.

Oh, Gray, what have you done to me?

And can you please do it again and again.

Chapter Nineteen

GRAYSON

"You never stop surprising me, little one." I'm still coming down from the high of our morning delight.

"I surprise you and me both," she says as I'm untying her hands and slowly rubbing them for her. "I kind of liked it, though." Her eyes look down away from me and her voice is a soft whisper.

"Me too, baby. Anytime you want to play on the wild side you just tell me. Playing around together is definitely on my list of favorite activities."

"As if that was ever in doubt." That little giggle she has when she's feeling embarrassed just gets me every time.

"Hey, what are you trying to say, that I like sex, more specifically sex with my hot girlfriend? That's no crime in my books." I lower my head down to hers that is lying on the pillow, her brown hair messed up and fanning out. "My main goal is to make you happy. It's just that sex seems to help me fulfill that goal." Kissing her softly on the lips, I lean back off her and roll to the side.

Tilly tries to get up and head to the bathroom without me.

"The only reason you better be going in there is to pee, otherwise we are heading in there together so I can wash you clean."

"See? Sex maniac!" she yells behind as she closes the door.

I give her a few minutes, but the moment I hear the shower I'm up and in to join her.

"You know I can dry myself," she says very matter-of-factly.

"Yep," I answer as I'm running the towel down her leg.

"You're not going to let me, though, are you?"

"Nope." I keep wiping the towel over the other leg.

She just stands there smiling.

"That's right, just let me spoil you. The day I stop, then start complaining."

"Fair enough. I'm not complaining. It's just new to me. You know I have so many things to add to your first list. You are excelling at this test, Dr. Garrett, just saying."

"I am pleased to hear that, my little one." I stand and kiss her on the nose.

"Now the important question. Today is your date day. What's happening? I'm a little excited to see what you've come up with. The pressure is on, you know." I'm standing in her room with just my pants from last night on. I need to get some clothes here for nights like last night where we end up here unexpectedly.

"Oh, like I can even compete with your date. Mine I must say is great, but very different. However, I have some sad news. You need to go home now."

I look at her pretending to be not impressed. "Really? Why? What if I don't want to?" I ask, faking annoyance.

"Stop being a child. You need to take Memphis home and then wait for the first part of the date. I didn't exactly plan on you being here last night."

Hearing his name, Memphis trots into the room looking for some loving.

"Did you get that too, boy? She's kicking us out. I'm so offended." Memphis walks over to Tilly and plops his butt down on her feet.

"You suck, you know, Memphis. What happened to the boys sticking together? You're Team Gray, remember?" I watch as Tilly bends down and pats him, then hugs him while his tail thumps on the floor.

"Yeah, I get it, she gives good cuddles. Okay, I forgive you for being a traitor. But just don't think you get prime spot on the couch with her. That is all mine."

Tilly is looking up at me with such a sparkle in her eyes. I'm so glad the nastiness of yesterday is forgotten.

"I'm not kicking you out. You just know how this works. When you ask someone on a date, you go to their home and meet them at the door to pick them up. Today is all mapped out, you know what I'm like. Now go home, get my little guy settled, put on something casual, and be ready when I come calling for you at ten o'clock."

I look at my watch and see that gives me an hour. I better get moving.

"Any clues?" I plead with puppy eyes.

"Not one, now shoo. Otherwise you'll be late, and it's rude to keep a lady waiting." She's waving her hands at me but there is no way I'm leaving before I've said a proper goodbye. I don't care if I'm seeing her in an hour's time.

Taking Tilly in my arms, I whisper the words that I can't keep to myself anymore.

"I love you so much, little one."

Kissing her like it's the last time I'll see her, I leave her standing in the love-drunk stage. Where your legs don't want to move, and your brain is in the clouds. The perfect state to be in.

"Memphis, door," I tell him, and he gives Tilly one more wag of his tail and is off waiting for me.

"I have to go now. I have a date with this super-hot chick. She also gets jealous of any other women who hang around me, so I need to be home in plenty of time. She's protective like that and I fucking love it." She giggles as I pick her up off the floor and spin her around.

"Don't be late," I tease her, "I get anxious if dates stand me up."

"You're crazy, you know that. Now get out of here before my boyfriend finds you. He's also very protective and has a vicious guard dog. His licks are his secret weapon." We're both laughing as I head to the door for our final kiss.

"Love you too, Gray. More than I knew possible." Her final kiss is in the palm of my hand. "Hold onto that until I see you again." She closes my fist around where she kissed me, and my heart is melting.

I can't really talk otherwise I might choke on my own words; she weakens me like no one ever has in my life.

I turn as I get to the elevator and blow her a kiss. She reaches out, captures it in her hand and lays it on her heart.

Yep, I'm done.

Signed, sealed, and delivered, I'm hers.

239

Now let's see what she's got in store for me today.

The buzzer in the apartment goes off at nine fifty-nine, and I know it will be Tilly.

Right on time.

"Yes?" I try to sound like I don't know who it is.

When a male voice comes through the intercom, I'm taken back a little.

"Dr. Garrett, your transport ordered by Miss Henderson is ready downstairs." Buddy, the doorman, waits for me to answer.

I finally snap out of it.

"Great, thanks Buddy, I'm on my way down." I grab my things and I'm out the door so fast. I feel like a little boy in the elevator wondering what she's up to. Now I realize what she was feeling on Friday night. We need to keep doing this in our relationship. I've never had so much fun, either from the planning or from the enjoyment of how she has planned something for me. As the elevator reaches the ground floor, exiting and walking towards the glass doors, I feel my heart in my throat.

It's hard to breathe looking at my girl leaning against a 1955 Cadillac Fleetwood 60 in a blue color. This was Elvis Presley's favorite car. I can't believe she found one. The fact that she is starting the date with something that is so dear to my heart has already floored me. I walk slowly to her, still taking it in.

"Hi, Gray." Her soft voice tells me she knows I'm emotional. Up on to her tippy toes, she kisses me lightly and then hugs me.

"Baby, you have no idea," I manage to get out.

"I kind of do. I couldn't get a pink one, but we have this one that will drive us to our next destination. With the top down on this beautiful day. Does that sound okay? Oh and of course the only music it plays is Elvis on every channel. So, I think you're set."

"This is more than okay, it's perfect, just like you." The driver then appears out of nowhere to open the door for us to climb into the back.

I burst out laughing. He's dressed in a full Elvis outfit. Gold sparkles and jewels over a white jumpsuit. The high collar, cape off the back of his shoulders, and the trademark glasses. I'm in heaven. Before we climb in, we get Buddy to come and take photos of us all with the car. I want to be able to remember this day forever and show Dad and Bella. They'll understand what this means.

Cruising down the freeway, wind in our hair, Elvis pumping through the speakers for an hour is so much fun. We've been talking, laughing, singing, although Tilly is much more in-tune than I am. I've spent time explaining things I know about the songs that I remember my mom telling me in the kitchen. She would sit me up on the kitchen counter while she was preparing dinner and we would chat about the music. Then for her favorite songs she would grab me down and we would dance around the kitchen.

I remember coming downstairs one night for a glass of water and caught my parents slow dancing to Elvis in the family room. I sat on the stairs and peered through the railings watching two people so in love. It was when my mom started to unbutton my dad's shirt that I took off back to my bed and decided I wasn't thirsty anymore. Although it was weird at the time, it is a treasured memory I have as an adult of knowing how much in love my parents were. I've never told anyone that story until just now. Tilly gets tears in her eyes and agrees I was blessed to have that memory. I understand why it is so hard for Bella because she doesn't have the memories I have. As much as I try to share, it's just not the same.

The driver takes the next exit. I look to Tilly and she's about to bounce out of her seat.

"Welcome to Chicagoland Speedway, Grayson. I know you love cars, and this graceful trip in the old lady has been fun, but your next car will go just a little bit faster."

I blink and look at her again.

"What have you got in store, baby?" I'm praying it's what I think it is.

"First you are going to do a few fast laps with a driver in a Nascar race car. Then after you have lunch with some of the team and drivers, they will send you out for your own drive around the track."

"Are you kidding me!?" I yell a little loud as the car comes to a stop at the back of the pit area.

"I'll take that as a happy reaction."

I grab her face in my hands and kiss her so hard she falls back into the seat. "Happy! Oh my god, Tilly. How did you even make this happen?" I'm just in awe and so excited I'm already out of the car and helping her from the back seat.

"Just like you listened to me when I asked you to slow down, well, sort of. You planned a beautiful slow romantic date. So today, because I know how you want to go a little faster and you love cars, I thought you might enjoy this. Plus, I know it will feed Mr. Competitive in you too."

"You are too good to be true. I'm not letting you go. Ever! Just so you know." I hug her tightly and start twirling her around again. Listening to her squeal is music to my ears. The happiness is infectious.

"Put me down, you crazy man. You don't want to be dizzy when you get in the car." We're both laughing together by now, and I turn to thank Elvis for the ride in his car. He poses for a few more pictures and then we are off into the track.

I still can't believe she organized some fast laps in a race car. This has been on my bucket list for a long time. Tate and I always talked about doing something like this and never got around to it. Wait until he hears I've been without him.

Approaching the gate, I squeeze her hand to let her know how excited I am. She just smiles at me and keeps walking. Matilda has her planner hat on now. She's in charge of my day and is going to make sure everything runs as perfectly as she organized.

Waiting just inside the gate is a man I recognize vaguely, whose face lights up as we approach. He opens his arms and Tilly lets go of my hand and goes to him. She falls into his hug and kisses him on the cheek. The hairs are up on my neck, but I'm holding it together.

After letting her go, they turn to me and Tilly sees the reaction on my face.

"Oops, I'll explain. Paul, this is Grayson Garrett, my very protective boyfriend. Gray, this is my cousin Paul Bonnet. He is the crew chief for one of the big Nascar teams. So, you can calm down now." She thinks she's very funny.

"Hey, man, nice to meet the man who has won our little Tilly's heart. No worries, buddy, I'm more than happy for you to be protective of her." He puts out his hand for me to shake.

"My nerves have calmed, and I will be teaching your cheeky little cousin here about jokes a little later tonight." I grab her around the waist and tickle her as she tries to struggle away from me.

"Tilly just happened to time it perfectly because we're here testing at the moment, and I've been trying to get her down to the track for ages. It just took a good man to get her here. Now let's get you suited up and in a car as we run some test laps. While you're out there, I can catch up with Matilda." He walks towards the garage and we follow like excited little kids.

The look on her face is one that shows how proud she is of her surprise. I kiss the top of her head as we walk and let her know that I'm so happy too.

Suited up and ready to race, Tilly is taking a thousand photos of me near the car waiting. I feel like a celebrity. Paul just keeps laughing at her. Finally, we are ready to roll. I get strapped into the racing harness and introduced to my driver Roger who is a test driver for the team. He asks if I'm okay with fast, and I nearly choke on my answer. That's a no brainer for me. Yes, all the way. The faster the better.

Tilly pops her head in through the window to give me a kiss before we pull out on to the track.

"Love you, time to take this relationship full throttle." I chuckle and kiss her back before the pit crew lifts the safety net up on the window.

The car roars to life and we start the crawl out of the pit lane. Through my headset I hear Roger talking to the crew in the pit. This is so much more than just a lap in a car. I'm getting the full experience.

"Holy shit!" I yell as Roger plants his foot on the accelerator and the car heads up the track and the G-forces hit me.

I can hear both Roger and Paul laughing at me.

"We were waiting for that reaction," Paul says through the headset.

Spending thirty minutes in the car, doing various speeds as they adjust different settings on the car, is one of the greatest experiences of my life. As we pull into the garage, I see the smiling face of my girlfriend. Beside her are a few familiar faces I wasn't expecting.

Climbing out of the car, I grab her and hug her as tight as I can, kissing her as I let her go. Then it's time to find out what's going on.

"What are you boys doing here?" Tate, Lex, and Mason all smile like Cheshire cats.

"We've come to see Tilly own you on the racetrack. She is totally going to ruin you."

I look to her when she raises her hands on either side of her and shrugs her shoulders to tell me it's possible.

"Am I racing you?" I start laughing because this day keeps getting better.

"Settle down there, big boy. Paul isn't silly enough to put both of us on the track at the same time. We will be racing our times." Tilly puts her hands on her hips.

"I get to go first, and you get to see if you can match me. I know you love a bit of rivalry. I thought it would be a great idea to invite the boys to see me smash your time. That way you can never dispute as I have witnesses."

"Very confident there, baby. Let's just see how well you are up against the master. What have I told you before? I'm an overachiever." The boys all break up with laughing and smartass comments.

"First I just want to say you obviously haven't slept together if Tilly is calling you big boy." Mason takes control of the conversation. "Secondly, since when have you overachieved against any of us? You're all talk, Doc. I can't wait to see your woman totally blow you away out there." Putting his arm around Tilly, he proudly looks at me and says, "Team Tilly all the way."

"For fuck's sake, not you too. I thought we agreed, baby, I got to keep my friends. You've already claimed my sister and the dog. Give me a break. What about you two suckers?" I look to Tate and Lex who turn around to show the backs of their shirts at the same time Mason turns, revealing "Team Tilly" plastered across the back.

"Are you serious!" Everyone can't stop laughing at me, and I'm actually happy, for once, to be joining in. I love how easily Tilly fits in with my friends.

"Paul, I'm sitting with you at lunch. These dickwads are in the enemy camp."

"You aren't having much luck. Remember cousin? I'm Team Tilly all the way, man." With that, Tilly comes over and puts her arms around my waist, looking up with those beautiful eyes that suck me in every time.

"I promise I'll give them all back when I've whipped your ass today."

I grab her on the cheeks and tilt her face up to hold her looking at me.

"I love you and your cheeky ass. But you can keep the cocksuckers. They have crossed the line. You will regret taking them. They're just a pain in the ass anyway. Now where is this lunch you promised?"

We all head into the mess area where the caterers have set up for the crew and we're joining in. I know the guys are loving chatting to the team and finding out different things about racing life.

Me, on the other hand, can't get enough stories out of Paul about Tilly when she was little. This is my one chance to get ammunition against her before

Arabella spills all my secrets. We're laughing so much at times Tilly is crying at the stories and memories. Today meeting Paul is giving me a real insight into her childhood and what makes her the beautiful woman she is.

We're laughing about the time that Tilly wanted to be like the big boys and climb the tree to the treehouse only to get stuck halfway on a branch. They had to get the fire department to rescue her. Paul then looks at the time and declares it's time to race. We have one of their test cars, thank goodness. I do not want the responsibility of the top car and me breaking it.

I'm actually not sure how I feel about Tilly in danger out on the track, but I know I have to keep that to myself. I will get crucified if I say anything. With her now strapped in the car, it's my turn to kiss her and wish her luck. She doesn't look at all nervous. Perhaps I should be a little more worried that she may be better at this than me.

"Stay safe and don't do anything silly. Just remember it's a bit of fun." I want to say all the safety warnings like, don't you dare crash and get hurt, but I don't want to jinx her. I'll admit I am freaking out, though. It has taken me so long to find her, I can't imagine losing her. My heart would not take it.

"You just want me to go slow so you can win." She chuckles as she pulls away and out towards the track. I like that she's being a little cautious on the first lap, but by the time she gets around in front of us for her second lap, she's going full throttle. Well, full speed for amateurs like us. Paul has put a headset on me without me realizing so I can hear everything that's being said between them.

It's then I know I've been set up. She knows exactly what she's doing out there. The language she's using is totally above my head. I've lost before I've even gotten in the car. Well played, my little one.

I stand watching in awe as she throws the car around the track with ease. As she rolls the car into the pit lane, ready for me to change into the car, I can see the guys making fun of me. They knew all along, I'm guessing. Well, let's see what I can come up with. It's not over yet.

Climbing out of the cockpit, pulling off her helmet, Tilly leans up and whispers in my ear, "Try your hardest, but I want you to stay safe. Remember it's just a bit of fun." Walking away swaying her cute ass, this woman knows exactly how to play my games. I knew from the beginning we're perfect for each other.

Listening to the brief as I sit in the car, I zone everything else out. It's like when you operate on a patient. You need to be totally focused. I am determined to get as close to her lap time as possible. I rev the car and take first gear as I pull away and start to climb the hill of the track. Picking up speed, I take my time to find a rhythm in the first lap. Then as I get into the second and third lap, I'm pushing the envelope, hoping I'm setting a good pace. I can hear Paul in my ears, but I can't talk at the same time. It's taking all my energy just to keep the car on the track. My last lap is intense, and I give it everything I've got. No matter what happens, I'm not going any faster than this. I can feel the car starting to control me rather than me control it. So that tells me it's time to back off.

I don't even need to ask. Rolling the car into the pit area, I can see Tilly and the boys jumping up and down. Fuck, I've been beaten by a girl and in front of my buddies. I thought this date was supposed to be about me. I get out and walk over to get the roasting I know is coming. Tilly comes running towards me and jumps into my arms. Screaming at me.

"You did it, you did it. Congratulations!" I'm so confused I look at the guys who all turn around with their shirts now having stickers over the top that say, "Team Gray – Bro code always."

"Congratulations, man, even with her inside knowledge you beat her by two seconds. It was so close." Paul pats me on the back.

"You get to keep your man card," Lex yells out to me. I give him the finger behind her back.

I look at Tilly in my arms, legs wrapped around my waist.

"Tonight, when I have you alone, I can't even begin to tell you how much I want to punish you and fuck you hard at the same time," I quietly tell her. "This adrenaline has me wanting to take you on the hood of this car, but I sure as shit am not sharing you with anyone." Her eyes smolder at the thought of being fucked on the car.

"That's right, baby, you feel it now too, don't you. No one gets to take my man card away from you." We both kiss like no one is watching. The cheers and whistles of the guys remind us that's not the case, but we don't care anyway. As I slow down the kiss, I lean my forehead on hers.

"I can't thank you enough for today, baby. It's just hard to believe you're real. No one has ever done anything like this for me."

"It's not over yet. Time to move on to the next part of the date." I slowly put her down, and taking her hand, we head over to the peanut gallery of the boys behind the barriers. Looking up to me, Tilly offers that beautiful smile that's so full of life.

"You don't get to bring your support crew with you, though. They get to stay here and have a little drive themselves. Time to say goodbye."

"With pleasure. They're just trophy hunters, anyway, jumping teams when it suits." We all have a laugh together and I wish them well in their laps, making sure someone is videoing so I can watch later.

Waiting for Tilly to change out of her fireproof race suit, Paul comes up and takes the opportunity to give me the talk. The big brother talk, from a cousin's perspective.

"Watching you two today, I can tell Matilda really loves you. I haven't seen her this relaxed and playful in a long time. She's been working so hard I think she's forgotten how to live. You've brought the fun-loving Tilly back to us. I'm really happy for you both. Just know that if you hurt her like the last douchebag did, I will hunt you down."

"You will never have to worry about that. She told me about him, and if I knew where he is, I would hunt him down now. He really did a number on her. I won't hurt her, I can guarantee. I can tell you now she's it for me. When the time is right, I will be making sure I make this permanent." I know I can trust Paul. He and Tilly seem close, and judging by the stories over lunch, they grew up like brother and sister.

"Good to hear, man. What he did playing around on her, and then he didn't even care when she lost the baby. That is such a dick move." I can feel my heart stop dead. What baby?

"Oh fuck. She didn't tell you that bit, did she. Fuck, don't tell her I told you. I'm sure she'll tell you when she's ready. It nearly ripped her apart." My mind is going crazy as I hear her voice coming towards us. I'm still staring at Paul, trying to make sense of what he has just said.

Why didn't she tell me?

I think back to that night in my office.

I knew there was more, but I was called away.

No wonder she was so upset dragging all that back up, and I had to cut her off. By the time I saw her again, I know she had buried it back down deep.

I don't want to wreck her plans today, but this is something I need to tell her

I know. To comfort her and make sure she knows I would never leave her if that happened, I'd be right by her side, for as long as she needs me.

Forever.

No matter what life brings to us, good or bad, I will always be by her side.

To me that is what real love is.

Chapter Twenty

GRAYSON

L eaving everyone behind at the track, I was expecting to head to the carpark, yet Tilly has me walking in a different direction.

In the distance, I hear a noise that sounds like it's getting closer.

"How are you with heights, tough guy?" she asks as I see a helicopter come into view.

"Really! Wow, you must have spent a fortune today, sweetheart. I'm feeling guilty. I'm not sure I'm worth it." This stops her still in her tracks to look at me with a mad look on her face.

"No other person in my life is worth more to me, than you. Don't ever say that again. I might not be rich, but if I want to spend every last dollar I have on making you happy, I will." Shit, I think I stepped on her toes.

"I didn't mean it like that, I'm sorry. Baby, you have to remember most women I've dated are only looking for either my money because I'm a doctor or for the reputation of being with me. No one has ever done anything like this for me. I just don't know how to accept it and believe that I deserve it. I know you feel the same, so hopefully you understand. It will take me time to appreciate that I am worthy of you. Does that make sense?"

Her face softens and she hugs me so we can connect how we do our best communicating. No words, just our hearts beating to each other.

"Sorry, I'm just so sick of defending myself, being an independent woman and not relying on any man for money or my lifestyle. I know you didn't mean it. I do understand what you're saying and it's something we can work on together." By now she is shouting as the helicopter comes in to land. I pull her in tighter as the dust is kicked up and the skids of the helicopter touch the ground. The co-pilot jumps out and opens the back doors. We duck our heads and run to climb in.

Passing us our headsets, they run through the safety instructions as we get strapped in. I've flown plenty of times in a plane but never a helicopter, so I'm excited to see Chicago from the air.

I can't believe how awesome the city looks from up here. Flying over landmarks that you know but they look so different from this angle. I've taken many photos in front of the Cloud Gate sculpture. It looks like a giant mirrored bean, which is the local nickname. From the air it looks so different, the way the sun sparkles on the rounded shape is so mesmerizing. Tilly keeps tapping my leg and pointing out different things that she knows. We both kiss as we see the Ferris wheel at Navy Pier that holds some special memories already.

The pilot announces that we are coming in to land at their heliport in the city. It is all over too quickly and I make a note to bring Tilly again at nighttime. I can only imagine what the view would be of all the lights across the city.

After the helicopter winds down and we leave the heliport, there should be no surprise that there's a car here to pick us up.

"Where to now, little one? I'm guessing this is not the end of the road." I can tell she still has more planned because she's busy organizing something on her phone.

"Okay, it's time for a relaxing afternoon beer at a nice bar, Cindy's, before we move on to the last part of the date."

"I think you've stretched the rules a little here, Tilly. I only got a night and you've managed a whole day and now we're heading into the night. How did I not see this coming?"

Standing next to the car before we get in, she turns and puts her arms around my neck.

"Technically you had the night, the whole night through to the next morning. So, if we're going to count hours...." Smacking her ass, I just smile and open the door for her to get in and settle back in my arms as we are whisked off to the next destination.

"If you think you won't still be with me when you wake up tomorrow morning, then you are dreaming, baby, so just admit you cheated. Just like at the racetrack, where you obviously have some prior experience. Well played, sweetheart, well played."

Laughing at her obvious victory, she feigns her innocence. "I didn't realize this was a competition. I just thought we were trying to plan a special date for the one that we love."

"Yeah, that too, I'm on to you. Next time I will make sure the playing fields are even, right down to the last second. You wait for the next dates, it's game on, baby."

"You're such a boy." Tilly rolls her eyes at me while still smiling like she loves it.

"Umm excuse me. All man here, baby, you've seen the proof." I lean down to her ear. "You've felt every inch of that manhood too. No denying that."

Her smile becomes a little gasp and her mouth opens. Oh, how I'd like to fill that mouth with this manhood who's now getting impatient because it's been too long since he's been making friends with my girlfriend. I'm starting to think she might be right. Tilly is turning me into a sex maniac.

The car is getting close to our destination of a rooftop bar, Cindy's. From up there, we can look over the bean in the park that we just saw from the air. It has been such a big day that I could really use a beer right now.

Still playing on my mind is everything Paul said earlier, and when I look at my girl, I just want to shout to the world that no one ever gets to hurt her again. I can't do that until we have the discussion that we are both needing. When the time is right, it will be so good for her to learn she is not on her own anymore, no matter what.

Entering the bar, I look across to the window and see my dad and Arabella sitting with a drink each and two spare drinks. Bella is madly waving, like I haven't already seen her. Tilly starts to walk towards them, but I pull her back to me.

"What's going on here, baby?" I can't look away from her eyes, they're dancing at the moment.

"I know how important your family is to you. I thought it might be nice for us to spend a little time together and get to know each other, like a first date of the family. Is that okay? I know a date is supposed to be us. I asked you to slow down and you did that, but I know you really want to speed things up. So, it's meet-the-family date time." She doesn't wait for my answer and starts dragging me over to my family.

Bella is up out of her seat and wrapping her arms around Tilly before she then comes to me. It makes me happy, but I can't resist making a point.

"I can't believe I've been replaced so easily as your favorite person. Big brothers should always be number one." I squeeze Bella a little as she wriggles to get away.

Dad then pulls her into his arms. "Not a chance, son, dads should always be number one in their little girls' eyes. One day you will understand that, when you have your own daughter. From the moment they first open their eyes, they suck you in, and for the rest of their lives they will always be your special girl." He has already said hello to Tilly and held her chair out for her.

I am sitting here in heaven, with my three favorite people. It's like Tilly has known everyone for years. Her sense of humor and friendly banter fit perfectly with us all. Bella hasn't smiled so much in a long time. I think it has a lot to do with another female to keep her company. We get onto talking about the foundation function which strangely has Bella turning quiet. I see Tilly has noticed it too.

I'm about to say something but Tilly gives me the look to say I need to leave it to her.

"Bella, you don't seem very excited about the function, is there something you don't like?" Bella is looking down and fiddling with the straw in her empty glass.

"I can fix anything you would like to change. That's what I'm here for. To make the memory of your mom come to life." Tilly reaches across and places her hand on the top of Bella's on the table.

"That's just it. They're just memories. I don't even remember her. My own mother, I have no memories. Everyone will be asking me about her, and I have to lie and say things that I can't even remember." My heart breaks at the sight and sound of her tears. Dad and I both go to grab her but instead she turns and falls into the arms of Matilda. It finally all makes sense. All these years she has craved the touch of another woman who she can call family. It may be early days, but we all know Matilda being officially part of this family is just timing now.

"Bella, I'm so sorry you feel like this, we didn't mean to hurt you in any way."

Dad looks torn. Wanting to honor Mom but his baby girl is hurting in the process.

"Sis, why didn't you say something in the beginning?" She raises her head out of Tilly's shoulder and lays it to the side. Not leaving her arms but just so she can see us.

"You both want this so much, that I wanted it for you. I just didn't realize what I had buried for all these years." My beautiful girlfriend is stroking Bella's hair and soothing her just like a big sister would. For everything I've tried to protect my sister from, I can never protect her from herself.

"Arabella, I think you need to look at this from a different angle." Tilly looks down at her, waiting for her full attention.

"We all understand the devastation you feel, but don't look at the function being about remembering your mom. This is the start of you making memories of your mom. From what I hear, she loved to help people. By starting this foundation, you are bringing your mom to life again. Be the woman your mom would be proud of and make memories of good deeds that your mom would be doing if she were still here. Be her earth angel. Fulfill her dreams and I think you might find you will be fulfilling some of your own too. Don't be your mother, but be the woman your mother would have worked side by side with. Making others' lives better and giving them the chance at life to make their own memories."

Tears are falling, not just on Bella's face, but Dad's and mine too. This woman sitting holding my sister and bringing her into the world of her own finally, takes my breath away. Part of me knew that Mom sent me Tilly, but little did I understand she sent her for all of us. She is the key to the next stage in this family. The one where we all need to let go and move on. Always together but on our separate roads, without Dad and I standing over the top of Bella and putting her in our shadows. Mom is telling me that I should let her shine on her own. As hard as this will be, I know it's time.

MATILDA

I knew there was something holding Bella back, but I had no idea it was as deep as what she has just finally let go. Holding her tight I can feel the tension leaving her body with the tears that are falling down her cheeks. I know what it's like to hold deep feelings and never sharing them. You can only keep them down there for so long and eventually they surface. I miss my sister when she's traveling, and I know Bella has never known a close woman in her life. Our friendship will be a treasure for us both.

Looking across at Gray and Milton, I can't help but feel this family has just turned an important corner. My big strong cocky man has been brought to tears from the pure love for his sister. That is the kind of man I have longed for all my life. A man who is not afraid to show his emotions at times that mean so much, yet tie me to a bed and have me screaming his name too. The best of both worlds.

Milton stands and walks to his daughter and takes her in his arms to comfort her. I think it is as much for him as it is for her. Gray pulls me out of my chair and into his lap, burying his head into my neck as he takes his own moment. He whispers just loud enough for me to hear, "I can never thank you enough for what you have just done for Bella. You are my angel."

We stay like that for a moment and then, being in a bar, know we need to pull it together. I sit back in my chair only to have Gray drag it so close to his I may as well still be sitting in his lap.

"Here's to making new memories of Mom." Bella lifts her glass and we all cheers to that. We continue to chat a little about the function until the alarm on my phone sounds. The smile on Gray's face tells me he knows I have another surprise planned.

"I know this is a date for Grayson and me, but I really thought we could all enjoy this part together." Everyone looks at me with intrigue.

"I have organized a rock-and-roll dance class for the four of us. We get to learn the moves and have fun dancing away to Elvis among some other sixties classics."

"Oh my god. I can't believe it. Thank you." Bella is out of her seat and hugging me. "Gray always tells stories of Mom dancing in the kitchen with him."

"Now you can make memories of dancing with your old man." Milton laughs at himself as he smiles. "I haven't danced with anyone since your mother passed away. It's about time I get my feet moving again. What do you say, princess, you happy to have your toes stepped on by your dad?" We're all laughing and talking as we leave the bar.

Gray is walking with his arm around me, having me tightly tucked into his side.

"You tried to tell me your date wasn't as big as mine. You were right, little one. This is so much bigger. I can't even tell you how much today means to me." He leans down and kisses the top of my head and then goes silent again. Looking up at him, the look on his face tells me there's a lot going on in his head today.

When the instructors ask how much experience we have, I happily put my hand up.

"Zero, and I was born with two left feet. So good luck with me, Gray."

"Not sure I'll be much better, baby. We can crash land together, okay?"

Milton explains he can dance but hasn't for a long time and wants to take it slow, so Bella gets the basics. Slow sounds like a great plan to me.

We've been dancing for about an hour, laughing, stumbling, looking ridiculous but having the best time together. Being the end of the class, each couple performs a dance for the other couple to watch. Milton and Bella are amazing and make it look so easy.

They dance to the fast-paced Elvis song *Follow that Dream*. It was just a perfect moment for them both.

Applauding their great display, it's time for Grayson and me to take the floor.

"My baby likes things nice and slow, so it will give us a chance to get this right."

Milton slaps him on the shoulder and smiles. "You've got this, son. Just feel the music."

"Don't help him, Dad. Let me at least be better at something in my life." Bella laughs from the side of the dance floor.

We stand in the middle of the room, and as the music starts, I know I'm done for. *Love me Tender* plays through the music and Gray looks down and smiles. I have a feeling I have been set up. As we start to move slowly around the floor, in our own little world, Grayson sings me every word with such love in his eyes. The feeling of longing that is coming with every word has me floating on air.

Forgetting there are others in the room when the music stops, Gray's hand slides up my neck and into my hair. Tilting my head to place his lips on mine.

Slow and sensually his mouth moves in sync with mine. The kind of kiss that makes you weak at the knees, takes away all rational thought, and releases the butterflies in your stomach. The kind that lets you know deep into your soul that you have found your other half. The person who will own your heart until the day you die.

As he slowly releases me and looks deep into my soul, he voices the only words that I need to hear.

"Love you, Matilda, and I always will." We stand together for a few moments just savoring the moment until there is the faint sniffle from the side of us. It's enough to bring us back out of our love bubble.

Bella is tucked in her dad's arms crying a few tears at us.

"That was so beautiful, one day I hope I can find what you two have. Now can you stop making me cry today?" She pulls herself together and the seriousness of the moment is broken.

"I know you two are ditching us now, so Dad, can I take you to dinner?"

Milton smiles down at her. "No, but it would give me great pleasure to take my daughter and beautiful dance partner to dinner. Plus, we need to celebrate, we totally whooped their asses on that dance floor."

There's a lot of contention on who are the better dancers as we all hug and say our goodbyes. Today has been a lot more emotion than I ever expected. It makes me glad that the last part of my date is quiet and will end the day perfectly.

"You have me to yourself again, so what do you plan to do with me?" Gray stands on the sidewalk waiting for his next instructions.

"We need a cab, kind sir. I'm taking you home."

His hand shoots into the air.

"Taxi!" he yells looking straight at me. "Best thing I've heard all day. Be prepared, Tilly, I'm ready to completely devour you." Kissing me on the forehead, he's concentrating on getting us a taxi as fast as he can.

"I need to feed you first, big boy. I'm thinking you may be using a lot of energy later."

"You will be feeding me, that I can guarantee. The food part can come later." I feel the heat of my cheeks blushing.

Sliding into the taxi, Grays's hand is already running up and down my leg. Each time getting slightly higher. I think it's lucky for the taxi driver that Gray's apartment is not far from here. Otherwise he may be getting more than he bargained for from his passengers.

The ride in the elevator tells me the rest of this date may not go exactly as I had planned but I'm totally okay with that. I'm trying not to laugh at Grayson who is standing with his back against the elevator wall. Hands clenched tightly together. He hasn't touched me since we entered this small confined space. He knows if he does then he won't be stopping.

The walk to his front door is fast and direct.

No words.

Door open, and I'm directed straight in. He closes it behind me, and the lock is engaged. He is making sure there are no interruptions this time from unannounced visitors.

I stand looking across the room towards the large glass floor-to-ceiling windows. The sun is almost set, and the lights of the city are already twinkling. Before us on the floor, is a cozy setting I arranged for Arabella to lay out. Pillows, twinkling tea lights, fruit platter, wine chilling in the cooler along with the antipasto platter.

I feel Gray behind me, his fingers delicately pulling my hair to the side of my neck. His hand slides from my shoulder down my front and rests on top of my breast, delicately squeezing. He must be using all his restraint to go so slowly. My breath is quickening as he then starts to lick and kiss my exposed neck. His free hand is now moving across my stomach and pulling me hard back against him.

A light moan escapes my mouth as I feel his hard cock pressing into me.

"Oh baby, tell me I don't need to wait. I need to fuck you so badly. You have been driving me wild since you stepped out of that race car. Suit unzipped and your tight tank top underneath. So fucking hot!" His hands are now roaming my body and I just want him to take the ache away.

Words aren't coming easily between the moaning. My body is rocking into his hands as they press and stroke the places that take away my clear brain.

"Let me fuck you, then feed you, then fuck you again. Tonight, I don't want to stop."

"Gray!" I cry out as he takes over my body. I willingly give him my all.

"I'm going to strip you bare and bend you over this couch, Tilly. Then every time I walk through the door, I will picture you here waiting, with your fucking sexy ass and pussy on show just for me." I don't want to stop him. When he talks like this it makes me so wet and my body is on high alert.

"Enough talking. Do it." I'm getting impatient now, he has me begging for it.

"You want me, baby? Tell me you want me."

"Fuck me, Grayson, please!" I gasp as his hand slips under my shirt and I feel skin on skin. "I want you so bad. You've made sure of that."

Both his hands take my shirt and drag it up my body, throwing it to the ground then quickly unclasping my bra. My pants are down around my ankles and I'm kicking them to the side as Gray drops to his knees behind me. Using his teeth, he is pulling my lace panties down for me to step out of.

"Legs apart, baby, and lean your body forward. I'm suddenly very hungry." I'm already quivering as his tongue starts its way up the inside of my leg. His hands on either ass cheek, he spreads me as his tongue swipes right through my pussy.

I let out a loud cry as he sucks hard on my clitoris with no warning. I'm so close to my peak that I know I don't have long until I let go.

"Oh, oh…oh god…oh my fucking god." I'm racing to an orgasm that I know is going to rip me to my core. Without waiting, he stands and pounds into me from behind. Burying himself as far into me as he can. He completely fills me with immense pleasure. Pulling out and pounding into me while his fingers grip my hips so tightly. My nipples are grazing on the leather couch as he pushes me hard.

Just as I'm about to explode Gray grabs my hair and pulls my head up to look at him.

"So perfect, you are so fucking perfect."

The pain and pleasure simultaneously have me screaming out as my orgasm hits like a rush of ecstasy.

"Grayson." I'm pleading for him to make me come again as he continues to slide into me over and over with such feeling, until finally, he thrusts and groans as we both explode together. Slumping forward for the couch to hold us both up, I'm breathless, sweaty, and in heaven.

Catching our breath only lasts a few seconds as Grayson stands, pulling me up and scooping me into his arms. He walks and places me in the pile of pillows on the floor. Grabbing a blanket off the arm of the couch so I don't get cold, his eyes never leave mine. He strips the rest of his clothes off and kneels down next to me with his face above me.

"I'm keeping you, Matilda Henderson. There is no way I can let you go. One day when you're ready, I'm going to ask you to marry me and we will live happily ever after. I can't promise to wait long, but for now I'll go slow like you asked." I place my hands on his cheeks, dragging him down to lay with me.

"Not yet, but soon. When the time is right, my answer will be yes. I can't breathe anymore without you."

Time for talking has finished and our lips are finding the love we have expressed. We lay enjoying the quiet, and each other's bodies for a while. Eventually we remember the food when Gray's stomach growl breaks the moment.

"We need to eat, otherwise your little growl will turn into a hangry Grayson." I sit up to reach for the platters and place them next to us on the floor.

"You will learn, nobody needs a hangry Grayson, it's not pleasant." He passes me a glass of wine as I pull the blanket up over my breasts and tuck it under my arms as I lean back against the couch.

"I think the queen needs feeding." He places a strawberry in my mouth that has juice running down my chin as I bite down.

"I'm supposed to be feeding you, it's your date." He chuckles as he cut some cheese and loads the cracker before putting it into his mouth.

"Why are you laughing at me?" I ask as he puts more food in my mouth.

"Baby, your date finished the minute we got in that taxi and all I could think about was fucking you. The rest of the night is just about us. Date done."

Smiling, I lean over and kiss him on the cheek.

"I can live with that. I didn't realize how hungry I was until now. You've worked up my appetite."

"I hate to tell you, baby, but it takes two to play the games we're playing. You can't blame just me."

"Fair enough, but I'm still saying it's your fault so feed the princess."

"It's my pleasure." Crawling under the blanket with me, Gray puts the food on our laps and continues to feed me as we talk and laugh.

Feeling full and now lying with my head in Grayson's lap, I look back over the last few days, and they couldn't have been any more perfect.

I know there is just one more thing I need to do before he has all of me. I promised myself when I found the man I will marry, that there will never be any secrets. I was crushed once before by lies and deceit. Never again will I let that happen. It's now or never.

"Gray," I whisper.

"Yeah, little one."

"I need to tell you something, and it won't be easy, but I need you to know."

"I'm always here to listen, take your time." His strong hand is now sitting on my naked shoulder, squeezing me for strength.

"When I went home to see Henry, it wasn't because I missed him." I pause knowing this part is hard. "Um, it was more than that."

"It's okay, you don't need to do this," he offers quietly.

"Yes, I do, for me I need to tell you." He just squeezes my shoulder to let me know he understands. Facing the window is easier, but I know to do this right I should be looking at him. Rolling on to my back so I'm looking up at him, I take a deep breath and then let it go.

"I was pregnant and was going home to tell him. After I walked in on him, in all his glory with her, I screamed at him that I was pregnant and that he has wrecked everything. He told me straight he didn't want anything to do with the baby and to fuck off back to the city." Little tears are pooling in my eyes, but I don't want to give him the power to hurt me anymore.

"I was so devastated at what he did and said, that I lost the baby in a miscarriage a few days later. It ripped me apart and I blamed myself. I ran back to the city and I've hardly been home since. It just hurts too much." I'm looking at Gray trying to wonder what he feels about what I've said. He leans down and kisses me ever so softly on my forehead, holding it for a few seconds.

"Tilly, I know about the baby and I don't care. I promise you the miscarriage wasn't your fault. I can give you all the technical reasons why, but they don't matter. All that I care about is you knowing that it had nothing to do with you and that the past is the past. I love you and I will care for you for the rest of our days."

"I don't understand, how do you know? And aren't you worried I might not be able to have children?"

"Not at all. If we are worried, I know a good gyno who we can ask. If that doesn't work, then just know you are enough. I just want you, Tilly, anything else that happens in our life is a gift."

He kisses me hard then pulls away as he whispers, "I just want you."

Chapter Twenty-One

MATILDA

"Do we really have to get up? Can't we just sleep here on the floor. It's been just fine for all the rest of our nocturnal activities tonight." Gray just shakes his head and rolls his eyes.

"You are not sleeping on my floor, I paid good money for my bed. I need to get value for money from it. Now give me your hand and I'll pull you up." I get the giggles trying to coordinate myself out of the blanket and all the pillows I'm buried in.

"I think maybe I had a little too much wine, GG." Trying to stand up is proving a little more of a challenge than I was expecting. I get little head spins as Gray sweeps me up into his arms.

"This is easier, that way I know you'll make it to the bed safely without falling over. It's not a hardship that you're completely butt naked either." I lay my head on his shoulder to stop the room from spinning.

"That was a silly challenge, wasn't it?" My speech is becoming a little slurred.

"Not for me, baby, I could have kept going all night. I just don't think you drinking a full glass every time I make you come is safe for you. Because let me assure you, I can keep you screaming over and over."

"Nope, not possible. Girls can't do that. Only once is normal for me. You're just this super GG and have this magic cock. My GG who is the master of the G." I know I need to stop talking, but it just keeps spilling out of my drunk mouth.

"You're adorable drunk, baby. I have a feeling GG means more than my name, doesn't it?" Gray places my head on the pillow gently and then starts to pull the blanket up.

"Ssshhh, don't tell anyone. GG is my gorgeous gyno. He is all over the G. You know his name is Gs and then he is GG and he knows my G-spot ssssoooooo good. Oh and then he makes me say God all the time. He is just my multiple-G man." In my head I'm telling myself to shut the hell up, but my brain is not working with my mouth. I'm so going to regret this in the morning. Lord help me that hopefully I won't remember it all.

I'm fooling myself if I think Grayson will let me forget anyway.

"You need to stop laughing at my drunk words, Gray. I shouldn't have told my secret. Don't tell anyone. I don't want to share my GG." My eyes are starting to get heavy and the room is still spinning a little too fast.

"Sweetheart, your secrets are safe with me. I love every G that I am to you. Now go to sleep. You're going to regret this in the morning, and I can't imagine I'm going to be a popular GG." Walking around to the other side of the bed, he crawls in behind me and pulls me close.

"You are in trouble because you are too good at sex. Who makes me come nine times, or ten, I can't remember now."

"Tilly. Go to sleep. The morning will be here soon enough and so will your headache." His voice is stern.

"GG, Grumpy Grayson!" I giggle like a little girl.

"Matilda." Now I know he's done with my drunk ass.

"Mhmm, love you, Grumpy Grayson."

"For fuck's sake, I will gag you in a minute and not for a good time. Sleep, woman, you're ..." That is the last I heard.

Ugh, that light is not my friend.

Mmm don't move quickly. Head is banging.

I hear a door open, but I don't want to open my eyes.

"Morning, Princess. How's the head?" Grayson's voice gets closer to me, coming from the direction of the bathroom.

"I hate you and your super sex," I groan which sends him into a fit of laughter.

"First time you've complained about the super sex from your master of the Gs"

The bed dips as he crawls on to lie down next to me.

I slowly open my eyes and put my hand on my forehead.

"I can't believe I told you that. What did you put in my drinks last night?"

Kissing my cheek, he just smiles. "It's not what was in the drink, just the amount you consumed, little one. It is like a truth serum for you. That's a trick I will be keeping up my sleeve for later."

I slap him on the shoulder for being annoying.

"You should have stopped me. You know, responsible service of alcohol and all." I lean into his shoulder to get a cuddle.

"Tilly, you brought up some pretty deep feelings to me last night. You deserved to let go completely. I just may have overachieved, as I do, on the pleasure part. Which then had you overachieving on the drinking part. You have to admit, though, it was a pretty spectacular day and night."

I can't deny everything he said, yet I seem to be the only one paying for it this morning.

"Why am I the only one with a hangover? You are way too chirpy."

"Because I'm working today and need to be sober to operate on people, it's sort of mandatory, besides that, it's a really good idea. The patients seem to prefer it that way. You, on the other hand, can dose yourself up with coffee and put on some dark sunglasses. Then sit in your office and bitch with Fleur and Deven all day about what a bastard I am for giving you a headache."

"Ugh, I'm going to need more than coffee. Where are the pain relief drugs, Doctor?" Standing as he walks to the bathroom cabinet, I admire the view of his tight naked ass. I might be hungover but I'm not blind. That vision will never get old.

"Take two of these, here is some water, and then shower. I'll make you some bacon and eggs to help get the body working again."

"Thank you, and coffee. Triple-strength coffee this morning."

Pulling on his gym shorts, he walks out of the bedroom while I lie here psyching myself up to move off the bed to the shower.

My head might be hurting like a bitch, but I'm the happiest I have ever been.

Leaning my head against the shower wall, the hot water running over my body, all I can think about is how much I have missed my life being carefree. It feels like forever since I was out on a Sunday night having fun and waking up the worse for wear on a Monday morning for work. I wonder when I became such an old lady and forgot how to live. Grayson has changed my world for the better. Well, maybe not this morning with this cracker of a hangover, but in general, life is so much better.

Now I have one thing left to do and that is go home once and for all and face that demon. My poor mom has missed me terribly, I know, but she never complains. She knows why I struggle and has never pushed. It's time to bury the past and live from today and into the future.

By the time I come out of the bedroom, Gray is already dressed for work. I try not to drool at the sight of my gorgeous boyfriend serving me breakfast in his tailored navy pants and grey shirt nicely fitted over his hot abs and arms. I really hit the jackpot.

"Feel a little more human now, Princess?" He looks up as he plates the last egg.

"Enough of the princess, this morning there is nothing in this body feeling all pretty." The frying pan drops into the sink and before I can even move, he has me wrapped in his arms.

"No matter how you look or feel, you are always a princess to me, and I will always treat you as such. Got it?" Waiting for my answer, I just nod at him. He kisses my nose and then directs me into my seat.

"Now eat. It'll help, and we also need to get moving soon, it's already seven o'clock. Bella also messaged and said she's off work today so is keeping Memphis until this afternoon. He'll be here when we get home."

"What time do you finish today?" I look up from my coffee.

"The magic question. I should be finished by six, but it depends on what's happening at the time. This is part of the gig, Tilly. I live a fluid life to some extent. I can't always be reliable for being somewhere on time. I will always try but some things are just out of my hands." He looks worried at how I will take this.

"It's okay. I understand. I knew what I was getting myself into. You were honest from the start. There are times that my life is the same, when I'm trying to fix last-minute problems. We will just work through it together."

He picks up my hand and kisses it then we both get stuck into eating. I'm also inhaling my coffee like it's my lifeline this morning. There will be a few more of these needed before I'm functioning on a normal level.

As we're clearing the dishes and loading the dishwasher, I stop and just blurt it.

"Gray, can you come home with me this weekend? Meet my parents and help me lay some demons to rest?" It all came out rushed. I don't why I'm worried about taking him home. I'm not ashamed of where I grew up, it's just been hard to go back for so long. I don't know if I want him to see me go through this.

He stops stacking and grabs me around the waist, hoisting me onto the counter. His hands are on my face and he's looking into my eyes.

"Nothing would make me happier than to meet your mom and dad and to be your prince and slay your dragons, baby. That's my role. I get to be the protective tough guy now. Nothing you do in this life, you ever do alone again. I hope you understand this. The two of us aren't singular anymore. We are an us. One perfect package. Now call your mom and tell her we're coming, and she better not be old-fashioned and want me sleeping in separate beds. Otherwise book a hotel because there will not be another night that our bodies aren't together in the same bed. Okay?"

Before I can answer, he kisses the air out of me and continues to make me totally understand everything he said. Once we finally pull our lips apart, I whisper, "Okay and thank you for loving me."

"Always, baby. It will never stop."

I bury my head in his neck, getting one last tight cuddle and taking in the scent of his cologne that will get me through today.

He lifts me down, turns me towards the bedroom, and gives me a gentle smack on the ass.

"Now go and quickly finish getting ready for work before my pager goes off. I want to drive you to work. Get that sexy butt moving, woman."

He knows just what I need every time.

When to treat me softly, when to play hard, and best of all when to make me laugh.

My perfect GG.

GRAYSON

Walking through the hospital doors this morning, I feel like a different person. Life feels lighter and I'm thinking of things I never imagined I wanted before Matilda came along.

I can't wait to take her home and see her parents. They sound like great people from the stories I got from Paul at the racetrack. Meeting them gives me a chance to let them know how much I love their daughter and that I will never hurt her.

I almost make it to my office when I run into Tate in the corridor. "Hey there, stud. How did your day finish up yesterday?"

I just put my arm around his shoulder still walking towards my office. "Let's just say it didn't finish yesterday, we may have stretched it a little further than that."

Tate just looks at me and rolls his eyes as I unlock my door. "No boasting, okay."

"You will never get details from me. What Tilly and I have is not being shared."

"Like I want to know anyway. That shit is a vision I don't need to picture."

Dropping my bag and turning on my laptop, I get to work while he makes himself comfortable.

"Jokes aside, Tilly is great, Gray. I mean, what woman takes her boyfriend and his best friends Nascar driving on a date? Seriously, how did you get so lucky?"

"It's my charm, buddy, do I need to share my secrets?"

"Not a chance. I'm doing just fine on my own, thanks."

"You're right, though. She is one special lady and there is no way I'm letting her go. I'm thirty-seven years old, man. I'm not messing around."

"Marriage, shit. Are you talking about marrying her?"

"Damn straight I am, as soon as she's ready. I'll tell you one thing, though. She better not take too long, because patience is not my strong point."

"Happy for you, man. I really am."

"Thanks. Now who won the race yesterday? You better have video for me to watch."

"Fucking Lex! Can you believe it? I thought for sure it would be me or Mason, but the quiet little angry man blitzed us. He was driving like someone was on his tail. Wait until you see the video." Tate leans back in his seat with his hands linked behind his head.

"Is he alright, did you talk to him about it?" I ask trying to think if I have noticed Lex a little off lately.

"Yeah, but as if he'll tell us anything. You know he keeps everything to himself. It's not until the world is going to end that he explodes and then we're picking up his drunk ass off some bar floor late at night. Listening to some slurred words about something that makes no sense at all."

"True. What about you?" I look for his reaction, but none comes.

"What about me?"

"You all good?"

"Let me see, spent my day off at the racetrack in a Nascar, then talking shop with the boys. Life is good, man. Now I just need to find me a Tilly." We both laugh.

"Well, this Tilly is taken, so back off. Go find your own." As I finish, I look at emails that have just loaded on my screen.

"For fuck's sake. Like I've got time for this shit today. A fucking meeting with the Chief of Staff." I slam my fist down on the desk. "Kitty is going to be the death of me. I have a meeting about my poor treatment of her at a hospital-endorsed function. She's lucky that she's a woman because if a man said what she did about Tilly, I would have decked him."

"Do you need me to come with you? I'll tell them what a crazy bitch she's been for months."

I know what I need to do and there is no way I will be the one walking out of this meeting with my tail between my legs.

"Thanks, but I don't think it will help. Do me a favor, though, call Fleurtilly and get hold of Fleur. Don't let Tilly know what's going on, I don't want her upset. I need the names and phone numbers of a few of the guests at the function that I can call from the meeting. Message through to my phone." I reply to the email that I am on my way for the meeting and then take myself offline for paging. I need to sort this problem once and for all.

Standing outside the Chief of Staff's office, my phone buzzes in my hand.

Fleur has sent me at least twenty names. Along with a long message of what she thinks of Kitty. She also offered to pull the CCTV footage from the venue if needed. I laugh a little to myself. I would hate to piss Fleur off. I'm much happier she's in my corner for this battle. I quickly shoot off a message letting her know it's okay at this stage and thank her for the help. I promise I will be in touch once I'm out.

Knocking, I get called in and here is Kitty sitting in the chair opposite the boss, Professor Carden. Kitty's dressed in a tight short black skirt, very fitted white shirt with her tits pushed up nice and high. Her face has the bitch look like she is ready for blood.

"Dr. Garrett, please take a seat." The boss signals next to Kitty.

"Hello, sir, thank you. Kitty." I nod at her, barely acknowledging her.

"I won't keep you long, Dr. Garrett, as I know you're on shift and we need you downstairs. I will get straight to the point. Kitty contacted me over the weekend to talk about how distressed and embarrassed she is with the way you treated her at the function in front of her peers. You weren't an invited guest, and I understand you were just there because you're having some fling with our new contractor, Miss Henderson. Is that correct?" He sits back in his tall black leather chair, hands clasped together giving that school principal look down his nose over the top of his glasses.

I could do one of two things here. Get angry and get fired up at the load of bullshit I've just heard. Or I can calmly put her in her place. I want to do the first one, but I know I need to hold it together and be the bigger person here.

"I will say part of that story is true. I wasn't an invited guest and yes, I'm in a relationship with Matilda that is far more serious than a fling. I was contacted by one of the Fleurtilly staff informing me that Kitty was at the function, drunk, and if it was a work function for her then that is obviously an issue, however we aren't here to discuss that. The staff informed me that she was being extremely rude to my girlfriend and thought I should know. I don't know about you, sir, but if the woman you love is being attacked just because she is in a relationship with you, wouldn't you want to protect her too?" The look on his face is one of confusion.

"Kitty, do you care to explain the night a little further? Had you been drinking?"

Her huff tells me she is about to wind up for a big speech. "Of course, I had a few wines, we all do at these events. I was not drunk. I was merely pointing out to Miss Henderson how poor her services were, and she is very jealous of the relationship Dr. Garrett and I have, so she got nasty." I didn't even give the boss time to reply.

"Enough of this bullshit, Kitty. We are not, nor have we ever, been in a relationship. We slept together once, that's it. As for Matilda, she was doing her job and removing you from the function because you were severely intoxicated to the point you couldn't walk straight. When I walked in, you were in the middle of the room screaming at her, calling her a whore. Now if you want to keep up this crap then I have the names of twenty independent witnesses on my phone who were there that night that I'm happy to call right now on speaker phone for us all to ask their opinion."

"I can't believe you would do this to me, Grayson. What we had was perfect. Now you're making up things to hurt me." Kitty tries to look like she's about to cry.

"That's it. I have tried to protect you by not putting a stop to this, but I can see you aren't going to let it go. Professor Carden, sir. I think Kitty needs some help. She is an alcoholic and dependent on prescription drugs, I believe. I have suspected for a little while by watching her actions, but I believe if you test her right this moment you will find both in her system."

I turn to look at her. Face frozen and mouth open. It's the first time she has been speechless.

"If you were a doctor here, I would have reported my suspicions earlier, as we have people's lives in our hands. I hope I'm proven wrong, but Kitty, you need help. It's an illness and you are in the right place. It just can't go on anymore. You're hurting other people now with your delusions but most of all, you are hurting yourself. Let us help you. It doesn't have to leave this room." I look to Professor Carden and he nods a little to agree.

There is silence for a few moments then her head drops into her hands. The tears start and I'm sadly proven right. She keeps looking up slightly at both of us and looks so ashamed. Like a small child who knows they have done something wrong and they're trying to work out how to explain their way out of it.

"You don't understand the pressure of being a woman in this job. Always being judged. Everyone watching and waiting for you to fuck it up. There just aren't enough hours to get it all done. I just need help to keep going and keep me awake. That's all. I don't do it all the time. Just when I need it. I can stop at any time." She continues to fall apart as I reach for tissues and pass them to her.

"I think you're needing it more often than you realize. I know the pressure of long hours and intense situations. You just can't rely on those to get you through. Get more staff or find another job that suits you better. The damage you're doing to yourself is not worth it just for a job. Please, Kitty, let us get psych up here to help and start you on the right path."

"Dr. Garrett is right. We can help you get better. You will be put on leave until we can get this sorted, and as far as the staff know you're just on annual leave. We can do everything to put this in place, but you need to want to get better, Kitty. Otherwise it's a waste of everyone's time."

"Kitty, take the leap. You will be happier and healthier when you come out the other side. It won't be easy, but you're a tough woman, we've all seen it. What do you say?" We both sit waiting for her to process everything.

"I don't have much choice, you asshole. You always thought you were better than me. I was never good enough for you. I don't need to do anything, but I have to do it, don't I, or I'm going to lose my job otherwise. I know things have to change and I was going to do it myself. Now you're making me do it your way. I suppose I better listen to the almighty male doctors."

I look at her and know that in her head she still doesn't see she has a problem. But the first step is to start getting help so hopefully we've given her that push she needs.

"I think you can leave now, Dr. Garrett. Sorry for the misunderstanding. Thank you for bringing this to my attention." He puts out his hand for me to shake. I stand and shake his hand and then turn to Kitty, crouching down so I'm eye-level with her.

"I had fun when we went out, Kitty, but we aren't meant to be together. You are a beautiful woman who will make another man very happy. Get yourself better and then you can find your One. I promise there is a man out there for you. Do it for yourself." She looks up and shocks me.

"Fuck you!" Then her head drops again, and I take that as my cue to leave.

Standing outside the office after I close the door, I let out a long sigh. That was tough but I knew I needed to do it. I had suspected her drug abuse for a little while, but seeing her the other night just confirmed my thoughts. I hope Kitty gets the help she needs. Then all the pain will be worth it.

I shoot a quick message off to both Fleur and Tate letting them know that everything is fine, and it was a misunderstanding. They don't need to know Kitty's private issues.

Fleur replies that she'll knee her in the bitch balls next time she sees her. I don't even know what that means, but I'm happy that it's over. Tate just replies with a thumbs-up, which means he's busy.

Once I'm back in my office, I just sit for a few minutes taking time to clear my head. I have a big day today and my patients deserve me to be at the top of my game. As soon as I think back to yesterday with Tilly, my body starts to calm. She has that effect on me.

Setting my pager back online, I know I have thirty minutes before I'm needed for my first patient. A text message arrives from my girl which has me smiling before I even read it.

Tilly: My head still hates you, but my heart and body love you lots
Already miss you

GG: You have no idea how much I needed this message.
I miss you too, baby.
Don't worry, by the time tonight is over, your head will love me again too

Tilly: Are you okay?

GG: Yeah baby, I am now. Some days are just tough.
You always make it better.

Tilly: Good. Now, can you make my head better?

GG: I'll kiss it better tonight.
Maybe I'll kiss it ALL better
Gorgeous Gyno GG xx

Tilly: Oh God, you will never forget that will you.

GG: No way. I'm getting a tattoo that says

G master
On my hands, for all to see.

Tilly: You are such an idiot.
Lucky I love you.

GG: Yes you do, and I have it in writing now
That's a contract.
You're mine now baby

Tilly: Where do I sign?

GG: On my heart

Tilly: *heart melting* If you sign mine too

GG: Already did

Tilly:I know

Just as I'm about to reply, my pager goes and the moment must end. I'm not sad, though, because I'll take all these little stolen bits of happiness for a lifetime with her.

GG: Need to go- paged
Love you, talk later
xx

Tilly: Love you more
xx

Those three words have me smiling for the rest of the day. It's one competition I'll be happy to have with her for the rest of our lives.

Showing how much we love each other is the best game I can think of playing.

Chapter Twenty-Two

MATILDA

This last week since our two dates has flown by so quickly. There hasn't been much sleep happening in between work and Grayson. Not that I will ever complain about that.

Sometimes it may be only for a few hours between Gray's different shifts, but every night we've been in the same bed together. Sometimes it's mine and sometimes it's his, but every time we are together. When Gray works at night, I spend the night with Memphis, and he keeps me company. Curling up at the end of the bed, keeping watch until Gray comes home in the middle of the night. Without a fuss he then trots back out to his bed and lets Gray take over the shift.

I have never felt so treasured.

I just wish I wasn't feeling so anxious right now as we drive home to see Mom and Dad for the weekend. Fleur is covering me, and Gray swapped some shifts so we could do this. I knew if I didn't do it now then I'd lose the confidence to finish it once and for all.

My mom was beside herself when I called and told her we were coming. I can imagine she's had Dad cleaning all week. He'll be complaining she's dragging him away from the garage and she's fussing for nothing. Although I'm anxious, I can't wait to see them. Nothing beats a hug from your mom and dad. Well, maybe not nothing. Grayson has some pretty special things, but that's a whole other story.

"You okay, baby?" Gray squeezes my hand that he has had hold of the whole trip.

"Yeah, I will be. It's just a little hard, but it's time."

"Remember you aren't on your own. We've got this." He lifts my hand to his lips and kisses it which still gives me tingles every time.

"We're almost there. About five minutes away. Are you ready to be attacked by my mother? I'll just apologize now for all the hugging, talking, feeding, fussing, and any other mothering she will be smothering you with. Both my sister and I haven't been around much for the last few years, so my poor dad has been putting up with it all." I know I need to warn him about the whirlwind that Mom will be when we arrive. I'm surprised she hasn't got a sign in the main street welcoming me home.

"Baby, I doubt your dad is complaining about having his wife fuss over him and all that time alone in the house without his daughters listening."

"Grayson!" I yell. "You did not just say that to make me think about my parents having sex, did you? Oh my god, I can't unthink that now. I told you everything revolves around sex with you. Christ, you look at women's vaginas all day. You are obsessed."

We're both laughing and Gray tries to defend himself. "Here is a little secret that if you tell anyone I'll have to kiss you to death. I might look at vaginas all day, in a medical way which is not like you think. All I see is flesh of someone who I want to keep healthy and help in whatever way they need. But when I'm playing with your pussy, it is totally different. She calls me to do lots of naughty things to her. She's the only one that talks to me."

"Oh my god, why would you even say that? I mean, you sit there all straight-faced and tell me I have a talking pussy. You are a mess, you know that. I will never be able to concentrate when your head is down there again." I groan as he keeps laughing at me.

"You have no idea, she says 'come and eat me, G master'. How can I resist?"

"Ugh, stop already. You are just gross. Remind me again why I chose you?" Without realizing, we've already pulled up at my parents' house and he's looking proud of himself.

"You didn't, you tried to run but I chased you down. Now I may be gross, but I managed to take your mind off the nerves and now we're going to walk straight in there and get this over and done with. Because the way the curtain in the front window is moving, your mom is going nuts inside. I think we need to go and save your dad." I look out the windshield to the place I always felt safe. Where there is always love for me no matter what.

"Thank you for everything. For loving all the parts of me." He kisses me on the forehead so softly.

There are so many kisses in this world.

There are family kisses, on cheeks, on hands, the polite hello and goodbyes.

Then that first kiss with someone is all on its own, when you're fumbling through that initial touch.

That hot and steamy, "I just want to eat you" kiss. The kiss that can be placed anywhere on your body and you feel the intensity of it.

A romantic "I love you" kiss can be the one that reminds you that your heart belongs to them and there is no other way to express how they feel.

Then there is THAT kiss!

The one on your forehead. Your face held in both his hands.

It's so soft and longing. Telling you how absolutely treasured you are. It's not sexual, it's loving, it's everything.

Grayson is telling me I'm everything.

That strength is enough to take on anything.

The moment is broken with the tapping on the window.

"I told you." Sighing, we break apart and I don't even have time to say another word before my mom has the door open, pulling me out and into her arms.

"Welcome home, Matilda. It's time for you to finally come home." I can feel Mom's tears on my cheek where we're touching. The guilt of what I have put my mother through is there, but as Gray told me, we can't go back to the past, we have to live for today and into the future. That's what I'm doing, I'm living.

"Let me breathe, Mom." I laugh a little as she steps back and then pulls me in again. "I'm home, Mom, I'm not leaving you alone anymore." Now we're both crying.

I can hear my father's voice next to me.

"You must be Grayson, Todd Henderson, nice to meet you." Shit, I should be doing that.

"Mom, I need you to let me go for a minute." Dad helps me out and pulls her towards him.

"Grayson, this is my mom, Shelley." Before he even has time to say anything, she wraps him in a hug, which looks kind of funny. She's only a small woman and seeing her trying to hug Gray is quite a sight.

"Thank you for bringing our girl home. Thank you." My mom keeps babbling.

"Shelley, for god's sake, woman. Let the poor boy go. You'll send him packing." She giggles and comes back to my dad who has just let go of me.

"It's okay, I understand. I'm very happy to meet you both. I have heard a lot about you from Tilly and Paul."

"Don't you listen to that cheeky little Paul. That bratty little boy was always up to mischief. I'm sure he didn't tell you the stories of him getting into trouble all the time." Mom is already linking arms with me and we're walking inside. She knows Dad will help with any bags and the boys will follow.

"Now I've made scones, cake, and my homemade lemonade. Go and wash up and meet me out back on the deck." Mom is already off in the direction of the kitchen which means we're about to be fed within an inch of our lives.

"Lemonade, who is she kidding? Up for a home brew, Grayson? My last batch is a good one." Dad is already slapping him on the back as he heads for the garage.

We're both left standing in the front hall just looking at each other. I put my hand over my mouth and try to keep the noise of my laughter hidden from Mom. Gray is smiling and trying to hold it in too.

Grabbing his arm, I drag him up the stairs to my bedroom with our bags. Shutting the door, we both collapse on the bed in a rapture of laughter.

"They are adorable. They love you, little one, and have missed you," Gray gets out after he calms down.

"I know, and they're trying so hard to impress you. Mom only makes her lemonade for special occasions, and Dad, he doesn't share his beer with anyone, unless you're part of his inner circle. You've passed the test in the first five minutes."

"Of course I have. I brought their little girl home to them. Plus, I'm a pretty spectacular guy." He waves his hands down in front of him as if he's showing off a prize.

"Do not encourage my mother with your ego. She'll just feed it and we don't need it any bigger. Be careful of Dad's beer. It's like rocket fuel. It's only early afternoon and we don't want a drunk Gray as the first impression."

"Could make for a great story at the wedding, the night I met my future in-laws I was so drunk I was running around the backyard dancing, thrusting my hips while singing Elvis songs."

"I'm warning you. It's not even funny. I will cut your beer off and lock you in the bedroom if you get the slightest bit tipsy."

"Now that sounds like a great idea. Bring my beer, woman."

I just get up and walk to the door, shaking my head at him.

"I give up, I'm done. You're just crazy."

Gray jumps off the bed and is across my tiny room before I can get the door open.

"I might be crazy but it's just crazy in love with you, little one. Never forget that." He kisses me hard on the lips to make sure I'm paying attention.

"So this is your childhood room, Princess." We stand together looking around.

"Yeah, this room has a lot of good and bad memories. I would normally struggle to be in here. It was here I lost the baby. I associated the last time I stayed in here with pain. I don't feel that pain in here anymore."

"That's because the pain wasn't in this room, Tilly. The pain was in you and now that you've let it go it can't hurt you anymore. It's time to remember the fun times in this room and make new memories."

I look up into his eyes, with their twinkle. He still hypnotizes me with that look.

"There is no way we are having sex in my parents' house." I shake my finger in front of his face.

"Oh yes we are, and you will be having sex in your teenage bed and you will be very quiet while I make you come harder than you have before." He has that look of cockiness all over his face.

"Not happening," I tell him as I duck under his arm and out the door.

"Keep dreaming, Tilly, because we both know I'm very persuasive. I will win. Now where is this rocket fuel you talk of?"

Chasing me down the stairs trying to tickle me, we both head to my parents standing out on the back deck with both their offerings to the Grayson god. This afternoon is going to be one in a million, I can just tell.

"I can't believe I just had sex in my parents' house with them in the room next door. Damn you and your super sex powers, GG." I lay with my head on his chest whispering in case they can hear me.

"Never doubt my attraction to you, little one. The challenge of being the first boy to fuck you in this bedroom just needed to be on my list of firsts. Surely you agree." His hand is stroking up and down my back softly.

"What if I don't agree with you?"

"Then I get to fuck you again until you do," he whispers in my ear.

"I've created a monster."

"Ah, but such a loveable monster."

"Now that I can agree on. Time for sleep. I'm just warning you my mom will be up and making breakfast nice and early to make sure you get a good meal before you leave."

"Well, we better work up an appetite then."

"Grayson," I squeal as he rolls me underneath him and kisses me to shut me up.

Sliding his hand down my body, he is shushing me to remind me I need to be quiet.

We both stop dead and look at each other. Checking that the noise we're hearing is what we think it is. My mouth drops open and I try to put my hands over my ears as the squeak of my mom and dad's bed and the headboard hitting the wall signals that we aren't the only ones having sex in this house tonight.

If there is anything that will kill the moment, it's having your parents next door beating you to it. Grayson rolls back on to his back trying so hard to hold in his laughter. Me on the other hand picks up my pillow, places my head on his chest, then pull the pillow over my ears.

That is how I fall asleep. Listening to Grayson's heartbeat and nothing else.

Nothing else at all.

"Mom, please don't cry. You will see me in two weeks when you come and stay with us for the foundation function. I told you I'll visit more, I promise." Leaving is hard because Mom is fearing that I won't come back like last time.

"I know, it's just hard. You're so grown up, but still my little girl."

I hug her tight as Dad starts to pull her out of my arms and wrap her in his. "I'll call you during the week and we can organize your visit and meeting Gray's family. You'll love them too, including Memphis who thinks he's a human in this family."

"Hey, what are you talking about? You're the one that he goes to now. He joined Team Tilly from day one. You stole my little buddy," Gray complains as he puts his arm around my shoulders.

"Can't help it if your dog has good taste. He just traded up in the deal, that's all."

"You know you're not too big to put over my knee even in front of your mom and dad, don't you?"

"Shut up, you crazy thing, and say goodbye." We all hug again and say our farewells, which takes another five minutes.

Finally, in the car and driving through town, I'm smiling at all the memories of Fleur and me flooding in. Life was good here. I'm so glad I'll get to show Gray my home now as we visit more often.

Laying my head back on the headrest, I look across at the man sitting beside me. It's then that I realize that home is not a location for me anymore.

Wherever Grayson is, then that's where I feel the love and happiness you need to believe you are safe and the freedom to be yourself.

I ran away from home once before.

But I'm done running now.

Grayson is my home.

GRAYSON

2 Weeks later

"Thank god your mom and dad are staying in your apartment and not here with us. I'm not sure I can eat another mouthful after tonight's dinner." I rub my belly while Tilly's head is laying in my lap as we relax on the couch.

"I warned you on day one about her need to feed us constantly. I swear, I lost ten pounds the first month I left home."

"I'm not complaining. She cooks the best food. But I can't believe how much she turned up with. I'm sure she's been cooking since the day we left to prepare for this weekend." I run her hair through my fingers and listen to her breathing starting to slow. I know she's exhausted with how hard she's been working. Her normal workload has been doubled since they took on the hospital contract, and with the foundation function tomorrow night, she is pushing herself hard.

"She was nervous about coming to the city, meeting your family, and tomorrow night. She bakes when she's nervous. So be prepared for whatever else she has stashed over there in my fridge and freezer already."

"I love your mom and dad, they're so real. No crap, just real people."

"That's the way they raised me. Look for the good in people but also look for the realness which is just as important." She yawns as she finishes her sentence.

"Come on, we need to get you to bed. You're tired." Agreeing with me, she sits up and we both stand. Memphis knows what the routine is now. He comes to Tilly for his pat, then me, then heads over to his bed and settles down for the night. While Tilly then walks to the bedroom and starts to get ready for bed, I turn the lights off and make sure everything is locked up and turned off for the night. Usually I beat Tilly into bed by the time she's done all that crazy girl's stuff they do before bed with night creams and all the rest of it.

Tonight, though, I walk in to her already in bed and a light snore can be heard. I stand leaning against the doorframe just watching her sleep. I don't know how long for, but I just can't take my eyes off her. This beautiful angel sent from the heavens to make me whole. She will never realize how much it means to me, the extent she's going to for the function tomorrow night. Every detail has had its I dotted, and its T crossed multiple times. When Fleur told her she isn't working the function, I thought she was going to explode on the spot.

We had to explain we want her there as a guest, my girlfriend, and part of the family who this foundation is based on. Fleur and TJ will have everything under control, and she will be there if needed. She didn't like it but agreed to disagree.

I can't wait to see her in the dress she bought last week. She doesn't know yet, but we have organized for a bit of pampering for her and Bella tomorrow. With a hairdresser and makeup artist coming here to help them get ready. I want her to feel special and treasured on such an important day. Her and Bella both.

Turning out the light, I slide into bed next to her and pull her into her sleeping position. Tucked into my side, head on my heart. She told me late one night that the rhythm of my heart is what puts her to sleep and allows her to know she's home.

As I settle her in my arms, she murmurs those few words that mean the world. "I love you." Then the next little snore comes out. Even in her sleep she needs to tell me before the night ends.

"I love you more." Kissing the top of her head, I close my eyes and pray that tomorrow goes just like I've planned. I've waited so long for this moment I just can't believe it's finally here. Drifting off to sleep, I think of my mom and know this is what she would have wanted. I know she will be happy watching from above.

The night takes over and morning will be here before we know it.

"Grayson, where did you put that bag with my jewelry in it?" I hear her screaming from the bedroom. I don't dare go in there. She's like a donkey on the edge. Dad and Bella left a few minutes ago to pick up Tilly's parents and we'll meet them all there. We will have a little time together, alone in the town car to just breathe before the night gets crazy.

"Don't worry, I found it."

I don't even bother answering because I know she's not even listening to me. Looking at the time, I'll have to give her a hurry along shortly. Just then I hear her shoes coming from the bedroom down the hallway. As I stand there in my black tuxedo, I am absolutely in awe of the beauty in front of me.

"Matilda," is all that leaves my mouth.

She plays nervously with her handbag waiting for me to say something.

"Don't do that. Don't be shy. You look so beautiful you took my breath away." Walking up to her but afraid to mess her up, I just place my hand on her cheek. She melts instantly into it.

"My little one, you are just stunning. I am so blessed to have found you. Every man in that room tonight will be jealous of me. I intend to show you off to the world tonight." I lightly kiss her cheek, not wanting to wreck her makeup.

"Thank you. You look very sexy in your tux too. Love a man in a suit. Reminds me of another night I went out dressed up and there was this guy in a suit. He wouldn't stop staring at me. I was too frightened to walk over to him. He just looked so fuckalicious I knew he was out of my league."

"Tilly, that is where you are so wrong. It was you that was out of my league. I just knew, though, I couldn't let you go. There was something about you that made me keep chasing. I didn't know at the time what it was, but I do now. It was my soul. It found its mate and knew where it belonged, and that is together. I love you, baby. Now let's go and show the world just how much."

"If you make my makeup run from tears, you'll be in trouble from your sister. So, stop being so perfect." Her hand on my cheek, I can feel everything she is trying to say. "Let's go and make memories of your mom."

I take her hand and raise it to my lips as I lead her to the door and say to her, "Let's go and make some memories."

Pulling up to the entranceway of The Blackstone Hotel, I can feel my nerves starting to go. I'm not one to get nervous usually but tonight is special, for all of us. Tilly senses my anxiousness and takes my hand, squeezing it before we get out of the car. She looks at me with her beautiful eyes and repeats my words back to me, "We've got this."

I feel a wave of calmness wash over me as I take a big deep breath. "With you beside me, we can do anything."

"Exactly."

Exiting the car, I stand waiting for Tilly to slide across the seat and take my hand. I feel a light wisp of air brush across my cheek. No trees are moving and there is not a breath of air after it. I smile and know it's just my mom letting me know she's here. That everything will be fine.

Tilly stands and smooths down her dress, then straightens my jacket and bow tie. She looks up at me.

"Are you okay?" she asks.

"I am now."

Let's do this.

After the first hour I start to feel more settled. The night is going according to plan. Already we have raised more than we were dreaming about. The vibe in the room is so heartwarming and positive. Bella is circulating and looks happy like she has found her place. Dad is enjoying chatting with everyone and managing to drag money out of them before he moves on to the next person. Tilly's parents seem to be having a good time. Todd is over with Tate, Lex, Mason, and Paul who has flown in especially for tonight. After I told Tilly that it was Paul who had told me about the baby, she called him and thanked him for watching over her all these years. They talked for a long time and she asked him to come along.

Shelley, on the other hand, keeps getting in trouble with Fleur for trying to help the waiters. God bless her, she just wants to help and that's the way she knows how. We have now given Hannah and Deven the job of keeping her busy before Fleur blows a fuse.

My ever-efficient girlfriend has just come over to send me to the stage. Fleur was five steps behind her about to do the same thing. We both just shake our heads at her. She might not be working officially, but she may as well be.

Having everyone's eyes on me and the room becoming so silent is a humbling experience. Standing up here telling the world about my mom and how she loved to help others.

"By starting this foundation, we hope to grow it, so every woman, no matter what her income, race, or social standing will still receive immediate attention and the best care. With your help together we can save lives."

The crowd is all applauding loudly, and I feel elated at the sight of everyone keen to help fulfill our dream.

"There is one more thing I would like to do tonight. I want to introduce you all to the most important woman in my life. My girlfriend, Matilda Henderson. Come up here and join me, Tilly." I see her blushing as she walks through the crowd to join me on stage. "This beautiful lady has worked tirelessly along with her company Fleurtilly to make tonight's function so perfect. I couldn't be prouder of her." Everyone cheers her as I take her hand and bring her closer to me.

"This foundation and my mother brought us together after a few misadventures. I have never felt so happy and loved as I do when I'm with you. From that first day, I knew I couldn't live without you. You are the air that I breathe. So tonight, as we start the Maxine's Angels Foundation, giving it life, I thought it's the perfect night for us to start our new journey too. You asked me for slow, but this is as slow as I can go."

Dropping to one knee and pulling the box from my jacket pocket, Tilly's hands rush to curb the gasp of air she's taking in surprise.

"Matilda, my little one, my Tilly, I have never loved another like I love you, and I know now I never will. Will you let me love you with all I am for the rest of our lives? Will you do me the honor of marrying me? Will you let me be your GG and only your GG?"

Her tears are streaming down her face and she's nodding up and down. I smile at her, willing her to say the word. Her hands come down to mine as she whispers that one simple word.

"Yes."

As I slip the ring on her finger, I hear her beautiful voice just a little louder this time.

For all the letters in the alphabet I only needed three. Just three simple letters to strengthen the bond of those three simple words I never tire of hearing.

"Yes."

And then I hear my three favorite words.

"I love you."

Well, maybe make that four words.

"I love you more."

THE END

Epilogue

MATILDA

"Where do you think you're going?" Allison looks at Gray with the stare that would put the fear into most men.

"Into the exam room with my wife." He stands in the waiting room with his arm around my waist. Staring down his friend.

"I don't think so. This is doctor-patient privilege. My patient would like a little privacy. You can sit your butt back down on the chair like all the other husbands." I can't tell if she's serious or just doing it to annoy him.

"Not a chance. You do know she doesn't need to keep seeing you, she has her own gorgeous gyno. Plus, I can guarantee I know that area of my wife far better than you ever will." He huffs with a glint in his eye of having the upper hand.

"Grayson," I scold him for being so crass and he shows no remorse.

"Maybe so, *Mr.* Garrett, but if your skills are as good as you say they are, then why is she still seeing me?" I'm starting to feel like this is a bit of a pissing competition between two doctors.

I can't help it, I just start to giggle. "You two are ridiculous. Can we just get on with the appointment?"

Grayson doesn't wait, he just starts walking towards the examination room pulling me by the hand.

I'm still laughing while I hear Alison behind call out to him, "You always were an asshole."

"Not the first time I've been called that in your waiting room and look where it got me." We're all laughing now. Thank goodness this is an after hours appointment and no one else is in the office.

As I lie down on the bed, I look to both of them. "Have you two finished now? Can we play patient and doctor for a minute?"

They both smile at me, but I know full well Allison may as well step aside now because Gray will be over her shoulder.

"We can if Mr. Arrogance over here agrees to play patient, doctor, and patient's husband. Just remember there is only one doctor in that sentence and that would be me." She waves her finger at him to reinforce the point.

"Yeah, yeah, whatever. Can we just do this?" he huffs, pacing the room.

"Yes, hello, over here. Patient just wanting to get examination over with. Can you two argue the point of who has the biggest stethoscope later?" They both stop and look at me. Mumbling sorry, they start getting things organized.

Grayson comes and kisses me on the forehead and leans down to whisper in my ear but loud enough she can hear him. He knows how nervous I am and I'm sure he is just trying to distract me.

"Don't worry, baby, if the mean doctor lady hurts you or makes you uncomfortable, I will make it all better when we get home."

Allison just groans and rolls her eyes.

The look on my face as she picks up the ultrasound machine must have shown on my face.

"Gray," I whisper.

"Baby, we've got this. No matter the outcome. We will be okay."

I just nod my head and all the joking is gone between him and Allison as he nods at her to start the scanning.

I've known for over two months that I'm pregnant, and the only people who know are the three of us in this room. I didn't want to go through the hard part of telling people if I miscarry again, which is always a possibility. I didn't want a scan done until the baby was big enough for an external scan. I was scared that it may be too risky. As much as Gray assured me it's safe, I put my foot down and refused. The blood test confirmed the pregnancy and now it's time to finally confirm I have a little peanut inside me. Having a little spotting still each month, I just can't settle yet.

"Just relax, Tilly. This will be a little cold." She squirts the gel on my stomach and tilts the screen so we can all see.

To me it looks like just black and white shapes and a whole lot of noise. I keep looking between the two of them to read their faces.

Then it happens, the most amazing smile spreads across Grayson's face as we hear a heartbeat. I turn to the screen to see our little baby's heart happily pumping away.

"Gray," I gasp.

"Fuck," is all that comes from him.

"Yep, that's what did it. Gray fucked and now we have a little Garrett baby. Congratulations, my beautiful friends." Allison is also crying a little.

I can't completely let go yet. I need to know everything.

"Is the baby okay, is anything wrong, does everything look normal?" My breathing is a little fast and I'm squeezing the blood out of Gray's hand.

"Princess, just breathe, everything is fine. Give Allison a chance to finish the scan and take some pictures for you. But that amazing little baby on the screen is happily secure and growing nicely. We still have a ways to go, but we are out of the worst of the risk period. Now let's see how far along you are so we can find out when our baby is due." His voice and his touch just calm me every time.

"Our baby...we are really having a baby...that's our baby..." Finally, it all sinks in and I let go. I'm crying and laughing at the same time.

"Yes, little one, we're having a baby. A little GG. Another Gorgeous Garrett just like you."

"Oh, we can only pray for that," Allison teases. "This world can only cope with one Grayson Garrett, another cocky overachiever in your house will have Tilly going crazy, or crazier than she already is married to you." She continues with her scanning and doesn't even miss a beat with her reply to Gray.

That just makes me laugh harder which is not good when you're full of water for the ultrasound.

"Stop it or I'll pee on the bed."

"Gray, you're cleaning it up if she does."

He just rolls his eyes. "Oh, now she wants me to be the doctor. Too late. I'm happy sitting here being the husband and the dad. You're on your own, Dr. Fontain."

He leans down and kisses me with such love that I know what he's saying without even saying it.

Then he makes my heart melt when he moves down to kiss my stomach with just as much emotion even though it's covered in gel. He doesn't care.

With him back at my side, I look up into those eyes that captivated me that first night and have never let me go.

"We love you."

To which he replies the only way he knows how. My always overachieving Gorgeous Gyno.

"I love both of you more."

GRAYSON

I'm sure I'm being punished for all the years of laughing at the expecting fathers. Here I am on the due date of our little GG. I can't eat, I can't sleep, and I can't let Tilly out of my sight.

I think she's getting close to divorcing me, but I don't give a fuck. I promised I would always look after her for the rest of her life, and I'm just doing my job. Plus, she's carrying precious cargo. I know all the logic, not many babies are born on their due date, but I don't care. I'll be here waiting as long as it takes.

"Grayson, go take Memphis for a walk when you're finished. He looks bored," Tilly snarls at me from the couch while I'm in the kitchen preparing her a snack.

"Nope, no need. Hannah and Daisy are coming over to take him out for a doggy date shortly. You know I'm not leaving you."

"Ughh, you are ridiculous. GG has no plans of going anywhere soon, I can assure you. Apparently, it's comfy in there and they don't have to put up with their crazy overprotective father if they stay put."

"Your pregnancy humor is so funny...not!" She thinks she knows more about babies being born than I do. Damn woman is going to be the death of me. "You should just be thankful that it's Hannah and Daisy coming and not your mom and dad. Keeping your apartment for them to come and go as they please for visits was all good in theory, until you told them that there's a little GG on their way. I swear your mom has been here in the city more than at home in the last two months. Your dad is biting his tongue, but it's wearing thin, he misses his garage."

"Oh my god, Gray, if you let my mother in here today you will no longer be the G Master. You will be master of nothing because you will be getting nothing. I love her but she is driving me crazier than you are and that is saying something. I already feel stressed enough."

I see the look on her face change and show how tired she is. The pregnancy hasn't been easy on her because the whole way she's still had the fear of losing the baby. I didn't tell her I silently feared it too. For all my knowledge, if it was going to happen then I couldn't stop it.

Putting her snack on the table, I sit down next to her, pulling her on to my lap.

"I'll squash you," she protests.

"Not a chance." I run my hand up her neck and into her hair, pulling her closer so I can kiss those beautiful lips.

"What are up to, Gray?"

"Calming Mommy down. The stress is no good for GG. Besides, no matter how pregnant you are, I still think you are so fucking hot." Our next kiss turns steamier, and it doesn't take long for her to be moaning with my hand in her pants, stroking her pussy.

"You know I can't resist sex at the moment," she mumbles between kisses.

"Like it was any different before you were pregnant. Now stand up so I can strip down those pants and sit you on your favorite seat, me." No matter what, I can still make her laugh.

Stripping off my pants and then slowly lowering her down, we both moan at how good it feels. This is the best way to be connected. Nothing between us. As I lift her to bring her down again, she screams out this time.

"Fuck, tell me you just came super quick," I ask as my lap is saturated with fluid.

"Ummm no. You're good but not that good." She slaps my shoulder.

"Oh god, my super dick just broke your water. I don't think GG appreciated Mommy and Daddy having sex."

"Gray, I'm scared."

"I know, baby, just remember we've got this."

I pull her head towards me and kiss her forehead as I pray for today to be perfectly normal.

I'm torn where to be in the delivery room. I want to be there for Tilly, but there is no way anyone else is delivering my baby. We have Allison here to help me, but I can tell it's almost time for us to swap roles.

I look at my wife's face as she opens her mouth to yell at me. She's in pain, but I have a feeling she's about to tell me how much pain she wants me in.

"Grayson Garrett, I swear if you don't get this baby out of me in the next five seconds, I will cut it out myself."

"Baby, just breathe, you're doing great and the head is crowning."

"I know the motherfucking head is crowning because it hurts like a bitch, now get it out, or I will hurt you. That's a promise!" Tilly shoves me toward the end of the bed and Allison is trying not to laugh at me.

"Shut your mouth and look after your patient. I've got this," I yell at her as we swap places.

"Okay, Princess, now I need a really big push."

If her eyes could talk, they would be telling me to go to hell as she bears down as hard as she can. I look down at my baby's face for the first time and almost freeze until I hear Allison telling her to push again.

Shit, I need to concentrate.

"That's it, Tilly, shoulders are almost out, just a little bit more." As she takes another breath, my baby slides into my hands in all her naked glory. I hold her up and she lets out a little cry and I can finally breathe. The tears are flowing, and I lift her up on to Tilly. In all the years I have been doing this, I've never really known the true feeling of the moment when the baby is placed on her mother.

Two warriors who have just fought the toughest battle for each other. True unconditional love.

"We have a little girl, Gray, she's a Gorgeous Garrett. Our little GG."

I wrap them both in my arms and just gaze in awe at our little creation.

"Gorgeous just like her mom." I kiss her little forehead to let her know she is my everything. Both her and her mom.

"Welcome to the family, our little Grace Maxine Garrett. We will love you for the rest of our lives."

"Our little GG." Tilly smiles at me.

I can't think of anything better to say than, "I love you both so much more than just more."

Acknowledgments

Thank you to this amazing group of women who read my words before they make sense to the rest of the world. To Vicki, Nicole, Di, Brenda, Linda, and Shelbie. You have the patience of saints. Your feedback is amazing and hilarious all in one. Love you girls!

To Tara, thank you for having my back and proofreading at the last minute to save me. So lucky for our friendship.

Linda and the team at Foreword PR and Marketing. You girls are amazing! Linda, you have taken me under your wing and been unbelievable in your help and advice. Even if it is at weird times of the day and night. I can't thank you enough for teaching me how to navigate this crazy book world.

My mentor, your words that are planted in my subconscious push me harder every day. For all you do and say, I am so extremely thankful. My world is a better place since you walked into it. Eternally grateful for you, and our friendship.

Sarah Paige at Opium House Creatives, thank you for designing the perfect cover for my Gorgeous Gyno. You never cease to amaze me.

Thank you to Michael Scanlon for allowing me to use his image that was taken by FuriousFotog. Michael you are an amazing and kind soul. Thank you for all your help on this book. I am so grateful and feel blessed to have found a new friend.

Contagious Edits, once again you have done a wonderful job. Thank you for all you do for me. Nothing is ever too much of a problem. You make my books stronger with your talents.

There are four important people in my life who when I told them this year I was wanting to really concentrate on my writing, they never complained. Instead just give me love and encouragement every single day. My hubby and three kids, you are my reasons.

Lastly but most importantly, my readers. Thank you to each and every one of you for reading my books. I hope they give you as much joy as they do to me writing them. To all the amazing people in the book world, bloggers, promoters, reviewers, readers, and fellow authors. Thank you for your support, constant love, and encouragement. Grateful every day for you all.

Happy reading xoxo

Other books by Karen Deen

AVAILABLE NOW

LOVE'S WALL #1

LOVE'S DANCE #2

LOVE'S HIDING #3

LOVE'S FUN #4

LOVE'S HOT #5

Printed in Great Britain
by Amazon

25773893R00172